Don't miss th   's
extraorc

Book O
The Changeling War

Two worlds: One teems with life and technology. It is called
Earth. The other is a twisting maze of interconnected dwellings
and empty space. It is called Castle. Both worlds know violence. Both know greed. And now, in our time, they are about
to meet.

The war has begun . . .

Book Three of the Changeling Saga
The Magic Dead

The war between Earth and Castle has taken its toll on both
worlds. Now, the ruler of Castle—the insidious Pale Man—
plans to resolve the conflict by melding the technology of
Earth with the magical powers of Castle. For the Pale Man, it
means absolute victory. For all others . . . utter annihilation.

To stop him, long-embittered enemies must unite, and wage
one final assault against their common foe.

—✦—✦—

"Well-written . . . interesting."   —*VOYA*

"A clever blend of contemporary and magical adventure, enlivened by a set of intriguing characters."
                              —*Science Fiction Chronicle*

"What a wild, unpredictable ride! Original and fresh,
yet with enough common fantasy elements to keep me
comfortable, this one's an amazing addition to the
genre."
          —R. A. Salvatore, author of *The Demon Awakens*

The Changeling Saga by Peter Garrison

BOOK ONE: THE CHANGELING WAR
BOOK TWO: THE SORCERER'S GUN
BOOK THREE: THE MAGIC DEAD

THE CHANGELING SAGA

THE SORCERER'S GUN

Peter Garrison

Peter Garrison

ACE BOOKS, NEW YORK

THE SORCERER'S GUN

An Ace Book / published by arrangement with
the author.

PRINTING HISTORY
Ace trade paperback edition / October 1999
Ace mass-market edition / October 2000

The Penguin Putnam Inc. World Wide Web site address is
http://www.penguinputnam.com

Check out the ACE Science Fiction & Fantasy newsletter
and much more on the Internet at Club PPI!

ISBN: 0-441-00775-9

ACE®
Ace Books are published
by The Berkley Publishing Group,
a division of Penguin Putnam Inc.,
375 Hudson Street, New York, New York 10014.
ACE and the "A" design are trademarks
belonging to Penguin Putnam Inc.

PRINTED IN THE UNITED STATES OF AMERICA

10 9 8 7 6 5 4 3 2 1

THE
SORCERER'S
GUN

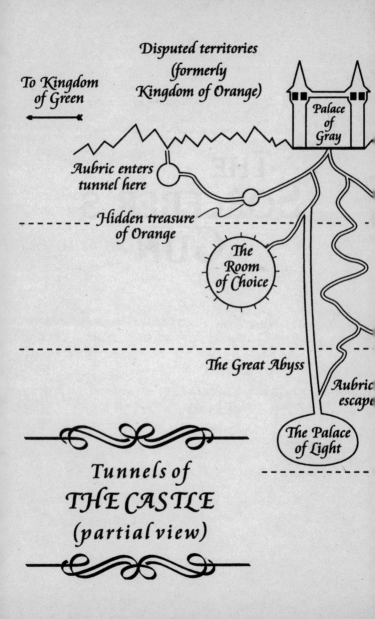

To Kingdom
of Green

Disputed territories
(formerly
Kingdom of Orange)

Palace
of
Gray

Aubric enters
tunnel here

Hidden treasure
of Orange

The
Room
of Choice

The Great Abyss

Aubric
escape

The Palace
of Light

Tunnels of
THE CASTLE
(partial view)

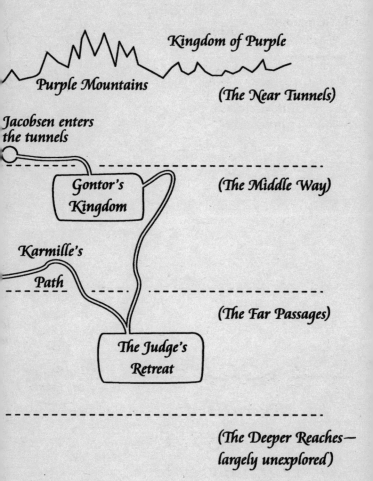

Kingdom of Purple

Purple Mountains

(The Near Tunnels)

Jacobsen enters
the tunnels

Gontor's
Kingdom

(The Middle Way)

Karmille's

Path

(The Far Passages)

The Judge's
Retreat

(The Deeper Reaches—
largely unexplored)

Prologue

THE SOUND WAS BARELY any sound at all.

The Growler did what he did best: a murmur, deep within his throat, little more than the purr of a cat; a sound he made when lost in thought.

He had much thinking to do.

Others tried to keep the Growler away. They thought their grip on power might last forever.

Nothing was forever.

All the players would soon be in position. A thousand years, or two or three thousand, what did it matter? The Growler knew it would have to change again.

That was why they—the instruments of change—were called Changelings. They were different from those they hid among, a difference that sometimes brought banishment or death. But those who survived grew strong. They would change it all.

The war had lasted almost as long as the Growler's memory, but the war would soon be done. There were so many players now, so many forces yearning to succeed. And the others, some with a thousand years of power, some who had been denied power for far too long, yearning to conquer it all.

They dreamt they could control the Growler.

There would always be dreams.

The Growler shifted.

The others were ready at last. He had woken his children. He would cause others to awake as well. All would soon be in place. And they would seek out the Growler. He had hidden for so long, most had forgotten he was even here.

Once they had the keys, they would have to come to him. He would make them remember.

Who would win? Who would lose? It depended, of course, who had them in the end.

They were designed to be most slippery.

He had slipped once, had almost lost it all forever. He had to rest, rebuild, restore.

He had to growl.

His knowledge was vast, but his powers were limited. This time, they might succeed in killing him.

There would always be dangers, in the world, the Castle, and that which was lost.

But great danger meant great prizes. After all, there was more than a single world to win.

Book One

―――――――――― ❧ ――――――――――

"No war, even one supported by seemingly endless re-serves of magic, would last forever. So it came to pass that the various factions realized the true desperation of their situation. Old alliances were shattered. New bar-gains were forged that might have seemed unimaginable only scant months before.

  "But none could imagine where these new bargains could truly lead, for they opened gateways that had been previously hidden; gateways that held forces that might change the very nature of the war, and, indeed, the very nature of the Castle itself."

—From *The Castle; Its Unfolding History*
(a work in progress).

.1.

The Castle

KEDRIK AWOKE TO SOME-
thing he had not known in five hundred years. His fine,
grey hair stuck to his forehead; his hands left damp impressions on the sheets of fairy silk. The room was impossibly dark. Where was the candle that always burned, the
silent servant who always stood guard?

He heard faint sounds in the darkness; a rustle of fabric,
a low grunt that might have been made by anything. He
wished for another voice, some words of reassurance,
wished his need for privacy had not demanded that he remove all his servants' tongues.

He knew he should raise his own voice, call for light,
call for his guards. Surely this was his own bed. Surely
there were half a dozen servants within the sound of his
cries.

Yet Kedrik hesitated. The same caution that saved his
life a hundred times as a young warrior was with him now,

a thousand years later. There was a stirring deep within
him, something he thought he had left behind when he had
come to rule. But it had not been so long that the High
Lord of the Grey did not still recognize the emotion.

Kedrik was afraid.

He felt a breeze upon his skin, a breeze that rose to a
wind in a room that held no windows.

He heard an exclamation across the room. He wasn't
alone!

"Brian?" a deep voice called. "You okay?"

"Yes, sir," a second replied.

"Call me Joe," the first said.

"Uh . . . Joe. Where are we?"

"In the dark. But not for long." A single flame erupted
in the middle of the room, sprouting from a metal box one
of the strangers held in his hand. The flame made the room
swirl with shadows. The stranger turned and saw Kedrik
upon his bed. The light went out.

"Shit!" the deep voice called. "There's someone
here!" A moment later, he added, "I've got a gun!"

What, Kedrik wondered, was a gun? How had these people entered his bedchamber? No doubt they meant to kill
him. He wished now that he had not decided to keep his
private quarters free of weapons. He had been worried
about angered servants. He had never thought he'd face
assassins.

"Kedrik!"

Kedrik recognized this last voice. It was Basoff, chief
among his Judges. "Judge!" he called back.

A dull green glow swirled in the middle of the room,
the beginning of one of Basoff's spells.

Kedrik swallowed a cry as a point of light far too bright
for fire appeared in the far corner of the room. Something
exploded. He saw two figures in the middle distance. One

of them waved a new metal object in his direction.

"The first one was only a warning!" the stranger's voice called. "Now I want you to tell us—"

"Begone!" Basoff replied. A shadow fell over the bed. "We tell nothing!"

The green light grew, showing the two in the corner to be a man and an adolescent boy.

Basoff clapped his hands. The two strangers disappeared, like a flame extinguished by the wind. The green flared to fill the room.

Kedrik shielded his eyes as he looked at the black-robed man above him.

"Kedrik?" Judge Basoff's voice sounded impossibly loud. "You are well? Then I was in time."

The light dimmed to the point where Kedrik's vision could accommodate it. Only Basoff, the first among the Judges of the Grey, would dare to enter Kedrik's quarters unannounced. The hooded Judge turned from the bed and strode quickly across the lord's bedchamber. The sorcerous light bobbed just above his head, throwing shadows that danced madly in the corners of the room.

The Judge sniffed at the air. "I was in time," Basoff said again. He shouted a quick string of words in the Judge's tongue, issuing commands against the dark, sure his voice would drive out whatever evil remained.

Kedrik's speech, in contrast, sounded faint and hoarse, as if he barely remembered how to use his voice. "Time?" he managed. "Time for what?"

"If I had not countered the spell, it would have been the time of your destruction," Basoff replied. Kedrik noted that the Judge did not look at him, but stared off at the moving shadows.

Still the Judge spoke in riddles. "Destruction?" Kedrik asked, his voice already stronger. He thought of the two

strangers. "Who would dare?" The fear was receding, replaced by the much more familiar anger. He did not care
to have even one of Basoff's skills talk to him with such
a condescending tone.

Basoff hesitated for a moment before he answered, as
though he realized he needed to choose his words more
carefully. "A fire Judge, I believe, upon the other world."

"The other . . ." The words were so simple, and so unthinkable. Someone had disobeyed the most basic of the
covenants. "Then the third world has been opened? Is all
we've worked for over?"

Basoff looked at Kedrik at last. "No, the Judge sends
his magic from within the second world. The seal still holds
upon the third; it will continue to hold until I—until we
say otherwise." The Judge's gaze left his lord again to scan
the corners of the room. Was the danger still present?

"The one who makes this magic has a terrible power,"
Basoff added a moment later. "But even he must realize
magic does not work well in that other place."

Kedrik nodded. He had been under the illusion that, on
the world of humans, magic did not work at all.

"I realize you must be unsettled." Basoff spoke far too
calmly. "Others are willing to resort to desperate measures." He paused before adding, "The rules no longer
seem to hold. We were, after all, willing to break the covenant in another way."

"As a final resort," Kedrik reminded the Judge. He did
not like this turn of events; it only reminded him that there
were others out there as powerful, and perhaps as desperate,
as themselves. "The war will destroy us all."

The Judge smiled at that. "Only most of us. I still intend
to be one of the few who remain." He bowed to his lord,
a gesture that did not appear to be totally sincere. "And

where would I be without your guidance? We have always been the ones to take advantage.''

The way he phrased it, Kedrik had almost become an afterthought. He was not so far gone in his dotage not to notice that.

The lord of the Grey repressed a sigh. So much seemed to have drifted away from him of late. He had spent far too much time consorting with those playthings that Basoff had brought—things not quite real, but all the more enticing— no. He couldn't let his mind wander that way. Not now.

So much had changed in these last few years. He thought of the way the last of his daughters, Karmille, played him. Well, he supposed it suited his purposes to give her a sense of independence—an independence that could be crushed in an instant. He had had seen the deaths of over a hundred of his children, had planned nearly half the deaths himself. Living this long did have its advantages.

Basoff stood before him, awaiting his command. Kedrik's mind had wandered away from the real. Despite all the Judges' magics, the High Lord of the Grey was feeling very old and tired tonight. Once he would have demanded a thorough accounting, taken immediate command of the situation, gathered half a dozen ministers from their beds, giving orders for both the mystical and the mundane. What was happening now? A thwarted spell from another world? He was aware of details, but the whole appeared to elude him. He had to wake fully, strike back at those who would strike against him.

He looked sharply to the Judge. ''This is not the end of it. We must strike back. What of your counterspell?''

Basoff sighed. ''The spell comes from another world. It is impossible for me to pinpoint its origin. I know only that the spell brought two who meant to do you harm, but they

were only instruments of a greater power. I had to send
them elsewhere.''

At least, Kedrik thought, he was well protected. Basoff
was an Earth Judge. Earth contained all four magics, and
bonded easily with the other three—the moisture of soil,
the spark of stone against stone, the swirl of dust in a wind-
storm. In Basoff's hands, earth magic seemed the strongest
of all.

But, Kedrik realized, those sent elsewhere had not been
destroyed.

''Where did you send them?'' he demanded.

''Again, we find the limits of magic. When using this
spell, you must know the other place—the place they are
sent—very well. A problem with spending all of my life
within the Grey Keep; it is all that I know well. Failing
somewhere, I had to send them to someone.''

Kedrik followed the logic. ''Someone you know.''

''I sent them to Karmille.''

Kedrik paused to consider this information. His daughter
had just this day sent an elemental to ask for help. Now
Basoff sent her this instead.

It would be a shame to lose the last of his daughters,
never to hear her laughter, never again to have her beside
him in his bed. But Kedrik no longer expected his heirs to
follow him. Either he would rule forever, or—he did not
care what might happen to the world if he was no longer
a part of it. His daughter's life was a small price to pay in
the greater plan.

And Karmille was far from the palace, deep within the
tunnels that honeycombed the great castle. Kedrik's palace
was only a tiny part of that castle. That, too, would change.

New questions flooded the High Lord's mind. Perhaps
he was awake at last.

''You tell me of a threat sent by magic, and that you

have sent it elsewhere. I only saw vague shapes in the darkness. And from the sound of the stranger's voice, he was as startled as I. You did not describe the danger.''

Basoff appeared the slightest bit uncomfortable. ''The portents were so strong I thought it best to act quickly. The spell sent two meant to do us harm. I sensed that, if they were not stopped, they would destroy everything we are working toward.''

''Two you say. Two of what?''

''Humans, my lord.''

''Humans?'' So it was more than magic that came from the other world. The answer was so startling, Kedrik found himself gripping the edge of the bed. ''Now we even have to worry about humans?''

Basoff nodded. ''The war has indeed changed everything.''

''And what do you know of these humans?''

''Little. I rid the Grey Keep of their presence at the first opportunity. I caught no more than a trio of names.''

Kedrik leaned forward, his curiosity engaged at last. ''Three names? Human names? But you said there were two.''

''Most decidedly human.'' Basoff frowned, as if he had to dredge the names up from deep in his memory. ''Yet, though they were two, they held three names. Ernie, and Joe—and Brian. Surely this confusion has something to do with the magic passing between the worlds.''

''I trust it is a confusion you can soon put behind you,'' Kedrik replied with a frown. ''Still, those names do not sound particularly frightening. Perhaps my daughter can deal with them after all.''

Basoff smiled ever so slightly. ''Your daughter is a most capable woman, my lord. Much is still possible.''

Kedrik looked longingly back at his scattered bedclothes. Sleep was beyond him for now. "Much is still possible," he repeated, half to himself. "Far too much."

"As always, I bow to my lord's greater wisdom."

Basoff did bow then, and turned and exited the room. Kedrik was alone in the dark, left to contemplate what had just transpired. This business of magic between the worlds disturbed him; it threw a new element into the delicate balance of the Castle. He trusted Basoff would soon bring this new sorcery under control; the Judge's power, and Kedrik's power as well, depended upon it.

Kedrik took a deep breath. Perhaps he should not be overly concerned. It was, after all, only a spell with humans, even if two of them did hold three names. No doubt it was an experiment by the Fire Judge upon the other world, a spell projecting something expendable among the High Lords, to see what might be done before the wizard revealed his true purpose.

Thought about in this way, the incident was nothing more than a warning. A dire warning, to be sure, but Kedrik was sure the Grey Judges were equal to the task.

Perhaps, then, Kedrik could afford himself a few more hours' sleep. Perhaps he could even reward himself with his special visitors.

Humans, after all. Hah! The castle could easily absorb a couple more of their useless sort. Most likely, even with that "gun," whatever it was, they would both be dead in short order.

To think otherwise would be absurd.

ALL OF THEM bowed as he entered the room.

Basoff looked silently at the half-dozen Judges he had gathered together. As much as they tried to hide it with both their attitudes and their sorceries, he could see discontent upon many of their faces. Their auras flickered in the darkened space, sending off multicolored sparks above their heads to mix with the last traces of those spells their leader's abrupt summons had disturbed. A touch of smoke rose from the robes of one, the hint of women's laughter settled about another, a third came from the distant echoes of a child's screams.

Basoff knew that the Judges' dissatisfaction came from more than being rousted from their late-night pleasures—or their beds. Their lord Kedrik liked to see results from his Judges, not necessarily the Judges themselves, so the brotherhood of the Grey only gathered for formal occasions and emergencies. While these Judges now before him might speak upon other plains a dozen times a day, they rarely met face-to-face, and never without a cushion of magic. In the Grey Keep, the successful Judge might literally be lost in a world of his own.

Except tonight. So Basoff had decreed in his summons.

"I will need your total attention!" Basoff announced brusquely. Now that they had been pulled from their comforts, Basoff would need to challenge more than their social graces. Four of the six were immediately attentive. The other two seemed distracted, as if still half lost in their recent sorceries.

"We have a crisis," Basoff announced. "We have long been charged with keeping the Grey supreme. And you have all won a place in the palace, thanks to your unique gifts." He turned his head slowly, looking directly at each Judge in turn. "I have asked you here in person because you must use those gifts more directly."

"Anything for the Grey."

It was Kayor who had spoken, his voice solemn, the sarcasm implied. Displays of patriotism and loyalty were not favored among the brotherhood. Kayor was the free-thinker in the palace, as difficult as he was talented.

"We are pledged to serve," Nallf spoke up next. The Judge at his side, Eaas, nodded his head. They were the most plainspoken of the Judges, and the most agreeable. Basoff had worked most closely with them over the years. They knew their best interest was his best interest.

But for all their attributes, they lacked both Kayor's humor and his anger.

He must strike a balance.

"I am planning to send some of you on a mission outside of the Keep," Basoff continued. "It involves the lady Karmille."

Basoff imagined he could feel resentment surge beneath the impassive faces before him. In the Grey Keep, loyalty had always been secondary. Fear was much more important as a motivating force. Kedrik was a master of spreading fear, and his daughter Karmille was his best pupil. As Kedrik's favorite, she echoed their lord's unpredictable power.

"The lady finds herself in danger, deep within the tunnels. Judge Sasseen is with her, but I fear he is unequal to the task. We will need a party to go and join them. Those who rescue them will be deeply rewarded."

"Those who rescue them?" Kayor asked. "Are you looking for volunteers?"

Basoff smiled. "Some of you must leave your comforts behind."

"Perhaps we might leave our boredom behind as well." Kayor was always good for the unexpected.

Basoff studied the remaining Judges. Two of them looked as if they were drifting, unable to concentrate totally on the real, lost among their sorceries even in a crisis. For an instant, he thought of sending the pair into the tunnels as a punishment. But no. Unknown forces were at work in

the vast spaces below. This small rescue mission might be
very important.

"Kayor, since you are so interested, you will be one of
those to go. Eaas, Nallf, you will go as well, to keep Kayor
in line. The rest of you are dismissed."

The other three disappeared—very quickly for the two
who had appeared distracted, Basoff noted. He would find
some even more unpleasant task for the pair. In the meantime, he needed to inform his chosen three as to the dangers
ahead.

"You will leave as soon as we have a few words,"
Basoff began.

"It is a rescue mission," Kayor agreed.

"Kedrik will supply some soldiers for an escort," Basoff continued, "to . . . protect you . . . and, of course, to
carry anything you might require. But none of us should
make light of this.

"The war has changed the world in ways that we had
not expected. We are doing this not just for Lady Karmille,
but for the fate of all the Grey. Especially the Judges of
the Grey. What you encounter in the tunnels below, and
how you deal with it, will greatly influence our continued
survival."

He had their attention now. For the first time, Basoff
spoke aloud a few of his most secret plans.

· 2 ·

The Castle

Eᴛᴛᴏɴ ꜰʟɪɴᴄʜᴇᴅ ᴀꜱ ᴛʜᴇ missiles bounced off the sorcerous barrier. They were nothing more than small boulders, catapulted from the hill on the far side of the battlefield. The rocks made a dull popping sound as they stopped abruptly, high in the air, often amid a shower of multicolored sparks at the juncture of rock and magic. Each boulder would hang that way for a long moment, sparkling as if the stone itself had caught fire, only to slide down to the ground an instant later, a lifeless rock once more, added to the ever-growing pile that littered the lower hillside.

Etton sighed. It was a sign of his fatigue that the usual distractions surprised him so easily. He had survived a hundred or more of these encounters, the two sides preparing for battle on either end of one of those great open expanses that had served this function for so long. Each side could plainly see the other, even on a night like this, overcast and

threatening rain, but each side was protected by the magics
of their Judges. Until the moment of attack, there was never
any hole in the sorcerous armor on either side. And yet the
opponent always tried to find some nonexistent weakness.
No doubt Etton's troops did the same—searching for any
defect, any advantage, no matter how slight.

Etton closed his eyes. He was battle-weary. What small
gains his army made were taken the following day. But then
the Green would take it back again. But at what cost?

Battle had taken most of his spirit. Lately, though, it had
felt far worse. Three months ago, his father, Tevard, had
returned to his Keep, trusting Etton to maintain the struggle.
Being placed in command had been no consolation at all.
So many in his service had died or disappeared. Lepp, Savignon, Aubric, his boyhood friends, all were gone. Not
that the four had been close since Etton had taken command. Judges ringed him constantly now, protecting him
from both friend and foe. But it had been heartening simply
to know his friends were near. Four days past, all three had
disappeared, victims, no doubt, of a raiding party of the
Grey. They were his connection with home, pieces of his
childhood, one more reason he could keep on fighting.

All gone.

And now?

Tonight was different. Battle after battle after constant
battle, Etton had seen no real advantages. Most times, he
had seen no surprises. Today, however, when Etton and his
army of the Green had reached the hillside an hour before
dawn, they discovered the Grey were not alone. The opposite hillside was packed with more troops than Etton had
seen in a pair of years.

"My lord." The deep voice at his side startled him.
Apparently, everything would startle Etton today. Dantis,

his chief Judge and advisor, had once again arrived silently
at his side.

"That the Grey would do such a thing," Dantis looked
over at the mass of men on the other hillside, an army flying
two flags side by side. "To ally themselves with the Purple
is a sure sign of desperation."

Etton looked at the far hill for a moment before replying.
"Perhaps the most desperate part is that we did not consider
such an alliance first."

"My lord?" Dantis pretended to be shocked.

"Need I say it out loud? The war goes badly, not just
for the Green, but for everyone. The war has lasted for so
long, it can have no other outcome. In a way, I am glad
that two of our foes have joined. Anything that can end
this thing might be considered an act of mercy."

"But even to speak with the Purple . . ." Dantis left the
rest of his thought unsaid.

Rumor had it that the Purple were the cause of this war;
the first cause, at least. They were the first to violate the
Conditions, the delicate weave of diplomacy and magic that
held sway over all of the castle. It had led to the first Great
Betrayal, in which the Orange had been destroyed. The
Brown and the Silver had been absorbed within the Purple,
frightened that, should they do otherwise, they would follow the Orange. The other High Lords rallied, first against
the Purple, then against each other. Soon there was more
than treachery between the houses—there was treachery
within some of the houses as well. The Blue had crumbled
in upon itself and declared a hasty neutrality. Was such
weakness within their house caused by the High Lords or
the Judges? Etton suspected it was some of both.

But the war had truly begun. By now, Etton believed it
would never end.

"Does my lord have any new orders?" the Judge by his side asked softly.

"Pardon, Dantis?" Etton replied to give himself an instant to collect his thoughts.

"We have come this day to fight the Grey, and found this instead. This—situation is most unusual."

Etton knew what his chief Judge really meant. The Green had marched here, initially expecting to meet an opposing army close to the size of their own. Instead, they found a force with close to three times as many troops, and who knew how many Judges? To do battle with an opponent of this strength would be foolhardy and wasteful; the results were bound to be tragic. Not that a Judge would say such a thing to his lord.

He gazed at the twin flags of his opponents, illuminated by the flares dotting the enemy's sorcerous barrier. What were his choices if he did not fight? He expected no reinforcements. The troops were exhausted. Even the Judges seemed harried, as if they approached the end of their sorcerous strength. His supplies were dwindling; the neverending war made paupers out of everyone in the House of Green. He had no choices.

He smiled at Dantis. "You are correct; most unusual. I believe we need to honor the occasion. Our foes deserve a very unusual response." He waved to the Judge. "Dantis, get my generals here, now. The battle begins before dawn."

"My lord." The words hung in the air, but the Judge was already gone.

Etton turned back to the enemy. The Grey had forged an alliance out of desperation, but it was a new alliance, and Etton hoped, one that was still untested. It would suit his purposes if the newfound allies could not agree. He resolved to give them something to fight about.

The rocks flaring against the invisible walls had given

him an idea. Not that Etton's plan was without substantial
risk. But his combined enemy had at least twice the troop
strength, and twice the number of Judges as Etton's small
band. It was the Green who would face true desperation in
this battle. Etton resolved to make the desperation work for
them.

"I WILL NOT!"

"It is the only way we shall win!"

"Win? You Grey barely survive. Only the Purple know
the way to victory!"

Both voices fell silent as Limon of the Grey walked into
the command tent. His brother, Zibor, stared enraged at
their new ally, Cantelus, while the Commander of all the
Purple stared upward as if he had never seen the roof of a
tent before.

Limon had hoped for better than this; he had hoped for
far too much. Their new alliance was not working well.
Cantelus and Zibor would never agree. Their verbal battles
over everything from troop placement to Judge protocols
to weather conditions would keep them from ever getting
close to a real, combined attack by their forces.

Limon believed they had needed a common enemy to
focus on, and had finally managed to convince the others
they should move their army to the battlefield. Once they
began to work together to defeat the Green, all their differences would be forgotten. Or so he had thought.

Of the two brothers, Limon was the diplomat, Zibor the
man of action. This alliance was largely Limon's doing.
Now he had begun to wonder why he bothered.

Their new ally sniffed to acknowledge Limon's presence. He nodded ever so slightly at Zibor. "You will follow
my recommendation."

The tone of Cantelus's voice said that it was not a recommendation, but rather a command. Not only was Cantelus High Lord of the Purple, but he was older than Limon and Zibor, the two surviving High Princes of the Grey. Cantelus seemed to think this made him some sort of father figure; his job in the alliance to show the youngsters the way. But Limon and Zibor had a father beyond equal; a father who was as likely to kill his children as reprimand them. When Limon thought of their father, Kedrik, he remembered spilled blood and cruelty; a father whose children learned to listen and obey as a simple matter of survival. In comparison, Cantelus was little more than a large sack of overheated air.

"The Green will be completely demoralized when confronted by our combined forces," Cantelus continued. "We will attack at dawn, first with magic, then with troops. The Green will attempt to flee, but not before we can decimate their forces."

Zibor spat on the parched dirt at their feet. "If the Green are so demoralized, why are they even here? Surely they have scouts that would have informed them as to the size of our forces. Perhaps they feel they should take a stand with whatever strength they have remaining." He smiled his half smile, the result of a dueling accident as a child. "Go down to glory—that sort of rot."

He looked to his brother, then to their new ally. "Why do we even have to attack? With our superior force we can surround the Green, choke them, weaken them. We cut their supply lines, force them to surrender."

No. Limon had fought the Green too long to think they might simply surrender, or be so easily surrounded. But if he could suggest a way to compromise and combine plans . . .

"They will guard against such a maneuver," Limon said, nodding to both his brother and the Lord of the Purple.

"Perhaps we can distract them. I think magic is in order—
in this, I believe Cantelus is correct. And we need at least
the threat of a frontal assault, if only to distract the Green
from our true purpose."

"A-a threat?" Cantelus sputtered. Apparently, he wasn't
interested in compromise. "Why do we have to take half
measures when it would be so easy to destroy our enemy?
The Purple do not sit back and wait! The Purple conquer!
The Green will feel that we are weak."

Cantelus's posturing was too much even for Limon.
"What do you care what the Green think if we win the
battle? We must be willing to adjust our strategy according
to the situation."

"Well, I suppose that much is true," the Purple lord
admitted. "And I, with my long years facing battle, have
the clearest view. We will draw the Green into a trap. And
I *will* oversee the fighting."

"So you insist!" Zibor threw up his hands in disgust.
"This gets us nowhere. I say we cast votes."

"Votes?" It was Cantelus's turn to show disgust. "You
mean your two votes to my one. I did not join with the
Grey to lose all my—"

"Sire!" An officer of the Grey stepped somewhat hes-
itantly into the command tent. "Forgive my intrusion, but
we have caused a breach in the enemy's defenses!"

"Explain, Captain," Limon said brusquely, careful not
to show how relieved he was for the intrusion.

"Our missiles are getting by their barrier, and seem to
be causing chaos. There is a large fire within their encampment, burning out of control."

Cantelus laughed. "See? Already our superiority breaks
down their sorcery. Here we argue while our Judges do all
the work. Enough talk! Let us finish the battle." He strode

past the captain to the door of the tent. "I'd like to see this chaos for myself."

Zibor looked sharply at his brother. "He is doing nothing without me." He quickly followed their ally from the tent.

Limon decided he would let the two of them annoy each other without his participation for the moment. He would find out more about this remarkable turn of events from a reliable witness. He strode over to the officer.

"Captain?"

The captain stared straight ahead. Officers of the Grey learned not to display emotion, no matter what happened around them.

"I have a question or two, if I may."

"Sire," the captain replied.

"How was it determined that the enemy's barrier was breached?"

"The missiles stopped flaring, for one. A set of stones were catapulted into total darkness, with no sorcerous reaction. There was noise, as well—screams and shouts, a commotion loud enough to be heard from our own hill. The Judges soon informed us that there was a change in the weave. All signs pointed to a broken barrier."

The weave. That was what the Judges called the interaction of their sorceries with those of the enemy. It was such a peaceful word for something often so violent, full of thunder and wind, rain and fire. So these "signs," as the captain put it, were all favorable. Why, then, did Limon hesitate? Oh, he was always the cautious one. Zibor was ceaselessly ready to rush forward into battle, and Cantelus of the Purple seemed, if anything, even more volatile. And what would Limon do as his brother and the prince of the Purple pushed each other into battle—sit in the command tent and worry?

Limon thanked the captain and quit the tent to find the
first light of dawn brightening the camp, turning the dark
mass of men that littered their hillside into a riot of silver
helms and pale faces, with clusters of purple robes popping
up amidst the grey, like flowers on a rocky hillside.

He turned to look at the battlefield, and saw that the sky
was full of clouds, but they did not appear to be of natural
origin. It was Judges' work, one of the most common ways
for the opposing magics to manifest themselves—by sub-
verting nature. The clouds were of two distinct colors: the
ones hovering above their hillside were, appropriately, a
deep, roiling grey with darker streaks of black and brown,
clouds that promised a storm beyond compare, the kind of
tempest that would uproot trees and level dwellings, leaving
nothing but destruction.

Opposing these clouds were another set, quite different
in color. These other unnatural clouds were somewhat
lighter, barely grey at all, but set through with long streaks
of deep red, as if these clouds were filled with blood. They
met the grey overhang in a line over the very middle of the
battlefield in all but one point, where the grey mass went
pouring through to reach the opposite hillside. *There* was
proof of the breach. It seemed a very dramatic proof, too.

Cantelus strode up to Limon.

"Your brother hesitates, waiting for a word from you. I
have sent my own troops ahead, to spill blood and gain the
glory. The Purple will destroy the Green!"

Limon suppressed any response. This man was insuffer-
able enough already. How much farther might he puff out
his chest if he claimed a solo victory?

Limon called to his brother, who was conferring with
his generals some distance down the hill, to join them. Perhaps, Limon thought, they could use their Grey army to

support the Purple advance, so they might claim some part of the victory.

"Pilar!" Cantelus announced before Zibor could rejoin them. "To my side!"

The Purple lord was joined by an elderly Judge, so old that even his magic could not keep him from appearing bent and wrinkled.

"Pilar is my eyes and ears. He has been the eyes and ears of my family for six generations." Cantelus smiled, happy at last now that he was in control. "Come, faithful Judge. How goes the battle?"

The Judge hugged his black robes around his emaciated form as he shut his eyes. His magic, after all, would allow him to see elsewhere.

"We rush across the lower foothills and onto the plain. No one stands in our way."

Cantelus clapped his meaty palms together. "They are so demoralized that no one confronts us. The Green will soon be history!"

"How close are their troops?" Limon demanded.

Pilar shuddered. "We are almost to their camp. A hundred men are screaming. There is a great fire. The path up the hillside is deserted."

Limon frowned as Cantelus roared with laughter. This was far too easy. "Surely there should be someone in their path, if only by accident. No spell could ever be that complete."

Zibor had joined them at last. From the deep frown on his face, he didn't appear to be sharing in the victory. Limon noted the way his brother's fingers drummed on the hilt of his sword; a first sign of Zibor's anger.

"There are a few bodies strewn at the edge of the clearing," Pilar reported. "All is chaos. They have fled before our assault!"

"Why do we rush? I think some caution is in order," Zibor stated loudly. "The situation among our enemy is not at all clear. Our Judges tell me there are certain confusing signals at the edges of the weave."

"Your Judges are jealous because my own have taken the lead!" Cantelus cheered. "The enemy is retreating, soldiers, Judges, and lords! We shall swoop down and take them from the rear!"

"If we must." Zibor's hand stayed on his sword. He turned to his brother. "Our captains are prepared to move into battle. They suggest flanking the Purple attack on either side."

"You'll mop up the few that escape the Purple net? Very well." Cantelus threw open his arms to embrace the battle before him. "You find me in a generous mood. I will let you share in our victory."

Cantelus's latest round of laughter was cut short by a weird, high-pitched scream. Limon realized the uncanny sound was coming from Pilar.

"No!" his voice quavered. "There are shadows where no shadows should be!"

Limon stared at the distant battle. Smoke from the raging fire seemed to obscure much of the opposite hillside.

"Brother!" Zibor called. He pointed skyward.

Limon looked up to see the clouds close above them, the red spreading like a great pool of blood, overwhelming the marching Grey.

Pilar screamed even higher than before. He fell to the hillside. Blood poured from his mouth and ears. The lord of all the Purple nudged the elder with his foot, then kicked him sharply in the ribs. Pilar did not respond.

"They have killed my Judge!" Cantelus shrieked.

"They kill more than that, you fool." Zibor nodded to

the distant battle. "The Green have released boulders from farther up the hill."

"No!" Cantelus's voice rose to a wail much like that of his Judge. "I will not allow this!"

But it was far beyond what the portly lord might allow. Limon saw a hundred boulders roaring downward, and then a hundred more. The first rocks had dislodged others, which had freed others still. The whole upper half of the hillside seemed to be moving toward the Purple. Some of those in the army's front lines saw the danger above them and were trying to retreat, but were stopped by the forward thrust of the ranks behind them. The troops were forced to a standstill.

No one was moving but the wall of killing stones.

Zibor cried out: "The Green show themselves!"

A few dozen archers in the uniform of the Green had appeared on the far edges of the hillside. Standing well outside the path of the avalanche, they sent a hailstorm of arrows to fall on those Purple closest to the plains. Unless Cantelus could quickly redirect his men, his army would be slaughtered.

Limon turned to their stunned ally. "Do you have someone else you can contact to relay orders."

"Pilar . . ." Cantelus murmured.

"Pilar is dead!"

Cantelus blinked. "Pilar . . . had an apprentice."

So he had another to communicate directly with his troops. "Find him! If you want to save your men!"

Cantelus appeared frozen in place. He looked wildly about him, at the two princes of the Grey, and the dead Judge at his feet. "I was lured into this, before I was ready. I will lose half my forces. And Pilar." His gaze returned to the brothers of the Grey. "Pilar! This is your fault! If you had not lured me here with your false promises . . ."

He turned back to the carnage on the hillside. "Our alliance may be at an end."

"What good is an alliance with a lord that has no army?" Zibor shouted. "We need your army if we are to succeed." He turned to Limon. "Those archers are vulnerable to attack from the plain."

What his brother said was true. "It is time to deploy our forces," Limon agreed. "Cantelus, you have drawn them out. Now the Grey will dispatch them."

"I will inform the captains." Zibor lifted his hand far above his head and brought it down sharply to his side. One of the captains and a Grey Judge both rushed up the hill to join their princes.

Cantelus stared at all of them, unable to say a word.

ETTON COULD NOT believe his luck.

The first wave of enemy troops had blundered straight into his trap. The rocks and arrows together would probably destroy half of the great wave that had assaulted his camp. Or what they had thought to be his camp.

Dismantling a part of the Green's sorcerous barrier, while a risk, had allowed certain of his Judges to be released for other tasks, especially the movement of boulders. This had produced a much more effective attack than would otherwise have been possible. Both enemy troops and enemy Judges were caught by surprise, allowing for a two-pronged counterattack. According to Etton's advisors, hundreds of enemy soldiers were dead, along with at least one enemy Judge.

But surprise was a fleeting advantage. He saw two more enemy legions advancing to either side of the first. His archers were exposed on the surrounding hillside, vulnerable to arrow, catapult, and directed sorcery. While they still had the advantage of position, they would not be able to overcome such a large force. And his infantry was only half the size of the legions that approached—legions that he suspected still did not reflect the full strength of the enemy. He had used up all his luck. Now there was only time to die.

He hoped it would be a final, glorious battle. Once his army was gone, his father's Keep would be overwhelmed. But perhaps the Green, like the House of Orange before them, would be remembered as warriors. They sang of the Orange throughout the castle. Etton hoped they would sing of the Green as well.

His Judges cried out from farther down the hill. Had the Grey increased their sorcerous attack?

"My lord Etton!" Dantis called. "We have visitors!"

Etton raced down the hill to find his Judges surrounding four strangers. The newcomers stood very still, making no move to attack.

They were not members of the Grey. One of them was a warrior dressed in the uniform of the same noble Orange he had hoped to emulate, a house that had disappeared long before Etton was born. And the warrior was the most normal of the four. Next to him stood a human—his father disliked the word. It was never used at court. When had Etton begun to think in such vulgar terms? He was another like his boyhood friend Aubric, but dressed in the strangest clothes Etton had ever seen; what was the design on the flimsy shirt the man wore—large, pink flowers? Behind the two stood a Gnarlyman, probably a servant of one of the others, and perhaps the strangest of the four, who stood slightly to the side of all the others. For this last man was made of solid, burnished metal—weapons, clothes, and all.

"We are privileged to make your acquaintance."

Etton was not at all surprised that it was the metal man

who spoke. Not that his lips moved, but the great, booming voice had to come from somewhere. "Etton, is it not? Prince of the Green?" The metal man bowed ever so slightly. "We believe you may need some assistance."

Etton bowed ever so slightly in return. No matter what, his father Tevard had always taught him to be polite. "And you are?"

"I think you will find us to be your friends."

Well, Etton hoped so. Not that he would trust these newcomers until he knew a bit more about them. He needed, quickly, to be back with his Judges and generals, planning their defense.

"We need friends, especially now," he called to the newcomers as he turned to rejoin his advisors. "The Purple have allied themselves with the Grey."

"I have been looking for the Grey."

Laughter boomed above the strangers.

"They may have a new ally," the metal man continued. "But you, friend Etton, have gained a god."

. 3 .

The World

JACKIE PORTER HEARD A SI-
ren behind her. She pulled her car to the side of the road
and let the ambulance roar past. Then she floored it, doing
her best to keep up with the speeding ambulance. If a local
cop came along she could flash her badge. It felt very important to be back there with Karen and Mrs. Mendeck
when the ambulance came.

Like all violence, it had happened quickly.

She had been perhaps twenty feet away from a pair of
men with definite ties to organized crime. And, at that particular moment, they were on her side. She had been far
more worried about the other man—the one that appeared
out of nowhere, and didn't appear to be precisely human.

Shots had been fired, but now they almost seemed beside
the point.

She had no explanations for what had occurred—people
appearing where they could not possibly be, then disap-

pearing a moment later. It had all been beyond her. She
was glad her companions, two teenagers and a short woman
in her mid-seventies, had seemed to know a lot more about
what was going on. Not that the teens, Brian and Karen,
weren't freaked by the whole thing. But the older woman,
Mrs. Mendeck, seemed in complete control. Jackie would
only be half surprised if Mrs. Mendeck had orchestrated
the whole thing.

Mr. Smith—that had been the stranger's name. She'd
learned his name, oddly enough, from her own Chief of
Police. He'd brought Smith to the hospital to question
Brian—question and maybe a lot more. Right then, the
Chief had seemed far too willing to allow Smith to do anything and everything, whether it was legal or not—even if
it involved kidnapping a child. Smith had appeared to have
some control over one of the two mobsters—Ernie was his
name. But then Joe—the other mobster—had shot Smith.
In an instant, Smith was gone. It was all over—or it had
just begun.

But Smith had done something to Ernie before he had
disappeared. The big man had collapsed and could not be
revived, like he had fallen into a coma. It had sent her on
this errand of mercy—to the nearest pay phone and help.

They had to get Ernie's body back to town. Mrs. Mendeck said it was much more than a coma. When Joe and
Brian had disappeared *somewhere else,* they had gone looking for Ernie's spirit. At least, that was Mrs. Mendeck's
story. For the first time in Jackie's life, she wished she
followed some of that New Agey stuff so she might understand what was going on.

The siren roared on the van in front of her. They were
easily doing ninety on the flat country roads.

Officer Jackie Porter's specialty was accident reconstruction; that was what the Parkdale Police Department had

hired her to do. She was able to take the unknown and give it a probable cause, given the speed and direction of collision; figuring in time of day, weather conditions, and whether or not alcohol or drugs were involved. Basically, she solved a puzzle given a set number of variables. She realized she wanted to do that, here, too.

She had gone into her line of work because of her analytical mind. Everything—even what happened with Mr. Smith—had a cause and effect. Again, she was dealing with a set number of variables. Except she had the feeling, where Mr. Smith was concerned, the variables just got increased by some factor beyond her imagination.

The ambulance was slowing down. Jackie hit her brakes. The scene—was it a crime scene? An accident?—was just ahead.

Jackie pulled to the side of the road after the ambulance. Ernie lay where they had left him, mostly on the dirt beyond the asphalt, but with a shoulder and arm flung out into the road. Mrs. Mendeck had thought it was best not to move him, so Jackie had put a couple of flares in front of him, and parked his car behind him with the warning lights flashing.

There was a county sheriff's car there already, pointing toward her on the far side of the road. Jackie walked over to the deputy and showed him her credentials.

"I was the one who called," she explained.

The deputy frowned at her. "Is this part of a case?"

It could be, Jackie thought. But what would she be investigating? Her chief? She shook her head. "Nah. I was taking a couple days off, went out for a ride in the country with a couple women friends." She waved to Mrs. Mendeck and Karen, who were standing off the road behind Ernie. They waved back, then turned to watch the medics with their stretcher.

"And you found him like this?" the deputy asked.

"Mrs. Mendeck was the one who saw him first." She didn't want to lie to the deputy. But how could she possibly tell him the truth?

The deputy nodded. "It was lucky you drove by here when you did. This guy's out cold." He walked over to talk to the medics. It was all over in a couple minutes; Ernie was strapped to the stretcher and loaded into the back of the ambulance, headed, the deputy said, for the county hospital.

The deputy pointed to the LaSabre. "This the guy's car?"

Jackie explained how she had moved it to alert any other cars to the body by the side of the road.

"Yeah, the old lady already told us. Quick thinking." He looked down at his notepad. "The car's registered to a Bisotti Construction. The guy's got no ID. We'll have to call the company. Maybe they have some idea who he is."

"Maybe," Jackie replied softly. It was probably for the best if none of them, Mrs. Mendeck, Karen and herself, officially knew Ernie's identity—but it still felt very uncomfortable to lie to a fellow officer.

"I'll get someone out here to tow the car." He flipped his notepad closed. "Well, Officer Porter. I hope the rest of your trip is quieter."

She shook her head and smiled. "You and me both."

The ambulance roared off back the way it came. A moment later, the deputy climbed back into his car and headed in the opposite direction.

Mrs. Mendeck smiled at Jackie. "It was best that we called that in. Ernie is only a pawn in the game."

But Jackie found herself very angry at this whole thing. "A game? Is that what this is? A game?"

Mrs. Mendeck sighed. "I think we will have to discover

exactly what this is, and very soon. Otherwise, Smith will win."

"Win? What does that mean?"

"Mr. Smith knows about us now, and he has marked every one of us. He does not forgive."

"Does that mean we can't go home?" Karen asked.

Mrs. Mendeck shook her head. "I think we have to. I have certain things at my apartment—in fact, why don't we all go to my place?"

Jackie thought the old woman made it sound like a slumber party. "You say that Smith does not forgive. But there must be some way we can stop him."

Mrs. Mendeck paused for a moment before she replied. "Oh, even someone like Smith will make a mistake eventually. He might accidentally alert the authorities here, or something even more powerful . . . somewhere else. But by the time that happens, it is likely that all of us will be dead."

Great. Just the sort of reassurance Jackie needed.

"I guess we'd better head for home, sweet home, then."

Neither of the others noticed her sarcasm.

HE WAS KNOWN by many names. On this world, some called him the Pale Man; others referred to him as Mr. Smith.

The Pale Man entered the room. The man without arms shrank back, hiding among the jungle of wires and speakers that allowed him to answer the phones. The Pale Man was pleased. The Pale Man lived for fear.

Recent events had gone badly. Mr. Smith did not approve.

He had thought, if he worked quietly, everything would fall into place for the next part of his plan. But, while he had been careful not to alert his enemies upon the other world, he had been careless with those who were closer.

He had not been diligent enough. He had tried to have others eliminate the potential threats on this world, either by killing them or adding them to his cause. His powers had located two in this town, both living as human teenagers—Brian and Karen—with the power he needed, while both were young enough to be molded by his will. He could have used either one of them, then disposed of the other. But another, more shadowy figure stood in his way, a figure it had taken him time to identify. And now, the one who called herself Mrs. Mendeck had interfered with the next stage of his plan.

He looked down at the remains of the gun wound in his arm. It would take hours to heal on this world.

The phone rang. "Problems solved," the man without arms answered on the second ring.

The Pale Man had to solve his own problem now.

He had underestimated them, and given them a chance to fight back. It made the threat to his plans all that much more real. While they might have some raw power, they had no true experience; they could do nothing without his carelessness. He was stronger, and older, than any of those who fought against him.

He had made mistakes. Now he would have to use his resources. He had made many deals since he had arrived, and had created many debtors.

They could be of use. They were all disposable.

In the meantime, he had a use for Ernie. He might have sent his spirit elsewhere for safekeeping. But the body—thickly muscled, easily recognized—would come in very handy for what he had in mind.

. 4 .

The Castle

WELL, THIS SUCKED.

Brian yelped at his side. Joe's eyes snapped shut as he was surrounded by blinding light. He felt a second, disorienting lurch, and the sense that he was floating in nothingness.

He was standing on solid ground. Apparently, they'd landed somewhere for a second time.

"I think we're alone," Brain whispered. "Wherever we are."

Joe carefully opened his eyes. After a moment of squinting against the newfound glare, he saw they were in a featureless white hallway. The bedroom they'd just left had looked like something out of a King Arthur movie. This place looked more like a space station.

"What the hell?" Joe muttered, not really expecting an answer. He heard what at first he thought was the echo of his voice in the antiseptic hall, but the words were new,

and the tone was even more upset than Joe was. Another
voice was shouting in the distance. He looked over at Brian.
"I don't think we're all *that* alone."

"Do you think we'll find Summitch here?" Brian asked.

That's right. The old broad had claimed she was sending
them to someone, or something, called Summitch. Joe
Beast had agreed to follow Ernie—well, "Ernie's spirit,"
that's what the old lady had called it—without giving it
much thought.

He guessed that was the Joe Beast curse—he hadn't
given anything in his life much thought. So he'd gone to
college, but had ended up working for his uncle and his
mob connections. It had started out almost legal with that
dummy corporation, but recently his involvement with his
uncle's business had gotten more and more hands-on, running less-than-legit errands with his cousin Ernie. Errands
that used guns. And when you've got a gun, you end up
using it, right?

He'd actually shot a guy—the father of a teenage boy
he was supposed to pick up and deliver to his uncle—and
was sent out, hours later, to kill a teenage girl. It seemed
his uncle, Roman Petranova, had made a deal with a certain
Mr. Smith—a deal that included killing kids.

There was something creepy about this Smith, besides
putting contracts on high school kids. He didn't play by
any of the rules. Hell, as far as Joe could tell, this Smith
wasn't even human.

Everybody had their limits. Joe guessed that kid-killing
was his. It all had to stop, no matter what his uncle said.
Joe ended up following his gut, protecting the boy whose
father he had shot and the girl he'd been ordered to kill.
They were only kids, after all, and they seemed a lot more
innocent than Joe had been in high school. So to hell with

his uncle's orders. He'd find some way to talk his way out
of this. Or so he'd thought.

But this had gone way beyond talking.

First, there was some kind of magical mumbo jumbo
involved. Smith had sent Ernie (or his spirit, Joe reminded
himself) to some other place, and the only way to rescue
Ernie was for Joe to go after it. So this Mrs. Mendeck, who
looked just like a little old lady, except she could do things
like a little old lady witch, set up this dark doorway between this country road and wherever the hell they were
going. She simply said, if they wanted to save Ernie, that
both he and the kid Brian had to go. And Joe had walked
right into it.

It was only when he stepped into the dark that he realized he didn't know anything about this place Mrs. Mendeck was sending him. Then he and Brian had ended up in
somebody's bedroom—a pretty nice bedroom, too. Not that
they were allowed to stay there long. The cordite smell still
burned in his nostrils. So much for using the gun. He
should probably save his bullets for emergencies. If he
could figure out what was an emergency around here.

The confrontation was over in an instant, but the whole
thing was still crystal clear in his mind, like he'd had it
etched behind his eyeballs. Their sudden appearance had
startled one pale guy in his bedclothes, but the second
one—the guy in black—was ready for them. And both of
those guys looked just like Mr. Smith. There was a cruelty
in their eyes that could match up with his uncle Roman.
But Roman Petranova, for all his casual cruelty, was different. Roman was family; that counted first and foremost.
It was the only reason Joe had survived all these years.
These guys had no such connection. There were no rules.

What if this new world was full of Smiths—pale guys

who lived to kill? Maybe the old lady had sent them to a
world of monsters.

Joe smiled when he thought of it. Well, the two pale
guys might have been monsters, but they sure as hell were
surprised to see Joe and Brian back in that bedroom. Maybe
surprise would help him to survive. Heck, if his uncle Roman figured out what Joe had let happen to Ernie, he was
dead anyway. This way, at least his death would be a little
more interesting.

In the meantime, they were standing in the middle of
some bright, white corridor, so cold it could make a hospital look homey. So much for Joe Beast, man of action.

"You think maybe we could call for Summitch?" Brian
whispered. "He should be around here somewhere."

Always that Summitch. But that wasn't the name of either of the two creeps they'd just left, and Joe didn't see a
welcoming committee here, either. He was beginning to
wonder if Mrs. Mendeck didn't know quite as much as she
seemed to.

"Wait a second, kid." The noise, while still faint, was
growing louder. Now that he concentrated on it, he could
make out two or three voices. It sounded like some kind of
fight. Of course. No matter where Joe went these days,
there was a fight.

He frowned at Brian. "Well, if this Summitch is around
here, I'd say he's busy."

"It sounds like it could be dangerous," Brain agreed.

"I'm beginning to get the feeling that everything here
is dangerous."

"Joe?"

He almost jumped. Who had said his name?

"Hey, Joe?" The words were faint at first, little louder
than the distant fight. But he knew that voice.

It sounded like his cousin. "Ernie?" Joe called back. "Where are you, man?"

"Hey, I'm right—I mean, I don't—man, why can't I feel—Joe?" Ernie's voice was getting louder, but there was no Ernie attached. It was like that bus sound they had heard back on the road, with no bus to go along with it. In other words, magic.

"Joe?" The voice was already growing fainter. "I don't like this, Joe." It sounded like he was headed toward the fighting. "I gotta find myself, Joe."

"Ernie, don't go." Joe shouted after the retreating voice. "Ernie, damn it, stay here!"

"Here?" Ernie's voice was already retreating, headed toward the voices down the hall. "Where's here? I gotta find a light or something. See that everything's all right. Joe—"

Ernie's voice was lost amid a new round of shouts from the fighting down the hall.

"That was Ernie?" Brian was back to whispering again.

"Well, it was at least part of him. You know what Mrs. Mendeck said about the spirit business." Joe frowned. Shouldn't Brian know more about this stuff than he did?

"So what do we do now?" He knew what Brian meant—did they walk toward the fight, or did they run in the opposite direction? Well, Ernie had sort of decided that for them. He had to follow that voice and try to rescue whatever was left of his cousin. That was the only reason he'd come here.

"I'd say let's see what's going on." He waved his gun. "My guess is that they haven't seen many of these before."

Brian nodded. Joe guessed it was up to him to lead the way. They started walking.

In a moment, they came to a place where the hall they walked down intersected at an exact right angle with another hallway, every bit as featureless as the first, save that this one held three figures clad all in black who rushed in their direction. Joe pushed Brian back into the hall that they had come from. He positioned himself so that he could see the three approach while keeping his gun hand hidden from sight.

"Stand clear!" one of the three called loudly, in a voice that might have held more authority if it weren't so panic-stricken. "Interfere, and you will feel the wrath of the Judges!"

So they had judges on this world, too? Not that Joe particularly respected them on the world he came from. Especially when they tried to throw their weight around. Joe wasn't about to stand around for anybody's wrath. Maybe it was time to show them his piece.

He stepped farther out into the corridor so they could see his .44.

The three looked at his gun and screamed; a real full-throated yell in three parts. There was a flash of light even brighter than their surroundings. Joe turned his head away. When he looked back, the three in black had vanished.

Joe looked down at the shiny metal in his hand. "Maybe they *have* seen a gun before," he said aloud. "Maybe we're not the first people from our world to show up here. This is starting to get interesting." He waved for Brian to follow him. "I think we'll find the action down where our friends were."

Unlike the never-ending hall they had just quit, the new corridor before them curved to the left, so they could only see a few yards in front of them. But they only traveled another hundred paces before the hall opened into a very large room with rows of benches around three sides, like some kind of theater. Most of the benches were empty, but down on the floor in front of them there was a small band of men in black—more Judges, Joe guessed, facing off against another small group, who, from their clothing, looked like they'd be more at home in that King Arthur bedroom than here in the spaceship-like white. The two groups did not appear to be completely friendly. In fact, there seemed to be some sort of standoff in progress.

One of those in black—Joe realized the new group was made up of both men and women—pushed himself in front of the others. "You must let us have him before the merging is complete!"

"Why?" a woman in the other group shot back. "So you can continue with your mock trial and condemn us all to death?" She showed them a tight-lipped, scornful smile. "I think the power has already shifted here."

Joe stopped dead when he saw the newest speaker. She was of the same pale-skinned race as Smith and the others he had seen—including those dressed in black. But the high cheekbones and foreheads of the three males he'd had close contact with had made them seem haughty and cruel. The same features made the woman seem . . . well . . . distant and commanding, but impossibly striking as well—her ivory skin framed by raven curls, her silver-grey eyes almost beyond color. Joe didn't want to take his eyes off her. She was one of the most beautiful creatures he had ever seen.

Another dark-robed figure stepped close to the beauty. "Beware, m'lady. Aubric need be no concern of ours."

She smiled back at the speaker, apparently her own personal Judge. "Dear Sasseen. I have always been fond of Aubric. Especially now that he might be of some use."

The woman was flanked by a number of fighting men of various shapes and sizes. A couple of them looked a little the worse for wear, with torn clothing and bruised flesh. One of them was missing a hunk of meat on one arm.

There was no bleeding, though. Actually, this last guy didn't exactly look like he was alive.

There was no sign of Ernie, either. Not that Joe knew exactly what to look or listen for. Neither one of the groups out on the floor paid particular attention to Joe or Brian; after all, it might disturb their staring contest. He tried to listen for other voices when the combatants weren't shouting at each other, but the only other noise was a low moan, like someone in continuous pain. It was coming from behind the woman. That couldn't be Ernie.

Joe realized that anyone, or anything, could be Ernie in this place. Back on the highway, Mrs. Mendeck had talked about Brian having something special about him. Right now, Joe wished Brian could use that specialness to explain what the hell was happening.

He felt a tug on his sleeve. Joe looked over at Brian, who pointed overhead.

Joe looked up.

There was something hanging just below the ceiling, like a dark and ragged cloud, except this cloud had a face.

"The merging goes too far," the cloud rumbled. "I cannot hold! I cannot hold!"

This seemed to spur the lead Judge to another round of exclamations. "You don't know what you do! We need balance! Otherwise, we will never survive!"

The woman laughed. "Balance? Like a thousand years of war? I think maybe it is time—"

The floor shook beneath Joe's feet for an instant. Great. Maybe this whole place was going to collapse.

"Do you think one of these is Summitch?" Brian asked.

Joe didn't think he could ask. It looked like there was too much going on for these strangers even to notice a gun.

"The signs!" the cloud groaned as the ground shook a second time. "Beware the signs!"

The battered guy—the one with the chunk out of his arm—shuddered suddenly. He shook his head and looked directly at the newcomers.

"Joe?" he asked.

Could that be Ernie? But how? Hell, why didn't he just stop asking questions? Joe started to walk toward him across the room.

"New forces enter the fray!" the woman's Judge—Sasseen?—shouted. It seemed that they liked to shout. "I fear, m'lady, that this is all beyond my control."

"Then, Sasseen, let us be gone from here! Aubric, I hope when next we meet, you will remember this little kindness."

"Ernie!" Joe called. They weren't going anywhere until he found out what was going on. He raised his gun.

They still paid no attention to him. Instead, the Judge with the woman waved his hands about in the air, causing a swirl of movement that spread from his hands to surround the entire group, immersing them in a surge of color— brown and blue and red and green, all twisting and merging until it looked like a curtain between Joe and the woman's group. The color evaporated like steam off a bathroom mirror. The Judge, the woman, the guy who might be Ernie— all of them were gone.

"Hey!" Joe shouted into the now-empty space. He wondered if he'd ever get used to this sort of thing.

"Look!" Brian called out. Joe realized the woman's party had left someone behind. A man dressed in chain mail was huddled on the ground, the constant moan coming from his lips.

Another tremor shook the room. The moan became a scream.

The Judges were gone, too. Joe hadn't even seen them leave.

Brian was headed for the man in pain. Maybe the kid knew something. Joe decided to follow.

"Mister?" Brian started. "Hey, excuse me. Is there anything—"

The man looked up and opened his eyes. Brian gasped and took a step back. The stranger's eyes were full of light. Even in this overlit room, they shone like two flashlights in the middle of the night. The man shivered violently, as if he had taken the tremors inside himself.

Brian looked back to Joe. "What should we do?"

Joe glanced around. It seemed like everybody was gone. It was just Brian and Joe and this guy who looked like he was going to explode.

Joe had no idea—where to go, what to do, how to stay alive—he didn't have a clue.

This place was too much for him. A cloud with a face spoke of doom; people popped in and out of existence. The only one without any magic was Joe. All he had was a gun.

THERE WAS ACTUAL sky out here. Not that strange, painted sky he had seen in Gontor's cavern, and anything but those claustrophobic torchlit tunnels Eric Jacobsen thought he'd never escape. And it was actually blue. Sure, the wispy clouds had some pretty strange colors in them, but you couldn't have everything.

Jacobsen took the deepest breath he had probably taken since coming to this place. He liked being out in the open. He realized he was actually beginning—well, maybe not to believe in Gontor, but to trust in his particular, peculiar abilities. Gontor kept telling Jacobsen how important he—Eric—was; maybe he really did have a part in all of this.

His newfound sense of freedom was tempered by a constant, low-level grumbling by his side. Jacobsen let out the breath with a sigh. Summitch was at it again.

"This is what I get for tying my plan to others," the short, very wrinkled fellow muttered. "Summitch works best alone. But I needed someone to help carry the gold, didn't I? Next time, Summitch will make do with less gold."

Jacobsen nodded to his short companion. "You do talk to yourself an awful lot."

Summitch glared back at him. "Most times, I am the only one worth talking to. There are bad times ahead, Eric Jacobsen." The Gnarlyman nodded. "The last time I teamed with another, it was a disaster. Summitch still owes a favor to that one. Of course, to collect it she'll have to find me first." The five hundred wrinkles that covered his face turned about into what might have been a smile. Jacobsen found the whole effect a little frightening.

"If you say so." Jacobsen made the safest of replies. He had long ago given up trying to decipher the fine points of the small one's muttering. Simply because he was unique—from what Jacobsen knew about this place, the other Gnarlymen did not have the ability of speech—did not make his words worth hearing.

Besides, there was a whole drama unfolding before them. Gontor had gotten the four of them away from the Judges, only to plop them in front of what appeared to be the headquarters of an army. Still, while the Judges seemed all too eager to attack, at least the head of the army was willing to listen.

"So," a tall, young fellow in a green tunic approached them. He smiled, but those who followed, a Judge and an older man also dressed in green, looked most unhappy. "I am Etton, prince of the Green." He introduced himself, a polite sign, Jacobsen thought, even though Gontor already knew—and had spoken—his name. But then, Gontor knew everybody's name. "But you say you have a proposal for our mutual benefit?"

"Most certainly!" the booming voice of Gontor agreed. Now that he had been around Gontor long enough, Jacobsen could hear the metal guy's excitement. After all, he had a new audience.

Etton looked down the hillside toward the remains of the recent battle. "Well, we are always interested in our mutual benefit. But perhaps we might discuss this quickly."

"We have some little time," Gontor reassured him. "The Grey—and the Purple—were quite taken aback by your little surprise. You have forced them to regroup. I will let you know when they are on the move again."

The second, older man in green frowned at the statement. "And how might you know that?"

He pointed to his metal chest. "I am Gontor." After a moment's stunned silence, he continued, "Those you see before you are destined for greatness." He waved his gleaming arm at his three companions. "We are far more than four. Allow me to explain."

There were no more comments from the men in Green. Jacobsen hoped this was a positive sign.

"First," Gontor continued, "may I present Tsang, the last soldier of the Orange." His next wave indicated Tsang's white robes and orange sash. Tsang glowered, his hands resting upon the hilt of his great curved sword. "He is pledged to restore the greatness of his noble house. Of the four, he is the warrior."

He nodded to Tsang and next pointed to Summitch, who, for the moment, had ceased his grumbling.

"This short fellow here is perhaps the most mysterious of all my followers. Who knows what secrets he still holds unrevealed, for Summitch is the schemer among us."

He turned then, and nodded at Eric. "Which brings us

to the one who has so far proven to be the most valuable of all who have joined me upon this quest. Eric Jacobsen, though he comes from a place foreign to us all, is without secrets, wearing his every emotion upon his face. I give you the noble fool.''

Etton nodded pleasantly, as though he might receive this sort of visit every day. ''So your band contains the warrior, the schemer, and the noble fool. But what of their leader?''

The metal man gave the slightest of bows. ''I realize that it is difficult to comprehend my greatness. Therefore, let me simply state that I am Gontor, a deity of no little power.''

The older, military man sputtered. ''S-so you say. A deity? What more have you to gain if you are already a deity?''

Gontor inclined his head. ''A fair point—General Naddock, is it not? Well, perhaps I could someday be a deity with even greater power. It is good for all of us to have our goals.''

''And what exactly are your goals?'' Etton asked.

''Why, we are on a quest for justice, of course.''

Jacobsen noted Gontor said nothing about the keys. They had searched the tunnels that honeycombed this world until they'd found two of these powerful items. The third key had been taken somewhere out in the world. It was the only reason Jacobsen could see for Gontor to leave his kingdom so far behind.

Etton appeared to take Gontor's words at face value. ''I am flattered that you equate the welfare of the Green with justice. Still, I feel your appearance has somewhat disquieted my staff.''

''Understandable. I am quite possibly the only metal being they have ever seen.''

''That is one thing I may grant you,'' Etton replied. He

turned to his advisors. "If we are to work together, we must understand each other. With your permission, I will let my staff ask you a couple questions."

"Gontor hides nothing," he said with a nod.

"General Naddock?" Etton prompted.

The general frowned even more deeply than he had before. "Gontor, is it? Very well. If you wish to make your presence known in the world, why not ally yourself with the Grey? With them, it would be easy to achieve victory."

Gontor looked up to the heavens, as if such a question might be beyond his understanding. "I would never work with the Grey. We have had certain . . . differences in the past. Besides, where's the fun in defeating a smaller army?" He waved at the hill before them. "This way, the few ragged defenders of the Green against the amassed might of Grey and Purple—well, the results will be far more impressive."

When the general appeared to have nothing more to say, Gontor turned to the man in black.

"And what of you, Judge Dantis?"

The Judge opened his mouth, then closed it again. He stared at Gontor for a long moment, then smiled.

"No," Dantis said. "I believe you are who you say— more or less. Let us work together. I imagine it will be quite interesting."

Gontor bowed. "It will be interesting at the very least." He turned back to the hill. "But the Purple and Grey make their move."

Jacobsen looked away from the local drama and down to the valley and the far hillside. He saw men moving down the other hill, filing out from behind rock outcroppings to march down worn dirt paths, great lines of troops dressed in shirts of beaten mail and helmets of dull silver, with robes of grey or purple slung across their shoulders. The mass of men fanned out as they crossed the foothills and reached the valley below.

There must have been thousands of them. In a matter of minutes, they covered the entire far hillside and a good part of the valley below them.

Gontor turned back to Etton. "Before now, I think you were outnumbered." He chuckled, quite taken with his own humor. "But if you will excuse me, I'll show you one of my abilities. It is best if I move some little distance away from the rest of you." So saying, he walked quickly until he was masked by a nearby rock outcropping.

Jacobsen thought he had some idea of what was coming. After all, he had seen it before.

Gontor's absence seemed to embolden the general. He strode forward, frowning at Jacobsen and his two remaining companions. "And how, may I ask, will the rest of these aid us in the fighting?"

Summitch scowled back at him. "Right now, I think it's best that Gontor speaks for all of us."

In other words, Summitch had no more idea than Jacobsen about what was going on. Jacobsen tried hard not to smile.

Upon reflection, there was little to smile about. Sure, he was out under the open sky, but it wasn't much consolation to be out of those tunnels if all he was going to do was die out here. If the battle came to him, what could he do? The others fit into this world, and into the fight. Tsang the Warrior would be in his element, and Summitch could use his peculiar magic. Jacobsen still had his gun, but the bullets were going fast. Noble fool or no, how could he contribute once the gun was empty?

Etton had turned to his advisors and was issuing orders. "Call our men back behind the rocks. We do not have the numbers to fight them one-to-one, and I doubt that we can draw them into another ambush.'' He looked at the three newcomers. ''Perhaps you have another suggestion?''

''Ask Gontor.'' Summitch waved at the rocks where the metal man had disappeared.

The general shouted because Gontor chose to show himself again. His head emerged above the rocks, perhaps ten times the size it had been when the metal man had left them. Gontor had been this size when Jacobsen and Summitch had first stumbled upon his kingdom, astride a great chair at the chamber's center, like a statue seated upon a golden throne.

''I am ready for battle,'' Gontor announced as he rose to his true height, perhaps fifty feet or more.

Even from their position, high atop the hillside, Jacobsen could hear cries of alarm coming from the army below.

''One-sided battles are so boring, don't you agree?'' Gontor called down from far above. ''What do you say to destroying the might of the Purple and the Grey, once and for all?''

. 5 .

The World

ROMAN PETRANOVA LOOKED down at the cigar he held between his pudgy fingers—a cigar that had gone out five minutes before. "So where are they?"

Vinnie glanced over to his boss. You didn't tell Roman Petranova that it was all his fault. Not that Vinnie was in the habit of telling anybody anything.

Mostly, Vinnie did things for people—Roman's cousin, Roman's brother-in-law. These last few months, he'd actually been asked to sit down at the second table in the banquet room when Roman held court. So far, he hadn't done anything else but sit.

Even Vinnie could see what was going wrong.

Roman Petranova had sent his son Ernie and his nephew Joe on an errand for somebody they never should have gotten involved with. Mixing it up with that Smith character was bound to end badly.

Now the two of them hadn't called in for over twenty-four hours. It didn't look good.

Vinnie didn't talk. Nobody talked. Roman Petranova took turns staring at everyone in the room, all of them gathered around two tables at the back of what the sign said was DELVECHIO'S BANQUET ROOM. Vinnie had never seen a banquet take place back here in his twenty-six years of life. It was, instead, where the boss held court, the place you'd come when he sent for you. Now—besides Ernie and Joe—everyone was here.

At one table sat the boss, with one of his musclemen to either side, Johnny T to the left, Larry the Louse to the right. They were both quick with their guns, and would die for the boss. Between the two of them, they had maybe one brain.

They looked where the boss looked, their hands resting on the table, ready to go for their guns.

Nobody said a word.

The four other family members present—Sal, Vinnie, Mike, and Earl—sat at the second table.

Sal was Roman's cousin, and held a position in the family halfway between elder statesman and bum. He ran the pinball/amusements concessions for the family, and could remember everything that happened to the Petranovas for the last thirty years, if his cousin would ever let him talk about it, which wasn't very often. Vinnie and Mike were both younger generation, doing the occasional score, filling in when Ernie and Joe needed a hand. And Earl? Who ever heard of a made guy named Earl? He had gotten into this thing through marriage. Once he had run the numbers. Now he ran lottery tickets. Mostly, he smiled and kept his trap shut. He would never amount to anything in the organization.

Nobody talked, but everybody knew.

Everyone was here because Roman Petranova wanted them here. Over the last few weeks, Vinnie had seen a change in the boss, stepping back from his usual hands-on approach, even questioning one or two of his decisions out loud. Ernie and Joe had been doing all the legwork while the rest of them just stood and watched.

Maybe Roman felt he was getting old and wanted to pass the torch. More likely it had something to do with his wife leaving him. Even Ernie and Joe didn't know about that. Vinnie was the eldest child of the wife's sister; on the right side of the family to get the word. That Roman Petranova would let a woman hurt him like that—he'd kill Vinnie if he even breathed a word.

Nobody breathed. You didn't tell Roman Petranova bad news that he already knew.

Yesterday, Roman had been out of the driver's seat. But that was yesterday. Now that there was a crisis, he seemed back to his old self, ready to shoot the first person who gave him the wrong answer. So, like usual, nobody was answering.

The boss slammed his fist on the table. Both Johnny T and Larry the Louse reached for their shoulder holsters.

"I'm not going to stand for this." Roman looked one more time at those in the room. "Vinnie."

Roman Petranova was calling him out?

"Yeah, boss?" He did his best to return Roman's stare.

"I'm gonna need your help on this."

"Sure, boss. Sure. Anything you say." Half of him was excited, the other half was scared out of his mind. The boss was personally calling him out at last. Ernie and Joe were gone, and Roman was calling on him to find them—and to take their place. It was either a great opportunity or a death warrant.

He looked at the others in the room. They were

breathing a little easier now that Roman had started talking. The banquet room didn't feel right when Roman wasn't in control.

"Vinnie, whatever happened to my son and Joe— Smith's responsible. There's got to be a way to get to Smith. Find out where he lives, find out who works for him, find out everything you can. Take Johnny T with you. You're gonna find out what he did to Ernie and Joe. Maybe you'll find them, too." He regarded his unlit cigar for a moment. Larry the Louse fished out a lighter. The boss shook his head. This was important. "Smith's got a couple things to find out. Roman Petranova don't take orders. And he don't let anything happen to his family."

So he was supposed to find Ernie and Joe? The first thing Vinnie thought was the one thing Roman wasn't saying—that maybe the two of them were out there, but that maybe they were dead. He wouldn't want to have to tell the boss that, not without giving him Smith's head on a platter along with the news.

Vinnie said the words that would seal his fate. "Okay, Boss, you got it. You got any idea where to start?"

"A couple people at the phone company owe me favors," the boss replied. "We'll get you the address of Smith's private phone lines." He turned to the muscle on his left, a man with shoulders so big that they seemed to swallow his neck. "And Johnny. Take some firepower with you. I got the feeling that you're going to need it."

JACKIE PORTER GAVE up. It was impossible to drive when Mrs. Mendeck was making that kind of noise. What came from the old lady's throat was as remarkable as it was annoying; a high keening sound that would have seemed more in place originating from a bird rather than a human being.

She pulled into a closed gas station and turned to the woman in the passenger seat. Karen grimaced at her from the back.

"Why must you do that now?" Jackie realized how harsh the question sounded as soon as it was out of her mouth. She had started on this trip right after her last shift on patrol, driving out with Mrs. Mendeck as soon as the chief had given her a little extra time off. She hadn't slept in over a day. Her exhaustion was catching up with her.

"I know how I sound." Mrs. Mendeck looked quite cross herself, in that distracted way she had. "I should have done it a long time ago. I'm afraid I don't often perform my secrets out in the open. As you can see, there are practical reasons for some of them to be kept private. But I must contact Summitch. I should have spoken with him a long time ago."

She leaned back in the car seat, her curly grey hair matted with sweat. "This is not going as well as I had hoped. He should have answered when I first started calling."

"Why is this so important?" Jackie asked, trying to keep the frustration from her voice.

Mrs. Mendeck shook her head. "He has no idea that I've sent Brian."

Karen leaned forward in the backseat. "You mean, you haven't spoken with Summitch before now?"

The old lady sighed. "Well, we have—but not for some years, no. But he knows what to expect."

Jackie was glad that Karen had started asking questions. She somehow felt better knowing someone else couldn't understand the old lady.

"You mean he doesn't know anything about Brian," Karen pressed, "but he's expecting Brian?"

Mrs. Mendeck pursed her lips. "Well, he's not specifically waiting for Brian, but he is—I need to explain." She looked to both Jackie and Karen. "Those of us, like my-self—and Summitch, for that matter—are specially trained for a time like this. We are born waiting for the likes of Brian"—she paused to smile at Karen—"and you, my dear. We knew the time was near. The fact that there were two of you brought into this world within months of each other meant the signs had been right all along."

Jackie remembered now how Karen had mentioned that Mrs. Mendeck had a way of explaining things that didn't explain things at all. Everything out of the old woman's mouth sounded good, but none of it was very specific. *Why* exactly were they waiting for Brian and Karen? Who exactly *were* Brian and Karen? The time for *what* was near? Jackie tried to figure out which question to ask first.

That awful sound started again in the back of the old woman's throat. Mrs. Mendeck shut her eyes, her frown turning to a look of pain. She gasped.

"Oh, dear. This is not at all good."

"What?" Karen demanded. "What isn't good?"

"There is something blocking the path that I usually take—something that is very angry—something that threatens to overwhelm the other world and then our own." Her eyes snapped open. "I'm afraid that I can do no more. Until he finds Summitch, Brian is on his own."

This didn't sound very good at all.

"And what about us?" Karen asked. "You sent Brian there. Could one of us go after him, maybe bring him back?"

Mrs. Mendeck shook her head emphatically. "No. We are needed here. All of us are a part of this now. I think, very soon, we shall have our own battles to fight."

This was news. By helping Mrs. Mendeck and Karen, apparently, Jackie had signed up for the war. Well, perhaps she had volunteered long before that, when she helped

Brian to escape from Mr. Smith, and her own Chief of Police. Now that she was going back, she'd really have to find what the Chief's part in this was.

Jackie turned back from where she had been gazing off into the early morning light. The car was very still. She looked to her passengers.

Mrs. Mendeck nodded back. "I'll be quiet now if you would like to drive."

Jackie Porter put the car into gear and headed home, back to a job with a chief she didn't trust, back to a city where a mysterious figure who called himself Smith seemed to have far too much control.

THE RIGHT REVEREND Billy Chow, chief spiritual advisor of the Church of the Unbroken Word, took a quick look at himself in the darkened store window. He looked sharp, dressed in his trademark dark suit with sharp creases, direct from the finest tailors in Hong Kong, set off with the gold tiepin and cuff links, just the right bit of polish to complete the ensemble. He always looked sharp.

At times like this, he liked to reflect on the course his life had taken over the last three years. He had gone from hundreds of followers to hundreds of thousands. They kept him in the suits and cars and cuff links. But his new life-style required a certain amount of maintenance.

There was always a price to pay.

He rang the small white button at the side of the door. He was ushered inside and taken down a long hallway with a thick, grey carpet and mahogany paneling on the walls. The inside was so much larger and grander than one could possibly guess from the outside. This place, he thought for maybe the hundredth time, must take up the whole block of darkened storefronts.

Those who met him at the door simply nodded. In all the many times he had been called here, they never spoke, and he never spoke to them. They knew what he wanted. People came here for only one reason.

They took him to the office of the one responsible for the reverend's good fortune, and so much more, leaving him just outside the door. Smith only spoke with those most important to his needs.

The reverend knocked. The door swung open without a sound.

Mr. Smith looked at Chow with his cold silver eyes. He sat in his usual place, behind his desk, still wearing the dark coat and hat. Chow had never seen Smith without them.

"So, you asked to see me?" Chow said.

"I have a use for you."

At moments like this, the reverend always felt a little defensive. "Haven't I always done exactly what you asked? More, sometimes?"

As usual, Smith's voice was a raspy monotone, his face without expression. You could read whatever you wanted into every word he said—the fear, the guilt, the outright paranoia—most of it came from inside the listener. "You have realized the true nature of our relationship, far better than some."

Chow shrugged. "Let's say I just know what side my bread is buttered on."

"You may say whatever you like. As long as you fulfill those things I ask of you."

The reverend pulled at his left cuff link—a nervous habit. He forced his hand away. He would not be nervous.

"Heck, Smith, you don't ask, you tell."

"Some do not realize that. There are those who would move against me."

Reverend Billy smiled, something he had trained himself to do automatically. "You gave me a handy miracle when I needed it. Now I just have to pay and pay."

Smith's thin lips turned upward into a ghost of a smile. "Some do not see it that way."

"You know how good I am at making believers."

Smith nodded. "And those who will not?"

"I guess there's always going to be those who believe in free will. I knew I was damned a long time ago."

"That's why, Reverend, you and I will continue a profitable relationship."

Chow had had enough of the small talk. He pulled his hand away from his cuff link. "And what profitable relationship are we talking about today?"

"We are having some continuing difficulty with Mr. Petranova. I have it on good authority that he plans to move against us."

Chow found himself genuinely surprised. Not with Smith . . . he was totally predictable. But the people under Smith's thumb could sometimes do the unexpected. "Some people will never learn, huh? I thought you had Petranova handled."

"It seems finding someone responsive to Mrs. Petranova's needs was not enough. Perhaps we shouldn't have taken his son so quickly. People like Roman Petranova appear to put far too much stock in family."

The reverend nodded, quietly pleased with himself. He thought Smith was taking too much of a risk when he got into bed with the local version of organized crime. Reverend Chow would have advised against it, if Smith had ever solicited his advice.

"I want you to get in Petranova's way."

Chow almost lost his smile. He might not just wind up

damned, but dead. His fingers pressed into the smooth gold edges of the jewelry on his left cuff.

"How exactly do you want me to help you?"

"We will attack him at his weakest point. I may need you to accompany a friend of ours." He raised his voice slightly. "You may come in now."

The door behind Smith swung open, and a tall man walked stiffly into the room.

"Meet Ernie Petranova—the instrument of my vengeance."

He was a solid fellow, but his face was so still it made Smith seem positively expressive. If he hadn't moved, Chow would have doubted that there was anybody in there.

"Fella doesn't talk much, does he?"

"His spirit is elsewhere, but I only need his body."

"Waste not, want not," the Reverend Billy Chow agreed.

· 6 ·

The Castle

KARMILLE TOOK A DEEP breath, careful not to show how much recent events had disquieted her. Sasseen's magic had brought them out to the safety of the older tunnels—those rough-hewn corridors of stone and packed earth, lit by sorcerous torches placed there so long ago that no one quite remembered. She had been beaten about a bit in the confusion, but aside from some dirt on her riding outfit, she looked much the same as she had when she began this journey. Karmille looked at the others in the perpetual torchlight. They all seemed in fine shape: her personal guard, whom she called Blade, and her assassin, who called himself Flik, then Sasseen himself and the Judge's two soldiers, Sav and Lepp, one completely dead, the other merely on the way.

They were quiet, they were safe. But they had lost Aubric, whom they had trailed as a spy. He had led them to a whole hidden community of Judges, and introduced them

to a whole new race of beings, creatures that seemed to be
made of nothing but light. But Aubric had appeared to work
for neither. The renegade Judges had wanted to destroy
Aubric along with the rest of them; the light creatures had
ended up using Aubric for their own purposes.

And what of Karmille and the others? Certainly they had
all survived. But they had gained nothing from the exchange.

Karmille felt herself grow angry. How could she possibly defeat her father if all they did was run from danger?

"We have done nothing!" she cried out to the tunnels.

Sasseen smiled benignly at her. In his formal black robes
and hood, the uniform of the Judge with a single band of
grey upon the sleeve, he was the picture of calm, which
only served to make her more furious. "We have our lives.
Without that, all else is nothing."

She knew he was right, but she would not acknowledge
it. She turned from the others and stared off into the tunnel.

"We have gained information," Sasseen continued.
"This hidden world of Judges will surely unbalance the
war. For now that we have discovered their secret, they
will be motivated to move against the world above."

So they would bring about a new wrinkle to the
thousand-year war. While perhaps diverting, she could not
see it having a lasting effect. But Judge Sasseen had piqued
her interest despite herself. Still not looking at the others,
she asked, "What can a few hundred Judges do against the
entire might of the Castle?"

Sasseen did not answer immediately. It was difficult to
maintain her resolve and continue to look away from the
others in the mounting silence. She thought she heard
something coming out of the tunnel before her—a high,
distant sound like a woman wailing in misery. What else,
she wondered, might be in these tunnels?

"If they attacked all of the remaining lords?" Sasseen finally replied. "The renegade Judges might be the one thing to cause all the opposing elements of the Castle to band together. And that would not serve our purposes at all. No, we must use these Judges, convince them that they would be best served joining one side in the battle—our side. After we have won, we will offer them some reward, a haven within the Castle itself, say—someplace at a distance from us—perhaps the Kingdom of the Green."

So Sasseen planned for all of them. Karmille was pleased that her purpose had become the Judge's purpose as well, and so soon after they had joined together in pursuit of Aubric. He knew as well as she that, while they might never completely trust each other, they would use each other to gain the power that otherwise might forever elude them.

That thought particularly cheered her, since the only way they could truly gain that power was by destroying her father. Her father, the noble Kedrik, High Lord of all the Grey.

Every time she thought of her father, she thought of the thousand times he had entered her sleeping chambers, unannounced, unwanted, unavoidable. She could feel his hands upon every inch of her body, smell his sour breath upon her face. No one in the kingdom, including the princess, could deny anything of the supreme ruler of the Grey. Now she would give him a final gift—his death.

She brought her thoughts back to the matter at hand. "Work with these Judges?" she asked. "It would be a most uneasy alliance."

"But one quite necessary for their survival," Sasseen insisted. "They have hidden themselves from the true Castle for hundreds of years. They would have no knowledge of those in power, their strengths and their weaknesses.

Combining Judges, who have had a thousand years to de-
velop their own powerful magics, with those"—a wave of
his hand indicated Karmille and himself—"who could
serve as guides in the treacherous Castle today; they would
have to agree."

Karmille considered the possibilities. She turned around
at last to regard the others. "The renegade Judges hate all
of my kind. They will attempt to destroy us all eventually."

Sasseen acknowledged her statement with a dismissive
nod. "Eventually, no doubt. But our own Judges will know
many of their secrets by then, and have a way to counter
their attacks."

"M'lady!" her personal guard called out. His sword was
out before him as he looked down the tunnel where she
had so recently turned her attention. Karmille could hear it
now, too; no longer a weeping, but a great howling sound
that seemed to be roaring toward them.

Down the tunnel, in the distance, she saw a cloud of
dust rushing in their direction.

"Surround Karmille!" Sasseen cried. "Down on the
floor! Cover your heads!"

Her guard and her assassin both pushed her to the
ground, handling her in a way that would necessitate their
deaths under other circumstances.

She covered her head as a great wind descended upon
them. Others clutched at her sleeves as the wind threatened
to lift her, perhaps lift them all, and dash them against the
tunnel walls.

She could sense moments of darkness through her half-
closed eyelids. The torches—torches lit by magic, torches
that should burn forever—sputtered beneath the gale and
threatened to go out.

It was over. The wind vanished, leaving silence behind.
It had passed in an instant, but Karmille was certain that,

had they not taken precautions, it might have destroyed them all.

The others helped her to her feet, much more respectful now that the danger had passed. She would forgive them their trespasses; after all, this far beneath the Castle proper, they could not easily be replaced.

"What was that?" she asked softly, barely able to raise her voice above a whisper.

Sasseen looked down the tunnel where the wind had gone. "It is the change in the nature of things. Something—the Judges' attack, the creatures of light—perhaps something else we have not yet encountered—is throwing off the balance maintained for a thousand years. It causes the existing spells to react strangely, or perhaps reawakens spells long dormant. Now, all will change."

Then that was a spell? Karmille felt like shivering, although she would not allow the others to see such a thing. The wind had seemed like a living thing. "And what do we do when the balance is gone?"

The Judge stared down the tunnel where the gale had gone. "Rather than run before it, we must confront it, and make the change benefit ourselves."

So now they would ally themselves, not just with renegade Judges, but with spells that had the force of nature. "And how do we few confront such a thing?"

Sasseen paused again.

Her personal guard spoke instead. "Forgive me, my lady, for speaking out of turn."

"What is it?" she demanded. She knew, from his training, that he would only speak when he found it might harm her not to do so.

"We have sent for reinforcements. Certainly, with more Judges and men-at-arms, it will increase our options."

Karmille frowned. Did she need her guard to help her

remember something so basic? Perhaps she had not wished
to think of it. When they were certain—had it only been
moments ago?—that they would be overwhelmed by the
renegade Judges, they had indeed turned to her father.

She looked to her own Judge. "I am no longer so sure
I want my options increased."

Sasseen sighed. "The situation appeared far more simple
at the time—and our lives appeared to be in far more immediate danger. If your father does send help, it will be no
more than a Judge or two, with a handful of troops. We
may use them as well, with their consent or without. All
of them, even the Judges, are expendable."

It was true. Her father could choose to ignore her plea
for help and send no one at all. Odd that that would now
seem preferable. No, she thought it likely that her father
would send a small force. On the small chance that Karmille might succeed and return, the myth of unity among
the royal family must be maintained.

"Perhaps," Karmille suggested, "should these newcomers arrive, we might win them to our cause."

"Perhaps—if we might sufficiently engage their self-
interest." Sasseen still sounded doubtful, as though he
knew Judges far too well. "I believe they might be controlled, and the other Judges brought, however temporarily,
over to our cause. But we have another worry we have not
discussed."

Did Karmille need to be reminded of everything? But
they had avoided the most dramatic event they had so recently witnessed.

"Sir Aubric," Karmille said for both of them.

"Or whatever it is that Sir Aubric has become," the
Judge amended. "In his present condition, Aubric may be
too dangerous to be allowed to live."

Karmille considered this. "I have certain creatures that may be of assistance."

The Judge raised a single eyebrow. "The ones that you sent after Aubric before?"

Would this Judge constantly annoy her? They spoke of that same bit of magic he had previously detected, a little something she had dabbled in while in the Castle. Only Judges were supposed to use magic. It was forbidden of the High Ones. Of course, she realized that killing one's father would be almost equally frowned upon. Still, Sasseen knew far too much about her for her liking. "I used the creatures to herd Aubric and the Gnarlyman to me. It would be convenient to use them again. They know Aubric's scent. Surely, enough of it is left about him, even with his change, that they might find him again. This time, I will make certain that they kill. The light creatures will pose no threat once we destroy their mortal shell."

It would be Aubric's death sentence. She sighed. "It is a shame to waste such an interesting man, but sacrifices must be made." It would, after all, have taken a great deal of work to bend him to her will when she had no time for such diversions. She supposed that was the reason he was so appealing. Soon, she would be Queen of all the Grey, and could have whomever she wanted. In that, her father had trained her well.

She looked to the others but spoke to Sasseen. "Where now?"

"We must find some representative of the Judges. Ideally we might find a member or two of their community who have been separated from the others, to give us a chance to talk before they try to kill us again. I also believe we should keep moving, so that it will be difficult for others to find us. Once we are in a safe location, perhaps it would be a good time to release your creatures again. We do not

want the things who have taken Aubric to become too powerful.'' The Judge looked first down the tunnel in one direction, then the other. He chose the first direction. "We
go this way.''

Karmille and her two guards turned to follow the Judge
as Sasseen barked a command to his two sorcery-bound
servants.

Savignon and Lepp did not move. Karmille realized they
had seemed frozen in place since they had come to this
place. They still appeared to stand like statues, staring off
who knew where.

"Nothing ever goes as smoothly as one hopes,'' the
Judge said with a sigh. "One of our many recent encounters
seems to have interfered with my hold." He waved at Karmille to start down the tunnel. "Go on ahead. There is
nothing I can sense in the tunnels nearby. Once I re-
strengthen their spells, we will join you shortly.''

"Very well,'' she replied. He obviously did not wish to
have Karmille observe his sorcery on his slaves. The spell
must be simple enough that even she might be able to handle it. With an army of obedient slaves at her back, she
might not even require the services of a Judge.

"Come with me,'' she called to Blade and Flik as she
walked away. She and her guards would do well to have
some time alone. As well as their alliance had worked so
far, it was wise to have some private plans.

"I WILL NEVER forgive you for this!'' The lord of the Purple waved both fists over his head.

Limon would never cease to be astonished by this fellow. Even in the height of battle, he could think of nothing
but to bring him back here to the tent in an attempt to quiet
his complaints. And yet the lord of the Purple was shrieking

so loudly, he'd be heard not only in the command tent but halfway down the hill beyond.

"What was I thinking of?" Cantelus shouted. "You forced my hand! You confused me, leaving my strategies behind!"

Limon thought it more likely that the lord of the Purple had left his senses behind. An hour ago, he gloated over seizing an opportunity. Now he seemed capable of taking no responsibility for his actions. How could such a man command an army? At this juncture, Limon was beginning to marvel that the army of the Purple existed at all.

At least, before this most recent outburst, Cantelus had still seemed malleable. Zibor had convinced the Purple commander to send out his remaining troops as part of a combined force. That way, if nothing else, they would gain revenge against the treacherous Green.

Cantelus paused, staring at the tent flap that led outside. "What is your brother doing? I would take over the army myself. But soldiers will betray me everywhere!"

A captain of the Grey burst into the tent. He bowed before Limon and Cantelus. "I have been sent by Zibor, my lord."

"What news?" Limon demanded.

"Not good news, I fear," the captain replied, still staring at the ground. "They have a new weapon!"

"What?" Cantelus shrieked. "You mean the Green will turn back this assault as well?" He threw his weight forward so that his bulk was almost touching Limon. "You assured me that our combined forces would easily overrun those troops remaining to the Green. Why do I listen to those who betray me? How many of the noble Purple will die because of your stupidity?"

Limon did his best to ignore the shrieking man. "You

say they have a new weapon." He addressed the captain.
"Is this some new ploy by their Judges?"

The captain shook his head. "It is not a Judges' spell."

"Then what is it?" Limon demanded.

The captain nodded slightly, still not looking to either
of the other men. "If it would please both my lords, it
would be easier to show you."

The captain quit the tent before either man had a chance
to respond. Limon followed close behind. Cantelus trailed
after them, his complaints for now reduced to a low mumble.

Limon gasped when he saw the golden giant striding
down the far hillside. He stated the obvious.

"It is a creature ten times the size of anyone in our army.
And you say the Judges have nothing to do with this?"

"That is what our own Judges claim."

"It is what we have determined." Limon turned to see
a Judge standing at his side. "This is not to say there is no
magic involved. But the magic is ancient. The senior Judges
believe it might even date from before the Concessions."

So long ago—before the Judge's caste was even created? Limon did not approve. Had the war gone on so long
it would even stir up something from antiquity?

"Have we taken countermeasures?" he asked the Judge.

"The generals mounted an attack as soon as the creature
came upon the field," the Judge agreed. "Arrows and
spears have no effect." The Judge confirmed what Limon
had seen with his own eyes. "They simply bounce off the
thing's metal skin."

The giant seemed to treat all the missiles thrown at him
as something no more worrisome than small, buzzing insects. One of the batteries on the hill had armed a catapult
and sent a large rock flying straight for the giant's head. It

caused him to pause long enough to swat away the boulder with a flick of one immense metal hand.

Cantelus moaned as the huge being reached the first of the troops. The giant's method of battle seemed to be to pick up a soldier in either hand and toss them into the ranks beyond. The troops nearest to him were panicking, backing from his swinging arms. If, Limon thought, their command did not come up with an adequate defense, the Grey and Purple might soon be faced with a full-scale retreat.

"There must be a way to stop it!" Limon shouted, as though he wished his voice to reach the troops far below. "What says Zibor?"

"He is upon the ridge just ahead, my lord!" said the captain who had first brought the news.

Limon looked to Cantelus, whose whole corpulent form seemed to be quivering.

"Let us see what we might determine—together." With that, he turned away from the other lord and strode toward the ridge. He heard the other man's heavy breathing as Cantelus trotted after him.

"He goes for the Purple first!" Cantelus's voice was more of a shriek. And, indeed, though the giant had first discarded a half-dozen or so of the Grey, he quickly strode into the midst of a gaggle of Purple robes.

Zibor turned from the battle scene at the sound of the Purple lord's hysteria. Both his hands rested upon the hilt of his sword. "You have heard—" he began.

Cantelus rushed over to confront Zibor. "You have led me into another trap! I should never have listened to you! I am withdrawing my troops immediately!"

Zibor frowned. The usually still lines upon the ruined side of his mouth twitched slightly. He would no longer listen. He was ready to act.

This was neither the time nor the place for the command

to fight among themselves. Limon moved forward to place himself between the two other men.

"Surely, we are all suffering under this new attack," Limon insisted. "Cantelus, we can still reach an agreement, find a way to compensate you for your loss. Perhaps we can give you two-thirds of the kingdom of Green."

Cantelus hesitated, frowning at the battle below them. No doubt, he realized that if he left the alliance, he also left behind great personal gain. "Perhaps, if we can find some way to turn this giant about, we can turn the battle to our advantage."

"He is large and ungainly," Limon said after a moment's thought. "Surely we can trip him, then overwhelm him when he hits the ground."

Zibor smiled, but the corner of his mouth still twitched. "A wonderful idea, brother. Instruct the troops to bring some rope." Both men called to their generals and Judges to devise the best plan for bringing down their giant enemy.

"We will turn this latest surprise aside in a matter of moments," Limon called to Cantelus.

"And we will crush the Green!" The Purple lord seemed to be calming at last.

Zibor strode over to Cantelus. "Calm heads will prevail. Now, if you will precede me into the command tent, perhaps we can make this agreement more to your liking."

"You'll put it in writing?" Cantelus actually smiled in return. "Two-thirds of the Green, you said? Perhaps the day will work out after all."

Zibor continued to shout orders to those around them as the three walked back toward their private meeting.

Cantelus paused as he was about to enter the tent. "What was that?"

Limon was afraid to confirm what he had just heard; but the great, booming sound from the valley had sounded like the giant's laughter. He turned back to look at the battle.

The first attempt to trip the giant was a disaster. The metal man grabbed the nearer rope, and looped it around half a dozen of their troops, tying them close together so he could pick up the lot of them and dash them into their fellows.

And the soldiers of the Green were now making full use of the chaos in the valley. Three lines of them poured down the opposite hillside. Following the giant, they met with little resistance.

Cantelus stood at the entrance to the tent, horrified, watching as all his remaining power was stomped into the earth before him.

"They will kill all of them. I will not listen to either of you for another instant." He took a step toward Zibor, who stood blocking his way. "My Judges to my side!"

"No, Cantelus." Zibor stepped forward, using both his hands to push the older man. "I insist we conclude our bargain." Cantelus stumbled back into the tent, with Zibor close behind.

There was a moment's silence, then a shout. Limon rushed to the command tent. As Limon pushed the tent flap aside, he heard Cantelus make a strangled sound. He leaned against a tent pole just inside the door. The older man's face was quite surprised, but his eyes were devoid of life. A sharp piece of metal protruded from his chest, his tunic dark with blood.

Zibor had smoothly impaled Cantelus with his sword.

"I have lost none of my speed." Zibor placed a foot upon the Purple lord's back and withdrew his sword, letting the body fall to the ground. "Though it does seem a shame to sully my sword with such tainted blood." He smiled at his brother; his face was once again relaxed. "The command of the troops just became far easier."

Limon was still a bit surprised. "You'll tell them you killed their lord?"

Zibor looked at him in mock horror. "Nothing could be further from the truth." He stepped nearer, continuing in a lower, conspiratorial tone. "The Green are more desperate than we even thought. A spy has penetrated our headquarters, killing the leader of the Purple before he could be stopped. The Purple now must avenge an even greater wrong."

"A fantastic story," Limon agreed. "I would not have believed it if I had not seen it with my own eyes. And the Purple?"

"They shall fight against the Green to the last man."

Zibor wiped his sword on the old man's robe, then replaced it in its sheath. "Shall I?" He left the tent.

"Guards!" Limon heard his brother shout outside. "There is a traitor in our midst! He cannot get away! Cantelus has been mortally wounded."

Limon supposed a stab in the heart was as mortal a wound as one might have. He kicked the corpse a couple of times in payment for having to listen to all of the old man's drivel.

Then he, too, left the tent. There were more important tasks at hand. They must find a way to defeat this metal giant. After all, it would be a shame to waste a battle in which they had already added another kingdom to their own.

· 7 ·

The Castle

FOR THE FIRST TIME SINCE
Brian had come to this strange place, it was quiet.

The man that the others had left behind had stopped
moaning and thrashing. Instead, he lay flat on his back, his
open eyes throwing flashlight beams at the ceiling.

Joe stood on the other side of the man, frowning down
at the body. "You really want to help this guy?"

Well, Brian would probably try to help anybody. But
another good reason had occurred to him. "How else are
we going to find our way around?"

Joe nodded, looking slightly surprised. "Good thinking.
We're just tourists here. He's a local."

Joe seemed like the kind of no-nonsense guy that could
take just about anything in stride, even a guy with light
shining out of his eyes in a room in the middle of nowhere.
Brian was glad, for now at least, that Joe and he were on
the same side. Brian was surprised he wasn't more freaked

out by this whole thing himself. Mrs. Mendeck had hinted
that he had a special purpose in this place. Did some part
of him already know what that purpose was?

The man with the light in his eyes moaned softly.

"Do you think this guy is named Summitch?" Brian
asked.

"His name is Aubric."

They both turned at the sound of the woman's voice.

She was young, perhaps only a couple of years older
than Brian, and wore what must have been a simple white
gown before it had gotten torn and dirty. Brian imagined
she had spent some time down in the tunnels. She looked
at the floor rather than at the two of them. "Forgive this
intrusion. I am a person of no importance."

Joe pulled on the lapels of his jacket. Brian realized he
had been reaching for his gun. "Hey, you're somebody else
from around here. That's pretty important to us right now."

"Do you have a name?" Brian asked gently.

It took her a moment to answer, as if a person of no
importance did not deserve a name. "Well, Aubric called
me Runt."

She didn't look very Runtlike to Brian. Between her
low-cut gown and long red hair, she looked, well, very
mature.

"Aubric and I were brought here by those creatures who
now live inside him." She bit her lip, then continued, "I
served the lady Karmille, but she seems not to want me
anymore."

"Well, I'm sure you can help us. Do you have any idea
how we can help this . . . Aubric, here?"

She stepped forward to get a better look at the fallen
man. "No, his condition is quite recent. He—" She paused
as she looked up at the two males. "You're human, just
like me."

Joe smiled at her. "Where we come from, humans are mostly all there is. I guess it's a little different around here."

She looked quickly down, as if even a man's smile might be too familiar for her. "I guess so."

Aubric moaned again. He sat up.

"Hey!" Joe cheered. "He's doing it all by himself. You need a hand, buddy?"

Aubric grimaced, making one odd expression after another, as if he had to reconnect with the muscles of his face. His voice, when he spoke, was halfway between a human's vocal chords and the sound of bees. "Forgive us. It is so long since we have held mortal form."

"Oh. Sure." Joe shot Brian a "what the hell is going on here" look. Maybe, Brian thought, it was time for him to take over.

"Who are we speaking with?" he asked.

"We speak for Aubric," the voice full of bees replied. "We are many. We are eternal. But Aubric is still a part of us."

He stood, a bit unsteadily. He waved away both Brian and Joe as they stepped forward to help. "We must learn to move as though this body were our own. This body is our own. We are Aubric. Aubric contains the last of our kind."

Aubric turned his head one way, then another. He tentatively swung his arms. "We were unfairly banished, long ago. Now we will have our revenge. Now we will destroy the corrupt, those who do not deserve the power they have held for these thousand years."

Aubric swiveled his head so that he faced Joe and Brian. The light had dimmed somewhat in his eyes. Now, rather than twin beams glaring out from his sockets, his eyes seemed full of a hundred sparkling points of brilliance. "It is most interesting that you have found us as we are being born. Our fortunes are intertwined.''

Aubric held out a hand toward them, and in that hand was a bouncing ball of light.

"You are not of this world. Your fight is our fight. We were banished long ago. We will take our rightful place. Now that we have found a vessel, we can walk beneath the sky, with a power that will dwarf the sun. You will help us learn, and we will help you survive and take what you will.''

"Then you can show us the way out of here?'' Joe asked.

"We can show you the way to rule the world.''

Brian wasn't exactly sure about ruling the world. But perhaps someone as powerful as this might be able to help them in another way.

"Do you know where we might find Summitch?''

Aubric looked at Brian a moment before he replied.

"Summitch has helped me before. I'm afraid he has recently fled this place. He now serves another.''

Joe grinned and shook his head. "Well, I'm glad Summitch was at least here. I was beginning to wonder about Mrs. Mendeck.''

Brian felt a flash of anger. How could he possibly doubt Mrs. Mendeck? Of course, she could be sort of vague. And the spell that had gotten them here did seem a little sloppy.

Brian persisted. He asked Aubric, "Do you think you can help us find Summitch?''

"We will see Summitch again. He is no longer in the tunnels. We will see him on the surface. We will walk beneath the sun once more.''

Brian guessed that was a yes.

"We should begin,'' Aubric said.

"Lead the way,'' Joe agreed.

• • •

THE JUDGE'S SPELL was not complete.

Savignon, soldier of the Green, still held a spark of consciousness. He and his dead friend Lepp might be trapped in this obscene bondage, their bodies mere vessels for Judge Sasseen's commands. His magic forced them into service to Karmille, lady of the Grey. But one corner of his mind was free. And that corner had seen a friend he was sure was no more.

Aubric was alive! And he was free of the Grey, on a quest beyond Savignon's understanding. The Judge's spell left little room for understanding. But the spell did not reach everywhere. Now that he had seen Aubric alive, he felt the first stirrings of a very private hope.

The Judge shouted words at both Savignon and his dead compatriot. Sav did not understand the words, but his body responded, moving slightly to the Judge's command. The spell's tendrils gripped his muscles and tried to push away his thoughts.

No. Sav would not be denied.

Lepp spoke.

"What the . . . Where am I? What are you doing?"

It was not Lepp's voice. The Judge cursed. Whatever spell he was using was not entirely under his control.

It was another diversion that Sav might use. He was hopeless no longer. He would take control, first of his thoughts, then of his body. He would wrest Lepp from the Judge's control, drain whatever sorcery now troubled him, and allow him the peace he deserved.

He would break free. He would kill his captors if he could, escape if he could not, to lead others against them.

While he was alive, he would never surrender.

The spark inside him was growing.

The Green forever!

THIS TIME, IT was Flik the assassin who made the overture.

"M'lady, if I may speak?"

Karmille nodded, hiding her surprise. The assassin rarely spoke, preferring to do his work in silence.

"Please do so," she replied. "This might be our only opportunity for privacy." They were some distance down the tunnel, and Sasseen was still otherwise engaged.

"Should we not have a plan to rid ourselves of the Judge if things get difficult?"

"This is a strange territory," she replied carefully. "His life ensures our own."

"Still, there are other forces at work here. Should he choose to ally himself against us . . ." She knew Flik referred to those other Judges. Should they reach an agreement, the alliance might be much more to Sasseen's advantage than to their own.

Karmille nodded. "And should you think my own life in danger—"

"I would be so pleased to kill a Judge."

"Flik, you would be pleased to kill anyone."

"All save one." He managed to bow as he continued to walk at her side. "You give me my reason for living, m'lady."

She smiled in return. "I've given you many people to kill." This situation invited familiarities she would not otherwise allow. Still, even these familiarities served a purpose.

She looked from Flik to her guard, Blade, who walked upon her other side. "We will all find ample reason for living. Once the kingdom is won, you will both be re-warded.''

It was the first time she had ever depended upon others. And perhaps, if this ended as she hoped, she would reward them, and Judge Sasseen as well.

Unless they reminded her of her dependency. The lady of the Grey was never weak. Should any ever imply such a thing?

Then she would kill them all.

''Hush!'' Flik called softly. ''I think I hear someone approaching.''

The sound of quick-stepping boots filled the hall behind them. Karmille held up her hand, indicating that they should stop and wait for the rest of their party.

The two soldiers appeared around a distant corner, both running at a steady pace. Sasseen sat atop the living one's shoulders.

''Halt!'' he called when the two were some twenty paces away from Karmille. The two stopped with four additional steps. Sasseen jumped from the soldier's back.

''All has been mended,'' he said as he strode toward Karmille. ''As you see, I am once again in total control.''

Karmille gave him the slightest of smiles. It was time for a distraction to prevent any questions. ''I have had a thought while you were away. If the time is right, we might have a final use for my maidservant.''

Sasseen appeared surprised. ''We did not think to bring her.''

Karmille gave a dismissive wave. ''She is better left be-hind. She is only useful if she is with Aubric.''

''Which is likely. She would need him for protection.''

Karmille thought of the maid's little finger, which she still kept stuffed within her sash. ''And she is very easy to find. You wish to dispense with those things that have taken

Aubric.'' She pulled the finger from its hiding place for all
to see.

"Perhaps we should send them a little present.''

Sasseen considered that for a moment, then nodded.
"Were we to deal with Aubric, it would please the other
Judges greatly.''

"The other Judges,'' she repeated. Yes, they were the
other element to this drama. "What of those from my father?''

"It will take them time to find us. When they do, perhaps we will give them a choice. When they arrive, we
must all fight together''—he bowed slightly to Karmille—
"under my lady's command.''

"And if they refuse such an offer?''

"A small force from the Castle, no matter how brave,
would crumble before the renegade Judges. I think their
refusal is not an option.''

"We coerce the Judges of the Grey to join us, then use
our combined might to form an alliance with the renegades?
Is that possible?''

Sasseen bowed even more grandly. "You have not yet
witnessed my negotiating skills.''

"Haven't I?'' To Karmille's thinking, Sasseen spent
every moment trying to twist things to his advantage.

"Believe me, m'lady,'' he replied without the trace of
a smile. "I have more to offer than you might imagine.''

She nodded. "Very well. Then we shall set the stage for
your negotiations by ridding ourselves of another annoyance.'' She took a deep breath, silently recalling the method
she must use. "I will send the creatures now. I will send
them for Aubric, but they may destroy others. My creatures
are always very hungry.''

"Very well,'' Sasseen agreed. "You will do your part
and I shall do mine.''

She nodded as her hands began the intricate movements. "Behind me!" she called to the others. "I will conjure them and direct them!"

Karmille smiled. At last she felt she was in control.

. 8 .

AUBRIC MOVED VERY CARE-
fully. The muscles of his shoulder pulled to raise his arm,
and his arm flailed above his head. He managed, after a
great deal of trial and error, to stand, propping himself
against one of the featureless white walls. Not that the wall
looked so plain as before—with his new eyes, he could see
not only the surface, but the spell that held the surface
together—small, yellow swirls of power that bound the
ground stone as a length of rope might tie a sheaf of grain.

He was learning. Aubric had to begin again, as though
he were a small child, discovering everything for the first
time. All his senses, all his movements, all his thoughts—
he remembered how to do all these things, and yet they
were totally new.

Aubric felt very strange.

He was both himself, and more than himself. His throat
felt a little sore, as though all the voices he held within

might strain his vocal chords. His muscles were so full of energy they seemed to burn. He might not be able to walk, but he felt that he could easily leap twenty feet in the air if the ceiling was not there to stop him.

And his eyes. Could he still call them eyes? They saw so much more now, he thought he might need a new word to name them. Oh, he was still aware of his immediate surroundings. But, with a thought, with the flex of a muscle, behind his pupils, that he had never felt before, he could see beyond the tunnels, his vision passing through the greys and browns and reds and yellows of earth and rock to the very center of the world, and to the Castle far above.

The voices buzzed inside his head now.

Have a care. You must proceed slowly. We all must proceed slowly.

Their words of warning almost made him laugh. "What do you mean? It comes so quickly!"

We attempt to muffle the sensations. We do not wish to drive you mad.

Mad? He had no time to go mad. He had so much to learn. He felt exhilarated. Why didn't they let him see it all?

Aubric had always known he was different. He had learned the name of his true nature once he had met Summitch. "Human" was not a word used among the Green.

Now he had met other humans—one a kitchen maid, two more from another world. But now Aubric was far more different still.

There were so many voices, so many noises inside his head. How could he listen to them all, much less understand them? But he heard another noise, too, a noise outside himself. Someone spoke, one of those separate entities that was not a part of him. He pulled his vision back from where it looked beyond miles of rock, let his consciousness float up from deep within. He blinked and tried to focus on someone at his side.

"So, you spend a lot of time talking to yourself?" It was the one who called himself Joe. A human from another world, along with the youngster named Brian. They had introduced themselves when they first arrived. Before he had been able to move, Aubric was able to listen.

"I am no longer a single entity," Aubric admitted. Now he spoke to those outside his form. But, apparently he had also spoken aloud before. When those within him spoke to Aubric, did they speak through his mouth as well? "This is something that I have difficulty comprehending."

"Right around now," Brian admitted, "we could believe anything. But I was hoping you could tell us more about this guy we were supposed to meet. Summitch?"

They had spoken of Summitch before, even though they came from another world. That surprised Aubric, but not the beings who shared his body.

"Summitch and I traveled together for a time. We were briefly reunited a few minutes before you arrived. But I am afraid we have lost Summitch for the moment." Aubric tried to twist the muscles of his face into a weary smile, but felt them form into more of a grimace before losing whatever tension they had. "I would like to find him myself. All of those inside me would like to find him."

Joe nodded. "Why the interest?"

"I believe Summitch to be a creature of many talents." On this, Aubric and those who shared his form agreed. "We are powerful. But we have forgotten what it is to be mortal. We will need talented allies."

Joe smiled with an ease that Aubric envied. "Well, I guess we were sent to this Summitch for pretty much the same reason. Fellow seems kind of slippery, though."

Slippery? Perhaps that was one of the talents Aubric was looking for.

But he couldn't accomplish anything unless he could learn to move his arms and legs. He tried to lift his right leg very slowly. The leg jerked forward, his boot heel jarring as it came down on the floor. But he did not fall. His left leg moved forward more easily, not quite as spastic as the right. He swayed a bit, but the balance was there. His right leg came forward even more easily the second time. His muscles and his mind were becoming reacquainted.

"Do you have any idea where Summitch has gone?" Brian asked the next time Aubric paused.

"You mentioned something about . . . outside?" Joe added.

"Outside? Above the tunnels? Yes." Aubric considered the request. With his new powers, it would be far easier to find the Gnarlyman. "We believe that is where he went—at first. Summitch can move very quickly.

"I will do my best to locate him," he added after a moment. "I can see quite a distance."

But he had to learn to use his eyes in much the same way he learned to use his legs. Aubric frowned—his face seemed to work for that, now—and stretched out his sight. His vision pushed through miles of rock, far past their current, austere surroundings, into tunnels of rock and brick and cut stone. "He is no longer in any of the nearby tunnels." His vision extended farther still, looking through the passageways and caves, chasms and stairways that made up this world beneath the world. "He is no longer in the more distant tunnels. He must be somewhere above."

There was no sign of a Gnarlyman. He saw a dozen or so retreating Judges—where had the others gone? He saw the lady Karmille and her party, some surprising distance away. Near to the Castle, he saw another small party of soldiers and Judges in Grey livery, walking deeper into the tunnels. Perhaps they would meet with Karmille.

And there was something else. Aubric wasn't sure which side of him, human or otherwise, realized it first. It was something he could only see from the corner of his far-seeing eye. It was something moving very quickly through the tunnels.

"I must stop my search," his many voices said aloud. "Something, or someone, is coming for us."

Recognition flooded his many selves. It was something he had seen before. Something that had almost killed him. Something that had killed the brethren of the lights, sacrificed for the food of the future, sacrificed so that they might once again gain mortal form.

He heard the many voices speak within him. *Lady Karmille sends her underlings. We must prepare.*

That was what the lights within him called them? Underlings? Aubric could only remember how they had torn apart m'lady's guard. He had been a sacrifice, ordered to give his life by Karmille. For, once these creatures were loosed, they could not be stopped before they had tasted blood and souls. The things attacked too fast for the eye to see, save for a glimpse of a snapping jaw, a ripping talon, and an instant of blood, spurting forth from the guard like a fountain. Aubric wanted to shudder, but could not yet remember how.

Then the creatures were gone. The price had been paid.

This time, Aubric knew, Karmille sent the creatures for him. She could not control him, especially now that he had been joined by the multitude. He suspected that, with Karmille, that which she could not control she would destroy.

The creatures came again. The part of him that was Aubric felt panic, but the rest of him was very calm.

"What do you mean," Joe asked, "something's coming?"

Aubric quickly explained what was approaching, and what had happened last time they had followed Summitch and him. Joe and Brian looked less than happy at the news.

"That's what's coming?" Joe asked.

It is better if we take them by surprise, the lights murmured softly within him.

"Surprise?" Aubric said aloud.

Before, you could do nothing but run. Now, we have other methods.

"You bet I'm surprised," Joe replied, "among other things. I don't think I signed up for this."

"I think Mrs. Mendeck signed up both of us," Brian added.

"Fine," Joe replied. "Either way, we're dead meat. Super-fast things that tear you apart in an instant? What are we going to do?"

Aubric nodded. "We need to go and meet them." This time, when he smiled, his face muscles actually obeyed. "They'll never expect that. It will give us the upper hand."

"Go and meet them? I guess it'll be over quick." The one named Joe laughed. " 'They'll never expect that.' You're beginning to sound like my uncle."

As far as Joe could figure out, this whole scene went something like this.

Mrs. Mendeck had said she was sending them to this guy named Summitch. Except, somehow, her spell got messed up, maybe by the Smith guy, and they ended up in the bedroom of a couple of pale freaks. But only for an instant, because the freaks bounced them down to this place, where, apparently, Summitch had been until very recently, which might have been a coincidence, but Joe didn't think so.

Joe did have plenty of time to think. He and Brian were being led, forever it seemed, down this austere white tunnel, like a corridor in a hospital where there weren't any doors. This guy named Aubric had taken charge; Aubric, who was a friend of Summitch's, was now a friend of theirs. Which was good, since between his glowing eyes and the way he seemed to know his way around, Joe was just as glad to have this Aubric character on their side.

Apparently, the folks Aubric and Summitch were up against were the bad guys. Whatever. Hey, Joe was sure, back where he came from, working for his uncle's organization and all, that lots of people thought of him as a bad guy. But Joe knew different. Like everybody else in life, he was just getting by. At least, that was the plan until he had showed up here. Now Joe was going to have to learn a brand-new set of rules to survive, in a place where the nature of things seemed to change from one minute to the next.

When they had first started out, Aubric—despite his sword and armor—had looked pretty geeky, as if he didn't quite know how to walk. But Joe had noticed a change as they traveled—there wasn't much else to look at with these white walls. Every step Aubric took was more confident than the one before. The light in his eyes, while still there, had dimmed somewhat as well, so now Joe could actually look directly at his face. Besides having flashlights where his pupils should be, and being dressed in kind of medieval clothing, Aubric didn't look all that different from your typical man on the street back home.

Joe still wanted to figure out the angles. As much as he wanted to find Ernie, he also wanted to get both himself and Brian out of here in one piece. Up till now, there hadn't been much to see, but there had been a lot of time to think.

The young woman who called herself Runt walked to their rear, so quietly that Joe might forget she was there. She was a good-looking woman, despite the fact that she was missing the little finger of her left hand. Joe imagined it must have been some sort of accident; he wouldn't think the medicine was too hot in a place like this. Mostly, though, she was quiet.

Joe never trusted the quiet types. In his family, if you had something to say, you said it. Heck, sometimes with his cousin Ernie, it was impossible to get the guy to shut up. Damn Ernie, anyways. For better or worse, they had spent the past thirty years as a team, since they were kids. Now Ernie got himself messed up with a guy named Smith, and got some part of himself sent who knows where in this wacko place. Whatever happened, Joe would get him back, or he wouldn't come back from this place himself. It was more than having to face his uncle Roman if he failed. Ernie was family.

They came to a crossing of corridors, the third intersection they'd passed so far, looking just as featureless as the first two. Aubric hesitated for an instant, then pointed off to the left.

"We go this way."

"How are you sure?" Brian asked. The kid didn't seem at all spooked by the soldier with the glowing eyes. Joe, on the other hand—well, he was just glad he still had a gun.

"It is one of the two things I am sure of," Aubric replied. "Thanks to the changes in me, I have a new sight that lets me see every tunnel that is, and what lies beyond those tunnels as well. I want to find the quickest way through the tunnels. We all want to get out of this place. It has been so long since we have seen the sun."

Aubric shuddered, and when he spoke again, it was with a hundred voices rather than one. "We will have our vengeance."

"You said there were two things you were sure of?" Brian prompted.

Aubric nodded. He spoke again with a single voice. "It does not matter where we travel. M'lady's creatures will find us."

The white corridor ended abruptly. The corridor was blocked by a curved outcropping of jagged stone.

"I should have expected something like this. They have rolled a rock into our path."

"You mean those really fast things?" Joe asked. It didn't make any sense.

"M'lady's creatures?" Aubric paused, as if listening for a noise that only he could hear. "No, they are still a little distance away. The Judges seek to slow us down. As if something as simple as a boulder might do that."

Aubric narrowed his eyes until all Joe could see were two slits of white. "I could pass through the rock, but I could not take all of you with me at once, and I would not wish to leave any of you vulnerable upon the other side. Therefore, I will have to remove the obstacle." He paused, then looked to those behind him. "They're telling me you should stand back. You do not have my protections."

"I guess we'll take your word for that." Joe grabbed Brian's shoulder and pulled him back. Runt had already retreated twenty paces, and had turned herself toward the wall. Joe thought her shoulders were shaking. Maybe, he realized, there was a reason she was quiet. Maybe she was really scared.

He pulled Brian back to Runt's side as all hell broke loose.

• • •

THE CREATURES INSIDE Aubric spoke for him.

"Now!"

Aubric felt a surge of warmth blossom from his forehead as he stared at the boulder.

The rock exploded. The world shook.

Even Aubric, and all those within, found himself stumbling backward.

We must learn control.

Most of the force of the explosion had been directed outward, or into the white walls to either side. The hallway outside was filled with rubble. The once-smooth walls now sported great cracks all the way back to where his three companions stood huddled together.

Aubric noted that a few small fragments of stone had cut into his arms. There was a fair amount of blood, but he felt no pain.

We cannot risk the vessel, the voices said within. Aubric was the vessel. *We must learn caution.*

He—or they—sensed something was near.

"They come again," Runt said in a low tone. So she could sense them, too?

"That's the Judges?" the one named Joe asked.

"Not the Judges," Runt answered in a near monotone. "This is sent by the lady Karmille."

"The creatures?" Joe looked critically at the serving girl. "You don't seem terribly upset."

The serving girl looked down at her trembling hands. "My life is the lady's. I accept whatever she wishes to do with it."

A roar echoed down the hall, a sound loud enough for even Joe and Brian to hear.

"Well, the lady doesn't own me, and she never will."

Joe laughed and pulled something from his jacket. "Let's
see what a little of this will do."

Joe held something small and shiny in his hand. It
looked like the exploding machine Jacobsen had used on
the Judges.

New sounds echoed toward them down the newly
opened passageway—a great growling like a pack of animals rushing for the kill.

"What, have they got dogs?" Joe shouted.

"No," Runt replied. "Nothing so simple as dogs. . . ."

Aubric had seen them long ago, but now they were close
enough for the others to see as well.

"They're coming straight for us! By destroying that
boulder, we've left ourselves open to attack!" Joe was
shouting all the time now. "Aubric, what were you . . . Je-
sus, what *is* that?"

Aubric saw them plainly now, his new eyes so much
clearer than they were before. Three beasts, each with three
heads, with some of the worst features of the wolf, the tiger,
and the bear. They ran forward with alligator talons and
dragon claws, their eyes lit from within with a sorcerous
heat and their fang-filled mouths already open in anticipa-
tion of their coming meal.

"I'll handle this!"

Joe was at Aubric's side, the silver device in his hand.
He moved a single finger, and the device boomed, sending
a projectile toward the rushing creatures. Joe squeezed
again and again, five booms, five projectiles, then nothing
but quiet clicks.

"Oh, shit," Joe whispered.

Aubric looked to the rapidly approaching beasts.

The loud projectiles had had no effect. No, it was worse
than that. The creatures had swallowed the metal—it was
food for three engines that could not be destroyed. If any-

thing, the power they had absorbed made them come faster.

"Everything makes them stronger." It was Aubric's turn to whisper. The knowledge came from the lights that shared his form. Deep inside, Aubric could feel a little ball of fear.

No. Things upon the physical plane give them nourishment. We know their weakness.

Aubric could feel the heat gather within him again.

The creatures were almost upon them.

The power surged out from him again, catching the three marauders, holding them still enough so that the others might see them clearly. Runt screamed. Joe swore. Brian was very quiet.

The things roared in frustration, a tiger head crying to the ceiling while a crocodile snout snapped mere feet away from Aubric. He felt those things within him swirling about, generating the force that poured forth, a force great enough to create a protective barrier between them and the sorcerous beasts. But the things did not seem weakened by this force. Instead, it turned their anger into fury, which in turn seemed to make the creatures stronger still.

Crocodile jaws snapped shut a foot closer than they had before.

They were stronger than the lights within.

No. Our power is too diffuse. We are unused to our union. We will find a way.

But Aubric could already feel his legs shaking. His strength was flowing away with that of the creatures of light. And m'lady's beasts, snapping, snarling, clawing, growling, inched ever closer.

It was all Aubric could do—all those things inside him could do—to keep the barrier from shattering. The enemy would drain them all.

• • •

NOW THIS, JOE thought, *really* sucked.

He figured a gun in a place like this would be great. A couple of quick bullets would have stopped these monsters before they even knew what hit them. But he'd emptied his piece, and those horrors hadn't even felt it.

He had retreated, without thinking, really, as those things had rushed in to destroy them. But then Aubric had done his thing—now, his skin was glowing along with his eyes—like some radioactive guy from a bad sci-fi flick. Whatever he was doing, it only slowed the things down. They hung in midair, looking like every nightmare Joe had ever had, but had driven out of his mind: an obscene combination of bestial force that looked like it only did one thing—destroy. Mrs. Mendeck never told him he'd be coming up against something like this. And now there was nothing he could do about it.

"What can I do without any bullets?"

"Maybe I can help." Brian was at his side. He nodded toward Joe's gun and held out his hand.

"But there's no—" Joe began.

"I know," Brian replied as he gently pried the piece from Joe's fingers.

Joe let it go. The clip was gone, and the spares were still back in the glove compartment of a car on another world. Brian could admire the gun all he wanted. If it made Brian feel better to hold the gun until those things killed all of them, well, he could give it up.

Brian frowned at the gun for a minute, then looked up at Joe and smiled.

"Try it now," Brian said. He handed it over.

The gun felt heavier than before. Nah, Joe thought, it's just this crazy, desperate situation. . . .

Aubric shouted and fell back a couple of steps. The monsters slammed against the barrier, forcing Aubric back even more. It wouldn't be long before it would all be over.

"Shoot it!" Brian yelled. "Shoot the gun now!"

Really? Oh, what the hell, Joe thought. If he humored the kid, it would give him something to do.

He raised the .44 and pointed it at the monster on the left.

"Bang," Joe said as he squeezed the trigger.

The slobbering thing exploded.

"That's it!" Brian kept on shouting. "That's what it's supposed to do!"

The gun did that? Well, Joe guessed there was only one way to find out. He aimed at the second creature. "Bang," he said as he pulled the trigger again.

The second monster blew up, blood and guts and who knew what flying everywhere.

"Yes!" Brain was cheering. "Yes! We're going to win!"

Joe did the same thing all over again. Scratch the final monster.

The tunnel was very quiet, the only sound a faint hum from Aubric's insides. Joe looked down at the gun in his hand.

Aubric had slowed them down, but it had taken Brian, and Joe's gun, to finish them off.

· 9 ·

The World

THIS WAS HIS BIG CHANCE.
Vinnie had to keep telling himself this.

He'd never been particularly comfortable around Johnny
T. The muscleman had a way of glancing at you that said,
well, maybe he'd talk to you, or maybe he'd twist your
head around till he broke your neck. That was okay, Vinnie
figured, when Johnny was protecting the boss. Now,
though, it was just the two of them, driving down to Funland. Every time Johnny pushed the stick shift, every time
he turned the wheel, every time he even turned his head,
muscles stood out on his arms and neck. When Vinnie
looked at Johnny T, he didn't really see a person. He saw
a killing machine.

Johnny T didn't talk much. All that silence made it
worse.

The boss had sent him out with Johnny T. This was his
big chance. Johnny T was the muscle—that meant Vinnie

had to be the brains. Funland. It was a big old warehouse of a place, 90 percent of which was taken up with arcade games, Skee-Ball, and a snack bar—all flashing lights and blaring rock and roll. It also had a very private room with a separate entrance in the back where Roman Petranova liked to bring people who wouldn't cooperate. The games and rock music in the arcade were so loud, you could do whatever you wanted in the back room.

He didn't like to think of himself as squeamish, but it could get pretty bloody back here. Vinnie never came out here unless he had to.

Now Vinnie had to be the brains. It was his big chance.

Johnny T drove the Caddy down the entire length of the long alley behind the arcade. The back of the place was deserted. Nobody came back here if they knew what was good for them.

They got out of the car.

Johnny T unlocked the reinforced steel door and led him inside. The door slammed shut with a ringing sound, steel on cement, that echoed across the high-ceilinged room. The place was lit with overhead fluorescents; they made the cold place look even colder. Johnny T waved for Vinnie to follow, walking past the special chair—the one with the straps to hold "visitors" in place. Vinnie noticed brown marks spattered on the cement floor, close enough to the chair so they might be blood. Cleaning up wasn't a priority around here. Their boss had a few city officials in his pocket, after all. Everybody knew better than to come snooping around Funland.

Vinnie was led past a workbench on which were scattered all sorts of things you might find in a workshop—hammers, screwdrivers, a blowtorch, and an electric drill—things no doubt to use with the chair. Johnny T didn't seem to notice, striding briskly past a ragged hole in the floor, a dark gap in the wood the size of a dinner plate. It looked like a shotgun blast had left a little souvenir. He stopped at the far end of the room and kicked some apparently empty cardboard boxes out the way to reveal an old wooden door Vinnie had never seen before.

Johnny T jerked the door open so hard Vinnie was surprised it stayed on its hinges. He flicked a switch, revealing a set of stairs heading down.

"Come on," Johnny T said as he took the stairs two at a time. The steps groaned as the big man stomped down them. They only creaked when Vinnie followed.

"I never knew there was a basement," Vinnie said.

"Nobody does, except the boss, Larry, and me. This is the boss's secret stash. A little firepower for a rainy day." Vinnie had never heard Johnny T string together so many words at once. This was probably as excited as the big guy got. He got to the bottom of the stairs and disappeared around a corner, out of sight.

Vinnie hurried to follow. He turned the corner at the bottom of the stairs, and walked into a huge room, so big it probably ran under both the back room and the arcade space above.

The place was filled with metal cabinets. He could see a hundred of them, maybe more. Vinnie had never thought of Roman Petranova as the kind of guy who kept files.

Johnny T took a key from his pocket. He unlocked one long cabinet and pulled aside a large metal door.

Now Vinnie understood.

Instead of papers, these cabinets were filled with guns. The hardware was hung in four rows, six to a row, on the metal sheet inside, everything from machine pistols to shotguns. Johnny T moved on and unlocked another three cabinets with similar contents. "I wanna give us some choice," he explained. The second cabinet had what Vinnie thought were a couple of bazookas and a rocket launcher. Vinnie started to think this basement might be like the Noah's Ark of armories—a place where his uncle could gather together a couple of every weapon ever made. He wondered if other cabinets held crossbows and atomic warheads.

You're a funny guy, Vinnie thought. He was supposed to be the brains. But he knew nothing about guns. This was still Johnny's part of the show.

Johnny T waved at all the stuff around them. At least, Vinnie *thought* it was a wave. Johnny T was so muscle-bound, he sometimes had trouble moving. "We gotta choose our weapons carefully. Some of these aren't legal in this country. It would be stupid to be arrested before we got the job done. Too bad. Even a guy like Smith couldn't do much against a rocket launcher." The big guy chuckled at the thought.

"We'll take stuff we have papers for. And we'll take a few extras . . . you know, for insurance. You always wanna have enough firepower." He waved for Vinnie to come closer. "Hold out your arms."

Vinnie did as he was told. Johnny T started loading weapons into his outstretched hands. A couple of magnums, a couple of semiautomatics, four boxes of shells, half a dozen grenades, a big block of what must have been plastic explosives.

Vinnie thought his arms were going to break.

"Uh, Johnny, what are we going up against, here?"

"That's the problem, Vinnie," Johnny T replied as he grabbed a couple of pump-action shotguns. "We got no idea."

He frowned at the other cabinets. "Okay. Let me grab a couple more things and we'll take them up to the car."

Vinnie nodded. Maybe once he got out of here, he really

would have a chance to be the brains. He had to get these things upstairs without dropping anything. He carefully slid his right foot forward, then his left. He was surprised he could move under all this weight. So long as his arms didn't break, he'd be just fine.

He managed to get up the stairs and barely beyond the doorway before he heard Johnny T bounding up the stairs behind him. He glanced over at the big guy and saw he was carrying even more than Vinnie.

"Okay!" the muscleman called as he strolled on past. "Let's get this loaded!"

Vinnie nodded, sliding one foot in front on the other. He just didn't want to trip over that hole in the floor.

By the time he got across the room, Johnny T stood there by the open door, balancing his load on one muscular arm.

"Here. I'll get the trunk."

The big guy ran past him, popping open the Caddy's trunk, then reaching down and pulling up the carpeting. The trunk had a false bottom.

"These big cars have their points," Johnny T said. "Dump your stuff here."

Vinnie dropped the guns as quietly as possible. He heard a chirping sound. Johnny T reached inside his coat pocket and pulled out a portable phone.

"Go." He listened for a minute. "Got it." He flipped the phone closed as he loaded his half of the weapons on top of those Vinnie had already deposited.

"In the car," the big guy said. "They found out where Smith answers his phones. It figures."

With that, Johnny T got in the car. Vinnie hurried to get over to the passenger side. "What figures?" he asked as soon as he'd snapped his seat belt. Johnny T was not the slowest of drivers.

"The place is over on Dundalk Street. In the Heights."

Vinnie saw what the big guy meant. It was a great place not to get noticed. Despite its name, the Heights had been one of the city's poorest neighborhoods before they'd razed a quarter of it to put the new highway through. Now one side of the highway had gone upscale, restoring the grand old buildings of the Heights to their original glory. The other side of the highway, though, was like a no-man's-land. All of the industry and most of the people had moved out of the area. Housing and industrial developments kept getting announced for the place, but every one had fallen through. Of the whole area, which took up maybe eight city blocks, the only life was left on Dundalk Street, and that mostly from homeless folks squatting in the deteriorating buildings.

Johnny T got them over there in a couple of minutes. He pulled up in front of a darkened storefront, one of maybe a dozen in a row on this side of the street. There was a small grocery open on the far corner, the lottery and cigarette ads in its windows covered by bars. A couple blocks down, they had passed a small, self-serve gas station. The lights from the two businesses were the only signs of life in the whole neighborhood.

"I bet nobody bothers Mr. Smith around here," Vinnie said, just to say something.

"Well, that's all about to change." Johnny T got out of the car. Vinnie scrambled to follow. He thought he'd have some say in what they did here, but so far the big guy was calling the shots. He wondered if he could remind the muscleman that this was supposed to be a team effort. He walked quickly to the back of the car. Johnny T handed him a shotgun.

"Hold onto this for me," the big guy said. "We got to be ready for anything."

Maybe, Vinnie thought, they should stop for a moment

and come up with a plan. "How much should we take?" he asked.

"How much can we carry?" Johnny T replied.

To Johnny T, Vinnie realized, blowing Smith to kingdom come was the plan. Well, in a place like this, nobody was going to hear them. There could be worse plans. Johnny T passed Vinnie four handguns and four extra clips of ammo. Vinnie fit them all in his belt and coat pockets.

Johnny T tossed Vinnie a couple of grenades and a .44 magnum as he grabbed a couple more pieces for himself. He slammed the trunk closed. "Let me have the shotgun."

Vinnie picked up the gun from where he rested it against his knee.

Johnny T pumped a round into the chamber. "Let's go."

The door to the place opened before they could cross the street. Vinnie aimed his Magnum, while Johnny T pumped his shotgun.

"What the hell?" Johnny T said as he saw the large figure that blocked their way. Vinnie forgot all about firing his gun, too.

It was Ernie Petranova.

EVERYBODY STARED AT the Chinese guy in the suit. Nobody, but nobody, burst into the banquet room. Or at least nobody had until Smith had barged his way in here the other day. But Smith was crazy at the very least. What was this guy's story?

On top of all this, Roman Petranova knew this guy from somewhere.

"I thought I told you nobody gets in here!" he shouted at Larry. If The Louse couldn't watch the door, what was he paying him for?

The Louse scratched at his greasy scalp. "He acted like he didn't care if I shot him or not."

Oh, well. Maybe there was an upside to this. You couldn't get much information out of guys after they were dead.

"Why don't you give us one reason we shouldn't shoot you," he said to the newcomer.

The guy smiled like people said that to him every day. "You don't shoot somebody like the Reverend Billy Chow!"

That's who this was. Roman knew all about him. He came from Korea or 'Nam or someplace like that. Penniless, and all that, but for his faith. Roman knew the whole routine. The local TV stations showed his crusades late at night. He sometimes watched them. All that singing and preaching helped him fall asleep.

It figured he worked for Smith. Two peas in a pod. This Reverend Chow probably funded his crusades with little old ladies' bank accounts. Besides, neither one of them was a real American.

"Look, Reverend," Roman shot back, "we gave at the office . . . except we don't have an office!"

The other guys laughed at that. Even the reverend smiled.

"I am here to give you a message," the Chinese guy continued. "You have taken an unwise action."

"I've probably taken more than one of those," Roman agreed. He sort of liked the formal way this guy talked. "Which one are we referring to?"

"You have sent two of your own to confront our Mr. Smith. That is not allowed."

Now Chow was pissing him off. "Not allowed? Smith did something to my son Ernie! Is that allowed?"

Chow's pleasant face creased into the slightest of

frowns. "Smith realizes that events may have taken an unpleasant turn. Therefore, he is willing to return your two underlings if you—"

Roman smacked his hand down on the table. "Smith does not dictate terms! Not anymore!"

But he didn't want to go flying off the handle. Not until he'd considered his options. Smith was smart to send somebody like this, a public figure with a respectable front. Not that Roman Petranova would think twice about offing someone like Chow. Like he was thinking before, the way these televangelists fleeced shut-ins and little old ladies, it would be fine to take one or two out of commission. But even Roman had to admit it would look bad if anybody found out.

He waved his finger at the smooth-talking holy man. "I already told your boss he shouldn't show up here without an invite. So now he sends one of his stooges? Smith has my son. Smith is gonna pay!"

"He thought it best if he gave you a chance to back down. Mr. Smith has resources you can't even imagine." So the reverend wouldn't give it up. Chow was nothing but smooth edges. Now that he thought of it, Petranova hated smooth edges.

"Really? But maybe you can. Maybe you know a lot about Smith's organization. And maybe you'll tell us everything we need to know. I think it's time for a little trip to Funland."

A couple of his guys laughed at that, too. Hey, he didn't have to kill him. He just had to make Chow disappear for a few hours. Get him someplace private, where he'd be willing to give up Ernie's whereabouts. What could he say? Smith wouldn't want to go to the police any more than Roman did.

"This would be most unwise," Chow said quickly. "I am a neutral emissary."

It looked like he was getting under the reverend's smooth edges. Roman grinned. "Maybe we can make a little exchange. If not, we got ways of amusing ourselves. That's why they call it Funland."

"If I do not contact Mr. Smith—" Chow began.

"Who cares about Smith?" Roman was getting more pleased with every passing minute. He guessed even somebody like Chow could sweat. "Louse, get out the white Caddy."

The reverend's eyes darted from one side of his head to the other. "No, you don't want to do this. Smith will get angry."

"Smith don't mean nothin' here."

"Smith means whatever he wants to mean. You haven't seen what he can do. . . ."

Roman stood up. "And you got no idea what I can do. If Smith wasn't holding onto my son, you'd already be dead."

"You don't know anything!"

He was sick of this guy's talk. He took four quick steps forward. "That's enough from you." He took Chow's neck in one of his massive hands and squeezed. "Smith is dead one way or another. We get enough from you, maybe you live. Maybe you don't. It's up to you."

Chow's vocal chords did a good imitation of a garbage disposal. Roman let go. The guy still had to be able to talk.

"Come on. Let's go to Funland. I'm gonna take care of this, personal."

THE RIGHT REVEREND Billy Chow seldom questioned the rightness of his path. This moment, however, might be one of the rare exceptions.

You did not question or contradict Smith. You obeyed, and Smith would reward you. Not that the Reverend Chow had a conscience, but he knew he was doubly damned. Smith was just a very special part of his damnation.

But with Smith, he knew exactly where he stood—until now, when Smith had sent him into the lion's den. Who knew what Roman Petranova was crazy enough to do?

Hadn't Smith guaranteed him his protection? Here he was, in the backseat of a car, Roman Petranova on one side of him, some foul-smelling goon on the other. He was only supposed to deliver a warning. And now?

The Reverend Chow wished he was naive enough to pray.

He heard sirens.

"Cops!" the foul-smelling guy yelled. Chow felt fingers dig into his shoulder. "Should I off this guy, boss?"

Roman sighed. "And what would we do with the body?" He tapped the driver on the shoulder. "Stop the car. We don't need a police chase. Besides, we ain't done nothing wrong."

Yet, Billy Chow thought. As a rule, cops weren't particularly his friends, either. Was there a way he could alert them to his predicament without getting himself killed?

The driver stopped the car and rolled down the window. "Yes, officer?"

"You have someone in this car we very much want to see." A blue-capped head appeared at window level. "Reverend Chow? If you could step out of the vehicle?"

The police wanted to see him? What now? Consorting with known criminals, maybe? Had somebody from the D.A.'s office finally uncovered one of his scams? Smith had given him assurances that that wouldn't happen, either.

Roman slapped Chow on the shoulder. "Well, I guess we'll have to end it here, then."

The reverend stared at him. "What?"

"Get out, go to the cops. Larry, let the guy out."

The foul-smelling guy opened his door and scooted out of the car.

Petranova's voice followed him as he climbed out of the car. "Reverend, now that we know you're involved, we'll be talking again."

The Caddy door slammed. The car drove away. This was all very unreal.

The Reverend Billy Chow turned to the police officer. He felt very tired. "What do you want?"

"We'll give you a ride wherever you want to go. Call it returning a favor for a friend."

Really?

He should never have doubted. Smith had people everywhere.

Chow followed the policeman back to the patrol car. He should feel more relieved. Smith had rescued him.

But the Pale Man had also stuck him in the middle of something that even the Right Reverend Billy Chow might not survive.

. 10 .

BEFORE THIS, JACOBSEN HAD simply felt useless. This was far worse.

"Mendeck!" Summitch moaned, straining against the Judges who held his arms and legs. His whole small body shook as he screamed. "Send! Send! Protect them! Lost! Lost! Lost!"

"Hold him down!" the black-robed Judge called as they gathered around the thrashing Summitch. "Make sure he doesn't hurt himself."

First, Gontor had waded into battle, leaving Jacobsen with a small package for safekeeping. Tsang the Warrior had tagged along with the big bronze guy, while Summitch had gotten into deep conversation with the Judges of the Green. Jacobsen, as usual, was left feeling like a fifth wheel.

Here he was in a strange world, given a job he didn't understand in the least. Noble fool—that's what Gontor called him. The words might seem to insult him, if they weren't always spoken in such a reverent tone.

Then Summitch went crazy. The small fellow had started to twitch, his eyes crossing, his wrinkles shimmering in a palsied frenzy. The spasm appeared to spread from his head to his other extremities, as the Gnarlyman began to shout what at first seemed to be nonsense. Summitch fell to the ground, punching and kicking with ferocious energy.

The fit seemed to go on forever. Summitch was the only one he'd ever been able to talk to. Well, not that he could really talk to anybody, really, but at least with Summitch he could pretend to have some mutual self-interest. After all, there was always that gold the Gnarlyman had talked about.

"The Growler!" Summitch shrieked after a particularly violent spasm. "Help me, Growler!"

The small fellow grew still, the fit passing as quickly as it had arrived.

Summitch opened his eyes. "Oh, dear. How inconvenient." He smiled up at the Judges, an expression that, on the face of the usually frowning Summitch, looked a little creepy. "I'm quite all right now, thank you." He shook his head quite violently. "I had hoped I was over all of that."

Jacobsen frowned. Who knew what some of that ranting was about, especially that Growler bit. He could swear he'd heard one of those names—Mendeck—somewhere before.

The Judges stood, releasing Summitch's arms and legs. Dantis looked down at the Gnarlyman. "Most interesting. Our large marauding friend says you hold many secrets."

"A few too many, I'm afraid." Summitch shuddered. "If you step back and give me some air? I believe I'm quite over my fit, now."

The Judges withdrew as Summitch regained his feet.

"Are you all right?" Jacobsen asked as he reached the Gnarlyman's side.

His wrinkles shook as he nodded his head. "The channels are imperfect. I'm not sure if that's fortuitous or not."

"Forgive us," Dantis called as he and the three other Judges turned to go. "Now that you are past your crisis, we must attend to the fight."

"Crisis?" Summitch snorted. "Is that what they call it?"

"What would you call it?" Jacobsen asked. "And what do you mean by 'channels'?"

Summitch studied him for a moment before he replied. "It was an attempt at communication, from another world. Your world. I should have known, once you showed up, that this sort of thing would start all over again."

His world? "Does this have something to do with me?"

"I doubt it. Mrs. Mendeck—that's what she calls herself over there—was trying to tell me about somebody else. I think she is expecting to send others my way." The small fellow snorted. "Perhaps I should start offering tours."

"Mrs. Mendeck." It came back to Jacobsen now. The apartment building where he was sent by Smith to kill the teenage girl—except he found that he could never kill somebody that reminded him of his daughter. Besides, he never had a chance, with Mrs. Mendeck defending her. "Mrs. Mendeck! That was the name of the old broad who sent me here!"

"Of course it was. She can be a mean old broad, too." Summitch shivered. "Whatever you do, never end up owing her a favor. You do, and next thing you know, you're having a fit on the ground."

"You said something about a . . . Growler, too?"

Summitch looked up at him with alarm. "I spoke about

the Growler? Damn that Mendeck woman! I must have been delirious!''

But Jacobsen was getting straight answers out of the small fellow for a change. He didn't want to stop now. "Who, or what, is the Growler?''

The Gnarlyman looked down the rocky hillside. "Better you don't know.'' Doubt clouded his extremely wrinkled brow. "I didn't ask for his . . . help, did I?''

"It sounded like that to me.''

"I won't be able to escape a single debt,'' Summitch said very softly. "No!'' he continued much more force-fully. "I've put that negative thinking behind me. Sum-mitch is going for all the gold!'' He placed a cautionary hand upon Jacobsen's elbow. "Let us not speak of the Growler again.''

"Why?'' Jacobsen wasn't ready for Summitch to go evasive on him again. "Would the Judges know about this?''

"What can they do? They're only Judges!'' Summitch shook his head. "Enough about this! When Mrs. Mendeck wants into my head, I can't refuse her. But I won't dwell on her, either, or . . . other things. We have a battle to attend to. And we'd better attend to it quickly.'' He pointed out into the midst of the melee beneath them.

"Gontor's in trouble.''

Jacobsen looked down the hillside to the battle below. The metal man was surrounded by men with ropes and nets. He would tear through one line as another snagged at his legs and a third twisted about an arm. Tsang was at his side, slicing through ropes and enemy soldiers with equal ease. But a dozen new teams of soldiers with ropes and nets rushed to join those that surrounded the pair. Tsang could only do so much against so many.

The Gnarlyman nodded. "Time to get to work.''

"To work?"

"Follow my lead. We've got to help our fellows."

"Help?" It was amazing, Jacobsen thought, how quickly he could get confused all over again. "How?"

"Any way we can. I've got my knives."

Well, bully for Summitch. Jacobsen still had the short blade that the Gnarlyman had lent him back in the tunnels, but he didn't particularly relish the thought of wading into the battle with nothing more than that single knife. Of course, he still had his gun, but he was surprised it still had any bullets.

"And me?" he prompted.

"You heard Gontor." Summitch frowned as he studied the surrounding ground. "You're one of the four. Don't worry, you'll think of something."

Jacobsen guessed it had all worked out so far. It was just a little hard to believe in destiny when you were someplace where even the sky was a little strange. Still, the more action he saw, the less time he had to think.

His companion kicked at the ground with his toes. "Now if I can just concentrate for a moment. These tunnel entrances are everywhere."

"They are?"

"When you're a finder, they are. That's what I do. I find." He looked away from the ground before him, first down, then up, the hill. "Ah." He pointed to a stone outcropping perhaps a dozen feet away. "This rock looks good." He glanced at Jacobsen. "Are you coming?"

Jacobsen hurried after the smaller fellow. He definitely didn't want to be left behind.

Summitch stomped around the boulder, raising a great cloud of dust. "There!" He dug into the earth with both hands. With a grunt, he pulled up a square of soil, a trapdoor to a tunnel below, and glanced sharply at Jacobsen.

"The battle's not going to wait for us, you know."

He might never understand what was going on, but he'd never give up trying. "Why are we doing this, exactly?"

Summitch waved toward the battle down the hill. "It's not every day you team up with a bronze giant." He jumped into the hole beneath the trapdoor, so that only his head showed. "Even I am not exactly sure where all this is going to lead, but hey, I'm not going to waste this kind of an opportunity." He waved for Jacobsen to follow. "Come on. I'll show you a thing or two."

Jacobsen climbed into the hole, descending what he saw were a short set of stairs down into a rough-hewn tunnel that looked no different from the miles of corridors he and Summitch had already traveled. Summitch pulled at what looked like an exposed root jutting from one of the rough dirt walls. The door above them slammed closed as a dozen torches magically sprang to life down the length of the corridor.

The Gnarlyman looked back and forth down the span of the tunnel, which seemed perfectly level, and quite straight in either direction, despite being built into a hillside. "This way, I think."

Jacobsen thought it best to follow in silence.

"Ah," Summitch murmured after a few moments' walk, and Jacobsen saw they were at the head of a long stairway. They quickly walked down the stairs, which stretched for some distance, with a new tunnel branching off every fifty steps or so.

After they had passed four of those side tunnels, he heard a muffled sound above him, like a gong being struck repeatedly. Or perhaps like something hitting a bronze giant over and over again.

"Nice of our enemy to signal like this," Summitch confirmed his suspicions. "Now let's see how we can get up there."

The Gnarlyman hit a bump on the wall that, to Jacobsen at least, looked no different from twenty other bumps. A rope ladder fell from somewhere above them, followed by some shouts of surprise from overhead. The torchlight vanished as sunlight filtered down from above.

"Apparently, some of the soldiers don't approve of being displaced," Summitch quipped as he rapidly climbed the ladder. Jacobsen looked up to see a bright square of daylight above. He hurried to follow. Summitch was already almost to the top.

The Gnarlyman had disappeared by the time Jacobsen reached the top of the ladder. Cautiously, he poked his head out into the sun.

Chaos surrounded him. Gontor was perhaps thirty feet away, enmeshed by ropes and nets. And the enemy was using his comparative immobility to throw everything they could at him—spears, arrows, and rocks. The missiles made a hollow, ringing sound as they bounced from Gontor's metal shell—even the occasional catapulted boulder didn't make a dent.

Gontor didn't even appear to notice that part of the attack. Nor would he be captured easily. Twenty soldiers, maybe more, were attempting to secure the nets, anchoring them into the ground with long stakes. But Gontor refused to stop moving, pulling up a stake here, lifting a soldier off his feet there.

"Ah!" boomed that voice from who knew where that belonged to Gontor. "Friend Jacobsen!" So the bronze giant had seen him arrive despite all of this. "How long has it been since Gontor has had any real exercise!" His laughter rang out over the battlefield. "My body may be an efficient machine, but my mind is full of rust. Nothing a little exertion won't fix!'' He lifted a net with half a dozen soldiers attached from the ground and tossed it aside.

Jacobsen saw Tsang, then, as the warrior turned from a recently made corpse to cut at the bonds surrounding the giant. His bloody sword cut ten ropes, then twenty, but Gontor was covered with a hundred more. The Grey troops rushed with a yell at the warrior of Orange, causing him to whirl and defend himself. Two quick strokes disposed of two of the enemy, but the third soldier parried Tsang's blade, proving to be a more bothersome adversary. From the way the warrior pushed back the enemy, Jacobsen thought Tsang would easily better the other, but in the meantime another score of the Grey threw nets over the giant to replace those so recently destroyed.

Where was Summitch?

There! Jacobsen was surprised to see him quite close to Gontor, weaving his way around the enemy soldiers who, if they even bothered to look at him, looked away as if there was nothing there. On this world, Gnarlymen passed without notice. Or so Summitch had told him—repeatedly, on their long trips underground.

A soldier with a purple helm kicked at the Gnarlyman as he reached the edge of the ropes. The soldier screamed, a knife stuck deep in his thigh. He fell to the ground, aided no doubt by Summitch. His screams stopped abruptly. Jacobsen didn't even see the stroke that killed him.

The Gnarlyman walked on. Jacobsen noticed that the knife in the soldier's thigh was gone. The knife was back with its owner, one of the two in Summitch's hands. He cut one rope in the growing forest of hemp, and another, then stole between the others, crawling under and into the mass of netting.

''Who are you?''

Jacobsen started. The voice came from behind him.

Hands grabbed his arms and pulled him roughly from his hiding place.

Jacobsen guessed he wasn't going to be allowed to be a spectator anymore.

"He's not one of ours!" The hands spun him around to face a trio of soldiers in the uniform of the Grey.

"Kill him and be done with it!" one of them said.

"But what if he has information?" asked the one who had pulled him from the hole. "Better we take him prisoner and torture it out of him."

"Careful!" the third one cautioned. "The enemy is full of tricks today."

The soldiers held him loosely, if at all. Maybe, he realized, they might be as afraid of him as he was of them. Jacobsen wondered if it was time to use one of his precious bullets. Maybe he could cause the same kind of chaos he had before. If only he knew where, or who, to shoot.

A great shout rose behind him. The soldiers let go of Jacobsen as they shouted as well.

He turned around to see the source of the noise.

Gontor had been forced to the ground. The amassed legions of the Grey and Purple surged forward to overwhelm him. But where were Tsang and Summitch?

His captors rushed past him, eager to share in the glorious victory. He was forgotten, and free, at least for the moment!

But what did his freedom mean if all his friends were defeated?

Gontor was overwhelmed. Tsang had probably been defeated, too, if only by shear force of numbers, and Summitch apparently had run away! All hope was lost. And what could he, Eric Jacobsen, do, alone against an army?

Well, it had worked before.

He pulled out his revolver and shot a bullet into the air.

Everyone stopped—the whole army, thousands of men swarming to overwhelm the fallen giant—everyone froze, as if the great drama around him had turned into a snapshot. And everyone turned his way, to look at the man with the gun. An entire army stared at him.

Now that he had their attention, what was he going to do with it?

Maybe Jacobsen would be lucky and they wouldn't kill him instantly or throw him in whatever passed for a prison around here. Maybe, if he kept on grinning, they would realize he knew absolutely nothing. He could be an ambassador of goodwill or something. Maybe even the palace fool, if there was an opening.

More likely, he was about to be very dead.

The silence was broken by a new set of cries.

Jacobsen strained to make sense out of a hundred voices screaming questions and commands. The shouts of the Grey had turned from celebration to alarm. The mass of ropes and netting was considerably smaller than they were before. Apparently, Gontor had disappeared from beneath them. The bronze giant must have had a final trick up his metal sleeve.

A number of the soldiers turned again, to look back at the last representative of the enemy upon the battlefield.

Only Jacobsen was left to face all of the Grey and Purple troops. A very frustrated, angry force of men. Now he was truly alone!

They were trained fighters. He knew next to nothing about wielding a blade. So be it. He pulled out his knife with his left hand, raised the gun in his right. Although it would probably be over in an instant, he would go down fighting!

"Well, are you coming?" a familiar voice demanded.

Jacobsen looked down to see a trapdoor open by his left foot.

Summitch grabbed his leg and pulled him into the hole.

"WE WILL DESTROY the Judges—and the Lords. We will destroy the Judges—and the Lords."

Kedrik found himself filled with a nervous energy that he hadn't felt in a century or more; an energy he remembered from his long-ago youth, when he was about to go into battle—a mix of fear, excitement, and something like joy.

They had found a new enemy. He and Basoff had sent his daughter and a lesser Judge after spies and Karmille and Sasseen had sent them this.

"We will destroy the Judges." The Imp who carried Sasseen's message would parrot the same sentence endlessly. "And the Lords." They were words from a new danger, a group of renegade Judges hidden within the tunnel far below the Castle. For so long, Kedrik had fought a war with the other Houses of the Castle; a war that, through his superior forces and strategy, he was slowly winning. But these Judges posed a new challenge, an unknown danger, a force that might tip the great battle, might even undermine the Grey. But how? And when?

"You claimed there was more," Kedrik demanded of his first Judge. Basoff glanced at his lord only long enough to frown before returning to his examination of the elemental, a black flame that seemed to absorb light rather than shed it, trapped now under glass.

"There is, I am certain. I have gotten past the message Sasseen implanted on the thing, but it seems frozen upon this single moment."

There were so many who vied for power within the Castle. The intruders from last night proved that they must act quickly. At first light, Kedrik and Basoff had sent a small band of soldiers and Judges to his daughter's aid, half a dozen in all—it made no sense to send more through the tunnels. But Basoff had claimed there was more to be gained from the elemental. They were complex creatures, and tended to record not only the message the Judge wished to send, but all of their surroundings. If they might pry a bit deeper into the creature's memory, they would gain a much better view of the situation below.

Or so said Basoff's theory. In reality, they had spent hours on this thing, and accomplished practically nothing.

"Are you useless?" Kedrik demanded. "An old man whose powers have deserted him?" He knew, as soon as the words were out of his mouth, that his outburst expressed his fear—not just of Basoff, but of himself.

He rubbed his finger absentmindedly over the scar the Green had given him so long ago. The owner of that sword was long dead. All of Kedrik's generation, and a dozen generations after him, were dead and gone to dust. Kedrik was no longer precisely mortal. For a thousand years, Basoff and his fellow Judges had exposed Kedrik to certain of the Judges' arts; spells forbidden to all but the Judges themselves. Or so said the Covenants.

But this war meant the end of the Covenants; or, at the very least, a rewriting of the rules. Soon, Basoff and Kedrik would be above Lords and Judges and Covenants. Or they would be dead.

Basoff balled the hand that felt the scar into a fist, willing himself to concentrate. The spells were not perfect. Sometimes Kedrik's attention would wander. He needed his relaxations more than ever, depended upon those lovely creatures of Basoff's creation to get him through the day.

He had many of the habits of an old man; a man waiting for a death he prayed would never come.

And what of Basoff? Had he slowed so much as well? Perhaps that was the Judge's problem—he could no longer acclimate to this sudden need for haste after so many careful years of planning.

Kedrik hoped it wasn't so.

"I will show my lord my usefulness," Basoff replied at last. "Sasseen thought he was clever enough to hide this from me! Here."

The Judge waved a hand at the creature beneath the glass, prodding the elemental with the most delicate of spells.

"We will destroy . . ." The force caused the black flame to shiver. The creature hissed.

A torrent of voices erupted from the flame. Some came, no doubt, from the rebel Judges, voices threatening, voices demanding information. But Kedrik recognized other voices—those of his daughter Karmille and the Judge Sasseen.

"These Judges have great power . . . we cannot fight them ourselves . . . I have to go to my father. . . . But what if we can work with these renegades . . . rule it all . . . destroy Basoff . . . kill my father . . . rule it all."

The words did not overly surprise Kedrik. All the High Lords of the Grey were ruthless. If he ruled with fear and violence, he could expect no less of his children. His only error was in not guessing the strength of his daughter's ambition.

"More!" he demanded of Judge Basoff. "Get the elemental to tell us more!"

"As you wish, my lord." The black-robed Judge turned back to the glass, making a series of passes with his hands above the elemental.

The creature's hiss turned into a wail, as if it were recalling every voice it stored and releasing them all at once.

"No!" Basoff called. But whatever spells he tried were not enough. The flame dissolved, shattering into smaller and smaller sparks of darkness, until it vanished.

The Judge turned to his lord. "Forgive me. Sasseen had installed certain counterspells I did not see until too late. While he doesn't quite hold my skill, his talent is admirable."

"As befits a Judge of the Grey," Kedrik agreed. He felt a cold fury building within him; a fury he could not afford to unleash on Basoff. He had a much better target, after all. His beloved, traitorous daughter, Karmille.

Perhaps she had forgotten the ways he had to make her obey. No matter. She would remember soon enough. He would not kill her. No. Instead, he would destroy her freedom.

But that—as pleasant a thought as it might be—would only come in time. His lovely daughter might still be of use. He looked to his Judge.

"We have work to do, Basoff. We must speak with the party we so recently sent to the tunnels and—amend their instructions." But that was not enough. Kedrik realized he had given his daughter too much autonomy. If he were to use her properly, he would have to know everything she was planning.

He studied the now-empty jar. "Tell me, Basoff. We have lost our Imp. Could you make another?"

"Most certainly," the Judge agreed. "In unlocking its secrets, I had far more time to study it than either you or I might have preferred."

"And could you disguise this new Imp to seem like the one created by Sasseen?"

"I believe my skill is great enough. But why?"

"This Imp shall do more than deliver a simple message. It will act as a spy upon my daughter and all she encounters."

"Most wise, my lord." Basoff bowed. "If you would excuse me, I will begin work upon it immediately."

Kedrik dismissed his Judge. Yes, the feeling was back, the battle edge. A new group of Judges, with powers unlike any of those mired in the thousand-year war. He would let his daughter take the risks, and gain the knowledge. But if there were alliances to be made, power to be gained, Kedrik would let no one stand in his way.

He chuckled. The energy surged through him in a way he had almost forgotten.

Kedrik would indeed live forever.

· 11 ·

"**M**'LADY! NO!"

Sasseen turned at the guard's cry. The lady Karmille had collapsed, silently, upon the floor of the tunnel.

Something had gone amiss with her recent spell calling forth the beasts to rid them of the threat of Aubric. It was a crude spell, but it should have been effective, unless Aubric was far stronger than they suspected, or he had had some sorcerous help.

"Are you going to help her?" the guard demanded of him.

"I will if I can," Sasseen replied curtly, bringing his attention back to the scene before him. The lady Karmille could still be a most valuable ally. Besides, should anything happen to her, it would give First Judge Basoff an excuse to destroy him.

But this was a most delicate matter.

There were practical reasons why the untrained should

not dabble in sorcery. A part of oneself was involved in every spell. Judges were trained to isolate the spells to minimize the potential harm. The lady Karmille had had no such training.

He looked down at the princess of the Grey. She was still breathing; perhaps the backlash of the failed spell had done no more than render her unconscious.

"Help her!" the guard demanded. Her assassin, Flik, had moved silently to Sasseen's side. Would they threaten a Judge?

"It is in my own best interest to do so." He looked directly at the assassin as he approached the lady. "It is in none of our interests to kill each other. But these things must be handled delicately. I would not wish to harm the lady further."

He knelt by Karmille's side and placed a hand upon her wrist. Her heartbeat was slow but regular. He whispered a few words, sending a trickle of power through her form. She moaned. Perhaps a bit more energy might wake her. He closed his eyes, concentrating the force that bled from his fingers. She spasmed suddenly, her whole form going into convulsions.

"What have you done?" the guard demanded.

Sasseen removed his hand as quickly as the problem began. Her spasms reduced to a palsied shivering, then she was still again.

The Judge saw movement behind him. The assassin held a knife. Sasseen would not be threatened. A few more words, and the knife grew hot enough to singe flesh. Flik grunted and pushed the knife toward the Judge. Sasseen made a motion with his hands and the knife ceased to be, leaving only a black and blistered mark on the assassin's palm.

"I said it is no one's interest to kill!" Sasseen shouted

at the two. "If you continue in this behavior, however, I will oblige you. She will be very displeased when she awakens and finds you gone." He took a deep breath. "The lady Karmille was caught by her own spell. Whatever has taken her, it resists my first efforts to revive her. I am afraid I came upon this journey without much of my equipment. It may take me some time to determine the cause and affect a cure. Or, she may simply restore herself and wake on her own."

"So what do we do?" the guard asked grudgingly. "Wait?"

"I must study those tomes that I brought with me." The Judge frowned. "But we cannot remain here. Anyone powerful enough to overcome a spell as strong as that provided by m'lady might also be able to track the spell back to its source. We would be better served if we removed ourselves at least from that place where the spell was generated; it will make it more difficult for counterspells to find us."

The guard was still not convinced. "Is it safe to move the lady?"

"I believe so," Sasseen replied with more conviction than he actually felt. Until he knew exactly what had caused her to lose consciousness, every action would have a certain element of risk. "She breathes easily and has no fever. And it is not safe to remain here."

He clapped his hands. "I can have one of my soldiers carry her." Savignon and Lepp both stepped forward, fully under his control again. "I can instruct them to be quite gentle, and they never tire."

"No," the guard replied. "I will carry her. It is my responsibility."

"Very well." Better they take the accountability, he realized. It would leave him free to deal with other threats. And whoever could turn back the beast spell was a very great threat indeed. The renegade Judges, the thing that was once Aubric—when Sasseen had touched Karmille, he had looked for traces of their power in the lady's condition, but had found none. Did that mean there was a third force at work in the tunnels?

So much had changed in their day or two in the tunnels. When Karmille had first proposed their alliance, he had seen it as a simple bid for power, a way to get the upper hand within the Keep of the Grey. But the more time he spent within the tunnels, the more secrets he found they held: powerful secrets that, if what happened to the lady was an indication, might destroy them long before they ever returned to the Grey stronghold.

Sasseen would not allow this to happen.

"Gather her up, then," he called to her two servants, "and hear my pledge. I will find a way to wake her, and I will find a way to strike back at those who did this."

Her servants regarded him coldly as he stepped away from Karmille. They would force him to prove his words.

He would have to be the leader now. In a way, he imagined he should be glad he no longer had to make allowances for m'lady's whims. Perhaps it would even be easier for him to forge an alliance with the renegades—Judge to Judge—without the interference of a High One.

If only he understood the magic that waited for them in these tunnels. If only he knew who brought that magic, who attacked the woman he was sworn to protect.

Her guard knelt to pick up the lady. Karmille screamed, a high, piercing sound, but then appeared to return to sleep.

The guard known as Blade looked to the Judge. Sasseen nodded. The guard lifted Karmille from the ground. This time, she slept peacefully.

The Judge gave the command for his soldiers to follow them. He, who usually knew everything about his spells and his world, now felt like he knew so little. Once, mere days before, Sasseen was ready to rule the world. Now he would be content to keep his party alive.

No. He was learning that these seemingly empty, seemingly endless tunnels were rife with magic; sorceries strange even to a senior Judge. He would not simply protect the lady. He would grab the magics swirling around him, discover a way to harness the sorcery that threatened them and turn it to their advantage.

A few moments before, he had made a pledge to the servants of m'lady. Now, he made a secret pledge to himself.

After all, he was the second greatest Judge among all the Grey. With a few of the secrets he would find on his journey, he would soon be the greatest Judge of all.

IT WAS ONLY after the monsters were gone—blown into little pieces—that Joe thought to look at the gun.

"How did that happen?"

The bullets were all gone. The gun had been empty before the monster had even made the scene. Not that any regular bullets could cause monsters to explode. He looked at Brian.

The kid looked more scared than Joe felt.

"Did you do something?"

"I—I thought it would be really good if you had more bullets. But I don't think I did anything."

Aubric regarded the boy for a moment before he spoke in that multivoiced way of his.

"You're one of the . . . others, aren't you?"

This guy with light in his eyes was talking about others?

"What do you mean, others?" Joe demanded.

The light flared as Aubric spoke again. "My kind has

been on this world since the beginning. We were banished for a thousand years, but only a thousand. We know of the natural order of things. We are a part of that order, as is the one called Brian."

So now the kid comes from this place? Joe was really getting to hate these surprises. Maybe he was the only regular guy around here.

The regular guy had a question. "So, because Brian was one of the others, he made new bullets for the gun?"

"Brian is one of the Strangers," Aubric replied. "We have no quarrel with the Strangers."

"And Strangers make bullets?" Joe persisted.

"There are many Strangers. Some are senders. Some are finders. The rarest of the Strangers, though, is the maker."

"So he *made* me bullets?"

Aubric shuddered. When he spoke again, it was with a single voice. "Those inside me are still new to this form. Much of their strength has been taken by the recent battle. They need to move, to leave the tunnels behind."

Joe was getting pissed. "Hey! I want to figure out just what was stuck in my gun!"

Aubric paused a moment before replying. "They are tired. This new world blurs before them. Once we see the sun, all will be revealed."

"I wish we could see Summitch," Brian added.

Joe wished he could see Ernie, and get the hell out of here.

But Aubric was already marching away. Joe and Brian hurried to follow.

Imp was happy. Imp was free. Imp had a purpose.

Imp had a message for one group and a mission for another.

There was another Imp before. Imp was brand new, but like the other. He was the other, they told him to say.

Imp was happy to obey.

He flew through the tunnels quickly, sure of his destinations.

"Judge Nallf!"

Three Judges, six soldiers, headed down the tunnels, headed to the same place as Imp. Imp would get there first. Imp could fly.

The soldiers cried out. The Judges made warding signs. They had nothing to fear from Imp. Imp only brought a message.

"Judge Nallf! Basoff sends you greetings, and a change in your instructions. You were sent to assist Karmille, and report on her actions. You will still report. However, it has come to our attention that someone within Karmille's party is planning an act of treason. Make no mention of this upon meeting them. However, at your first convenience, you will disable Sasseen. Kill him if necessary, and take the lady prisoner in such a way that you do not do her harm. She should be returned to court as soon as possible. This by command, not only of Basoff, but of High Lord Kedrik himself!"

The Judges shouted questions at Imp, but he had no answers. In fact, he had already forgotten the message he had relayed. As he had been instructed.

Imp flew on to his second destination. The Judge Sasseen, who had made the first Imp (ah, but *he* was the first Imp); the lady Karmille, who must be both watched and protected; and his final instructions.

Imp was happy. Imp was free.

Imp had a purpose.

. 12 .

WELL, VINNIE HAD TO ADmit, if anything was going to keep them from going after Smith, this was it. It had totally freaked both of them. Freaked them and stopped them dead. They had backed away from their original plan and run into an alley across the street. Johnny T was normally a shoot-first-and-ask-questions-later kind of guy. But you didn't ask questions later when it came to Roman Petranova's son.

They had been going for the quick attack, using surprise to disrupt Smith's organization, and maybe get to Smith. Now Ernie Petranova stood there, barring the door they had planned to break through, their guns blazing.

"This is crazy," Johnny T breathed in Vinnie's ear.

Vinnie knew just what he meant. The guy looked like Ernie, and then he didn't. The way he posed there, not moving, no expression, he was more like a statue than anything alive.

"So what do we do?" Johnny T whispered.

Getting the guns, driving over here, the muscleman had pretty much been calling the shots. Now, with the first surprise, Vinnie realized that he was the boss.

This was his big chance. So he kept telling himself. Vinnie had never been very good at making decisions. He'd better start making them now.

The more nervous Johnny T got, the more he talked. "Why doesn't he do something? Ernie's always talkin' or gruntin' or scratchin' or something! Why does he just stand there?"

They weren't going to find anything hiding in this alley. "Why don't we ask him?" Vinnie replied.

Johnny T thought about it before he nodded. "You gonna call to him?"

If Vinnie was going to do this, he'd do it all the way. "Cover me. I want him to see me, too." He stepped out into the street. "Hey, Ernie!"

No response. Ernie acted like he didn't hear him. He acted like Vinnie wasn't even there.

Wait a minute. Not even there.

Vinnie, if you're going to make decisions, you're going to have to start thinking. What did the boss say about Smith?

"It sure looks like Ernie." Johnny T had walked up behind him. "If it was Ernie, wouldn't he say something?"

The big guy was still doing the statue bit. Vinnie decided to tell the muscle what he was thinking. "You know, they say Smith is kind of a magician. This could be some kind of illusion or something."

"It's a *trick?*" Johnny T's voice got considerably louder. "There ain't *nobody* there?"

The statue didn't blink.

Well, Vinnie realized, there was one way to find out.

"Let's throw something at him. Ernie's tough."

"Yeah." Johnny T grinned. Here was something he could understand.

The muscle examined the street before them. There was enough junk out on the street to start a war. Vinnie guessed that was one of the advantages of being on the wrong side of town. Street-cleaning was not a priority.

"We gotta get something big enough for him to notice." Johnny T picked up a rock the size of his fist. "It won't kill him, but it'll get his attention."

"Ernie couldn't ask for more," Vinnie agreed.

Johnny T lobbed the stone underhand straight toward Ernie. The rock hit his shoulder and bounced away. The statue didn't even flinch.

Johnny T looked down at the rock as it rolled to a stop. "Well, if that's Ernie, he's not himself."

That, Vinnie thought, was the understatement of the year. "So we can't go through the door. Let's try a window."

The whole block was empty storefronts. A couple of the stores were boarded up, but most of them were plate-glass city.

"Like the window next door?" Vinnie suggested.

Johnny T grinned. "That's why I brought my shotgun."

"Do it," Vinnie said.

The muscle took out the window with a single blast, a six-by-eight-foot piece of glass disintegrating with a crash. It was noisy but efficient.

Ernie still didn't do anything.

"I think it's time for us to stop looking at statues and get to work."

Vinnie led the way, his shoes crunching on broken glass. The room beyond the broken window was lit by those streetlights that still worked outside. It housed a battered desk and half a dozen file cabinets, like somebody had been using it for an office. A glass door led out to a hallway in the back.

Johnny T crunched after him. Vinnie pointed to the door.

"There's a light back there. Maybe these stores connect toward the back."

Johnny T pumped his shotgun. "If they don't we can make some more holes." He stepped quickly across the rubble and pulled open the door. Now that they were moving, the muscle was in charge once more. Vinnie rushed to catch up. He had one gun in his hand, another in a holster under his coat, one in his belt, and another pair thrown in his pockets. Johnny T held the shotgun, and had a couple of automatics stuck in his belt where Vinnie could see them, and who knew how many more under his jacket. The rest of the hardware was still back in the car, so they were dependent on what they carried. Vinnie hoped it would be enough.

The first hallway they walked down intersected with another after only about twenty feet. With its bright yellow walls and carpeted floor, it looked more like a corridor in an office building than the storage area at the back of a store. A row of doors broke the right-hand wall at regular intervals, leading back into what once had been empty stores. Who knew what was in there now? Maybe this whole block was a front for the pale guy's operation.

"I think Smith's got himself quite a setup here."

Johnny T frowned. He wasn't much for conversation once the action started. "Which way?"

Vinnie guessed it was decision time again. He nodded to the right.

"Let's move that way. There must have been some reason Ernie was blocking that particular door. We'll have to go in the back way."

The muscle must have agreed; he was already on the move. This hallway was empty, too. They weren't exactly sneaking around back here, either. Vinnie had expected to run into some kind of fight. Maybe Johnny T's shotgun blast had scared everybody away.

Maybe they were walking into a trap.

Well, they might as well get this over with. He tapped his partner on the shoulder.

"Johnny! The door!" The first of the doorways was already on the muscle's right. This should be directly behind the space Ernie was guarding.

The muscle used his foot to kick the door open.

Vinnie crowded in behind him. The place was full of machines. A pair of computers sat in the middle of a dozen black boxes, some with displays, some with flashing lights. There were cables and wires everywhere. This was probably the nerve center of Smith's whole operation.

"What are you doing in here?"

If he hadn't spoken, Vinnie thought he never would have seen the man buried in the midst of all the electronics. At first glance, he looked almost impossibly skinny. Vinnie realized there were wires where his arms should be, as though he were part of one of these machines.

Right now, Vinnie didn't care what his story was. They had a job to do. "We're here to kill you if you don't tell us where Smith is."

The armless man looked away as if dismissing them. "I'm sorry. That's quite impossible."

"We're the ones who say what's impossible." Johnny T was in his element. He pushed his way into the maze of wires, yanking out any that got in the way of his shotgun.

The armless man pressed his back against another wall of electronic gear. "Once you work for Smith, you realize that only he makes the rules." He jerked his head toward the wires erupting from his shoulders. "You see what he's already done to me—some of it, at least."

"Smith did that to you?" Vinnie asked. "Why?"

"I tried to leave. He tore my arms out of my sockets. And more. A lot more." He giggled. "I don't know how—or why—I'm still alive."

The phone rang.

"I have to answer that."

"I don't think so." Johnny T propped one of his guns under the armless man's chin.

"Careful," Vinnie cautioned. "Let's let him answer some questions."

The phone kept on ringing.

"I'm not afraid of much anymore." The armless man nodded so that his chin nudged the business end of Johnny T's automatic. "Maybe you could kill me, but I doubt it. I might be dead for a minute or two, but Smith would still find a way to bring me back."

This guy who was maybe half machine was a real sign of the Pale Man's magic. And this was the guy they were supposed to take down? It looked like Roman had a real problem on his hands.

The armless man shifted his weight, did something with his feet.

The ringing stopped abruptly.

"They're here!" he screamed. "Get them here!"

"Oh, hell." Johnny T pumped three quick rounds into the armless man's chest. "Goddamn freak!"

The armless man smiled as the bullets entered his body. He jerked spasmodically, pulling free of some of the dozens of wires that hung him between the machines.

"Here!" he wailed. "Here!"

Johnny T put three more bullets into him, scarring metal and ripping flesh. The armless man made a noise that seemed half scream and half electric hum, cut off by a final convulsion.

The force of Johnny's bullets had disrupted the delicate spiderweb that kept the armless man in place. His now-still body swung back and forth, banging from one display to another, the metal edges tearing at his flesh, his careening torso causing showers of electricity as it dislodged wires and dials.

His mouth opened a final time.

"Help," he said as a stacked tower of electronic devices crashed down upon him.

He died in a shower of blood and sparks.

Vinnie heard movement out in the hallway.

"Johnny! Behind you!"

Before he died, the armless man had called in the cavalry. A couple of goons had shown up on the other side of the glass door to the hall, both of them armed. At least neither of these guys looked like Ernie.

Johnny T and Vinnie both opened fire, smashing the glass doorway. The goons stood there and took it. The bullets punched holes in their clothing, but they didn't bring out any blood.

The bullet holes didn't seem to faze them. The two goons raised their weapons to return fire.

"Duck!" Vinnie called. Both he and Johnny T hugged the floor as bullets screamed overhead.

"We gotta get out of here!" Johnny T called. Once again, the master of understatement.

But how? Maybe, beyond all this machinery, they could find another door.

Something crashed behind them. More of the black boxes tumbled to the ground, pushed by somebody on their far side.

Vinnie guessed that somebody had found the other door

for them. A shadow blocked out the harsh fluorescents over-head.

Vinnie looked up.

It was Ernie.

The boss's son stepped out of view almost as soon as Vinnie had spotted him. Two more men with guns took his place.

"Hey!" Vinnie called to Johnny T. "At least Ernie isn't trying to kill us."

"That's great fucking news!" Johnny T agreed.

They kept on shooting.

JACKIE PORTER INSISTED on walking Mrs. Mendeck and Karen back up to their apartments.

The muscles in her legs and shoulders ached as she stepped out of the car. She had been behind the wheel for close to twenty-four hours. She was used to double shifts from her work as a police officer. It made it easier to rec-ognize her exhaustion. Fatigue was a problem. How would she react to danger? She knew she had lost her edge.

But she knew she'd feel better once she finished the job. Mrs. Mendeck had assured her that she and Karen would be fine once they reached her apartment and certain "safe-guards" she stored there. But men had been in this building before, men threatening them with guns. There could be equal danger now.

This town was always so quiet during the day, but parked here outside the brick apartment building, the quiet seemed anything but calm. The afternoon felt like it was waiting to explode, like that moment of stillness before all hell broke loose. Maybe it was her exhaustion. Maybe she was being too much of a cop. Right now, everything seemed threatening.

So there might be guns? Jackie knew how to handle guns. She leaned back inside the car, unlocked her glove compartment and pulled out the .44 she kept there for emergencies. She slipped it into her jacket pocket, mostly out of sight.

She turned to Mrs. Mendeck. "Give me your key. I'll go first."

The old woman handed over her keys without a word. Jackie walked cautiously up the front steps. She could see no one in the foyer or the front hall. She unlocked the door and stepped inside. She was alone. She waved for the two others to follow.

They climbed the stairs single file. Everything was still, everything was normal, until they passed the second floor.

There was too much light on the landing above. Officer Porter pulled out her gun. But the third floor was empty— of people. As for the light—the doors on two of the apartments were glowing.

"I think we have a different sort of ambush," Mrs. Mendeck announced.

"My door," Karen said in little more than a whisper, "and Mrs. Mendeck's."

What was it? Some special paint? An electrical charge? Jackie stuck the gun back in her pocket and slowly approached the left-hand door.

"You can see it, too?" Mrs. Mendeck called. "Interesting. That means the spell is either very strong, or very rushed. Karen and I would notice it at once—but you?"

Jackie wondered if she had just been insulted.

Mrs. Mendeck smiled at her. "Well, some humans can see this, too. We're quite closely related, you know, humans and, well, what we are. But Smith believes he can intimidate us. That's what this is all about, you know."

Jackie supposed she did know.

"He thinks this is going to stop me?" Mrs. Mendeck smiled down at Karen. "I think our Mr. Smith is starting to panic." She turned to Jackie. "Dear, it's best that you go now. What we have to do now can be dangerous for humans."

Jackie was starting to think her instincts had been totally wrong. Mrs. Mendeck was probably better able to protect herself than anyone in the world—at least against the likes of Smith.

"We won't be staying here," the old woman continued—if she really was an old woman. "Not now that he's trying this. But I need to gather a few things. Once I know more, I'll give you a call."

"Then I guess I'd better be going," Jackie admitted.

"Good-bye, Officer Porter." Karen waved. "And thanks."

"Oh," Mrs. Mendeck added, "and—with what you're planning next—be very careful."

Now how, Jackie thought, could Mrs. Mendeck know about that?

· 13 ·

THE TRAPDOOR SLAMMED
shut overhead, cutting off the cries of the enemy. The
torches sprung back to life. The way they flared up in an
instant took his breath away every time. How *did* they do
that?

Jacobsen felt a heavy metal hand on his shoulder. "Back
in the tunnels again, friend Jacobsen."

Jacobsen almost hurt himself whirling around.

There before him were his three companions. Tsang and
Summitch looked a bit worn from battle, but both seemed
steady on their feet. Jacobsen surmised that the blood spattered on their clothing largely belonged to others.

Their leader stood between the other two. Gontor was
returned to more—normal—dimensions, only a bit taller
than Tsang now.

"Your timely intervention was most appreciated. That
gun of yours proves to be a most worthy distraction." Even

though his face was incapable of expression, Jacobsen thought he heard a smile in the metal being's voice.

"Thank you, I guess." He had never thought of using his gun as "timely." "Desperate" was more like it.

"Then you didn't discuss your strategy beforehand?" Gontor asked, once again acting as if he could read Jacobsen's thoughts.

Summitch shrugged. "I figured he'd know just what to do."

"The very reason I asked you to join us!" Gontor boomed. "Summitch knows how to play the odds."

So now his life was reduced to a game of chance? Jacobsen sighed. Wasn't it wonderful what a little panic would do? If he really knew what was going on around here, he might end up getting angry.

"Come now, friend Jacobsen. A little celebration is in order. We disrupted the battle, with little damage to ourselves, and undertook a more important task. One of my long-range goals, so to speak."

"We have goals?" Jacobsen asked. "I mean, besides the stuff with the keys?"

"I particularly want the Grey to take notice of me."

"It's hard not to notice a giant," Summitch acknowledged. "But what else?"

"We have a quest. We have a score to settle." Gontor paused to study his companions. "We have many scores to settle. We are all too complicated." He looked overhead for a long moment, as though he could see through the packed soil to the battlefield above. "Come, we will return to the Green encampment. I will explain a thing or two along the way."

Tsang turned silently, Summitch followed with a grumble. All three of them, Jacobsen included, quickstepped behind Gontor as he marched down the tunnel.

"The Grey are very much a part of my plan," the metal man said after they had gone some distance.

"Do they have the last key?" Jacobsen asked, hoping to prompt more explanation than the occasional vague statement Gontor was prone to.

"I believe they control the third key. Whether or not it is the last key is open to speculation."

What? Jacobsen swore Gontor had mentioned "the three keys" before. And now? That was the problem with this world. No one ever stuck to their story around here.

"So you're saying there may be more of these keys around here?" he asked.

Gontor nodded his large, metal head. "There may be a fourth, but I doubt it is on this world."

"So why do you want the Grey to notice you so badly?" Summitch asked before Jacobsen could ask another question to add to his confusion.

"Once they notice me, they will try to kill me," Gontor answered.

"And this is what you're looking forward to?"

"It is very difficult to kill me, friend Jacobsen. It will bring out the most powerful among them."

"Which means?" Summitch persisted.

"Their fortifications, their armies, and their Judges make it very difficult for us to infiltrate their Keep. Better to have the Grey come to us."

"Don't we have them immediately above us already?" Jacobsen asked.

"Forgive me. We are looking for a very specific member of the Grey." Gontor again looked to the packed earth above them. "Not that we are at all done destroying the rest of them. We must worry them enough for them to do our bidding."

It was Summitch's turn for a question.

"Which is what?"

"Oh, it is much too early to make definitive plans. We must keep ourselves open to a number of options. If a key presents itself upon another world, we must be willing to pursue it. But not, I think, before we collect all those here."

Jacobsen noticed that, as usual, no matter how many questions he and Summitch asked, Gontor's replies were not growing all that specific. "You keep talking about some other world—"

"Which you, friend Jacobsen, know well."

Wait a moment. Was he talking about Earth? Was there a chance he might get home from this place? Up until now, Jacobsen had been too busy surviving to think about going anywhere.

"C-can you—I mean, is there a way that—uh—"

"There is a reason you are here," Gontor interrupted. "Perhaps there are many reasons. Friend Jacobsen, before you first set foot in these tunnels, you had met the owner of the other key."

He had?

Smith. It had to be that pale bastard. Pale like almost everybody in this place. Maybe, after he'd hooked up with Smith, all the rest of this had been inevitable.

The tunnel turned upward before them, a gentle rise, perhaps paralleling a rise in the hillside above. The added elevation did nothing to effect Gontor's stride. Jacobsen noticed that his own muscles weren't complaining as much, either. A few days of terror and confusion on an unknown world, dropped into the middle of a war beyond his comprehension—apparently it was the ideal way to get back into shape.

"But that path still lies well in our future," the metal man boomed. "In the meantime, I'm sure the Orange would enjoy some additional revenge." Gontor paused and hit the wall with the flat of one metal hand. A trapdoor swung open immediately overhead. "Let's make some more plans with the Green."

Gontor climbed up a rope ladder that hadn't been there a moment before. Tsang and Summitch followed. Jacobsen grabbed the ladder last, and clambered up after the rest.

They were back on that hillside, in much the same place as when they had first left the Green camp. A cluster of officers and Judges stood less than fifty feet away.

Gontor strode over to Etton, once again flanked by General Naddock and Judge Dantis. Tsang followed, as if that was the only thing to do. Summitch sighed deeply and trundled after them, waving for Jacobsen to follow.

"I hope you found that little episode satisfactory," Gontor boomed to the leaders of the Green.

"I suppose we must. You have given us a temporary advantage." Etton waved down the hillside. Jacobsen turned to take a look below.

The troops with Grey and Purple helms were quitting the battlefield, perhaps one-tenth of their number remaining behind to hold off a line of soldiers of the Green, while their fellows streamed up the hill to the other side.

"So, they're retreating?" Jacobsen called.

"Running away like whipped dogs!" Summitch's slightly raised voice seemed halfway between a cheer and a grumble, making even the most positive of statements seem something like a complaint.

"Our troops are spent as well," Judge Dantis told his lord.

"We will recall them as soon as it is safe." Etton glanced at the four newcomers, then added, "The Grey are prone to deception. We will have until tomorrow to collect our wounded and our dead. At least, so far, the Grey have not violated that basic rule of combat."

Etton appeared to be doing his best to be polite. But from the frowns on the faces of Naddock and Dantis as they regarded Jacobsen and his companions, the others were far from pleased.

"You have shown a certain facility in battle." The general cleared his throat. "But speaking of basic rules of combat—"

"Yes," Etton quickly agreed. "While I am all for springing the occasional surprise or two in battle, I would appreciate it if we—whom I believe are supposed to be your allies in this struggle—had some indication of your plans."

"Our plans," Gontor rumbled.

"We weave an intricate web here," the Judge quickly added, "interweaving our magic with the actions of our troops. It is all too easy to upset that balance."

"If we are to work together," General Naddock added, "we need to know your intentions."

Gontor nodded. "Sometimes, even I do not know my intentions. I am unused to working with others. It comes from so many years hiding underground." He nodded at Etton and his men. "I will do my best."

So Gontor was capable of humility. And perhaps of working with others. Summitch started to mumble, as if he didn't believe any of this. And Jacobsen noticed that Naddock and Dantis were still frowning.

"Very well," Etton said. "If you would give us a moment?"

The general and the Judge conferred quietly. Etton nodded at the two. A moment later, Jacobsen saw the soldiers of the Green were quitting the field as well.

The first of the officers soon reached the camp.

Etton nodded as the man approached. "Report, Captain."

The man removed his helmet and bowed before his lord. "We lost a few, but it could have been far worse. The metal man's arrival on the battlefield was a potent distraction."

"Good to hear. Any idea of the casualties?"

"No more than one in ten." The captain had some difficulty keeping his focus upon Etton, his gaze repeatedly wandering over to the metal man. "Pardon, my lord, but who is our new ally?"

"They call me Gontor," the metal man said before Etton could reply.

"I think," the general interjected, "that we will be speaking soon to all our troops concerning Gontor."

"Very good," Etton said to his captain. "You may retire."

The captain turned smartly and walked down the hill to rejoin his troops. Jacobsen heard him call to the others: "They say he is called Gontor."

A cheer rose through the returning troops.

"Gontor! Gontor! Gontor!"

"It feels just like home." The metal man sighed, the sound of wind blown into a bottle.

While the brass might have its doubts, the troops took to him at once. Jacobsen remembered, when he and Summitch had first arrived in Gontor's underground kingdom, how all of the metal man's followers would stand around and cheer just this way. And Gontor appeared to encourage it.

If he were Etton or a member of his staff, he'd be doubly worried. The Green could lose their army to a self-proclaimed god.

"Well," Summitch said close by Jacobsen's ear. "This is just fine, isn't it?"

"What do you mean?" he asked.

"We are free of the tunnels," the small fellow replied.

"We are free of that immediate danger that followed Sir Aubric and myself. I told you about that."

Perhaps he had. During their long walk through the tunnels, Jacobsen swore that Summitch had told him about *everything*.

"Refresh my memory."

Summitch grunted. "We had been captured by Karmille, the first lady of the Grey. Both of us escaped—separately. I was seeking him out when I found you instead." The Gnarlyman paused to snort. "Who knew the tunnels could hide so many humans?"

Jacobsen nodded. Running into Summitch so soon after he got here was probably the main reason he had survived.

"We ran into m'lady again down in the city of Judges," Summitch continued. "Gontor got us out of there, but where do we end up? On a hill someplace, confronted by the entire Grey army."

So what he's saying, Jacobsen thought, is we ended up fighting two different versions of the same enemy. He still couldn't see why Summitch was so discouraged.

"But didn't we win?" he asked.

"We won the day. That's much less than winning the war. Now that they have absorbed the Purple into their ranks, the Grey are stronger than they have ever been. In fact, I feel the Grey are very close to winning the war."

"I see." From what Jacobsen knew of the Grey, their victory would not be a good thing. But this was not his world, and Summitch didn't seem to want to get involved, either. "What do you plan to do?"

"We cannot stay here forever. There is too much death here for my liking. I like surroundings where I am more in control of my own fate." Summitch's frown seemed even deeper than usual. "We'll leave as soon as I find someplace safe to go."

So it was time to get out of Dodge. Jacobsen would miss having the protection of someone as powerful as Gontor. Except, now that he thought of it, since he'd met Gontor all they'd done was get into bigger and bigger trouble.

"Gontor and Tsang will have to fulfill their own destiny," Summitch continued. "Even I am a bit uncomfortable around a warrior of the Orange when we are about to take all his gold."

Ah. The part about the gold. This Jacobsen remembered. Summitch had described the great lost treasure horde of the Orange a number of times on their journey. And each time he told the tale, the amount of riches within the hiding place seemed to grow. According to Summitch, wasn't there more gold there than a thousand men could carry?

He looked hard at Summitch. "We're going to take *all* of it?"

Summitch grunted. "You are right. It doesn't pay to be greedy. Besides, trying to move all those riches at once would no doubt depress the market." He looked down, digging the toe of his shoe into the dirt. "And I do feel for Tsang. Perhaps we'll even tell him about the treasure room, once we've made ourselves wealthy. With all that gold, there's bound to be enough left to finance an uprising or two."

First Gontor had showed humility, and now Summitch showed compassion. Jacobsen tried not to look too surprised.

"Forgive me for intruding."

Jacobsen and Summitch both turned around. General Naddock had quietly moved in behind them.

"You were both an important part of what happened in the battle. You, my small friend, know how to use distractions to your advantage."

"That is one of my talents," Summitch agreed.

"Gontor has been telling us how you came by your reputation as a schemer," the general continued. "You will have to tell us of your plans, too." He clapped Summitch on the shoulder. "Those stories Gontor tells. If you weren't on our side, we'd have to kill you.

"Eric Jacobsen." The general nodded. "There is something about you that just feels trustworthy. As Gontor says, you are the right person at the right time. Take a word of friendly advice—don't listen overmuch to Summitch."

The general laughed as he clapped Jacobsen on the shoulder. He turned and walked away.

Trustworthy? Jacobsen thought. He guessed he had to go world-hopping for that to happen.

He noticed Summitch looked even less happy than before.

"The odds may have turned permanently against us. Very soon, it will be time to go."

"Why don't we just go now?" Jacobsen asked.

Summitch shook his head. "To escape when they are watching you is no escape at all. But that is one advantage to war. It is nothing but one distraction after another."

What could Jacobsen say? It appeared his situation would be changing again.

LIMON HAD ALWAYS felt it was not good form to spill too much blood in the command tent. He was afraid his brother did not agree.

"They're gone?" Zibor was ready to unleash his full fury upon the Judge. "What do you mean, they're gone?"

The Purple Judge, though among the youngest advising the battle, was calm in his reply. "We have not yet determined the exact nature of the giant. Apparently, he was able to elude our troops through some means we are not yet aware—''

"Not yet aware?" Zibor raged. "That is unacceptable. The giant cannot be allowed to murder any more troops!" He grabbed the hilt of his scabbarded sword. Zibor had killed Cantelus only moments before, and he looked like he would be pleased to reuse his blade.

Limon stepped between the other two. Judges were too difficult to replace to kill them in the middle of a battle. And now that Pilar was gone, the youngster—his assistant—was the main conduit to half of their troops.

A moment ago, before Limon had reentered the tent, he had seen it was still chaos on the field beneath them. The giant had vanished, and the Green had used the ensuing confusion to regain the high ground and rain missiles down upon their enemy.

Limon had called together the commands of both the Purple and the Grey and ordered a strategic retreat. To continue the attack under the present circumstances would only result in unacceptable losses to all their forces. But a single battle was not the war. They still held the superior numbers, in both troops and Judges. Etton had visited two surprises upon them in a row while the two brothers and Cantelus had hid in the tent and argued. The prince of the Green was far more clever—and perhaps far more desperate— than they had given him credit for. But even surprises could not last forever. They would simply have to be ready for whatever Etton threw at them next.

But readiness meant working together, not satisfying your blood lust. Now was not the time for Zibor to vent his anger.

"Call the other Judges! Both Purple and Grey!" Limon instructed the youngster before him. In the confusion around them, he had not asked for the young Judge's name.

"We must regroup! We will leave a force behind to guard the lower hill while the remaining troops are gathered for a counterattack!"

Zibor's hand slipped from the hilt of his sword, but he could not keep still; Limon saw a wild mix of panic and anger in his gaze. *"Someone* must pay for this!"

Limon would have to remain calm enough for both of them. "Someone will pay, but not now. Our troops are at a disadvantage. Enough have died for one day."

Who will pay? is what he didn't say. They were all to blame for this disaster. All of them, Zibor included. It was already late afternoon. Tomorrow they would plan more calmly. Tomorrow they would take more direct control over all of their troops.

"Our father does not allow failure!" Zibor looked down at the ground as though the answer lay hidden in the trampled grass beneath their feet. "Perhaps there is some way we can strike back. We can mount a sneak attack while they tend to their wounded. Infiltrate their troops with our soldiers, wearing uniforms stolen from their dead."

Their father would love Zibor's attitude. What did they care for the rules of civilized combat—especially if there were no enemies left alive after they had broken them?

But this was not the time. This fiasco had all begun with them rushing into a trap. He wanted full reports from their scouts before he considered any other action. Limon shook his head. "Impulsive actions have already led us to disaster. Decimating our army—any of our defenses—would be the true failure. We cannot risk Judges or soldiers to either anger or foolishness. In an equal attack, our forces shall win." He clapped his brother on the shoulder. "We have won a hundred battles. We will win this one in the end. We know too much, we are too strong, to have it otherwise." He added the one other point that was no doubt on his brother's mind. "Neither can our father dispose of either of us until the war is won."

Limon nodded to the young Judge. "Leave us now!"

Zibor seemed to calm a bit after the others had gone. Still, his angry discourse made a certain sense. The giant reeked of magic. The Judges should have anticipated his attack. They had failed.

Yet it was all a matter of perspective. Limon knew, seeing his brother's mood, that he could not mention their responsibility in all of this. If he did so, Limon would be looking at the point of Zibor's sword.

At the proper time, the death of a Purple Judge or two might discipline the others—both Purple and Grey. They would win by any means. Limon sighed. Cantelus's death might be a little inconvenient, but the command tent was now a much more peaceful place.

Limon realized that might be a way to calm his brother. Cantelus could be as convenient a scapegoat as he was a victim.

"Cantelus has already paid with his life," he began. "I'm afraid we allowed his demands to distract us, but you have assured that that will not happen again.

"We must make certain that the Purple swear fealty to us immediately. Once we have assured the loyalty of our own forces, we will devise a plan using our superior strength to destroy the Green."

Zibor agreed at last. "Then we withdraw for now. We must tell our father." He clapped his hands. "Let's get our own Judges in here!"

Limon made a sign to the guard at the door, then followed him out of the tent to confer with his officers.

The news was not good. The casualties were serious. They had lost half as many troops as they had gained. But there had been no dissension among the Purple after the death of Cantelus. Apparently, the High One had been as unpleasant to his own troops as he had to his ally brothers.

In addition, the Grey's reputation was well-established. To ignore or even misunderstand an order would mean a soldier's death. The Purple had no choice but to fall into line.

Limon was pleased with that, at least. That discipline would help them on the morrow. He returned to the command tent. He and Zibor needed to confer before they contacted their father.

When he reentered the tent, he found Zibor speaking with the three most senior Judges of the Grey. He nodded to his brother.

"A moment, please."

The Judges bowed slightly, then retreated to the far side of the tent.

Limon quietly spoke his concerns. "There is more than one way to report this to our father. We have many casualties, but we also have more troops than before. Perhaps we have now faced our greatest opponent. It is a small setback, nothing more. Knowledge makes us stronger. They will not surprise us again."

Zibor smiled slightly. He seemed the soul of reason, his outburst forgotten. "A wise decision. You were always the more prudent of our pair."

Limon nodded as he waved for the three senior Grey Judges to rejoin them.

"We must discuss recent events with our lord Kedrik," he said as they approached. "The Grey will not be defeated."

"ONE WILL HAVE to rise."

When the great voice spoke, all those who were a part of it realized its truth.

The Great Judge would pick one among them to lead them in their mission. One who might speak for all of them. One that might channel all their power. It was necessary, now that the time had come to leave their hidden kingdom.

It had been so long since one was truly separated from the whole. Their physical selves sometimes performed separate chores. Sometimes, they even used the names they had been given upon the surface world. But that was no more than using different hands for different tasks, than calling one hand left, the other right. They had no true separateness, no individual identities. They were a part of the One. That was a part of the Plan.

The Plan had been in place for a thousand years. But, in all that time, no one had truly challenged the Plan. Until now. Others had trespassed; others ignorant of the Great Wisdom; others with powers and desires unknown to the Great Judge. And all had seen the results.

Chaos.

Bloodshed.

An end to order.

That which was not part of the Great Wisdom, not part of the Plan.

But the Plan was within them all. Enemies came from above, from the defeated and imprisoned, even from the other worlds. But the Great Judge prevailed for all his many parts. Even now, they escaped those who would oppress them, those who would stop the Plan. And they remained united. One mind with many voices, many vessels of power, whose strength, made of the many different magics, was the greatest magic of all.

And the Great Judge presided over them all, told them when to run and when to hide and where to congregate, and gave them a new place for the Great Wisdom to begin. And soon, the Judge would tell them when to strike.

Panic was unnecessary. The tunnels were theirs, if they wanted them. None of those who opposed them could best them without the element of surprise. Now that the Great Judge was aware of the others, they could easily regain their first hiding place, or establish a second in one of those spots they had so carefully hidden.

But they needed more than the tunnels. They had hidden for so long for a reason. It was the first true part of the Plan.

In the world above were forces that might overwhelm even their power if they were not careful. Forces that had confronted them for the first time in their stronghold. Forces they would overcome; forces they would master; forces that would in turn become part of the Plan.

The Great Judge had grown complacent. Safe in hiding, sure he was the true ruler of the Castle, only waiting for the proper time. None of them who made up a part of the whole realized they could fail.

No. Until now.

Failure was temporary. Failure was not allowed in the Great Wisdom.

The intruders had been necessary to the Plan.

It had been up to these others to show the Great Judge that the time was now. This first defeat was the best thing that might have happened. It forced them to act. It reminded them that they lived only for the Plan.

The Great Judge had spoken.

And now the Great Judge would retreat, and choose one to be his voice. One who would lead them into the next stage of the Plan. One who would lead them toward wisdom.

The Plan.

All the Judges, free of the tyranny from above; all the Judges, four hundred strong, men and women, young and

old; some barely tasting magic, others steeped in the knowledge of spells; four hundred, together in a room that only
they could find. The Great Judge made certain of that. Four
hundred parts, all reaching toward the Great Wisdom.

Reaching.

Now.

SHE FELT A pause in the Wisdom, a hole in the All. It was
over in an instant, but the shift was shocking all the same.

"Xeria," the Great Judge rumbled. "That is your
name."

She was surprised—if only for an instant—by the call.
She had been a member of the Council who had governed
when the Great Judge's attention was forced elsewhere. She
found no reason not to kill those who opposed them, or
any who would question the Great Judge. She knew that,
in the end, the Judges would rule all. She would go to any
length to realize the Plan.

"Accept us, Xeria."

She stepped forward, past the front ranks of the four
hundred. And although the Great Judge surrounded them,
although each one of them was part of the greater whole,
she looked up, for she wished the Wisdom to enter her from
the direction of the distant sky.

In that moment, the Great Judge filled her with its purpose. She saw her part, as those around them saw theirs,
all part of the Plan.

The tunnels were no longer enough.

It was an honor to be chosen; to be a part of the Great
Judge when the time was finally upon them.

Surprise would be on their side now.

A thousand years, always planning a revenge for tomorrow.

They would take the world.

Tomorrow was here.

. 14 .

FOOTSTEPS.

Joe Beast noticed the sounds as soon as the four of them
started moving, sounds made by somebody else, faint scuf-
fling noises that echoed down the tunnel.

He still had his gun. Not that he knew how the gun
worked anymore. In fact, it might never work again. Or
maybe it would never run out of magic bullets, as Joe blew
apart monster after monster.

Joe didn't trust these tunnels at all. These passageways
were closed in and claustrophobic, leading who knew
where. You couldn't see where you were going, or who
else was there. First they had been waiting for those crazy
beasts that Joe's gun tore to smithereens. What were they
waiting for now?

Bare feet padding on stone. Something else. Distant
whispers?

He always thought he'd meet his maker on some dirty

city street running some fool errand for his uncle Roman. He'd imagined the footsteps, some goons from a rival family, a hired gun, maybe even the cops. He dreamt about it sometimes. He could never see where they were coming from.

This was too much like his dreams.

Scraping, shuffling, and echoes that would stop every time the four of them did, so you'd think maybe you were making the sounds, or maybe you were imagining all of it.

A sharp noise ricocheted down the corridor, like someone had dislodged a large stone that had hit the hard corridor of this stone hall.

"What was that?" he asked the warrior in the lead.

Aubric paused. The glow flared where his eyes should be. The lights within his body seemed to hum. "Pardon. I was looking beyond our immediate surroundings. The noises are made by many. We are far from alone."

He turned his head slowly, as if only now studying his true surroundings. "This place is honeycombed with passageways. Tunnels are hidden within tunnels. Great battles took place here once. Great warriors fought one against another, attempting to use the confined spaces to their advantage.

"Those who shadow us are not warriors." He paused again. "Warrior." The word came from deep within his throat. "In a little while, I shall be the warrior reborn."

Whew, Joe thought. This Aubric guy was a little full of himself. Well, when you looked at his buzzing body, maybe he was full of a lot of things.

"What do you mean, we're not alone?" Brian asked. "Who's here?"

"Those who have also been hurt by the Judges," Aubric replied. "Those who were forced to serve the Judges."

So that group of Judges kept others stuck down here

underground? When Brian and he had popped into the middle of that little argument back there, Joe hadn't seen anybody but those guys dressed in black. But the black robes
didn't seem like the type who wanted to get their hands
dirty. It made sense that they had servants. But what kind
of servants? Were they like the kitchen girl who silently
walked at their rear? Or did these people work for the
Judges the same way he worked for his uncle Roman?

"What are they doing?" Brian asked. "Following us?"

Aubric cocked his head slightly to one side, as if listening to all those who were so very close. "They are staying
near. What do they know? The Judges have left them. They
need some new direction." He turned back to Joe and
Brian. "They have known nothing but fear."

Fear was something else that Joe Beast could understand.

"Without the Judges' magic," Aubric added, "they will
not survive."

Runt crowded in behind Joe and Brian. "What do they
want?"

"It appears they are afraid to ask." Aubric touched his
forehead with the three middle fingers of his right hand.
"We will make it easier."

Light flashed from his eyes. The right tunnel wall crumbled to dust before them.

Brian shouted. Joe realized he had shouted along with
him, covering his head, waiting for the cave-in. But the rest
of the tunnel seemed as solid as before.

The wall was gone. Now there was just an opening,
bordered by a scattering of stone. On the other side of the
rubble was a moderate-sized chamber—maybe as big as a
three-room apartment. With its rock outcroppings and rows
of stalactites hanging from above, it looked like a real cave
in the middle of all these unreal corridors. It was filled with

boulders and crevices, with a couple of side caves Joe could
see and probably a lot more that he couldn't. The cave must
have had dozens of hiding places, yet even the open spaces
were crammed with people. Joe could see fifty or more
from where he stood. Who knew how many more there
were in hiding, just out of sight?

The people in the front pressed back against their fellows, but those behind them were packed so tightly that
there was little real movement. Joe imagined the lot of them
would run if they had anywhere to go. They looked very
ragged and very frightened.

"This is most of them. There are more elsewhere." Aubric nodded up and down the tunnel.

Brian spoke up. "What do they want with us? What do
they want us to do?"

Runt stepped forward. "I think we'd better ask." She
smiled apologetically at Aubric. "They seem to be servants.
Much like me."

She turned to look at the humble masses. "I've spent
all my life afraid of m'lady. If she was to suddenly walk
down that tunnel, I'd fall down before her again. I am so
very afraid of her. I could be a hundred miles away from
her, yet I believe she might kill me with a simple thought.
I know what these people must be feeling."

She stepped over the rubble where the wall had been
and addressed the crowd directly. "They call me Runt. I
am a refugee from the Keep of the Grey, a place I would
rather not return. Where do you come from?"

No one spoke.

"Please," she said. "We cannot help you if we don't
know what you need."

One person pushed through the crowd to stand before
the others. "Very well. Once, we, too, served in the Castle
above. We thought it could get no worse. We were wrong."

He looked at those around him. "All of us found the tunnels. We ran from the Lords above and were trapped by the Judges below."

A woman spoke up from the edge of the crowd. "We only existed to serve them. If we became sick or troublesome, we would die."

"But not painlessly!" another man shouted from the crowd. "The Judges needed subjects for their experiments against the High Ones above!"

"We were trapped," the first man added. "Without their magic, we would surely starve. Life was barely worth living at all."

Other voices shouted from the masses.

"They ran!" someone cheered.

"And then you came, and tore the Judges apart. They left us behind."

"Behind to starve!"

"Or maybe, to find our freedom."

These last words seemed to exhaust the crowd, which once again fell into silence.

Aubric's eyes glowed as he surveyed those before him, but none of his voices spoke.

"What will you do with us?" asked another woman at the front of the throng.

Runt glanced at Aubric, then looked back at the crowd before her. "We are no friends of the Judges, but we have no argument with you."

"We'd like to leave this place," the first man who had spoken admitted, "but we don't know how. There are too many tunnels, and no way of knowing which lead to the surface. Some of us are the children of those captured by the Judges. We have never seen the light of day."

"Well," Brian piped up, "that's where we're going, right?"

Runt turned back to look at Aubric again. "It will do no harm to have them follow us, will it?"

The light dimmed in Aubric's eyes for a moment before he spoke with the voice of many.

"They must agree not to interfere with our purpose. In times of crisis, we might even ask for their help. Is this acceptable?"

The crowd answered with even more voices than before, as if the fear was leaving them at last.

"Yes!"

"Anything to get away from this place!"

"Anything to see the sun!"

"We wish to be free. We will follow your wishes until we see the sun."

"We will ally ourselves with none of the families within the Castle. Our home will be the open sky."

Aubric smiled at Runt, and spoke with a single voice. "I—or those who dwell within me—have not seen the light for a hundred lifetimes. We will be followed by an army, to reclaim the world above."

Aubric turned and began to walk away. Those in the cave began to move as well.

Joe waved to Brian and Runt. "Let's not get lost in the crowd!"

They hurried to follow the quick-marching Aubric.

There was no way to tell how many were behind them, but once they emerged from all the hidden crevices and side passages, those from the cave easily numbered in the hundreds. Sandals, boots, even bare feet echoed where they hit the floor.

Wherever they went, Joe thought, they weren't going quietly.

But they seemed content to follow. They would not interfere.

Maybe now, he thought, he could talk to Aubric. Joe had never spoken about his real reason for being here. The constant light in the warrior's eyes, and that buzzing sound, like he was full of electricity, well—it didn't make it easy to have a casual conversation.

Joe cleared his throat. "Excuse me, Aubric, but I'd kind of like to ask a favor."

Aubric said nothing.

"I was wondering," Joe continued quickly, "if you could help me find my cousin."

Aubric glanced at him as they walked. "Your cousin is also in the tunnels?"

"Well, he came with me. Or at least part of him did." Joe was surprised how easily he accepted this now. "His spirit. That's what the old lady told me. His body was left behind."

Aubric nodded. "Judges' work. I will see what I can do. But you will have to help me."

Well, that was easier than Joe had thought. "Sure," he replied. "Whatever."

Aubric stopped abruptly and put his hand on Joe's chest. "Forgive me, but this is the fastest way."

Joe felt an odd tingling sensation. He looked down at the glowing hand over his shirtfront. He wanted to speak, but couldn't. He couldn't move at all.

He watched Aubric's hand push into his chest, as though his rib cage wasn't even there. He was blinded by a flash of white.

Joe blinked. Aubric stood before him, the warrior's hand once again at his side.

"Your brother's name is Ernie Petranova. I have taken information from both your mind and body to help me locate his spirit. Such an activity is disorienting, but you should suffer no permanent harm."

Joe shook his head. He felt like he had just been in an elevator that had plunged twenty stories in a second's time. He took a deep breath, and was a little surprised to realize that his chest, where the phantom hand had plunged a few seconds before, felt just fine.

But back to Ernie. "So—you think you can find him?"

"I will look. If he is in the Castle, I will find him."

He sounded so certain—the advantage, Joe guessed, of having an entire race of creatures living behind his eyeballs. If Aubric could deliver, it would make Joe's life one whole hell of a lot easier.

"Look," he offered. "If there's ever anything I can do for you—"

"I know, Joe Bisotti."

Joe was a little surprised that Aubric had used his real name. Nobody used his real name.

"Those within me spent a thousand years," Aubric continued, "suffering for the treachery of others—the treachery of the Judges. You have shown me no treachery. You stood by me in the chamber below while all others fled." His eyes flared as he added, "We will help those who have been hurt by the Judges. It is a step in our rebirth. All those inside me must learn to live again."

"Oh. Okay." Joe still wasn't on very sure footing here. "Well, thanks."

So this Smith was a "Judge," then. Like all those other guys in black. It made as much sense as anything around here.

Joe realized he had just forged his first alliance down here. His uncle Roman would be proud.

"There are others in the tunnels ahead," Aubric announced after a time. "Two groups. One waits for the other."

So now there were complications. "Do we need to run

into them? These tunnels go all over the place, don't they?''

"They do—but I have reason to intercept these groups. Judges will be present. To confront them would be an excellent method of testing my growing power.''

Oh, great. Aubric wanted to plunge them straight into another battle. Maybe this alliance wasn't all it was cracked up to be.

"You have a reason to intercept these groups as well,'' Aubric added.

"What do you mean?''

"I sense your cousin's spirit.''

Joe couldn't believe it. "We've found Ernie already? Talk about dumb luck.''

Aubric nodded. "I believe there are other things than luck at play here. We must talk to those who follow us.''

He turned and held up his hands. Everyone stopped—Brian and Runt, followed by the ragged horde that walked, two abreast, stretching down the tunnel as far as Joe could see.

Aubric called to the masses: "We will need to confront a small group of Judges if we are to win free of these tunnels. These are not the Judges who held you captive, but no Judges are to be trusted, and all should be destroyed. The battle will not last long. We have abilities that should easily overwhelm the Judges, and grant us our freedom.

"The most important thing you must do is remain calm. If the need arises for you to fight, or to run, I am naming this man, Joe—''

"My friends call me Joe Beast,'' he quickly interrupted. No more of this Bisotti nonsense.

Aubric paused, as if waiting for Joe to continue. Well, okay. He could lead a starving army to daylight as well as the next guy.

"Listen to me!'' he called to all those who followed.

"We'll get you out of here! We'll get you to see the sky!"

"See the sky!" someone called from deep in the tunnel. "See the sky!" another couple of voices repeated the words. "See the sky!" the chant grew like a great wave rising above the shore. "See the sky! See the sky! See the sky!"

The chant faded as quickly as it had begun, but all in the tunnel were focused on Aubric and Joe.

Joe decided he could get used to this.

"Very well," Aubric continued. "If it is needful, you will take orders from Joe Beast. Now follow us quietly. We have work to do."

Aubric led the way, with Joe by his side. Hundreds marched after them.

Once they had resumed their march, the warrior spoke to Joe in a quieter tone.

"As we approach the enemy, I will be better able to determine their strengths and their defenses. Once we know more, we will determine whether we will need to use our followers."

Now Aubric was including him in the decision-making process. Out of all the strange things that happened in this place, Joe never imagined he'd be leading an army.

The warrior turned to the wall. His brow creased like he was using his special sight to look through miles of rock. "I pray I can use our power to defeat the Judges quickly."

"Our power?" Joe thought aloud. "Well, you've got your power, I've got my gun."

Aubric paused a moment before his many voices replied: "Brian is the most powerful among us."

Brian? Joe glanced over his shoulder at the kid, who walked behind them next to Runt. Brian looked like he was a little spooked by the whole thing. Well, being scared might be good for the youngster. After all, he was the one who had changed Joe's gun. And that was for starters. Who knew what else he could do with a little practice?

"So what's our next step?" Joe asked Aubric.

"We win," Aubric replied.

"How do we win?" Joe asked.

"We survive," Aubric said.

IN THE GREY Keep where Sasseen had risen to be second among his kind, there were no longer any surprises. He knew all the habits of all the Judges and Lords, and could count upon their self-interest and their standing to predict their behavior. He had not realized how reassuring he had found that order, that predictability, until he had descended into the tunnels and left all of it behind.

In the tunnels, there seemed to be nothing but surprises.

Now Karmille, the woman who had brought him upon this journey, appeared to be in a trance. She had not been properly protected from a spell she had produced that had gone badly. And not even Sasseen, with his years of expertise, could fathom exactly what the backlash had done to her.

She breathed regularly, and at times made sounds that seemed to be the beginnings of speech. But all of Judge Sasseen's skills could not wake her. It was the danger of spells used by the untrained. That warning was one of the basic tenets of the Judges' art, and unlike much that the Judges promoted, actually held the element of truth.

They had stopped to rest in one of those larger chambers hidden by the tunnel maze. His two soldiers stood at attention, once again fully under his control. Karmille's two servants seemed rather more upset. Her overmuscled guard refused to leave her side, as if Sasseen might kill the lady in her sleep. Flik, the assassin, had taken to playing with his throwing knives—prepared, no doubt, to cast a blade before Sasseen could cast a spell.

Karmille's condition had little to do with Sasseen, but it would do no good for him to attempt an explanation. Perhaps he could use the servant's fanatical loyalty to his advantage with the newcomers.

Sasseen had gotten his two soldiers to use the sacks and spears they had brought with them to fashion a litter for the lady, so they might continue through the tunnels. It had allowed them to move Karmille to this hidden place. However, since he was uncertain of the exact nature of her malady, he was loath to move her overmuch.

If Karmille died while in his care, Sasseen knew he would die as well. While he might be able to escape the wrath of her servants, Kedrik and Basoff would see to his demise.

For now, she rested comfortably, her servants standing to either side of her litter. For now, she was not the greatest of his worries.

Judge Sasseen had thought this quest within the tunnels would make him free of the petty day-to-day squabbles of the palace. But politics had followed him even here. It permeated every inch of the Grey Keep—perhaps every part of the Castle. Some of those he knew all too well from the palace of the Grey, those he had left behind, would be joining them shortly.

He knew they were near even before Imp returned. He, like any Judge, could smell the sorcery around the corner.

Flik shouted as the creature first zoomed into sight. The elemental, a small black flame that flew through the tunnels like a small, darting bird, circled around Sasseen's head.

"Imp, return!" Sasseen said sharply. "Imp, report!"

The elemental settled upon the Judge's shoulder, flickering excitedly as it related what it had seen. Sasseen let his thoughts enter the quivering flame, searching for pictures of what Imp had witnessed.

Imp knew all the particulars. The party sent by Kedrik was near. It had passed them upon its return journey, and it had recorded much in its passing. The approaching party contained three Judges and six soldiers—a surprisingly large compliment from the Lord of the Grey. It could be seen as a sign of concern for his daughter's safety. More likely Kedrik wanted to find a way to control his daughter and the renegade Judge he'd so rashly let go earlier.

Sasseen knew he had brought this on himself. It had seemed they would be destroyed by the renegade Judges, but then other players had arrived. The drama had truly begun, the renegades were thwarted, Sasseen had found escape.

Now, who knew what would happen? He had brought these new players to the table. Perhaps there was a way to use them—as sacrifices to the renegades, perhaps? Killing a few Grey Judges might convince the renegades that he was truly independent. Sasseen smiled. Anything and everything could be an opportunity. But he would have to tread carefully.

There was no need to panic. The Judges of the Grey had come, in theory, to aid him. Perhaps he could turn a Judge or two to his way of thinking before he sacrificed the others. If he were to rule the Keep above, as he still intended, he would need to be better versed in politics than ever before. He was simply starting a bit early.

The Judges would be here in minutes. He would gain as much information as he could from the elemental before they were interrupted, information on the palace of the Grey, before Imp had passed the Judges.

Imp was not quite the same as before. The edges of its flame were no longer sharp, as if the elemental had been dirtied by its visit to the Grey Keep. It was the least innocent of places, after all.

Sasseen asked Imp a series of questions he had embedded in the initial spell.

"Who did you meet?"

"A Lord and a Judge."

"What were their names?"

"Kedrik and Basoff."

"What did they say?"

Imp hesitated, for only an instant, but enough for Sasseen to notice. Someone had tampered with his spell.

"They spoke of many things."

That answer should not have been possible under Sasseen's spell. The Judge honed his words: "You are made to record their every word. What did they say?"

"Kedrik and Basoff are very concerned for the lady Karmille. Nothing can happen to the lady."

Imp was no longer direct. Basoff had tampered with the elemental, filtering its simple perceptions. Sasseen wondered how far the tampering had gone. If not tended properly, elementals could be quite dangerous; a small black flame could become a roaring fire.

Basoff had damaged his creation. This was why Sasseen had left the Grey Keep. Basoff needed to control everything.

Sasseen should have expected this sort of response. It was logical that Basoff and Kedrik would cover up anything of real value about themselves. Still, Sasseen had made sure there would be other ways he could pry into his creation.

Sasseen quickly performed an incantation to undo any alterations to his initial casting. He spoke to the others in the chamber as he worked, though his two soldiers were beyond all save simple commands, and he doubted the lady's guards had the sophistication to understand. It was another reason to miss the court-bred Karmille. Still, it helped him to think if he reasoned this sort of thing aloud.

"Imp has seen so many things," the elemental responded to yet another question. "Imp has been so many places."

"This is most interesting. The creature is still evading my questions." Basoff must have overlaid a very complex spell on this simple creature. He turned back to the elemental. "What did you see in the Grey Keep?"

"Judge Basoff and Kedrik kept Imp very well. Nothing should happen to Imp. Nothing should happen to Kedrik's daughter, the lady Karmille."

"It defends itself," Sasseen mused. "It defends others. Imp has become far more complex since it has left me."

His hands made a complicated series of signs. Imp's flame split down the middle; a motion designed to shatter any spell.

"Judge Basoff and Kedrik kept Imp very well. Nothing should happen—"

The elemental repeated the phrase and then repeated it again.

Sasseen worked quickly, attempting to find a way to dismantle his creation while still retaining the truths the elemental held within.

Yet while Imp had appeared the same upon Sasseen's first cursory examination, he could now see that the elemental was profoundly changed. It was most curious, and most disturbing. Spells sent to dissect the creature seemed to back up upon themselves, producing nothing but bursts of color and a new line of chatter. It wasn't that Sasseen's spells weren't working; it was more that they were reacting to the Imp in unexpected ways, as if the very nature of magic itself was about to change.

For the first time, if only for an instant, Sasseen doubted his ability to overthrow this kind of power. If this was Basoff's doing, what sort of forces did the elder Judge employ?

"Well," he murmured aloud. "There are no answers in misdirection, are there?"

Sasseen would have to delve into the very center of his creation. He had imbedded certain messages deep within the elemental, so that, should all else fail, he might reach that core and regain control. Perhaps, in finally turning the elemental inside out, he might find some clue as to Basoff's methods.

He reached a line of sorcerous energy into the elemental, grasping for the core. The line shot completely through Imp, melting rock where it hit the floor on the other side. No one spoke, but the Judge could feel both the guard and the assassin watching him. Sasseen realigned the power into a fine filament to strike directly at the elemental's heart. He tried again.

Nothing. The filament hit the same molten spot upon the wall.

Imp was hollow.

The core did not exist.

The messages were gone.

That was impossible, unless this was not even the same Imp as before.

Of course.

How dare he?

Basoff had created an exact double, filled it with a new set of secrets, a new set of commands. The first Judge of the Grey had taken Sasseen's spy and turned it against him.

It was a clever ploy. Perhaps, had Sasseen been under the same duress as when he had sent the plea for help, he might not even have noticed the change.

Sasseen was careful to control the anger he felt welling within him.

He had hoped that Kedrik and Basoff would grow careless. Instead, they grew arrogant, trying to pass off this quickly fashioned copy as the original.

Very well, then. Sasseen trusted that arrogance, like carelessness, could be exploited.

"Judge!" Flik called out. "Someone seeks entrance!"

It had to be now, didn't it? Well, at least Sasseen now knew something of Basoff's opinion of his talents. No doubt he would learn more from the newcomers.

He nodded his head. "Let them enter."

The secret door flew open, revealing the long corridor without. The underground hall stretched on forever, dark and silent, as if there was no one there.

"Sasseen!"

They called him as they first appeared in the distance, torches flaring to either side, their voices amplified by the Judges' art.

Sasseen sighed. The elemental was beyond him for now. It flickered in the air beside him, showing him the limits of his ability.

"Let us do this calmly and carefully," Sasseen said quietly to Karmille's servants. "We should assume that we can work together, until they indicate otherwise."

The guard called Blade positioned himself before the lady with folded arms. Flik simply looked skeptical.

Sasseen turned his attention to those marching toward them—nine in all.

He knew the three Judges. The soldiers, of course, he had never seen before. More precisely, it was likely he had seen them a thousand times, but had never thought them worthy of recognition. Two of the Judges, Nallf and Eaas, were Basoff loyalists. The third, Kayor, was uncommitted, a man taking an independent track much like Sasseen. The others would be directly accountable to Basoff. They would weigh their actions, if not with care, at least with a certain predictability. The third one, therefore, was the most dangerous.

"Sasseen," called Nallf, the eldest of the Judges, as his party reached the door to the chamber. He was heavyset for a Judge, his hairless face settled in wattles of fat where his neck should be. Sasseen had always thought Nallf held all of Basoff's snobbery with none of his charm.

"Kedrik sent us to your aid," Nallf added.

Sasseen bowed. "Your aid is most welcome." This part of their meeting was all ceremony. The interesting part, where they parried for position, would come later.

Nallf inclined his head. With his barrel-like form, bowing was out of the question. Eaas—the second of Basoff's men, as thin as Nallf was large, bowed deeply enough for both of them. Eaas was well-versed in the protocols of court. He, also, to Sasseen's knowledge, had never had an original thought in his head.

On Nallf's other side, Kayor bent forward in the vaguest of bows, the sardonic smile on his face saying this was all nonsense. Of all the Judges in the Grey Court, Kayor was the most independent—and the most perverse. He made a habit of pursuing distant cousins of the High Ones, young ladies who came to serve as governesses or handmaidens in hopes of finding a more permanent place at court. Kayor would choose one every season to share his particular favors. The lucky ones were only driven mad.

Interesting that Kedrik and Basoff would send the greatest thorn in their sides. Perhaps they hoped he would meet with some misadventure.

"What has happened here?" Nallf asked. "Our lord Kedrik relayed your message, but we have no further in-

formation concerning your situation." He frowned down at
Karmille, laid out upon her litter. "It appears to have taken
a turn for the worse."

Sasseen presented what little strategy he had had time
to prepare.

"The lady Karmille is ill. She has appointed me in her
stead. We had initially come to this place to find someone
we considered a spy. However, these tunnels have shown
us far greater, and more immediate, dangers."

As Sasseen had expected, neither of those with a will of
their own contradicted his statement. Sasseen, after all, was
a known evil to Flik and Blade—and had professed to work
for Karmille's benefit. These others—unknown judges and
soldiers no doubt a part of the King's Guard—could hide
all sorts of new treachery.

"Dangers?" Nallf frowned. "We will contact Kedrik.
He will tell us what to do."

"No!" Sasseen barked. If Kedrik became too personally
involved, all his plans would be ruined. "No one will contact Kedrik without my permission."

Nallf sniffed, as if such a plan was out of the question.
"We have been instructed otherwise."

But Sasseen could not back down. "And your instructions might get us all killed! We have already run afoul of
a society of renegade Judges who dwell within these tunnels. They number in the hundreds, their strength too great
for even the four of us to withstand. There is no simple
way to communicate with the palace of the Grey that these
renegades won't be able to intercept."

One of the soldiers spoke up. "Beg pardon. While you
discuss the fine points of policy, we have been instructed
to personally care for the lady. Forward!" He and his five
fellows crossed the room, stopping just short of the guard
and the assassin.

"Stand aside," the first soldier announced, "upon orders of High Lord Kedrik."

Flik and Blade simply stood and stared.

The first soldier stepped up to the guard and drew his sword. "I will take charge of the lady." With a single movement, he stepped in close and positioned his weapon an inch from the guard's throat. "I am quite good with this. Now, if you would back away? It would be a shame if the sharp edge slipped."

The soldier's eyes grew wide. His mouth opened as he fell forward, but the only sound was the crash of his armor against the cavern floor. A knife protruded from under his helmet, pushed up beneath his skull and into his brain.

Flik jumped forward to retrieve his weapon.

"My knife never slips," he announced as he pulled it free.

"What have you done?" Nallf demanded.

"No one comes between us and the lady." Her guard spoke at that. "We are all instructed to protect the lady Karmille, at any cost!"

"You are quite correct," Sasseen added quickly. "We will have to be most careful that there are no more misunderstandings."

Nallf appeared to be turning purple with rage. "You killed one of the High Lord's men!"

Eaas was encouraged to join in. "This is insubordination. We are three to your one! We could strike you down now!"

Flik still held the knife in his hands. He balanced on the balls of his feet, ready no doubt to jump at anyone and everyone—should the mood take him.

Kayor glanced from Judge to Judge. "I must say—I'm finding this much more diverting than I had ever imagined."

Sasseen needed to take control. Few Judges ventured far into the tunnels. Kayor might have some knowledge of these intricate passageways, but Sasseen was certain the other two had never before wandered far from the comforts of the palace.

It was time for him to finish the game. "Yes, you could strike us down, if you were foolish. You are new to these places. We have had some time to acquaint ourselves properly with our surroundings—and all those who oppose us. You could bind me, muzzle me, even kill me. We could all die in these tunnels."

Sasseen was rewarded with a moment of silence.

"Very well," Nallf acknowledged at last. "We will defer to you in this. We will let you lead the way—for now. If we are to help you, we will need detailed explanations of the dangers you have faced."

"I will tell you everything you need to survive," Sasseen agreed.

Flik fitted the knife back into its empty sheath, side by side with five other knives. His belt was a row of sheaths, the most obvious and least hidden of all the weapons on his person.

"There will be no more misunderstandings here," Sasseen continued. "We are all here to ensure the continued rule of the House of Grey. All of us—save one—are expendable."

None of the newcomers spoke. Their silence was their consent. Karmille's assassin had provided an excellent object lesson—excellent, and relatively cheap. It had only cost them one soldier.

"Karmille will remain alive," Sasseen concluded, "even if she is the only one."

Nallf nodded at this. "The lady Karmille is alive, but, by your own admission, she is in distress. Perhaps we have all acted a bit rashly. But it will do us no harm to examine the lady. Our combined expertise may be able to restore her to consciousness.

"May we?" Nallf asked. Sasseen stepped back and nodded to her servants to give way as the three Judges crowded around the unconscious woman. So long as the three were closely observed, their combined expertise might indeed be able to help. Sasseen doubted the Judges were here to kill Karmille—at least not in any immediate and obvious manner.

Nallf frowned. "She brought this condition upon herself."

"A beast spell," Eaas agreed. "The Eater of Souls."

"I know the beast spell well," Kayor added. "It is a crude spell. Like a club. However, it is usually quite effective."

The Judges paused as they used their skills to trace the path of the magic.

Nallf said it first. "The creatures were destroyed? Without taking a single victim? You have most powerful adversaries."

"Bravo," Kayor agreed. "This goes from mildly diverting to actively amusing."

"Basoff told us very little of your mission before we were rushed on our way," Eaas added. "You will have to inform us as to the exact nature of the enemy."

"There is more than one enemy here," Sasseen replied. "These tunnels are like a hornet's nest, full of those who might wish to destroy the Grey."

Nallf frowned. "Specifically the Grey?"

"Some will *specifically* destroy members of the Grey. Many more are looking merely to destroy the Judges."

Even Kayor looked a little shocked at that. "We are beyond civilization at last."

Sasseen nodded at that. "We must put away our most petty differences. We will need to in order to survive."

FROM THE MOMENT his associates had received the message from the front, Judge Basoff knew this had to be handled most delicately. Therefore, he would receive and relay the message himself.

His master waited, impatient to get on with his personal business. Basoff had known that, when Kedrik had sworn to put such pleasures aside, they would never let him be. They had a certain addictive quality that Basoff had counted upon for some years now to keep the lord both properly occupied and properly grateful. Kedrik might restrict their use—again with Basoff's aid—but it would be almost impossible for him to leave them entirely. Basoff was his Judge because he allowed Kedrik such indulgences, and then protected him from their worst excesses.

The two of them were alone now, with not so much as a tongueless servant to see to their needs, in the innermost room of Kedrik's private chambers. The High Lord sat upon a low couch that he often used for other matters. Basoff stood before him.

"We begin," the Judge announced.

Basoff raised his hands, fingers opened wide, the gesture of reception. The Grey Judges had developed certain codes. The way an introductory sentence was phrased, perhaps, or a color attached when the missive was passed from mind to mind, that would indicate what was to come. The Judges upon the front were prepared to relay their lords' report, but their introduction let Basoff know what followed would be very—what? Delicate? Difficult? A little of both, he supposed.

Basoff closed his eyes to better accept the signals—

signals centered on words but containing fragments from all the senses—then relayed the words of Limon and Zibor to his lord without comment. It was the safest course.

Their report began with the usual bromides. The glory of the army of the Grey, the wisdom of its Judges, the reputation and sanctity of their lord and father. Once through with the niceties, though, the initial report was very skimpy on detail.

Oh, there was the merest outline of their campaign. How they had finally gotten Cantelus to agree to an alliance. Cantelus's unfortunate death. The death of much of the Purple through Cantelus's rash actions, and its consequences for the Grey. The unexpected opponent—a metal giant who had allied himself with the enemy.

This was one of the few reports from the front that did not speak exclusively of victory. Basoff could see that the Grey troops under the High Lord's sons faced more difficulty than any of them had anticipated. No doubt Kedrik could discern far more.

The battle had turned against them. Even as the words came out of Basoff's mouth, he could see the two sons were attempting to place the blame on a dead man when the blame was shared all around.

The message was done.

Basoff coughed to indicate he had finished the over-simplistic summary, then waited for the outburst from his lord. Kedrik did not take losing well.

But Kedrik was still, staring off into the middle distance. "Tell me again about the giant."

The Judges at the front had seen the giant, too, and their impressions had been relayed along with the report of the High Lord's sons. Basoff quickly sorted through the images that filled his head. He saw a being made all of metal, a great booming voice, laughter as he killed the soldiers of the Grey.

"Spare me nothing, Basoff!" the High Lord urged. Basoff realized that the lack of an outburst on Kedrik's part did not mean he was unaffected. Rather, his anger was all held within—the cold fury of his countenance, his skin the color of ice. The High Lord was the most dangerous at times like this, when he was quiet.

Basoff chose his words prudently.

"So this—giant—made a mockery of our troops?" he said softly after Basoff had carefully related what the Judges had seen.

The Judge felt no need to reply.

"It is most interesting," Kedrik added after a moment. "I should have expected it. This whole battle—his appearance, his destruction of my troops, his disappearance, as quickly as he arrived—this is largely for my benefit."

"Pardon, my lord, but why for you?" Basoff asked solemnly, careful not to show his surprise.

Kedrik smiled without humor. "I knew the giant once when he was someone else."

The lord was silent again for a long moment. Basoff knew no further explanation would be forthcoming.

"What do you wish to do?" Basoff asked quietly.

"This brings a new wrinkle to our little war." Kedrik grimaced, as though the memories brought pain. "Perhaps I can use this as well. He has his resources, as I have mine. But he is an overconfident fool."

"Have I met our adversary?"

"I think not. It has been a thousand years. Before your time. Before anyone's time but mine." Kedrik rose from his seat, as if finding that an antagonist from his youth had restored some of his energy. He paced halfway across the large room, then spun suddenly to look at the Judge.

"I must find a way we may—safely meet."

"Is that wise?" Basoff asked. Kedrik had not left the spells and protections of the palace in hundreds of years. He was far too vulnerable outside the Keep.

"There is no other way. This is his message. He will continue to destroy our army until we meet." This time Kedrik laughed. "We knew each other when we were very young. We thought we knew each other well."

Kedrik looked at his shaking hand for a minute before making it into a fist.

"We have no time now for worldly pleasures. Perhaps we have not made enough—sacrifices of late. I need whatever strength I might muster. I need to be bathed in blood."

Basoff nodded. Fresh blood. They would need a dozen sacrifices for the most severe of the longevity spells. To dispose of so many could be considered wasteful, especially in wartime. But Kedrik had known nothing but wartime.

Basoff considered how best to fulfill his High Lord's need.

"Karmille's servants will do," he said after a moment. "They have nothing to occupy their time. Will a dozen be sufficient?"

"I think fourteen," Kedrik replied after a moment's thought. "I will need all the energy I can muster." He smiled at that. "It will be good to fight my old enemy at last. We have both struggled for so long. One of us deserves the world."

Basoff bowed, and left to arrange the bleeding.

Book Two

"*Only when the worlds converge will the war truly end. Only when the chosen are found will it be possible to have a new beginning.*"

—from *The Castle; Its Unfolding History*
(a work in progress).

. 15 .

JACKIE PORTER WAS SUR-
prised at how readily the Chief had agreed to talk to her.

She had found a phone message waiting for her when
she had gotten back home. It was the Chief, asking her to
call. And what was she doing home, anyway? How had she
let Mrs. Mendeck talk her into leaving the two women so
easily?

Maybe it was because Jackie was dead on her feet. She
was so tired, she wasn't thinking clearly. Still, there was
something odd about that Mrs. Mendeck—in the way she
spoke, and the way she looked straight at you sometimes,
Jackie felt like the old lady was looking right through her.

Why had she done anything? Maybe Jackie would think
about it again after she had gotten some sleep. In the meantime, she was glad she had gone home. Otherwise, she
would never have gotten the message.

Otherwise, she might never have made the call back.

   The dispatcher at the station put her right through. And
the Chief sounded, well, relieved to hear from her. He had
admitted to making mistakes, had told her he had some
explaining to do. It had thrown her off guard.

   She'd said yes, she'd meet him after work.

   He'd asked to meet away from the station, at the Wash-
ington Street Diner on the edge of town. It was the kind of
place that had been there for fifty years, the kind of place
where the Chief liked to sit down with the mayor and the
fire marshall on a Sunday morning. With all that had been
going on, the Chief had said it was best they met in a public
place.

   She had agreed, and had fallen asleep as soon as she'd
gotten off the phone. Now, eight hours later, she was on
the road, headed for . . . what?

   She had been too tired this morning to make any sort of
judgment call. She was still too tired. She thought of Mrs.
Mendeck's warnings. Could she trust anything where Smith
was involved? Even with the Chief involved, could this be
some sort of trap?

   The Chief had been with Smith in the hospital. The
Chief had tried to get Brian alone with Smith.

   The Chief hadn't said anything about Brian, or about the
events of the day before.

   Probably it was nothing more than a dead end. Probably
he wouldn't tell her anything. The Chief would deny any
connection to Smith. Probably he wanted to warn her away
from doing "anything that would hurt her career" or some
such.

   She had to try. She had to know. She had become a
police officer, an accident reconstruction specialist, because
she had to know.

   Would the Chief tell her? Why was it so important to
hear from him?

Maybe he was a little sedentary. Maybe he was set in his ways. Maybe he still reminded her of her father, the ex-cop who'd died of a heart attack six months after leaving the force.

Maybe it was because of that connection—a connection, she realized, that only existed in her own head—that she wanted to confront him, try to get him to see reason.

No. There was much more at stake. They were risking the lives of two teenagers here. And the Chief had been right in the middle of it at the hospital, getting Smith whatever he wanted, Brian included. He wanted Jackie to walk away without any questions.

Maybe he wasn't anything at all like her father.

She stopped for a red light, the diner only a block away. Her police-issue revolver was in her glove compartment, along with the shoulder holster. She could put it on, under her jacket.

The Chief had sounded desperate on the phone.

What could happen in a public place?

She pulled into the parking lot just after nine PM. The lot held only a scattering of cars. She was able to park almost at the front door.

She spent a final moment in the car, breathing deeply, focusing. Part of her wished she could leave the gun behind. Wearing a revolver meant she was looking for trouble—no. That was something emotional talking, something from her childhood maybe, something deep inside her. She'd been trained in gun safety. She knew the best place for it was under her jacket, where she knew where it was and could control what happened to it.

She walked inside the diner, which was just as empty as the lot outside. The last of the dinner crowd seemed to be leaving and the night owls had just begun to filter in. Two of them sat at the long counter that ran half the length of the place, both men silently studying menus. She heard her name called. The Chief had picked a booth in the far corner, as far away from the counter and the other diners as possible. As far as she could tell, he was alone.

She walked over, took off her jacket, and hung it on the hook next to the Chief's. The corner booth the Chief had picked gave them a surprising amount of privacy. He nodded as she approached. He didn't say a word about the gun.

"Sit down." He waved to the waitress. He had a half-empty bottle of beer in front of him. "Would you like something?"

Jackie ordered a cup of coffee just so she would have something to do with her hands.

They didn't talk until the waitress had brought the coffee and gone. She had never seen the Chief look so tired. The lighting in this place made his skin look grey.

"I'm glad you called back," he said before she could speak. He sighed. "Somebody had to do something." He stared at the nearly empty beer bottle before him for a moment before he went on. "I'm afraid we've had some misunderstandings lately. I know. That's an awfully polite word for what's been happening."

Jackie didn't reply. She wasn't sure what to say. Until the recent business with Smith, she had never had any argument with her boss. He had been the one to make the final decision on hiring her, after all. If, after that, they hadn't talked too much, well maybe he reminded her a bit too much of her father, after all.

"I guess everybody makes mistakes," the Chief continued. "Most people, when they make mistakes, don't want to look at them. They want them to go away. Especially when they've made a mistake that could cost them their job."

The Chief looked down at the table. "I made a couple

of bad calls. I didn't realize how deep I was into this. When you're in a position like mine, you've got a lot of—responsibilities.'' He exhaled slowly, something between a sigh and a groan. ''There were a couple of guys, wanting to cut a deal, who were in a bit too deep with the wrong—'' He stopped himself and sighed again. ''You don't need to know the details. Let's just say I botched up pretty bad.''

The Chief stopped. He glanced past Jackie's shoulder. He sat with his back to the wall, and could probably see the entire length of the diner.

Maybe, Jackie thought, he was too embarrassed to go on. ''What happened then?'' she prompted.

''Smith was there to clean it all up.'' He laughed softly. ''I thought it was a way out.''

He stopped and looked past Jackie's shoulder again. When he started to talk again, he spoke more quickly than he had before. ''Smith has a way of drawing you in, of oversimplifying the consequences. Then you discover you've gone too far. You're working for Smith, or else. From time to time, Smith would tell me to do something for him—get rid of somebody. Either arrest them or—something more permanent. Now, most of the people Smith deals with are lowlifes, guys who deserve to be taken down. You don't mind following up on that sort of thing.''

Jackie nodded. The Chief was telling her that he'd killed people for Smith.

''Then this started,'' the Chief continued. ''It was only at the hospital that I realized Smith was going after the kids.''

The Chief stopped to take the last pull from his beer.

Jackie Porter had been anticipating a lot of things from this meeting, both good and bad. She hadn't expected a confession. ''Why are you telling me this?''

The Chief's attempt at a smile didn't take. His face

didn't seem to want to settle on any expression but misery. "I've got to talk to somebody."

He paused to look past her again. Was he waiting for somebody?

He leaned closer. She could smell the beer on his breath. She guessed he had had more than one. "Porter. Jackie. There's another reason I asked you to come here.

"You're right in the middle of this. For whatever reason, maybe just because you're a good cop, you got into the middle of this. And because you're a good cop, you started working for the other side. But now that you're into this, Smith has—well—noticed you.

"Smith won't try to kill you—at least, not right away. I know the way he works. He'll try to recruit you. You will get an offer. Don't make the same mistake I did."

Jackie studied her boss. As much as he was telling her, she wanted more. "Who is this Smith?"

The Chief shook his head. "I wish the hell I knew. He tries to paint himself as a benefactor, a guy who can help people, but he's anything but. He's into a lot of really weird shit. I've seen stuff around him I couldn't even begin to explain."

Jackie nodded. "Other people have told me that sort of thing, too." She didn't mention that the "other people" included a couple of mobsters.

"You may know more about him than I do. Mr. Smith isn't very—uh—forthcoming." He sighed. "I've liked your style since you got here, Officer Porter. If more cops were like you, we'd have a better department. But watch your ass. Smith never leaves any loose ends. If we don't find a way to stop him, this whole town is going down.

"So what can you do? It's not worth joining him, take it from me. If you get in too far, you lose control. I don't know if I'll ever feel clean again. So the only thing left is to beat him.''

"Beat him?'' Jackie asked. "The way you describe Smith, he's got a lot of power, a lot of connections.''

The Chief nodded.

"How do you beat that?''

"Who do you trust?'' The Chief glanced up and out, down the length of the diner. He looked down at the table. "After what I've done for Smith, I don't know if you should even trust me now.''

Jackie glanced over her shoulder. She saw a couple of guys who must have come in after her, two men in business suits talking at the near corner of the counter.

Or maybe they were trying to listen.

"Look,'' he said more quietly than before. "I've got to get out of here. If I can help you, I will. I might only be able to warn you—and maybe not even that. Watch out for Smith. No, more than that. Smith's people are all over this town. If he knows you're between him and what he wants—you're gonna have to watch out for everybody.''

The Chief rose quickly and grabbed his jacket.

"Good luck, Officer Porter,'' he said in a more conversational tone. "I hope we can talk again.'' His voice lowered slightly as he pulled on his jacket. "I'm going to fight this—even if it destroys me.''

He walked quickly from the diner.

A moment later, the two men at the counter followed. Jackie hesitated only a second before grabbing her jacket and following.

She pushed the diner door open carefully, ready to drop to the ground at the first sign of trouble. She reached her hand inside her jacket, rested it on the handle of her gun.

She was greeted by silence. The night air was cold and still.

The parking lot was as empty as before. The Chief, and the men who might have been following him, had both left quickly.

Jackie walked to her car, her nerves on edge, waiting for an attack that didn't come.

Well, the Chief had been a cop for more than twenty years. He should know how to take care of himself.

She heard a siren in the distance.

Dear Karen,

Your father and I decided we needed to get away. I've checked with Mrs. Mendeck and she'll be glad to look after you while we're gone. We'll give you a call as soon as we know our schedule.

                                              Love,
                                              Mom

Karen stared at the note in her hands. Her parents, apparently, had decided to go on vacation while she was missing and out of town. Not that they mentioned any of that in their note. If it even was their note. Karen had never read anything that sounded more unlike her parents.

Karen marched right over to Mrs. Mendeck's place and pounded on the door.

She waved the note at the old woman as she opened the door. "This is something you did, isn't it?"

Mrs. Mendeck chuckled. "Ah, Karen. I can't keep any secrets from you." Somehow, her smile didn't look quite as kindly as it sometimes did.

"How?" was all Karen could think to ask. Her parents hadn't taken a vacation in years. Her father complained when he had to go down to the corner to get some milk. They never went anywhere!

Mrs. Mendeck stepped back from the door. "Why don't you come inside? We don't need to talk about this in the hall."

Karen nodded and followed the old woman into her apartment. As satisfying as it was to shout in the hallway, if she wanted to get Mrs. Mendeck to spill the beans, it would have to be a private conversation.

"About your parents," the old woman continued as she closed the front door. She led the way down a short hall into the living room. "It was just another little spell I've worked up. It was best if they were out of the way—out of danger."

"Danger?"

"The danger is here, with me and you."

Karen frowned. "You told Officer Porter that we'd be just fine."

"I sent Officer Porter away, too. Oh, I imagine she'll be back. She's a bit more aware than your parents. She may be able to help us, too."

Karen couldn't believe this. "Are you orchestrating *all* of this?"

The old woman raised her eyebrows. "Very clever. Your abilities are beginning to show. And no, I'm not orchestrating *everything.*" She shrugged. "I don't go out to recruit total strangers, for one. Oh dear, that sort of thing is far too time-consuming. But I had to find a way to get the proper people involved."

"Proper people? Who are the proper people?" Apparently not her parents, she thought.

"People with the right connections. And people who would be sympathetic to our cause."

Karen couldn't see this at all. "Like those—gangsters? Some of those *sympathetic* people have been trying to kill us."

"But they didn't—kill you, I mean. They never wanted to kill you, not really. I can tell that sort of thing. And just because Smith grabbed somebody doesn't mean we can't grab him back."

Karen couldn't keep her feet still. She wanted to know everything, and she wanted to know it now.

"Have a seat, dear." Mrs. Mendeck waved at the bright, flower-patterned couch. "You'll wear me out if I have to watch you pacing around."

Karen really did want to understand. "So you grab people, and send them to this other world."

"It's sort of a relocation program I have." She paused, looking at Karen with a frown. "I'm afraid I shouldn't joke. It's just such a relief to be able to talk about all of this with someone.

"You've seen how horrible Mr. Smith is. And getting to know him better is, if anything, worse than one's first impression. He is here to use people in any way he can to further his goals.

"No one wants to work for Smith. They're coerced into it. I simply specialize in offering them a way out. Sometimes, that way out includes a trip to this 'other world,' as you put it. I place people beyond Smith's reach."

She sat down herself, on the overstuffed chair across from the couch with the matching pattern of flowers. "The situation has changed. Things have accelerated recently. Mr. Smith had been among us for some time, working very quietly. Until something happened. I don't know what. I don't even know if it happened on our world. Now, the way the one we call Smith is blatantly acting—even killing those he thinks might stand in his way—everything's changed. The fate of this world is at stake as well."

Mrs. Mendeck made a sound—a sort of clucking noise

with her tongue—that Karen often heard when the old lady was lost in thought.

"There are levels of risk," she added after a moment. "I've sent Brian into a greater danger I'd hoped neither one of you would have to face. But we both must work if we're ever going to see him alive. I have much to tell you. And you, young lady, have much to learn."

Karen leaned forward. "Will we have to go to that place you sent Brian? That other world?"

"The other world?" Mrs. Mendeck frowned. "Soon, Karen, I don't think it will make much of a difference which world we're on. Of these two, I mean."

Karen started. Just as the old lady was beginning to make sense, she throws in another of those left-field remarks. "You mean there are other worlds besides the one you always talk about?"

"Well, yes, there is a third, of course. Dear girl, that's how this whole thing got started." She paused for a moment, as if thinking just where to start. "You see, that third world, that's where you and I both come from. Well, where our people come from. That was a very long time ago."

"So we come from another world?" Karen thought about all the times she felt like she didn't belong. Was this the reason? "Why can't we just go back there?"

"Well, that's the point, isn't it? I'm afraid everything began because of a war—one that should have been over a long time ago. But because of what happened in that first war, a second war began, that has lasted for over a thousand years."

"This war happened—where?"

"In a place called the Castle, a world so honeycombed with tunnels it has become a single, gigantic structure, although even many of those who dwell within the Castle do not realize this."

"Is Brian in the Castle, then?"

The old lady nodded. "I'm afraid so. We need his strength there, even though he hasn't been trained. His teaching will be up to Summitch."

"Summitch?" Karen asked.

"Another of our kind, dear, even though he likes to deny it."

"But if we're here, and Brian's in the Castle, what's the third world?"

"Even the name is forbidden. Only we remain." This time, Mrs. Mendeck shook her head. "They couldn't destroy us. So they had to hide us. This world, the Earth, became their dumping ground."

"Hide us? From who?"

"Perhaps from ourselves. They tried to take away our self-knowledge, too. And they almost succeeded. Almost."

She smiled then. "They have stolen the magic from us. But we can steal it back. We have been slowly moving back, moving closer to home. On this world, Smith stands in our way. Smith is relatively new here. As he learns, he becomes more dangerous. We must defeat him before the danger becomes too great."

She stood abruptly. "Come. It's time to begin your lessons.

"Lessons?"

We need to show you how to protect yourself, and who to contact when the proper time arrives."

"What will you be doing?"

"Hopefully fighting right alongside you. But Smith is a desperate man. I will teach you as much as I can. If Smith destroys me, you will be the only hope."

Karen did not find this at all reassuring.

· 16 ·

*T*HERE YOU ARE.

What?

I believe you've overreached yourself.

Who are you? How dare—

I can dare whatever I want. We are in my world now.

Your world? I warn you, I am Karmille, daughter of the High Lord of all—

I know who you are. That is why I have sought you out. But your station in life means nothing now.

Nothing? Wait until I call my . . . Where is everybody? Where am I?

Your spell did not work. You were caught in the backlash.

Backlash? I don't remember. By my lovely beasts? Magic should not affect me. I was in the tunnels, surrounded by my guards. I was under the protection of a Judge of the Grey.

Protections mean nothing when you attempt the magic yourself. Your Judges subject themselves to years of training for very good reasons. You could have been killed.

Then I am not dead?

Far from it. Instead, you've given me an opportunity to introduce you to my realm.

Your—realm? I don't really see anything. Why is it so dark? Where have you taken me?

I haven't taken you anywhere. You've gotten here quite on your own. As to the darkness, well, you will see when you are ready.

Am I dreaming?

A fair question, under the circumstances. This is a— different place. Not quite dreams, but close enough.

Let me go! I am the daughter of the High Lord of the Grey!

Please. Let us not grow tiresome. You are going to want to hear what I have to say, and our time is limited. You will be leaving us soon.

Leaving?

Back to where you came from.

(She found she had nothing to say.)

You will need allies in the struggle to come. Your father is one of those who is truly dangerous in this conflict. You want to kill him. And I imagine he would not mourn your death.

How do you know this?

People talk. I listen.

Why would I want to work with you?

I thought that this little—display would impress you. It isn't everyone who can speak to your unconscious mind.

I have my own plans! I don't need someone like you!

You don't?

(She didn't know how to reply to that, either.)

We will talk again. But the offer won't last forever.

What offer? The alliance?

Not even that. An exchange of information, the occasional helping hand, nothing more. Consider them resources to help you destroy your father.

My father? Perhaps we can come to some arrangement.

You can choose to remember this, or not. It's all up to you. Well, actually, it is up to me as well. I'll explain that to you next time we meet. We will be talking again.

Who are you?

You can call me Growler.

Growler? I should—what? I don't—what's wrong?

It starts already.

I feel like I'm being pulled inside out.

You are only being woken up.

No! It hurts! Make it stop!

It is not of my doing. It is sometimes difficult to get from here to there.

(She screamed.)

Soon.

ONCE HE HAD been a soldier in the army of the Green. Once—how long had it been? Hours? Days? Years?—he had been resting and joking with two of his friends, when they had been ambushed by the enemy. One friend escaped; the other was killed. And Savignon was merely knocked unconscious and left to the mercy of his enemy.

So he was helpless, locked into a spell controlled by Judge Sasseen of the Grey. So he obeyed, so he marched, so he carried. So he now stood, in a chamber deep underground, with his friend's animated corpse at his side.

The spell was designed to make Savignon Sasseen's

slave. Often, he could think of nothing but the Judge's wishes. Often, but not always.

They walked the tunnels, filled with nothing but time, time that filtered into his consciousness and gave him pieces of himself.

The Judge's spell was far from perfect. It left him both aware and unaware, his own personal damnation. Perhaps the magic would have been enough in the palace above. The tunnels were different. Every new force, every new event grated at the edges of the spell that bound him.

He remembered more with every twist and turn.

First, he remembered he had had a name, then the name itself. Slowly, over time, he recalled his history.

At the beginning, it was only moments, flashes of memory like the first stars you might see in a cloud-filled night. First it was only the aftermath of battle, the moment before his capture, then the battle itself. The days and weeks before battle came next, then other fights, other pieces.

The rest of his life fell into place like fragments of a broken mirror. Walking at his father's side. Growing with his friends. The woman he planned to spend his life with once he had finished with the campaign. So many pieces, swirling together to form a life.

A life the Judge would never have.

Fragments of consciousness. Pieces of what he once was. He remembered his other life now while he stood in the chamber.

The Judge Sasseen sometimes strengthened his spell. The Judge could push the pieces away, but they floated to the surface again.

He would remember more. He would find a way to regain the use of his limbs. He would find a way to fight. When he rested, Savignon could think. Lately there had been nothing but rest.

More Judges had arrived, more pariahs. They busied themselves with the fallen lady. Their soldiers hung back, keeping away from both the Judges' work and the servants of Sasseen. He and Lepp must smell too much of enchantment.

He enjoyed the soldiers' discomfort. He enjoyed the one soldier's death at the hands of the assassin even more. It was one advantage of being little more than a walking ghost. He might stand here and silently watch them murder each other.

He watched them where he stood, a forgotten statue. The four black robes huddled together, like crows picking at carrion. They spoke in low voices among themselves, only occasionally letting their words fill the room.

"She stirred!" one of them called excitedly.

"She has done that before," Sasseen replied. "It is a part of her condition!"

"No, she is responding. We can call her back."

"Gently. She has just survived an attack."

The black robes gathered even closer. In the torchlight it was hard to tell where one Judge ended and the next began. Now that there were more of them, perhaps they would keep each other busy for days. Perhaps he could benefit from their other mistakes.

He thought of the sun, and summer breezes. He remembered more with every passing minute. Memories led to awareness, awareness to reason. As he reclaimed his past, he would also reclaim his present and his future.

He would remember a way to escape.

As soon as he thought of escape, he heard the words.

"What? Who?"

The voice was like a whisper. No. The voice was no voice at all.

"I don't—what the fuck am I doing here?"

He didn't hear the voice, really. He was simply aware of it, like it was a part of him, as though it had taken residence at the back of his brain.

"Hey! Can't anybody hear me?"

If this was a part of him, Savignon thought, he could respond. He would think his way into conversation. He called out, another piece of the enchantment. Hearing the whisper had allowed him to find a whisper of his own.

He could think of only one origin for the voice. Could it be his boyhood friend, calling back from the dead? Nothing was impossible anymore.

"Lepp! Is that you?"

The voice took a moment to reply.

"Who the hell is Lepp?"

Sav's gaze shifted to the decaying statue to his left, the frame that had held Lepp while he was still alive.

There was a change in the dead man's eyes. Sav saw panic and anger where before there had been nothing. It was not Lepp, but it was alive.

"It's that goddamn Smith, isn't it? My cousin Joe was right. My cousin Joe is always right! He's made pretty damn sure I'm not gonna get anyplace near him."

Lepp jerked forward.

"Careful," Sav cautioned. "You don't want them to know you can move."

Not that Judges or their soldiers were aware of much. They were so busy tending to the lady Karmille that they hadn't noticed.

"What? Why should I give a shit about them?"

"You spoke about your enemies just now. Here, these are your enemies."

A sound erupted in Sav's head, a sound much like laughter.

"Yeah, you're right, they sort of look like Smith. So do you, now that I think of it. Where the hell am I?"

How could he explain all of this to a stranger? There was much he still didn't understand himself.

"Like me," he whispered at last, "someplace you had never wanted to be."

The stranger also took a moment to reply. "I just want to get home."

"That, my friend, is all any of us want to do."

"Be a pal and give me a hand. Ernie Petranova is the kind that doesn't forget a favor."

Sav thought he heard strength in that whisper; strength and a certain fearlessness.

Perhaps escape was just a little bit closer.

NOW THAT THE gunfight was over, Brian had time to wonder what happened. Not necessarily how Joe had used the magic bullets, but how the magic bullets had gotten into the gun in the first place.

When the moment came, Brian just knew he had to take the gun. And once he'd taken the gun, the bullets were there.

But how?

He felt different now that he was here. It wasn't just the tunnels. These underground passageways could have been anywhere, even under his old hometown—well, except for those magic torches that lit their way.

Mrs. Mendeck had put him here for a reason, and he would discover that reason, whether or not he found this Summitch. He felt like his heartbeat matched the heart of this world. He sensed a vibration, a feel to the air and rock and dirt that was different, and oh so familiar. Brian thought it was like finding a street, maybe, a place he had played as a child but had forgotten about for years, until that day

when he turned a corner—and there it was again—with its
houses and hedges and picket fences on the first day of
summer—like he had been away for only a moment or two,
rather than his entire life.

That was a part of it, but there was more. It felt like
everything in his life was nudging him toward—not this
moment, maybe, but something very soon.

So he would follow Aubric, and he would learn. A long
time ago, Brian had learned to listen. He guessed that was
one thing he could thank his mother for.

So he listened to Joe's questions and Aubric's explanations, often not quite understanding what was being said.
He would understand in time.

He listened, mostly, to the long spaces between conversation. He listened to Joe's grunts and Runt's sighs. He
heard hundreds of feet marching behind them from the otherwise silent masses.

He listened most closely to the secret sounds of those
within Aubric.

They said things through Aubric's mouth but they also
spoke within Aubric as well, a hundred voices pumping
through him like blood; an electric sound, at the edge of
hearing, something like insects, something like a great machine. Soon he'd be able to understand them, too.

The way the gentle buzzing rose and fell in strength and
pitch, it seemed more than simple conversation. It was more
like a never-ending song. The more he listened, the more
he understood. Not words, but those things behind words.
Joy, anger, regret—he heard more with every passing moment.

"Pardon, sire," a voice spoke just behind him. "But
may I ask a question?"

Brian paused to look behind him. The speaker was a
young man, perhaps only a couple of years older than him-

self. He had come forward from the army of refugees who trailed them, and looked as gaunt and ragged as any who followed.

"If no one else will speak, y'know," the young man said, "I will."

Brian nodded, not knowing what to say.

The young man jerked his head back toward all those who followed. "Don't mind them. They need to find their spirit again."

Brian glanced ahead. Aubric, Joe, and Runt had gone some distance ahead.

"We should walk," he said. He paced quickly down the tunnel, eager to close the distance with the leaders. The young man walked easily at his side; his thin arms and legs were bands of muscle.

The young man smiled then. Unlike many of the others, he still had all his teeth. "It is strange to be liberated, y'know. And by such an interesting company. We're a bit of everything under the Judges, or so I thought, until I saw the metal man and that fellow whose eyes glow in the dark." He chuckled. "We haven't seen one like you in a while, either." He peered closely at Brian, sniffing the air.

"You're one of them, aren't you?"

"One of who?" Brian asked. "I come from a different place, but so does Joe."

"It's not where you come from, y'know, but who you truly are. I've seen a couple more of your sort." He lowered his voice conspiratorially. "The Judges put them both to death. They were that afraid of them."

The Judges were afraid of Brian? Perhaps he was in even more danger than he thought.

"More power, I say!" the young man cheered. "That's what I think of the Judges! Good to have you around!"

Brian guessed it was good to be appreciated. Not that,

at the moment, he could do much to justify that appreciation. He could probably learn far more drawing the young man out about his own life.

"We haven't been introduced. My friends call me Brian."

"Pleasure. Rouss was my name, back when they let me have one."

Brian glanced over his shoulder again. Having one of their number come forward and talk made all the silence behind him feel even more creepy.

"Why aren't there more back there who wish to come forward?"

Rouss nodded vigorously. "I'm not like the others, y'know. Not beaten yet. New to the tunnels. Judges couldn't grind me into the dirt." He shrugged his shoulders. "I get by."

It was Rouss's turn to look back at all who followed. "I'll tell you the story of my capture if you tell me a bit about yourself." He glanced back at Brian and grinned. "It'll pass the time, y'know? Trust me, Brian, we've got a bit of the tunnel to go."

Perhaps it would be good to have someone to talk to.

There was none like him in the crowd. The Great Judge had ordered them destroyed.

Brian wanted to find out more.

. 17 .

XERIA TURNED TO LOOK AT
the new order of things.

A thousand years before, they had driven the unclean
lords from their hearts and their minds. They had escaped
from the pestilence of the Castle and formed their own
kingdom, deep underground. They had formed the Great
Judge, a higher order than any of those crawling upon the
surface would ever know. They had thought they had found
paradise. But they had not had to struggle against their foes
in a thousand years.

The chamber where they now waited and planned was
filled with Judges, all four hundred preparing for what must
come. The Great Judge no longer ruled, but all wisdom still
came from him. It was her duty to dispense that wisdom.
She had set the lesser Judges upon numerous tasks. The
great room that was their temporary home was full of half-
formed magic, their many voices chanting spells, their

many hands shaping sorceries. The old world was over. Now they must begin again.

The world below was no longer pure.

For as long as Xeria had been alive, she had believed in the perfection of her society. The One had taken her in the moment she was born. The Great Judge was parent, teacher, friend. She need never be alone. She had always been a part of something greater than herself.

She realized now that it was a false security, only real as long as they were separated from the Castle above. The war within the Castle was all-consuming. It was bound to extend far into the tunnels. It was probably most surprising that it had taken so long for the battle to come to them.

And now?

The Peace of the Great Judge was no longer the same, now that others had interfered. While not gone entirely, it felt tarnished. Only a great effort by the True Judges could make it clean again.

The Great Judge was no longer adequate to the task. While their power was never greater than when all the Judges were a part of the whole, their communal thoughts were not quick enough to fight this strength and variety of power. The opposition had won the first skirmish.

She strode among the Judges, some working alone, their faces wracked by the pain of creation. Others worked in small groups, their spells piling atop each other, an ecstasy of magic. Thus was the legacy of great sorcery—it might encompass all of life.

They would not be so easily defeated again. The One saw to that, and acted through Xeria.

The Great Judge would never be entirely gone. He would be with them, in the backs of their minds, in the air of the tunnels, in the lines on their faces, in the rock at their feet. He would be there for them to call upon, but they would no longer be a part of the totality. Xeria had been chosen to lead them, to tell them when to act alone, and when to act as One.

She had already seen problems—the sort of problems she had thought their great society to be above. They had had to leave their home. They had had to move quickly. They had had to leave their servants behind. The simple comforts they took for granted, all were gone. Before, she had actually heard a pair of Judges arguing, no longer sure the Great Judge could show them the way.

There was no time for argument now. Xeria had seen to that when she'd set the Judges to their tasks. All were busy, rebuilding their world piece by magic piece.

They would not want for food and water. For now, they could get their needs met through sorcery. She had set fully a quarter of those Judges before her to stockpile the necessities. But such petty tasks were wasteful of their gifts.

It was so much more important to discover what had gone wrong and make it right again. They would take those secrets they had discovered in their cloistered life and set them free, so that the children of the Great Judge might change the world.

Xeria looked within, at that which all of them shared, but often took for granted—their common history, their place among the One. The Great Judge had ruled his hidden kingdom for a thousand years. They had learned the secrets that held together the world—and they had held the keys. Four of them, until one was stolen by the world above, and another was taken to another world entirely.

And then, Gontor had returned.

When Gontor had escaped them, some time before Xeria was born, the One had thought it a small error. Gontor did not choose to turn against them, but founded a small settlement of his own, filled with refugees from above. It lim-

ited the One's pick of servants, but Gontor was not
confrontational, and his peculiar powers posed certain dif-
ficulties, even for the Great Judge.

It would cost effort and Judges' lives to destroy him, so
the One decided to contain him instead; let him rule his
petty underground domain. The Great Judge had considered
him an annoyance, not a threat.

This, Xeria realized now, was the Great Judge's first
mistake.

It was obvious now that Gontor, imprisoned among them
for centuries, had spent too long in the presence of the
Great Judge. He had learned too much. When he returned,
he had seen past their defenses and taken the two remaining
keys as though they had been left for him on a doorstep.

That was the truth Xeria must confront.

Their keys were gone. The balance was shattered.

But the two keys so recently stolen were still near, and
still relatively unprotected. Xeria strode to one corner of
the chamber where a small group tracked their progress.

Three Judges looked up as she approached.

"The ones we seek have found the surface," one of
them said. Now that they were true individuals rather than
individual aspects of the Great Judge, she was having some
trouble telling them apart. At the first opportunity, she
would have to find them all names.

"And the keys?" Xeria demanded.

"Gontor no longer holds them. They are in the possession of another."

Interesting. Was the metal man being careless? Or was
this another of his tricks?

"Another without Gontor's protection?" she asked.

"No. The metal man's protection still extends to this
other."

This was less than satisfactory.

"We need better answers," she demanded. "We need specifics—names and locations. What do you propose we do?"

All three rushed to speak at once.

"They are upon the surface. We have little experience—"

"They seek to elude us. Gontor has his tricks—"

"The exact nature of some of those we seek is—well, not very exact. . . ."

Xeria's frustration was growing with every word. She should have suspected something of this sort when Gontor was involved. He had spent hundreds of years as their captive, and the Great Judge still considered him a mystery.

Certain energies still eluded their control. It all derived from the Great Covenant, when the Judges were first created. Not that the Great Judge subscribed to the Covenant, but in reinventing themselves the Judges had had to overcome close to a thousand years of mystical tradition.

The third Judge shook his head at that last remark. "We are capable of determining *everyone's* exact nature. No one is beyond our reach, but we must reconfigure our magic. We may not be able to attack them directly, but we may be able to influence those around them. Many things go unnoticed in battle."

"Really?" Xeria addressed the third Judge directly. Here was an actual plan.

"They have stolen the keys from us," the last Judge continued. "We simply need to persuade someone to steal them back."

"Now there is an efficient idea," Xeria agreed. "Perhaps this new order will benefit us all."

"Subterfuge. Secrets. Outright deceit," the third Judge replied. "There are many things we must relearn."

Xeria studied the man, so thin he reminded her of the

most emaciated of their servants. "Have you ever had a name?"

"I would rather have a title. You are Xeria, the chosen of the Great Judge. It would please me to be Xeria's Counsel."

Xeria smiled at that. "Then Counsel you shall be." She would need clever people to work with; clever people who thought differently. Even though the Great Judge no longer ruled their lives, he still would provide.

The newly appointed Judge bowed before her. "Then I might make my first recommendation. Four hundred Judges of such power are too much for any one individual to oversee. With your permission, I would like to find perhaps two more to help us in organizing those who follow us."

"It seems a reasonable request."

"I have appreciated working with my fellows." He nodded to the other Judges, who seemed a bit overwhelmed by the current course of events. "They are quite good at their work. The problems we face are very real, but we were also devising ways to overcome them." He bowed to Xeria again. "As my first task in my new position, I will find a third to assist them."

Thus did she gain a staff, Xeria thought, and perhaps the beginnings of individual power. And yet, her Counsel's constant bowing made her a bit uncomfortable. She was flattered, but was his treatment of her all that different from what they once were forced to give to the Great Lords above?

She dismissed the fear as soon as it entered her mind. Why shouldn't one of their own be given the same privileges as the High Ones? Behind her leadership, they planned to supplant those same High Ones and take their rightful possession of the Castle. Weren't her fellow Judges the true elite? And hadn't the Great Judge picked her from among the four hundred?

Her Counsel was only giving her what she deserved. For better or worse, they now left the Great Judge behind.

The Counsel had turned away for a moment, discussing something with his former workmates. He looked around, quite excited.

"Xeria! We have made a connection." He pointed to one of his fellows. "Tell her."

The other Judge nodded, not looking directly at either Xeria or her Counsel, but at some space on the floor between them. "Well. At first I wasn't certain. The ones we have found are not—entirely conscious. But we are able to manipulate them. Their condition is to our advantage. They are tired. They are hurt. They will be easy to control."

Xeria smiled. Good news came quickly.

"Very well," she called, her voice loud enough for all to hear. "Let our part of the battle begin."

AUBRIC COULD SEE so much now.

He had no more need for sleep. Those who had joined with him seemed to have given him endless energy. He was a world within the world. When the others in his party chose to rest, he spent the time in quiet conversation between the parts of him that now made up the whole.

We have been away from the world of mortals for so long. Much will have changed. Much will have been forgotten.

What can you give us? What do you know?

Aubric felt unequal to the task. They were so great, and he was so small.

"I know about the Green, my people. I know about war. Nothing more."

Nothing?

Aubric saw his life spread before him, from his earliest memories to his meeting with Summitch and his first trip through these mysterious tunnels. He had thought it to be a simple life, but each passing memory was filled with sight and sound and smell and taste. The touch of a hand. The touch of a breeze. He saw colors that those inside him had forgotten, heard sounds that they had never known. The memories, hundreds upon hundreds, flew before him. They never seemed to end. His life was a far more complicated place than he had ever imagined.

The many voices within spoke.

No. You know life.

You recognize the world.

We know about energy.

We know about survival.

We look for revenge. It had consumed us, and left us lacking.

Together we are stronger.

Nothing will stand in our way.

Aubric found his own voice among the multitude. "What do you give me?" he asked.

We give you our history.

It was Aubric's turn to see things he had never seen before.

He saw a race of beings, tall and slender, their skin a bluish-grey, as if they might be equal parts sky and rock. He saw a time when they lived in peace with the pale-skinned High Ones; a time when they gave of their peculiar energies and talents, and formed skills that both they and the High Ones might use. He saw dozens of moments, image upon image, tale upon tale, and yet knew these were only the merest hint of what those inside him held.

The images told many small stories, and one great one.

Over the course of centuries, a caste system developed in the pale-skinned race, with some talented individuals devoting their lives to the pursuit of the power the two races might share.

These were the first Judges.

We were too innocent.

We did not know treachery.

We learned treachery.

They would have killed us if they could.

They could not.

They cannot.

We were banished.

We return.

With two images fresh in his mind, Aubric realized he was both these things together. One was a boy, growing up in the court of the Green, first as a servant, then adopted into the royal family; a boy who grew into an honored soldier of the realm. And he was also an entire people, and the memory of that people, an ancient race who had walked the face of this world until they were betrayed and banished. But they were not destroyed. They would never be destroyed.

Two sets of thoughts crowded his head. One was human. The other wanted to fill the world, and make it theirs once more.

He was one, and he was many.

He had the strength of one born anew.

He was fury, and he was compassion.

He was a leader of men. Others followed him already.

Others would help him reach his goal. He would use them, no matter what.

No, he would save them. He was already the savior of an entire race.

Aubric took a deep breath. He held totally opposing views within, and deeply believed them all.

Somehow, he would be true to all his selves.

Once we reach the sun, we will be reborn.

Those within had a plan—a plan so grand that much of it was still unclear to him. The beings within would regain the world. What, then, happened to Aubric, warrior of the Green? Who was master here?

He would find a way.

We will all find a way.

We have new hope in you.

Aubric saw: He looked down, and within his hand he saw another, with slender fingers and blue-grey skin, as though both his hand and this other occupied the same time and space.

The Judges seek us.

They will not find us.

We have not lost the scent of power. We will regain all that is lost.

We should not become complacent. Others already fear us, and wish our destruction. We will need to keep on moving.

We will regain the world.

The voices spoke of the Judges underground—that society below that their very presence had disrupted. They had escaped, but they had not left the Judges behind. Even now, Aubric could sense their sorcerous tendrils searching for them. The lights that lived within turned the feelers aside—for now.

He stood. It was time to wake the others. For all their sakes, they needed to leave the claustrophobia of the tunnels and seek a bigger world.

•   •   •

SUMMITCH WAS MOST uncomfortable. Now that the battle was over and evening was upon them, Etton had asked him to join the leaders around the fire.

He was not used to being consulted in a council of war. People weren't supposed to listen to him. He had spent much of his life as a Gnarlyman so that most people would not notice him at all.

As he trudged up the hill to the command tent, he saw that most of the others had arrived before him, where they all stood before the tent, around a roaring fire. Etton had gathered a dozen of his followers, half of them military, half Judges.

All the other members of Gontor's party were there as well. Not that it much mattered in a council like this. What would the others say? Gontor liked to talk in glowing generalities, while Tsang didn't like to talk at all. Eric Jacobsen would shrug and plead an understandable ignorance. Summitch, though, was known as the schemer. Summitch was the one who would have ideas.

No doubt they would all try to draw him out, make him the center of attention. He had seen it before, when Etton had first invited him to his little party, and the talk had turned to strategy. Every time he did so much as scratch, everybody turned his way.

Voices rose as he climbed the hill, the air filled with shouts and laughter. Summitch realized his fears were fully justified. He was walking into a social event.

The real council had not even begun. Instead, Etton had found a roast somewhere, which twisted above the fire that would soon be the council's center.

"A small celebration," one of the Judges called out as Summitch climbed the last few feet, "for, if not a victory, then another day of survival."

He was handed a metal cup as he reached the edge of

the clearing, and offered either wine or water. Summitch chose the wine, hoping it would calm him. He was too much on edge for a single cup of anything to dull his senses.

Gontor waved for the small fellow to join them, while others cheered at his approach. Summitch forced his feet to move forward. He realized he was being honored for his part in winning the day. He should be flattered at being included in such august company. But Summitch wasn't the sort to take to camaraderie. The very thought of sharing his plans with others made him feel trapped.

He remembered that other time he had had to work with another of equal power, that Mendeck woman, shifting others of their kind from world to world. She had proven most valuable, especially in rescuing him from some particularly nasty business with the court of Gold, but she had also left him promising favors he would rather not deliver. Not that he would ignore his promises. He did have a sense of duty. Summitch simply chose to ignore it whenever possible.

"Summitch, my friend!" called a captain of the Green that the Gnarlyman could barely remember meeting. "The way you made Gontor disappear! It was brilliant!"

"You open great new possibilities to our battle strategies," a second Captain agreed.

"Imagine!" the first continued. "Our entire army could take to the tunnels." He laughed. "Now *that* would surprise the Grey!"

The two captains seemed capable of quite a conversation without him. Summitch nodded and moved on.

One young Judge sat a bit farther away from the fire than the others, on a low outcropping overlooking the darkened battlefield below, his face only illuminated by the occasional bursts of sorcery overhead. His face had a sad, faraway look to it. He appeared even more miserable than Summitch.

He nodded as the Gnarlyman approached, but made no effort to talk, preferring to turn his attention back to the valley. Summitch felt better already. He was always more comfortable around those who did not quite fit in.

Summitch stood by the Judge's side for a long moment, doing his best to make out the movement in the valley. He saw dozens of dark shapes below, rescuing the dead. The sky flared overhead, orange twisting into green, a new collision in the Judges' never-ending clash.

The young Judge sighed.

"There is a certain beauty, even on the battlefield. It keeps one alive."

Summitch nodded. He could see beauty, too, in the shifting darkness, the flashes of color.

"My work as a Judge is largely illusion, but the battle is all too real." The youngster looked up at the sky as crimson battled with white. "It all appears so far away from this hillside. But that is another illusion."

Summitch studied the youngster for a moment. He seemed very atypical for a Judge. He seemed almost as much an outsider as Summitch.

"And how do you use your illusion?" Summitch asked.

The youngster seemed to bristle at that. "I have recently been promoted. Thanks to my unique talents. I do my job."

He turned then and looked straight at the Gnarlyman. He smiled.

"I am being rude. I fear it's one of my specialties. They call me Qert."

"A pleasure. And I—"

The young Judge smiled at that. "Everyone knows Summitch."

The Gnarlyman grimaced at the truth of that statement.

"You don't look terribly happy for one who helped to save the day," Qert remarked. "But I imagine you deal a fair amount with illusion as well."

Summitch, for once, didn't know what to say. What could this young Qert see?

Qert held up a hand, a motion for silence.

"Someone moves about the hill below," he said quietly.

Summitch turned back toward the valley. He saw movement in the rocks perhaps a dozen yards away. The dark shape was visible for only a second.

Summitch already had a knife in his hands.

Qert had moved silently to his side—a Judge's trick.

"The battle has a way of becoming real," he whispered. "I venture you are quite handy with that knife. Rather than bother the others, what say we go and bring them a small gift?"

With that, the Judge was gone, no more than a flying shadow. Summitch decided to concentrate on that spot where he had seen movement before.

There.

Whoever approached was keeping to the rocks as much as possible. But the command tent was surrounded—by design, no doubt—by wide stretches of open ground. Even if they carried bows or slings, the intruders would be forced to show themselves, however briefly, in order to attack.

Summitch saw the top of a head bob briefly above a patch of rock.

The Gnarlyman was good at silence, too. He dropped to the ground and rolled, letting gravity push him to the rocks just above his sighting. He caught the first stone outcropping with the heels of his boots to stop himself, then rose to hands and knees, knife at the ready, and crawled forward to get a better view.

Summitch saw a shape crouched at one corner of the

outcropping below. He looked to be one of the many wounded, bound head and foot with bandages.

What would a wounded man be doing so far from the healers? Such bandages, Summitch decided, might also make a very effective disguise.

Summitch vaulted from the low outcropping and dropped quietly behind the intruder. Apparently he was not quiet enough.

The bandaged man whirled, brandishing a sword previously held out of sight. He roared as the blade sliced toward Summitch.

The Gnarlyman easily parried the thrust with his knife. He felt very little force behind the blow. But the bandaged man lifted his blade to try again. He staggered as he stepped forward. Summitch took a step back to assess his opponent better. The other looked very unsteady on his feet. Perhaps, Summitch mused, if he moved the battle among the rocks, he might get his enemy to defeat himself.

The bandaged man fell silently forward.

Qert smiled from where the enemy had stood. Apparently he had hit him from behind.

"This is the third of them," Qert said. "The last, I think."

"Who are they?" Summitch asked as he looked down at the still form before him.

"That's the most upsetting part. These are our own wounded soldiers, turned against us. I thought it best to relieve this one of consciousness."

This particular soldier looked rather the worse for his experience. His bandages had turned dark red with fresh blood as though the movement had opened many wounds.

"Now for our presentation to the command," Qert continued. "Not as pleasant a task as I had hoped."

He made a couple of quick passes, and the wounded

man's body lifted from the ground. Summitch looked beyond Qert and saw that two more forms floated in the shadows.

With a wave of both his hands, Qert brought the other
two bodies forward to join the first. If anything, these bandaged soldiers looked even less able than the first. One had
a bloody stump instead of a right arm, the other's face was
entirely obscured by a bloody gauze.

"I shall bring them as gently as I can to the tent above."
Qert turned to climb the hill.

Summitch walked by Qert's side, the three bodies floating before them. Neither spoke. This victory held no thrill.

Summitch looked ahead and saw that their recent fight
had not gone unnoticed. A number of the command staff
watched their approach in silence. The celebration seemed
to have left all of those above as well.

Etton, the supreme commander himself, led those who
walked down to meet them.

Qert nodded to the Gnarlyman as the others approached.
Apparently, the Judge wanted Summitch to make the intro-
ductions.

"We surprised a few intruders," he said shortly.

"Intruders?" Etton demanded. "Why didn't our scouts
intercept them?"

"Because these men came from our own camp."

The elder Judges knelt down by the three forms as Qert
lowered them to the ground.

"These men should be with the healers," one of the
generals announced.

"I believe," Qert spoke up at last, "this is where they
came from."

"I want answers," was all Etton needed to say.

Three Judges spoke as soon as they had touched the
three separate forms.

"They have been compelled here by outside forces."

"They seek information and disruption."

"They were brought beyond pain. This very action may kill them all."

"What have the Grey come to?" Etton asked. "To use our own wounded against us."

"I did not believe even the Grey would stoop to this." Only when Gontor's voice boomed out did Summitch realize the metal man had joined them. For one so large, he could be as silent as a Judge.

"They used our own men against us," Etton continued. "From within our own camp. We talk, therefore, of another kind of sentry. How could they have gotten their spells past our Judges' defenses?"

"This has nothing to do with the Grey Judges," Gontor replied. "Your Judges, primed to defend you against their opposites among the Grey, might not even be aware of these first intrusions. I know these—*other* Judges perhaps a bit too well. We face a whole new sorcery."

Etton looked at the metal man at last. "What do you mean?"

"We four have had skirmishes of our own before we joined you." Gontor shrugged his metal shoulders. "We bring advantages to your fight, we bring disadvantages as well. Like all within the Castle, we have our history."

The human of their little group stepped to Gontor's side. "So these are the same characters we met down below?"

"I fear so, friend Jacobsen. I am sorry that these problems follow us. These Judges seek certain items in our possession. I had thought they would not be strong enough to follow."

There went Gontor, getting dramatic again. "Well, they didn't follow us, directly," Summitch pointed out. He waved at the bandaged men. "But this is their doing?"

"It is most assuredly them. They do not care for the lives of others. Our hosts deserve an explanation." Gontor turned to face Etton. "During our time in the tunnels, we disturbed a community of renegade Judges—this surprises you? They have existed for a thousand years and more in secret chambers deep beneath the ground. I thought we and the others who fought them had left them weak and disorganized." Gontor's great booming voice grunted in anger. "Nothing is too low for them to attempt."

"You and others fought a battle below," Etton repeated. "What happened?"

"It was a messy affair, I'm afraid, with a few too many factions. There were a few that fought not with us but against the Judges—a daughter and Judge of the Grey, who would at first fight against us and soon deserted us. Our primary ally, though, was a warrior of the Green. Aubric was his name."

Etton appeared astonished by the news. "Aubric is still alive?"

Gontor nodded. "Alive—and more. Time spent under the Castle can change anyone profoundly. I am living proof. But I am quite certain you will be seeing Aubric again."

Summitch noted how deftly Gontor had avoided any explanations of the reasons for the battle. The keys that he stole from the Judges down below had not been mentioned once, much less explained. Then again, Summitch reflected, Gontor had not really explained the keys in any detail to his own companions.

"It is a shame that you could not have brought Aubric with you. Still, I know the best outcomes are not always possible in battle."

"But what of these strange Judges?" objected Dantis, first Judge of the Green. "As much as we are thankful for the metal man's help, if he brings an enemy as treacherous as this—''

''At the moment,'' Gontor interrupted, ''I believe they are only able to influence the afflicted. If you will protect those prone to their control for a day or two, you will be safe. I believe you will also be safe in the meantime.''

''But what is their purpose here?'' Etton asked. ''To attack us with our own wounded? All this can truly do is to anger and warn us against them.''

Summitch had been around Judges long enough to have an idea about this. ''Because they destroy those who are already helpless? No. I think they are looking to make us afraid, to show that no one is safe from their power.'' What Summitch didn't say aloud was that he thought that most Judges would be capable of this, and worse, if given the opportunity. The only thing that made the renegades different was that they were no longer answerable to the Lords.

''These recent events make our war council all the more important,'' Etton said. ''I think Summitch's point is well taken, and shows what a valuable asset he and his fellows can be.''

Now he'd done it, Summitch thought. And with his own big mouth.

''It is time for business,'' Etton continued. ''Let us settle in front of the fire.''

The whole group moved over to a series of benches gathered in a semicircle to one side of the roaring fire. Etton instructed the others to sit. Summitch found a place between Tsang and Jacobsen. Gontor remained standing.

Etton spoke once everyone was settled. ''First, to Gontor. While we appreciate your help, I suspect that your motives are not entirely altruistic.''

Ah. Perhaps the metal man had not fooled the Green quite so much as Summitch had thought.

"Nor have I ever pretended them to be," Gontor's voice boomed. "Your greatest enemy is also a great enemy of mine. I seek to draw him out. Today was a good beginning toward that end. The Grey now know that I am here. I thought I might bother them for a moment or two in the morning, as well, to show that I will not easily go away."

"No doubt constantly surprising, the Grey can be most amusing," Etton agreed. "But what do you hope to accomplish?"

"We will divert the Grey's attention. I hope to gain the attention of Lord Kedrik himself. In fact, I expect him to rally his troops to chase me. When that occurs, you can attack whatever distracted forces remain."

So Gontor planned to put the entire army of the Grey on his trail? Their trail, really, for Gontor would no doubt expect the companionship of the other three. Summitch, apparently, could look forward to a life full of narrow escapes and near-death experiences. Until, of course, the time the escape didn't quite work and the near-death experience would get a little closer than near.

The alternatives to his present course of action were looking more attractive with every passing moment. He supposed it would be bad form to sneak away in the middle of a war council. But after this was over, Summitch planned to have a little talk with Jacobsen about the disposal of a certain room full of gold.

"Divide and conquer?" Etton asked. His voice brought Summitch back to the present.

"Anything that will keep that large Grey army off balance is most desirable," one of the military men agreed. "But don't you worry about fighting off Kedrik's entire army?"

"Lord Kedrik has not seen me lately," Gontor replied. "He does not know what I am capable of. Besides, I will not be alone. I will have the aid of my three companions."

So Gontor had gotten his delusions of grandeur right out in the open. Summitch couldn't get back to the tunnels soon enough.

"But what of this new threat," Dantis interjected, "from the renegade Judges? Do you have any idea of the size of their party?"

"Their numbers?" Gontor paused an instant before replying. "Four hundred, I believe."

"Four hundred?" Judge Dantis cried. "That many of our kind working together might be unstoppable."

"No court holds more than a tenth that number," another Judge agreed. "We would have to work with other Judges to have a hope of success."

"How might we get the courts to cooperate?" another asked.

"I don't believe we can," Dantis replied. "My lord, I believe these renegades are an even greater threat than the Grey."

"But," Gontor interjected, "the renegades are after us. Once we leave you, they will bother you no more."

So they would not simply be running from the entire army of the Grey? They would also be chased by four hundred Judges, driven mad by living a thousand years underground?

Perhaps Summitch could slip away from a war council after all.

"If you wish to make the offer," Etton said, "I suppose we must accept. But we haven't heard from our master strategist. Summitch, what do you think of all of this?"

To the Gnarlyman's surprise, while spending all this time thinking of escape, he had actually formed an opinion.

"The most important thing we have done to the Grey is damage their confidence," he began. "Should we be able to do that again, we can win another day. On the following night, we should withdraw. Perhaps Lord Kedrik will be here by then. If we can get them to pursue—some portion of our party, we might ambush them, picking off more of their numbers before we have to make another stand."

Etton nodded. "A most practical plan. Sir Summitch, you have a gift. What do others—"

"My lord!" Qert spoke up suddenly. "Forgive the intrusion, but I have a message from my scouts. The Grey are attacking!"

"At night?" one of the generals shouted. "In the midst of all these spells? Are they mad?"

"No," Etton replied. "Only more desperate for victory than we had imagined. To your posts!"

So the battle began anew. Summitch thought how easy it might be to slip away in the confusion.

"Tsang!" Gontor called. "Summitch! Jacobsen! To my side!"

Well, the confusion would last for quite some time.

Summitch trotted after the others.

· 18 ·

VINNIE AND JOHNNY T STOOD
back-to-back in the office, each one facing a door. That
way, they both had a clear shot at everything and anything
that came through those doors to get them. Not that it did
much good, with the way Smith's men were acting.

The two from Petranova's mob threw everything at those
other guys, and the other guys just kept on coming.

Vinnie's arms were aching. He had already discarded
one gun, and was just about out of ammunition on the second. He must have fired a hundred rounds already. The
twenty or so that had attacked them so far had looked like
people. They didn't die like people. Not that that was the
worst of it. The hallways were covered with blood. It hardly
seemed to matter. The bullets punched holes in their bodies,
but the first two or three wounds barely slowed them down.
They would never stop coming.

"Watch out!" Johnny T shouted. Vinnie heard Johnny

T's shotgun boom, and watched one of the guys Vinnie had already plugged four times get to his feet again. This time, Vinnie shot him twice in the face. The guy fell back down, quiet at least for now.

It was starting again. The men who refused to die always came in waves. That meant Vinnie and Johnny T could expect two or three more to come on through those doors, besides whoever else tried to get off the floor.

He wished for maybe the hundredth time that there was some way they could get a message to Roman, get a crew over here to help. Vinnie had never expected—hell, how could anybody expect something like this?

They were only supposed to scope out this joint, see if they could figure out what had happened to Ernie. Shooting was supposed to be the last resort.

Vinnie jerked his gun toward something he saw out of the corner of his eye. One of the half-dozen bullet-ridden bodies on the floor had shifted. Were any of them dead? Had any of them been alive?

One guy had had so much blood running down his face, he probably couldn't see. Others slipped around in their own blood until another dozen bullets brought them down. Some didn't seem to bleed at all.

Welcome to the last resort, Vinnie thought. They had gone sight-seeing and run smack into a war.

Another expressionless man stepped through the door, his feet sliding a bit on the gore. Vinnie started shooting.

He shot six rounds before the guy in the door could even get off one. The guy staggered forward and fell into the pile.

Vinnie wished he was better with a gun. Before this, the only shooting he'd ever done was at the gun club. Now, well, he'd better hit the target four or five times, or he was going to end up dead.

"Shoot out their legs!" Johnny T called. "They can't get you if they can't walk!"

Johnny T was too much of an optimist. Nothing kept them from moving. They walked or crawled or wriggled or rolled, using whatever limbs they had left to reach Vinnie and Johnny T.

Another guy came through the door as three more struggled to rise from the carpet. One of the risers was the man Vinnie had just shot.

They had guns, too, but it took them a while to use them. Their aim wasn't all that good, their moves slightly spastic. Vinnie decided they looked like puppets. Life-sized, lumbering puppets. It was that sluggishness that was letting Vinnie survive.

They were slow, but they were almost unstoppable. Another couple of guys staggered through the door as everything that still had limbs attached tried to push itself up from the floor.

It looked like this time they were coming for Vinnie and Johnny T with everything they had left.

Vinnie had emptied another gun. He threw it aside, knelt down, and grabbed a machine pistol from a hand no longer connected to a body that had landed by his feet. The hand didn't want to give it up. Vinnie kicked the fist away with his boot. The fingers worked wildly as the hand sailed across the room.

"Throw everything you've got at 'em!" Johnny T screamed. Vinnie was staggered by an explosion at his back. Johnny T must have thrown one of his grenades out beyond the door. "They're throwing everything at us!"

It was all or nothing now. This was the end.

Vinnie had two pieces still stuck in his belt, saved for this moment. He pulled them both.

Vinnie emptied the clips in both of his guns as Johnny T

blasted away at his back. Those men still standing danced in the hail of lead. They slipped. They fell.

Vinnie threw fresh clips in both of his guns.

The whole floor seemed to rise, a bloody mass of undying fury, arms and legs and faces rolling toward them through the gore.

"Die! Die! Die!" Vinnie found himself screaming alongside Johnny T.

Vinnie realized nothing was happening when he pulled the triggers. All his guns were empty. But the attack had stopped.

A few things still twitched out in that mass of blood and bone, but the bullet-riddled human fragments had at last lost their forward momentum.

He looked past the carnage. Nobody else came through Vinnie's door.

"It quiet back there?" he called to Johnny T.

"Quiet as a fuckin' church."

"Bloodiest church I ever saw."

They stood there, still back-to-back, for a long, much-too-quiet moment.

"What now?" Vinnie called.

"You got me."

"You think we got all of them?"

Johnny T laughed. "Nah. They're just gonna bring in more."

Vinnie realized he felt the same way. Even if they got every guy in the building, Smith would just truck more in from someplace else.

It was never going to end.

Enough of this quiet. Enough of this place. Enough of Smith.

"Let's get out of here," Vinnie said abruptly.

"You got any idea which way we should go?"

"I say let's pick one. We stay here, we're dead." He tried to laugh like Johnny T. It sounded more like a cough as it echoed through the too-quiet rooms. "If we die now, at least we're movin' toward something."

"Yeah," Johnny T said right away. He stepped up to Vinnie's side. "You pick the way out yet?"

So Vinnie was making the decisions again. He looked from one door to the other. Johnny T's grenade had probably blown up any lingering resistance, but it also might have blown out some ceilings and walls. The way was bound to be clearer through the other door.

"We go my way," he announced.

Johnny T nodded. "Let's move on out."

Vinnie led the way. They moved carefully through the carnage, afraid they might still get grabbed by a hand or mouth come suddenly back to life.

He felt a hand on his shoulder.

"Wait!"

Johnny T took out his Magnum and plugged a couple of unidentified things moving under the gore. They waited for another jerk of muscle, another ripple of flesh, but there was nothing more. For now.

Vinnie looked down at the few bodies with faces still more or less intact. Vinnie had never seen any of these guys before. Whoever they were, they didn't move in the same circles as the Petranovas. He had no idea where Smith had recruited all of them, maybe out of town, maybe even out of the country. None of them ever spoke, even when they were riddled with bullets, even when they died.

The two men stepped past the last of the dead bodies, into the empty corridor. The quiet hallway looked out of place after the carnage they had just left.

"Let's move," Johnny T said again.

Closed doors lined both sides of the hall at regular in-

tervals. Vinnie tried a couple of the knobs as they passed.
The doors were locked.

The hallway was nicer on this side, with mahogany paneling and a plush carpet. They'd walked into the VIP part
of Smith's headquarters.

"I think we're getting closer to Smith," Vinnie said.

"Great. Nobody's gonna stop us from doing that."

They kept on walking anyway. So far, this hallway was
empty. Ernie, thankfully, was nowhere to be seen. If he
was under the same spell, or trance, or drug as the rest of
those guys—and when they'd run into him outside, he
seemed to have as much personality as all the others—he'd
probably be just as ready to shoot them, too.

What could they do, then? How could they shoot Roman's son?

Hell, what did it matter when he didn't have anything
to shoot? Vinnie only held an empty .38. He couldn't kill
anybody. Vinnie nodded at the gun still in Johnny T's hand.
"You got any more of those?"

"A couple. Used up eight pieces already. Wish I had
some more shotgun shells. It always pays to come prepared."

Vinnie noticed Johnny T didn't offer to share.

They reached a place where the hallway met another that
ran off at a right angle. The fancy paneling and carpet ran
both ways.

"Which way now?" Johnny T prompted.

Vinnie tensed. "What the hell is that?"

A sighing sound came down the corridors, as if the
building itself was breathing.

Johnny T spoke for both of them. "I don't like this one
fucking bit."

"Hell," Vinnie said, trying to make a joke. "Maybe
somebody just left a window open."

Neither of them laughed, but it gave Vinnie an idea.

Vinnie looked down one hall, then the other. "These hallways go on forever. Who the hell knows where they lead? Maybe we can break into one of these side offices and find a window to the street."

"Now that's an idea." Johnny T walked over to the nearest closed door and tried the handle.

The door was locked, just like all the others. Johnny T kicked it open.

The sigh returned louder than before, like a wind that groaned in pain.

Vinnie knew they had to get out of here now. Whatever Smith and his people had done to Ernie, they could do to the two of them. He followed Johnny T into the room. The place was full of boxes and a pair of worn swivel chairs. The far wall was smooth and painted black.

"I bet that's a window," Vinnie said. "Let's just hope it leads out to the street."

"Leaving so soon?"

"What?" Vinnie spun around at the sound of the voice.

"You're not going anywhere."

The words were a strained whisper, a soft sound that carried all too well through the quiet building.

Vinnie knew it had to be Ernie—or whatever it was Ernie had become.

"This'll do," Johnny T announced. He picked up one of the ancient chairs and hurled it toward the black.

The chair broke through the window with a satisfying crash.

"No." The whisper grew louder. "You will stay. Mr. Smith has changed his mind."

Johnny T looked up, as if the voice came from the ceiling. "You mean he doesn't want to kill us anymore?"

"Maybe he never did," the whisper continued. "Maybe

he just wanted to keep you here. You destroyed all who found you, and escaped without a single wound. How many shots did your opponents fire?''

Vinnie didn't believe this. ''So you let all those guys die—for what? Some kind of demonstration?''

''They were expendable. We have a use for you.''

''Screw this.'' Vinnie waved to Johnny T. ''This is meant to distract us. To keep us here. We got a way out. Let's use it.''

''Aren't you forgetting about someone?''

Ernie stepped into the doorway behind them. Ernie—the guy Roman had sent them here to find.

He still had that same blank expression on his face. And he still didn't say a word.

Johnny T looked over at Vinnie.

''So what do we do now?''

Ernie stood there, still and solid. His hands were empty. At least he didn't have a gun. Vinnie wondered if the dozen or so men who were crowding behind him could say the same.

''What do we do?'' Vinnie replied. ''Convince him to come? Carry him? There's something wrong with Ernie. I don't think he even really knows we're here.''

Johnny T looked real uncomfortable with that. ''Jeez, Vinnie. We gotta try.''

Okay. Nobody could say Vinnie didn't try.

''Ernie?'' he called. ''Do you know who we are?''

''Oh, we know all too well.'' Ernie's mouth opened, and the words came out in that same hoarse whisper. ''Roman Petranova doesn't appreciate you. We will know how to use you properly.''

''That's not Ernie's voice!'' Johnny T stated the obvious. ''What have they done to him?''

The words still came from Ernie's mouth. ''Doesn't Ernie look like he's safe and sound? He feels no pain. He no longer has to choose. We can do the same for you. Perhaps even better."

"What the hell—" Johnny T began.

Vinnie put a hand on his partner's shoulder. "Listen, Johnny. Ernie isn't Ernie anymore. We gotta get back—"

"Those who reach this far into Mr. Smith's headquarters are not allowed to leave."

Ernie stepped far enough in the room to let the dozen behind him enter as well.

Johnny T had a gun out in his hands. "Out of here, Vinnie! Now!"

Ernie walked forward and reached for Johnny T's gun.

"Oh, hell." Johnny T jerked away the hand that held the gun. He had trouble aiming it at the boss's son. "Ernie, don't make me do it."

Vinnie had stopped just inside the window. Johnny T knocked a hand off his arm. Two more hands took its place. He tried to pull the gun around to fire. It was yanked from his hand.

"Get out of here," he called to Vinnie.

"Johnny! No!" A dozen hands were pulling the muscleman back toward the door.

Four of the men walked past Johnny T, headed straight for Vinnie.

"Somebody's gotta tell our boss what's goin' down," Johnny T said. "Hey. You were always better with words!"

Vinnie risked a final look behind as he stepped to the broken window. Johnny was surrounded. Silently, the men reached for him like they wanted to make him one of their own. Johnny T disappeared, lost beneath the crush of bodies like someone sunken in quicksand.

Vinnie jumped through the opening, tearing his pants on the broken glass.

He was in some kind of alleyway. This place hadn't seen a trash pickup in years.

The voice was still right behind him. The whisper followed him into the street. Vinnie burrowed deeper into the boxes, looking for a place to hide, a place to run.

"We're going to get you all anyway. Mr. Smith is much too strong to be stopped. Why not come over now, of your own free will? It's much easier that way."

Vinnie couldn't stand it. "Ernie!" he called. "Just shut up!"

He heard running feet. Whoever was talking through Ernie's mouth wanted to goad him, to give away his hiding place, to get him to give up one way or another.

He pushed on, wading as quietly as he could through the knee-deep filth. If he wasn't quiet, they would find him in the dark.

"Vinnie. We have you surrounded, Vinnie. There are so many more of us than there are of you. Give up now and you won't get hurt."

Vinnie climbed past another pile of boxes and saw a streetlight ahead. A streetlight meant a real street beyond this alley.

Screw quiet. Vinnie knocked over the pile of boxes and ran.

He was out on the street. Alone on the street.

Their car was where they left it. Johnny T still had the keys, but hell—hot-wiring was in Vinnie's blood. He just had to get the car moving before they attacked him again.

Maybe Johnny T could get out, too, or maybe he was lost. There was no way Vinnie could go back in there.

Vinnie opened the car door, glad they hadn't locked it. He saw figures running out the same opening he and

Johnny T had entered only moments ago. Smith had Johnny T. Smith didn't want to let Vinnie go, either.

Vinnie tried to get his fingers to move faster.

The wires sparked.

The car revved to life. Vinnie stomped on the accelerator. He had to get back to Roman.

He looked in his rearview mirror. His speeding car was leaving the silent, running men behind. Maybe he could get out of this with his skin and his soul intact.

Johnny T was gone. And Ernie was—what?

Maybe this was bigger than just Ernie now.

JACKIE PORTER HAD to get into her car and drive. She walked quickly out of the diner and got behind the wheel. She heard too many sirens for this quiet little town.

She wished she had been a moment sooner, so she could be following either the Chief or the car that went after him. So what was she doing now? Jackie didn't have a police scanner in her personal car. She didn't even know that the other men in the diner were planning to follow the Chief, much less do something to him.

But she had this feeling.

As an accident specialist, she had learned to follow her hunches. Sometimes they led to dead ends. But more often than not, they were some part of the final answer, hidden bits that let her see it all.

She had learned to trust her feelings. She decided to follow the siren anyway.

The Chief had surprised her with what he had told her in the diner; how he'd owed Smith a favor, and how he wasn't going to let Smith collect anymore. She wished he had opened up and told her more. Maybe he was trying to protect her. But by only telling half the truth, he ended up protecting the other guys.

Now she was driving. It was something to do. She needed something to do. Her exhaustion was gone. She felt a wild energy now. She was too far into this.

Things would never be the same.

After being part of all that with Mrs. Mendeck she felt a little empty. It would be tough to go back to her day job knowing Smith was out there, snatching children.

She would see justice done.

She headed out of town, back toward the interstate. The sirens led her on. She took County 26 out to the nearest interchange. She could see the flashing lights on the highway below her. She turned up the entrance ramp and headed west, toward the action.

The chase led her out of the city, back out toward the dark and quiet farms. She kept the blue lights in sight, doing a steady ninety miles per hour. Ten miles out of town, the sirens got off the highway. She followed.

The local road out here ran through a marshy area, with wild grass up close against either side of the road in front of great still lakes filled with half-submerged trees.

She had a feeling.

She pulled off on what little excuse she saw for a shoulder. One of the sirens was coming back her way.

The police car roared past her, sirens wailing, so fast she wasn't even sure who was driving. They didn't even look twice at her—no doubt chasing a specific car.

She had a moment's quiet to follow up on her hunch.

She grabbed the flashlight from her glove compartment and walked back fifty paces to where she had seen the flattened grass, the crushed bushes. She only had to walk a few feet from the road before she saw the car.

The Chief's car. It rested against a tree, the windshield smashed, a body in the dark interior.

It didn't take an accident specialist to know the body belonged to the Chief.

She carefully opened the passenger door, doing her best to disturb as little as possible. She frowned. Even with the flashlight, she could tell the wound on the Chief's forehead didn't match with the pattern on the windshield. His head looked like it had been mashed at the temple by some heavy object, an iron pipe or a baseball bat. She saw no blood where his head should have hit the windshield and no bits of glass embedded in the forehead wound.

This was no accident.

The Chief had a radio. She'd use it to call for help.

They had killed the Chief of Police.

Maybe this time Smith had gone too far.

. 19 .

"Now!" HE HEARD KAYOR announce. Sassen saw the first signs of life in the lady's face.

She moaned. Her guard and assassin rushed back to her side.

"We do not harm the lady!" he said quickly before Flik could draw another of his knives. Sasseen was finding the constant suspicion of these two the slightest bit tiring. Not that their loyalty couldn't be useful.

His servant-soldiers had their place. They were strong and could take great abuse, but the enchantments made them slow. Flik would be very handy when there was quick killing to be done, and Blade would no doubt hold his ground for the lady until his dying breath. Sasseen doubted that any of the soldiers who came with the second set of Judges would have such staying power.

Rescuing the lady was a most delicate process, one the

Judges had to negotiate most carefully. The four Judges each represented one of the four elements. Sasseen was allied with earth, Kayor with fire, Eaas with air, Nallf with water. Basoff had chosen the balance wisely, but it still took hours to discover the proper balance for this most exacting of spells.

Their work had precedent. Every Judge of the Grey had spent years attending to the war. The collective process of Sasseen and his fellows most resembled those days in battle when many Judges would labor to construct their sorcerous weaves to be strong enough to defeat their enemy.

Where those weaves were great, thundering engines of destruction, this weave was far more subtle, a scalpel rather than a sword. Instead of attacking an army, they were attempting to retrieve a part of the lady Karmille that had been attacked by the repercussions of the beast spell. Sasseen was greatly relieved when the Judges had come to their initial consensus. Her consciousness had been damaged, but, if treated gently, would heal.

While it was difficult to determine the exact passage of time in these tunnels, Sasseen guessed these initial castings had taken the better part of a day. As the hours passed, they had dined on foodstuffs brought by the newcomers, slept in shifts, and relieved themselves in those hidden shafts designed for that purpose. If you had the resources of a Judge, you might remain here forever.

Sasseen studied the others as they worked. All of the Judges were competent, but Kayor showed flashes of brilliance. If he had been willing to play at politics, he might even have taken Sasseen's position, second only to Basoff in power among the Grey. But Kayor appeared too much the thinker, ready to serve the Grey since they gave him a livelihood, but not ready to mingle overmuch. Sasseen was uncertain how much the Judge was to be trusted.

The lady moaned again. Kayor nodded. They had opened the way at last. The Judges looked to one another, ready to complete the spell.

Earth and air, fire and water, each balanced the other. They wove a spell like a spider's web, so fine it might be invisible to all but the most practiced Judge. Each contributed from his personal power—a breeze, a spark, a droplet, a single grain of sand, then the power was divided again and refined, so their magics became as concentrated as a droplet might be to the ocean, or a grain of sand to the shore.

Karmille's spirit was lost, deep within.

When Sasseen had made his first fumbling attempts at rescue, Karmille had gone into convulsions, spirit and body fighting each other. The Judges had had to reintegrate her two selves properly, so that she could not simply function, but survive.

The weave increased. Sasseen found his own thoughts bound to the other three, all four Judges directed toward the lady.

Search, they called.

Deep.

Dark.

Hollow.

Her consciousness was hidden deeper still.

Reach, they called.

Deeper.

There.

They saw distant light.

Sparks.

Two sparks, swirling in the dark.

Two? Was one some final energy from the beasts looking to strike again? The delicate spell the Judges brought had no defense.

Careful.

Closer.

Call.

One spark retreated.

Karmille.

The second spark shifted, gained a bit in intensity.

Karmille.

M'lady.

We are here to help.

We are here to bring you back.

The spark grew brighter still, drifting toward the weave.

Gather.

Gather.

Gather and lift.

The weave encircled the single spark, as insubstantial as an ember floating on a summer breeze. Should the weave be too loose, the ember would float between the strands. Should they try to capture it too quickly, the force might drive it away.

Something gave the spark an extra push. It tumbled forward to settle in the weave.

Gather and lift.

Lift.

Lift.

Back to wholeness.

Back to consciousness.

Back to those you so recently left.

Buoyed by the four magics, the spark lifted and grew. The weave guided that part of m'lady back into its proper place among the whole.

Now.

Gently.

There.

The spark flared bright, returned to its home.

The four withdrew.

Sasseen blinked, a separate consciousness once more.

The lady Karmille opened her eyes.

"I had a dream," she said softly.

"We are glad you are returned to us," Sasseen replied.

Kayor frowned down at her. "You had a—bad reaction—"

"To the spell of the beasts?" Karmille interrupted. "Yes. That was explained to me—in my dream."

The Judges glanced at each other. A dream? While they may have rescued her, they were still uncertain of many of the possibilities of her former condition. Sasseen wondered if she might have heard some of their discussions in her unconscious state.

"Forgive me, my lady, but who explained this?" Kayor asked.

"He called himself—the Growler. He never showed himself, I'm afraid." Her half smile faded, as if only now was she fully waking from the dream. "I'm talking as if he were real? I suppose, to a part of me, he was."

She looked away from the Judges, past her guard and assassin, to the others. "We are still in the tunnels? Who are these people?"

"These are the reinforcements you asked for, sent by your father," Sasseen explained. He quickly introduced the other Judges. "The four of us, together, brought you from your sleep."

"You four, and the Growler." She sat up abruptly. "I am glad you are here." She looked straight at the trio of new Judges, once again the High One in command. "We called you during a crisis. While the immediate danger no longer exists, the renegades are a greater threat than any

the Grey have ever faced.'' She paused and frowned.
''Much of my knowledge comes from within my dream.
Yet I know it's true.''

She looked up to her guard. ''Help me to my feet.''

Her guard did as she asked. Once standing, she dusted
off the riding outfit she had chosen for her trip through the
tunnels and turned once again to those before her. ''The
Growler did me a favor, and asked for a favor in return.
While I am not usually prone to bargaining, I think this
might be in our best interest.'' She turned to her assassin.
''May I borrow one of your knives?''

Flik presented her with one of his weapons—hilt first—
before she could finish the sentence. She smiled at her assassin and knelt back upon the ground, using the sharp
blade to sketch something in the dirt—a circle with a line
through it, with three lines rising above the circle, and three
more below. It looked to Sasseen like a crude representation
of a sunrise over water. It also seemed oddly familiar, as
though he should recall it from some ancient teachings.

''This symbol dates from before the Covenant. So long
as it is undisturbed, it will confuse any magic that pursues
us.'' She looked up to her guard. ''Blade?''

The large fellow helped her to her feet once more.

''Now we may move away from here undetected,'' she
continued, ''all thanks to the Growler. And we will do our
part in turn.''

The Judges all nodded their assent. If any of them knew
more of the symbol sketched in the dirt, none spoke of it.
Now that the lady Karmille had fully regained her wits, no
one would dare to question her actions.

The Growler—Sasseen was sure he was the strange
presence within Karmille that he had not been able to identify, and the second spark deep within the lady that had fled

the weave. He longed to ask questions of Karmille, to discover how this new player fit into the ever-growing mosaic of power that existed underground.

But he was trained well. He would ask nothing. As the daughter of Kedrik, Karmille would tell them the specifics of the Growler and his plans only when she was ready to do so.

Now Karmille resumed command. Sasseen's life and position were safe—at least for now. He should not neglect his duties. Seeing that Karmille's wishes were fulfilled was his responsibility.

He clapped his hands sharply. "Everyone gather their belongings. We return to the tunnels."

The five soldiers snapped to attention. The three other Judges gathered together those things they thought might be useful into the sacks the items had come from, and handed the sacks back to the soldiers. Flik and Blade fell in behind Lady Karmille. Sasseen waved to Lepp and Savignon, who had remained motionless in the shadows throughout this long ordeal. His two servants blinked and shook their limbs, their movement returned to them.

In only a few moments, the entire party was ready to move from that spot where Lady Karmille announced they were now vulnerable. Sasseen judged it a worthy first step.

However, he would appreciate it even more if she would then tell her party where they were bound. The Growler's truth would only show its real value if everyone could share in such wisdom.

Patience was an attribute of the successful Judge, Sasseen reminded himself again.

He instructed his servants to position themselves in the rear of the party. He would follow them, careful to make sure neither of his puppets accidentally defaced the symbol

scratched in the dirt. In addition, his position at the rear
would give him an opportunity to observe the others.

He knew all three of the other Judges reasonably well,
and trusted none of them. Nallf and Eaas were all too eager
to do Basoff's bidding, while Kayor was totally beyond
prediction.

To Sasseen, Basoff's choice of these Judges was a sure
sign of his mistrust. Could the first Judge know anything
of Sasseen and Karmille's plans? Basoff no doubt mis-
trusted everyone. It was a sure way to maintain power.

It would not have been prudent to quiz any of the others
until Karmille had been rescued. Now Sasseen would have
a chance to ponder his circumstances, and perhaps get a
better understanding of the role these others played—perhaps even the true purpose of this "rescue party."

Damn Basoff, anyway. Sasseen's thoughts returned to
his creation, who was his creation no more.

Imp was not what he seemed. Sasseen kept the elemental
dormant, in a jar carried by Lepp, waiting for further study.
Not that recent events had afforded him much leisure time.

Imp was not what he seemed. He wondered if any of
these others were the same.

THE HIGH LORD of all the Grey was screaming, "This is
not acceptable! Another day of this, and every second one
of you will be put to death!"

Basoff had never seen Kedrik this openly angry. His lord
was subject to the occasional rage, but such anger had always been cold and direct, and Basoff had always been able
to see the circumstances that brought it about. This emotion
was hot and immediate and threatened to erupt anew from
their lord at any moment, to be directed at anything in his
path.

He had seemed quiet and composed, until he had bathed
in blood. That action, which had taken years off his tired
frame in the past, now seemed only to have taken years off
his anger. He had erupted from the baths, demanding to see
first his personal guard and then the collected Judges.

Basoff had no idea of what passed between their lord
and the guard. He fervently wished he and his Judges did
not have to be here now.

At the moment, Kedrik's molten anger was directed at
all of them called before their lord in the great hall. The
High Lord of all the Grey paced before them, pointing fingers, shaking fists, but mostly screaming. He still wore the
loose white tunic they would have provided at the baths,
and Basoff could still see dried blood around his lord's ears
and beneath his fingernails. Kedrik seemed not to notice.
His anger was too great.

Kedrik continued. "This should have been solved, long
before now! Why do I provide for so many Judges when
you cannot solve my most basic problems?"

Most of the Judges accepted the tirade stoically, without
remark.

The High Lord of the Grey stared at the seventeen
Judges before him for a long moment. Basoff counted to
himself for the length of fifteen heartbeats. Kedrik sagged
down upon his throne, his breath seemingly spent.

"Perhaps," one unwise Judge ventured in the silence,
"if we knew a bit more about the nature of Gontor—"

That made Kedrik actually leap from his throne and
jump to the ground before the Judges. "You are Judges!
You know all! Or you have ways to gain such knowledge!
Basoff has assured me of this time and again!"

He waved his guards toward the unfortunate Judge.
"Take him to the dungeons. If there are no results, he will
be the first to die."

The guards led the Judge from the chamber. Basoff heard the subtle intake of breath, noted the rigid posture of many of his underlings. A High Lord should not kill a Judge for such a minor slight.

Kedrik stopped, inches from Basoff's face. "You foil me at every turn, Basoff!" His voice was no quieter. Basoff was careful not to wince. "You have already sent away the most capable of the senior Judges."

"They were sent at your command, my lord," Basoff reminded him as gently as he was able. "We needed to protect your daughter."

"On your advice, Basoff!" Kedrik turned away. "I am surrounded by fools! We dilute our strength when we need it most."

The appearance of this giant seemed to have driven their lord beyond reason. The High Lord's ill-chosen words would force a wedge between the Lords and the Judges. Nor would it serve Basoff to appear weak before his underlings. While the Lords were first, neither could exist without the Judges. If Kedrik were to kill a Judge on a whim, there would be serious consequences.

"Fools!" Kedrik muttered as though his audience were no longer there. "All fools!"

Basoff knew he had to speak. Should he follow the other Judge to the dungeons, the Grey would fall. They would all be dead. But Kedrik's current emotional course would be just as fatal.

"Your current course of action serves neither of us, my lord."

Kedrik stopped pacing, but he did not turn to face Basoff.

"You ask us to give you this Gontor," the first Judge continued quickly, "yet you tell us nothing about him. You must trust us to do our work. Once we know more about this enemy, no doubt he will be easily defeated.''

Kedrik spun at that. ''I trusted Judges completely a very long time ago. See what it has brought me!'' He shook his fist at the air. ''They were to serve me! To destroy Gontor forever! They turned their backs on me! And Gontor has returned!''

With that, Kedrik paused, as if only then hearing Basoff's remarks. ''There is so much to tell? Where do I begin?''

The High One sighed. ''Once, I knew Gontor very well. He might have been a member of this very court, but this court did not yet exist.''

A time before the court of the Grey? Basoff realized Kedrik spoke of the very first days of the Covenant, perhaps even before the war.

Kedrik reached inside his tunic and pulled forth a golden disc that hung about his neck by a golden chain. ''This is something I stole from him, long ago.''

''Your pendant of office?''

''That is what it has become. It had a somewhat different meaning, all those years ago.'' Kedrik sighed, as if the touch of the pendant allowed every drop of anger to drain from his frame.

''Basoff, I will tell you all those things I have tried to forget. But we waste time. We must confront Gontor while he is still upon the battlefield!''

So they were back to that again. Basoff had thought, after all this time, that he knew his lord Kedrik.

But Kedrik seemed no longer content to let his children run the battle. Kedrik was filled with a manic energy. This had not come from age or the pleasures of the flesh, but from anger.

Basoff had thought Kedrik's challenges were all in his past. But with Gontor, his past had returned to give him another try. Here was the lord who ruled through intimidation and rage. Here was the lord who had made the Grey the most feared of all the houses.

It was three days' forced march from the Keep. Basoff could have delivered his lord to the battlefield in a matter of minutes, but Kedrik demanded to be accompanied by all fifty members of his personal guard. And, of course, he also required the presence of Basoff himself, to command the Battle Judges. It was too large a force for the Judges to transport in safety.

And, for the first time in over a hundred years, Kedrik would expose himself directly to danger, with Basoff at his side.

"Then we go to battle," Basoff said to his lord. "I have already made the preparations."

"Gontor has done everything—for revenge," Kedrik replied. "But I will see Gontor one final time."

Basoff could only hope that, once that time came, Kedrik would let his wits speak louder than his anger.

"My lord!" A guard called from the door. "A Judge demands entrance!"

Calsus, the most junior of all the Judges, and the only one excused from Kedrik's audience, strode into the room and bowed deeply.

"Forgive me, my lord! Basoff bade me to come as soon as I was contacted. We have a report from Eaas!"

Basoff looked to the High One.

"Lord Kedrik? Will you accept this?"

"What? Yes. We need this business done with." He nodded brusquely as he regained his royal chair. He seemed himself once again.

Basoff clapped his hands and addressed the other Judges. "Leave us now. A few will come with our lord's party. Those I have chosen will be ready to depart within the hour!"

The other Judges, Calsus included, filed silently from the room. As soon as they were gone, Basoff provided Eaas with a special device so that he might also witness his report. He therefore quickly conjured a simple globe that hovered a half-dozen feet before the throne. Eaas's image appeared within.

"My lord!" exclaimed the Judge within the globe. "Thank you for accepting my message!"

Kedrik nodded impatiently.

Basoff announced, "Eaas, report!"

"The lady Karmille was not well when we arrived," Eaas began. "To our best determination, she had been stricken with a magical affliction. She appears to be on the way to recovery.

"There are now potentially more serious developments. If what Sasseen says is true, we may have to face a new enemy—a group of renegade Judges."

"They show themselves?" Kedrik sat up in his throne. "I should have known, when Gontor reappeared, that they would have forgotten all the bargains."

"Renegade Judges?" Basoff asked. He would have to quiz his lord about this later.

Eaas nodded. "From Sasseen's description, they are Judges who have left every House, and the descendants of those Judges. There are literally hundreds of them. The arrival of others in the tunnels seems to have left them disorganized, but they are sworn to the destruction of the High Ones. Should they gather their power . . ." He shook his head, unwilling to continue.

"Now new powers are turned against us?" Kedrik asked softly. "Who has turned them away?"

From the way his lord studied the floor, Basoff knew that Kedrik was not addressing them, but his own private demons once more.

"Gontor," the High One muttered under his breath. "It is Gontor."

"Your report is most—troubling." Basoff replied to Eaas.

"What do you wish us to do with Sasseen?" Eaas asked.

Basoff looked a final time to his master, but the old man was slumped once again upon his throne, oblivious to all around him. He would still get no help from Kedrik.

"I believe you should wait to verify these reports of renegades. Sasseen might be exaggerating the dangers to glorify his own importance."

"Such a thought crossed my mind," Eaas agreed.

"Or he may not be exaggerating at all." While they had had their differences, Sasseen had not seemed the sort either to preen or panic. That was the very reason Basoff had chosen him to protect the lady Karmille. "Determine the size of this force of Judges. Assess the danger to the Grey. Once you have done so, return to the Keep with all haste."

"And Sasseen and the lady?"

"Do what you must to fulfill your orders. The war is shifting, Eaas. It may soon be over for the Grey, one way or another."

"I will call when I have news."

Basoff waved his hands. The globe disappeared from view.

There would be only one way to stir his lord to action.

"Lord Kedrik!" Basoff called sharply. "Your servants

should prepare you. We go to face Gontor within the hour.''

He had no other choice. He only prayed that Kedrik was equal to the task.

. 20 .

"WE CAN GO NO FAR-
ther."

Xeria looked at all the activity about her in the great
chamber. A hundred spells were being created in this room
as she watched. But her Counsel was correct. They had a
world of power, and no experience in its use.

"We cannot experiment upon our own kind," her Counsel continued. "No doubt some would volunteer for the
greater good, but we are Judges. The spells will not react
in the same way that they would to those who do not hold
magic, or to those of purer blood."

"For every discovery," Xeria replied, "we find a new
problem."

She looked at the activity around her. Only hours ago,
the chamber had seemed filled with possibilities. Now it
felt claustrophobic.

"We need to leave this place. The Great Judge knew

this. That was why he gave us back our independence.''

"Soon," Counsel agreed. "We will do so soon. We are refining the control spells.''

Xeria didn't think such spells could be counted as successes. "They seemed rather disappointing when used against the armies above.''

"Perhaps we were too eager. Our first subjects were limited to those distracted by injury or pain. Not your strongest subjects, I'm afraid. But our different disciplines know many control spells. They had to be used sparingly, back among the High Lords. I believe we need to feel no such restraints.''

Xeria wished she could share her Counsel's enthusiasm. Perhaps he was right, and their magic was on the verge of greatness. Or perhaps he simply wanted to justify his self-created position.

Xeria did not precisely understand this malaise that had overtaken her. She had never known uncertainty when she was part of the Whole. The Great Judge had meant her to do far more than this.

As much as she wished to push them to the world above, she knew it was too soon.

"We are not ready for the surface.''

They were like newborns. They were afraid. The thought of all that open space made even her—the chosen—a little nervous.

They would have to take tiny steps to power.

Counsel waved to another group nearby. "We have found other magics that might still work well at a distance. These three are hard at work restructuring a sleep spell— an ancient thing that had been out of fashion when the first Judge had escaped to the tunnels. Ancient magics, forgotten by these modern Judges.''

"Perhaps. Perhaps not. This is nothing more than theory.

You yourself have said it. We need subjects untainted by magic.

"Counsel, let us talk." She told those nearest to her to stop their work for a minute and join her. She quickly recounted her discussion with Counsel.

"We need subjects," she concluded. "Who would be most likely candidates?"

"The High Ones would be the first to feel it."

"They are the ones we must destroy."

Xeria saw a certain wisdom in this. Perhaps, without the High Ones, the other Judges would come flooding to their side.

"No," Counsel interjected. "The High Ones are too far away, for now."

"Find those who are still in the tunnels. It is best if we come as a surprise to those above."

"They must be detained or destroyed. Secrecy is in our best interest."

"Our servants are not far," another remarked.

Now, Xeria thought, this suggestion held merit. Those who had served them had already been taught to fear. It would take little to get them to serve again. And what better lesson than to kill a few with their experiments?

"What has happened to those who served us?" she asked.

"As near as they are, they are not easy to regain," replied the one who had spoken last. "They are protected by the Ancient Race."

Xeria saw an image of the light creatures entering a mortal form—a memory from the Great Judge. They were beings so long forgotten they were beyond the common magic. It was they, as much as anything, who caused the Great Judge to crumble.

When next she spoke, the Great Judge seemed to be

speaking with her. "For now, perhaps, the Ancient Race are out of reach. But remember that they were controlled long ago, and banished into these tunnels. They could be controlled again."

All of them knew this deep within. All of them were part of the Great Judge, and that Judge was with them still. Xeria felt a bit of the old peace returning.

"Pardon!"

Another, so young he must have only recently been granted his Judgeship, burst into the small group. "I have news of import."

Xeria frowned. She could no longer see the speaker. Counsel had interjected himself between Xeria and the newcomer.

"You may speak," she called.

It was Counsel's turn to frown. He stepped away.

"You may speak," he repeated.

Was he protecting Xeria or usurping her power?

The young Judge nodded gratefully. "Thank you, O leader." He took a deep breath. "My group was charged with mapping the surrounding tunnels. We have detected another party. Some of them were in the presence of the Great Judge. They have been joined by others."

"Yes?" This was the great news? Xeria found herself becoming impatient. "There were many others below. Forgive me, but in the confusion, I have forgotten a few details."

"Something must be amiss with the party. They have not moved in some time. But I am not telling you what is most important! They have four Judges. And a number of highborn soldiers. And a lady of the High Court."

Now she saw the reason for excitement. This party's crisis would be Xeria's opportunity.

"Those will be our subjects!" Counsel cheered.

"Will they?" Xeria cautioned. "They will defend themselves."

Counsel laughed. "What are four Judges against four hundred?"

Even Xeria had to admit it was most exciting—that one of those they wished to destroy could be so near. Those of pure blood had always been beyond the common magic. It was one of the original Conditions, a part of the Covenant.

The Great Judge had rejected the Conditions long ago.

"Some of our number are working in a new direction," Counsel enthused. "We will find a way to attack their blood directly. Once this spell is complete, the High Ones will destroy themselves. Their bodies will literally tear themselves apart."

He laughed at that. "Think of it! There will be only Judges left to rule."

Xeria still did not share her Counsel's confidence. They had many obstacles to overcome. And yet, for the Great Judge to return, many of his parts would have to contribute.

It was time to take their thousand years of magic and destroy the so-called Lords.

They would make their future whole greater than what had gone before. Their misfortune would lead to greater glory. Instead of being separate from the world, they would be the world.

And when the Lords began to crumble?

Some of the other Judges would resist, but most would come flocking to them.

Perhaps, then, the Great Judge would return.

He would rule the world, greater than ever before.

. 21 .

IT WOULD NEVER END.

Summitch would be the first to admit he was far from perfect. He did not work well with others. He especially did not work well with large groups. Large groups in open spaces made him *particularly* nervous.

When there was trouble, Summitch preferred the closure of tunnels to the uncertainty of the open sky.

The chaos of battle would soon return. Far too many were involved. And not simply the Green, the Purple, and the Grey. Gontor had his own mysterious plans. Tsang's needs would deprive Summitch of his gold. No doubt even Eric Jacobsen held secrets.

None of this, though, was what made him truly nervous. The greater war intruded as well, a war these others did not even comprehend. He had been called by Mrs. Mendeck. And the others told him he had called out for the Growler? Not very likely. He had probably sensed the Growler sniffing around. But calling out his name? An accident. He would never do such a thing on purpose.

Sure, Summitch owed favors. Sure, he had worked with these others before. Certainly they wished to work with him again. But given a choice, Summitch would do it all himself.

He took a deep breath, pretending to be free.

He was seated upon the rock where he had first met Qert, the war council of the Green on one side, the valley on the other. He had come here to get away from the commotion and maybe watch the sun set.

But the war would allow him no such luxuries. The war would consume them all. Earlier, Gontor had called them all together, warning them to be ready for action at any moment. Now it seemed like that moment would never come. That, Summitch surmised, was how these formal battles worked: a great buildup before a sudden strike. And, while the Green watched their enemy gather below them, they seemed capable of endless debate.

The valley before them was a sea of metal helms. The combined might of the Grey and Purple were once again on the move. There was no subtlety to their movement. They were determined to destroy the Green by sheer force of arms.

"Summitch!" He turned around at the sound of his name. It was Jacobsen, standing halfway between the rock and the council fire, smiling as if there was something to smile about. "They're starting."

By this time, it was assumed that he would participate in the Council. He climbed down off his rock and went to discuss his future.

The Council began the instant he took his place.

He had done this enough times now that he was actually

seeing a pattern. First, Etton's various advisors would put forth their theories.

He listened impatiently, wishing he were anywhere but here.

"They move all their troops before nightfall," a captain remarked.

"They will establish positions before nightfall," General Naddock had informed the Council, "and try to trick us into committing ourselves against what we perceive to be the greatest threat."

"Perhaps they will try to get us to strike again at their weakest point," another of the captains suggested.

"It worked to our advantage before." Naddock frowned. "They want us to be predictable enough to try it again. At which time, the weak point will actually not be so weak after all."

Etton looked around the circle without speaking.

Gontor was unusually quiet. Tsang, as usual, said nothing. Eric Jacobsen simply looked exhausted. Summitch imagined that getting plunked down in the middle of battle was not his usual line of work.

A thought entered Summitch's mind. What did Jacobsen do, on that other world? In their trips through the tunnels, Summitch had done far more talking than asking. It was another of his faults. If only he didn't find himself quite so interesting!

He realized his mind was wandering.

The metal man spoke up at last. "I think we are better at reacting. When they attack, Gontor will find some countermeasure."

General Naddock shook his head. "This time, I fear that will not be enough." He sighed. "We can counter some of their advance. Turn back the first line of troops, neutralize their Judges' efforts with our own. But, our push against these attacks will leave us vulnerable to their main force.''

No one spoke after that. Everyone's energy seemed drained.

To Summitch, it looked like the luck of the Green was finally gone.

"Perhaps," Etton said at last, "we should get some sleep. New ideas often come with the morning light. We will meet here again an hour before dawn.''

The others rose from around the council fire. Summitch wandered back to his vantage point to catch the last colors of the setting sun. The troops below seemed to have stopped moving. They had settled in small groups, dark cloaks looking little different from the surrounding ground in the twilight. There would be no bonfires for either side tonight. Fires were much too easy targets.

Summitch stepped forward to the edge of his rock, and saw a line of enemy soldiers protecting the edge of their camp, a forward guard that would stay alert through the night.

The scene blurred as he watched, the soldiers below fading too fast even for the disappearing light. The valley below became obscured by a fog, no doubt of unnatural origin.

This would be their Judges' protection, against an enemy army so close. The Green Judges had already dispensed with the boulders upon this hill in the earlier attack, at least those not buried deep within the earth like the one Summitch now perched upon. He wondered if they might dig a few more up and try to pierce the fog. The way the enemy had spread itself across the plain, any missiles from above were bound to do some damage.

"Ah, Summitch," a voice called. "I see that you, too, prefer the open air.''

It was Qert. Summitch realized that the young Judge had not been a part of the Council.

Qert climbed the hill to the side of the boulder.

"I think that none of us will get any sleep tonight."

He then climbed the boulder as well, stopping at Summitch's side.

"I have done a little scouting of my own." He grinned. "I have determined the nature of the Grey's spell. They have posted Judges upon the far hill to lay down these clouds. I believe I can puncture this little deception."

He reached into his pocket and pulled out what at first appeared to be rich, brown soil. Upon closer inspection, Summitch noticed a few specks of gold glittering in the mix.

"It is a concoction of my own devising," Qert explained, "its sole purpose to disrupt large-scale spells. Shall we see if it works?"

He threw the dust in the air and let the wind carry it down.

The sky flashed below them, as if a bolt of lightning had ripped the fog in half.

A large hole appeared in the mist.

"I'd say it works," Qert congratulated himself. "And what were they hiding?" He pointed to a spot below.

Summitch saw two legions of the enemy crawling slowly up the hill.

"As I thought!" Qert sounded as enthusiastic as a small child with a new toy. "They continue their advance! I must inform Etton." Qert jumped down from the rock. "Or whoever else is about. Dantis! A moment!" He waved to the senior Judge, who stood in conference some fifty feet away.

Dantis met Qert halfway. Summitch could overhear the young Judge tell his elder about his recent discovery.

Dantis frowned skeptically.

"That is unlikely," Dantis began. "Our scouts—"

"As unlikely as a fifty-foot metal giant?" Qert suggested.

"This is true," Dantis agreed. "Show me your proof."

Qert led the elder back to the rock where Summitch still waited. Qert bounded back to the top of the boulder. As befitted a Judge of his seniority, Dantis floated up to join them.

The rift in the sorcerous fog was beginning to close, but was still large enough to display one of the columns.

"Two of them climb the hill, to attempt to surprise our camp," Qert explained. "Here, let me show you." He pulled another fistful of dust from his pocket and dropped it off the hillside. It was followed by another explosion. The fog cleared considerably.

"I should not have doubted you," Dantis admitted. "Young Judges sometimes tend to overreact. What was that powder—"

"It is worse than I thought!" Qert replied. He pointed down the hill. "Those columns hold more than soldiers. There are Judges among them!"

Summitch could see them now, with their arcs of power, eliminating any obstacle, living or otherwise, that stood in their army's path. There was a pair of them at the edge of each advancing column.

They had no time for subtlety, practicing the more destructive personal sorceries: great spouting lines of fire, howling winds, cracks in the earth, and lashing storms, all encompassing only a few feet in front of the sorcerers.

So much for a restful night, Summitch thought. It was time for a little action. He quietly began to check his knives.

"We must inform Lord Etton at once," Qert said.

"Consider it done." Dantis disappeared.

"Etton will be with us in a moment," Qert said to Summitch. "Senior Judges are so good at that."

Summitch reserved his comments on senior Judges. He was surprised how much he liked Qert. Usually he had no use for Judges at all.

Qert put a hand on his shoulder. "Step back a bit."

Dantis reappeared, this time with Etton at his side.

"Something goes on below us," were the first words from Etton's mouth.

"You know?" Qert asked.

"Only that the enemy has killed almost all of our scouts," Lord Etton replied. "One escaped, with a story of almost being swallowed by the earth. When we attempted to contact the others, we discovered they were gone."

"This young man discovered the Grey's treachery," Dantis explained.

"Only because I came to visit Summitch," Qert replied. "In a way, they take a page from the book of the Green."

Etton frowned, but only for an instant. "You are correct. In this battle, the unexpected is the only common ground."

"I understand we have a commotion nearby."

That was Gontor's voice. The metal man stood behind them. How had he found out about this so quickly?

"So do I have this correctly?" Gontor continued. "The hill is filled with Judges, away from their cloistered protections?"

"Well," Dantis replied, "the Judges have joined the battle. I am sure, being Judges, they still carry a protection or two."

Gontor laughed. "A few paltry spells? No doubt each Judge is also protected by a soldier or two. It only makes the battle more sporting!"

"They attack at night," Lord Etton said softly. "We see the end of the gentleman's war."

"Warfare has been polite for far too long," the metal man replied. "Now it will end. I spent nearly a thousand years tortured by the likes of those below. Now, I believe I should have a little exercise."

Gontor seemed to have regained his spirit.

"I believe it is time to surprise those who plan to take us unawares!" Gontor whooped, an unholy sound that echoed down the hillside. "A Judge in the open is a Judge who might be destroyed!" He waved to the Gnarlyman.

"Summitch! To my side! We go to hunt Judges!"

Summitch had never heard the metal man's voice so loud: it rumbled over the valley like thunder.

Lightning streaked across the sky. Summitch looked away for an instant.

"They are not prepared for Gontor!"

Summitch almost fell from his rocky perch. In an instant, Gontor was close to ten times his former height. He had grown right before him, and Summitch still hadn't seen him change.

The metal man's voice boomed overhead. "A moment's distraction is all it takes, hey, Summitch? I'll meet you down in the battle."

The fifty-foot Gontor strode from sight.

Summitch supposed he should get busy as well. The Green had treated him like a friend, made him feel at home.

Now he knew he had to leave. He was feeling downright domestic. But first he'd join the final battle. After all, a promise was a promise.

He took his cue from Gontor, waiting until the others were all lost in earnest conversation around the fire. He slipped away quietly, glad that, even in this camp, most didn't pay attention to a Gnarlyman overmuch.

He sought out the tunnel entrance just north of the command tent, and opened the trapdoor very quietly. He prob-

ably needed none of this stealth. He could hear screams and
the clash of metal on metal from the hillside below even
here, and the sky above was filled with another dozen sorcerous battles. People were too busy even to look his way.
Still, stealth made him happy. He dropped into the tunnel,
pulling the trapdoor closed behind him.

The muffled sounds of battle could even be heard down
here. The Grey had gotten far too close to the heart of the
Green's encampment. Perhaps a little later, Summitch
would lead a party of Green soldiers through the tunnels to
surprise their enemy. But this time in the tunnels, he had a
personal mission.

He was a finder. This time he would find himself a
Judge. He walked down one short corridor, then took a
stairway leading down. A second tunnel felt right.

Yes. What he was looking for should be directly overhead.

He lifted the trapdoor carefully. He emerged in one of
those areas halfway up the hill favored by the scouts—a
spot of bare earth perhaps the size of a small hut, surrounded on all sides by boulders. And yes, there before him
was a Judge, perched on a boulder, his back to Summitch.
The Judge used his locale no doubt to give him a little extra
cover to perform his handiwork. All well and good. It
should also give Summitch that little extra cover to finish
his task.

The Judge had two soldiers as his guard. They were still
on the bare earth before the Gnarlyman, but both stared at
the spells exploding overhead.

Even better. None of them expected the enemy to pop
up out of the ground at their backs. Summitch had planned
well.

The Judge cried out.

Gontor appeared above the largest of the rocks.

No! Not now!

Summitch resisted to urge to yell at the metal man to find his own Judge. Whoever ended up killing the enemy, the result was the same.

"And who do we have hiding here?" Gontor remarked jovially.

"We are ready for you!" the Judge called up to the giant. He did a complex series of motions with his arms. Great rings of green fire shot from the Judge's open palms to explode against Gontor's chest.

Gontor nodded. "A very attractive spell, indeed."

The spell did not seem to have effected him at all. "Now is it my turn?"

The Judge stared at him openmouthed. "A force that great should have caused you to explode!"

"It is a nice thing about having a reflective shell," Gontor replied. His chest clanged hollowly where he pounded it with his fist. "Very few things stick."

But the Judge was waving his hands about again. "That was not my only spell! Take this, fiend!"

Gontor glanced away. "Pardon?" He looked down again at his feet, then back at the wildly gesticulating Judge. "Sorry, you'll have to excuse me for a moment. Some other pesky Judges are demanding my attention."

With that, the giant disappeared from sight.

The Judge stopped mid-gesture, apparently lost in shock. Summitch couldn't see what was happening, but he could hear a series of three explosions followed by a great many more screams. None of the screams sounded at all like Gontor.

"We have a visitor," a voice said just past Gontor's shoulder.

Oh, no! Summitch had spent too much time admiring Gontor's actions. He had allowed himself to be discovered.

He twisted about to look at the soldier only a dozen paces away.

"A Gnarlyman?" the Judge called down from above. "How could a Gnarlyman be here?"

"It must be a servant, lost from the camp above," ventured the soldier who had discovered him as he continued to walk in Summitch's direction.

"That's his misfortune," the Judge replied. "Kill him quickly."

Summitch jumped back from the soldier's grasping hand.

"He's quick," the first soldier said. "He's probably just frightened. With good reason, hey?"

"Perhaps he's here as a distraction," the other soldier suggested. "The Green will stoop to anything."

"Wait!" the Judge called down. "He can have another use. I'll test what I've prepared for Gontor."

"As you wish," the nearer soldier replied. He stepped back from the Gnarlyman.

"This is a somewhat more difficult spell," the Judge explained. "I was not quite prepared to use it when the giant took me by surprise."

Summitch noted that both soldiers, rather than trying to capture him, were now walking as far away from him as the clearing allowed.

Well, if you chose to kill Judges, you had to face the occasional obstacle. They still thought of him as a dumb servant. He wondered how he might use that to his advantage.

The Judge made a weird, keening sound in his throat. His arms opened wide. Summitch pondered if he could cast a knife up that far. A blade to the chest would stop any spell.

Despite the Judge's earlier explanation, the spell was

taking shape quickly. A pair of interlocking circles appeared before him, spinning about like two shining ropes dancing in and around each other. The effect was quite hypnotic. Summitch looked away for an instant. But he at least had to be aware of the spell's location. After all, these glowing circles were meant to kill him.

He glanced back. The circles had grown.

The swirling lights made a whirring sound as they passed through the air. They flew about in ever-widening circles, whirling one minute side by side, the next in such opposition that they appeared to form a globe.

They were not only larger, they were closer. Summitch realized they were headed straight for him.

The lights seemed transparent as they leapt through the air, but the swirling ropes were all too solid, and all too sharp, digging into the dirt where they touched the ground, leaving a furrow behind as deep as the length of Summitch's leg to the knee.

These were deadly ropes. He wondered if he might be able to disturb their forward motion with one of his knives.

He chose one of his more substantial blades from where he had hidden it beneath his shirt, and waited for the twin circles to leap into the air once again. Now.

He tossed one to cut through the lower portion of the swirling spell. His aim was true. The knife spun straight to the bottom of the glowing loop.

The rope neatly chopped the knife in half. Both pieces fell to the dirt.

This was not good at all.

"The Gnarlyman is armed!" one of the soldiers shouted.

"And you see what little good it did him!" the Judge called back.

The whirring noise grew louder as the rope sliced off a piece of boulder.

The two other soldiers scampered up onto boulders to either side of Summitch.

"It is best to be careful," the Judge on the first boulder agreed. "The glowing strands are as sharp as knives. And perhaps a hundred times as strong. They should cut through that metal skin as easily as they cut that rock. But watch what quick work they make of the Gnarlyman."

Summitch would rather not. He did not have the metal man's protections.

The tunnel entrance was right behind him. But if he left now, with everyone watching, he was sure to be pursued. No doubt the Judge would make sure he was pursued by the killing rope as well.

So he would have to find another way around this. As he watched the thing approach, he noticed a certain pattern to its movements. Now, if the rest of his theory was correct . . .

Summitch quickly tossed a second, more disposable blade through the center of the circle. It clattered off the rock on the far side, unharmed by its passage.

"You've unhinged the small fellow now!" a soldier called. "His throwing skill deserts him!"

Yes. That was exactly what Summitch wanted them to think.

The deadly rope was quite close now, swooping down at him from above. The glowing circles had continued to grow. Perhaps now they would be large enough.

Summitch realized they had to be. And he had to time this perfectly.

Now.

He jumped to meet the circle, diving through the center, his elbows and feet only inches from the cutting rope.

But nothing touched. He was on the other side.

The side near the Judge.

"The rope!" a soldier called. "It spins about!"

"The spell has been designed to kill the Gnarlyman," the Judge assured him. "He cannot escape!"

Unless, Summitch thought, I destroy the spell's point of origin. He scampered up the boulder that held the Judge.

"What are you doing?" the Judge called.

"I just want to be close to you," Summitch replied reassuringly.

"I will stop it!" the Judge cried. "Out of my way, Gnarlyman!"

But Summitch had kept one eye on that circle of death. It would be almost directly overhead by now, swooping down for the kill.

He threw himself toward the Judge.

"No!" The Judge threw out his arms defensively to ward off the Gnarlyman. But Summitch had dropped to his knees, somersaulting past the Judge's legs.

The glowing rope was more direct. It caught the Judge halfway up the right arm, slicing it cleanly off midway between elbow and shoulder.

The Judge screamed.

The circles wavered in the air, their light fading.

The Judge, Summitch thought, must have lost his concentration.

The Judge fell to his knees. He stared at Summitch as the blood pumped from his severed limb. His lips were moving, trying to find words, trying to form some final magic. Did he want to save himself? To curse Summitch?

"Shhhh." Summitch covered the Judge's mouth with his hand. The Judge could barely struggle. He had expended all his strength within the spell. Now all that was left for him was to die.

Summitch found it all quite satisfying.

"So, Gnarlyman, you finish a dying Judge? Let's see how you feel being impaled on my sword."

Did soldiers actually talk like that? He looked up to see one of them approach him across the rock.

Summitch skipped out of the way of the first lunge.

The soldier stared. "Damn you, scampering—"

It was not polite to stare. Summitch got ready to move again.

He was grabbed from behind. He had blundered backward into the other soldier.

Damn you, Gnarlyman, Summitch thought. If there was ever an overconfident, arrogant—

The first soldier lifted his sword. "Hold him there while I finish him. I think the fool has been trained to kill."

The soldier grunted. The sword fell from his hand. He lost his footing, rolling down the side of the boulder to the ground below.

Jacobsen stood on the rock, directly above the fallen man. He had used the butt end of his gun to club him over the head.

"No!" he called down to the unconscious soldier. "You've got it all wrong. I'm the fool around here."

"Enough!" the soldier behind Summitch announced. "I'll kill all these unnatural—"

But in reaching for his weapon, he let loose his grip on the Gnarlyman. Summitch whirled about.

The soldier's boasting stopped abruptly as he toppled forward, a knife in his heart.

"Well," Summitch admitted, "it's not subtle, but it works."

Jacobsen was looking out over the boulder, at the field of battle beyond.

"The battle goes on without us."

Summitch walked the few steps to the top of the rock

and Jacobsen's side. A few of the Grey soldiers still climbed the hillside above them, but many more lay dead upon the field. Gontor was chasing another twenty down the hill. Summitch saw no sign of the other Judges. They were either dead or in hiding.

"The battle moves away for a moment," the Gnarlyman announced. He walked over to the dead soldier and retrieved his knife. Jacobsen smiled at him.

"You never know where you can get more of these," Summitch grumbled.

"We work well together, don't we?" Jacobsen remarked. "Maybe Gontor knows something after all."

"I suppose we do, except I have no idea why you're here."

"Where should I be? With the Council? Everybody up there has something to do. I feel completely out of place." He waved at the dead soldiers. "We've got to earn our keep, hey?"

"You still haven't answered my question. Why are you here?"

Jacobsen shrugged. "Hey, I have no idea what to do. So I followed you through the tunnel."

And Summitch hadn't even noticed? Now he knew he was preoccupied.

"Watch out!" Jacobsen called, pointing behind him.

Summitch whirled. Another pair of soldiers had started to climb over the rocks. They met another pair of Summitch's knives.

"Hey," Jacobsen called as the Gnarlyman retrieved yet another set of blades, "working together is our destiny!"

Destiny? Here was the one thing that made him truly uncomfortable. Summitch wanted to run as far away from destiny as possible.

"What now?" Jacobsen asked. "We're missing out on

the battle. Perhaps we should get back to it.''

Summitch felt he needed to point something out here. ''With what? The handle of your gun? You don't have a weapon!''

''I still have your knife,'' Jacobsen replied somewhat defensively. He patted the hilt of the blade stuck through his belt.

''And I expect it back. One can never have enough knives.''

Jacobsen looked around their little clearing. ''I think surprise is our greatest weapon. Let's climb down into the tunnels and see what else avails itself, hey?''

Well, Summitch guessed, it was as good a suggestion as any.

And, if there was nothing particularly appealing underneath the battlefield, perhaps they could simply keep on walking.

· 22 ·

THEY WERE BACK IN THE
tunnels again. Jacobsen trotted after Summitch through the
never-ending torchlit passageways. When he had first come
to this place, these passageways had seemed foreign and
dangerous. To his surprise, Jacobsen realized he was beginning to take a certain comfort in these enclosed spaces.

This honeycomb of tunnels was where he'd first arrived,
and where he'd spent all but two of his days on this new
world. As much novelty and danger as they'd found on the
surface, these rough-hewn corridors with their sputtering
torches felt more like home.

They headed back toward the headquarters of the Green.
The battle still raged above them. While it was not so pro-
nounced as before, Jacobsen could still hear the occasional
war cry or muffled explosion. From what he had seen from
his recent trip outside, Gontor seemed once again to have
disrupted the Grey's advance. But even a fifty-foot tall

metal giant could only disrupt so many out of such a large force of men. For Jacobsen's part, it felt good to have overcome the Judge and the pair of soldiers. Still, he imagined it would have little effect on the overall course of the battle. He and Summitch and Gontor and Tsang would probably continue to have such little victories until the Grey simply overwhelmed them.

They approached the juncture of two tunnels. Summitch stopped abruptly.

"We're not alone down here," he whispered.

"Who else is down here?" Jacobsen whispered back.

Summitch sniffed the air. "I smell stale magic. It hangs on Judges' clothes like smoke from a cooking fire."

"A Judge? One of the Green?"

"I doubt it. Perhaps Gontor wasn't as good at removing those other three Judges after all."

Then the enemy was near. The tunnels suddenly seemed a lot less friendly.

"What do we do?"

"If you're good enough to find things, you can usually avoid them, too." Summitch grimaced, his face twisting into even more wrinkles than usual. "We'll need a Judge or two of our own to confront this one. I suppose we have to return to the Green."

"It can't be helped, huh?" Jacobsen had never heard such regret in Summitch's voice. Apparently the small fellow really had had enough of this whole battle. "You handled one Judge already. Why can't you take on a second?"

The Gnarlyman grunted. "That was as much luck as skill. That last Judge favored flashy spells that had flaws I could use against him. Should the Judge in the tunnels discover our presence, I imagine he would kill us."

"Just—kill us."

"Quickly and quietly. The more practical Judges are like that."

Summitch placed a cautioning hand on Jacobsen's elbow.

"Here it comes."

A low, moaning wind blew around them.

Summitch nodded. "He's noticed us, too. That wind's a way of looking for us."

That didn't sound like good news.

"But it passed right over us."

"Of course!" Summitch looked at him even more skeptically than usual. "That means he's found us."

Oh, Jacobsen thought.

"What happens now?"

Summitch shrugged. "Endless possibilities. He could send a spell—bloodthirsty beasts, poisonous fog, something like that—that would kill us instantly. But that sort of conjuring tends to attract attention, especially since we've got to be close to the Judges of the Green. No, he'll probably simply appear around a corner and hit us with a contact spell."

"Contact spell?" Jacobsen asked, not really wanting to hear what it was.

"A more subtle spell that works best in close proximity. Turn us to stone. Burn us to a cinder where we stand. That sort of thing."

So much for the peace of the tunnels.

"So he knows where we are? And he can kill us any number of ways?"

Summitch nodded. "He's getting close."

Jacobsen was trying not to panic. "What do we do?"

"We simply cease to be where he thinks we are. Give me a moment. Ah."

Summitch walked two steps forward and kicked at the

floor. A trapdoor sprang open at his feet. "Behold the means of our escape. Tunnels within tunnels, secrets behind secrets. The only plan in the construction of these tunnels was total paranoia. It's saved me more times than I would like to count." He waved for Jacobsen to follow. "Down we go."

He jumped into the darkness. Jacobsen was a bit more cautious. He swung his legs down into the opening, then hopped down to the lower floor as the torches around them sprung to life. The trapdoor overhead closed with a solid slam.

"Follow me," Summitch instructed.

"Is this enough for the Judge to be thrown off our trail?"

"Well, it will confuse him for a moment. But Summitch is not done with his schemes." He led Jacobsen another fifty paces down the passageway before he stopped abruptly.

Jacobsen had a thought. "Don't you think we should warn the Green about this enemy Judge underneath them?"

"If they are worthy Judges, they will know soon enough. We need to save our own skin first." He ran his hand over the rough stone wall. "Ah. Here it is."

He pulled on something that looked like a buried tree root.

The floor disappeared beneath their feet.

Jacobsen's rear end hit some sort of chute. They were traveling downward at tremendous speed, guided by a trough that also seemed to carry a bit of water. Jacobsen was reminded of those amusement parks where he used to take his daughter, when his ex-wife would still let him see his daughter. Now, all that seemed not just like from another world, but from another life.

"Landing straight ahead!" Summitch called.

Jacobsen saw a ring of torches still some distance below. As he slid closer, he realized they surrounded what looked like a small pond.

Summitch vaulted from the end of the chute, landing with a considerable splash.

Jacobsen tried to slow himself down, opening his legs so that his shoes rubbed against the sides of the trough, hoping for a softer landing. But he flew from the chute as well, landing four feet short of the Gnarlyman. Jacobsen's splash seemed just as big.

"Now that's the way to travel!" Summitch called as he climbed from the pool.

Jacobsen's feet found the water's bottom. The pond came up to about his waist. All his clothes had gotten rather wet, but otherwise he was fine. He waded out of the shallow pool and onto a walkway beneath a high ceiling, one that stretched all around, walk and walls and roof, made of cut stone.

"Well, now that should put some distance between us," Summitch added. "Let's see what this particular passage-way has to offer."

Summitch strode forward, oblivious to the fact that his clothes were soaked through. Jacobsen shook his own pants out as best he could and hurried to follow.

Summitch stopped and looked down at the wet spot growing at his feet. "A moment, friend Jacobsen." He mumbled a few words and waved his arms. The torches to either side flared abruptly for an instant, and then returned to normal.

Jacobsen realized his clothes were dry.

"Just another little something I picked up on my travels," Summitch confided. "Onwards."

The ceiling lowered a bit and the walls narrowed as they walked on, but the corridor was still twice the size of the normal tunnels. The torches to either side flared in great stone mountings, some in the shape of hands, others depicting birds and small animals.

"This is one of the older tunnels," Summitch explained as they walked, "when the builders still took real pride in their handiwork. At first, these tunnels served as meeting places of secret societies, spots for assignations among the early royalty, things that politely weren't meant for the light of day.

"Then, of course, the war came and the entire Castle fell apart."

The tunnel opened abruptly into another high-ceilinged chamber. Summitch stopped.

A single torch burned in the middle of the room. A figure sat beneath the sputtering flame.

"Well, you certainly took your time."

It was a Judge in the livery of the Grey.

Jacobsen took a step backward.

The Judge chuckled. "Where could you run? My spell would catch you before you took a step."

Summitch didn't move an inch. "You have us. Why haven't you killed us already?"

"One has to have a little drama at the end of a chase. Where's the satisfaction otherwise? Now how would you like to die? I believe you mentioned burning? Or was it being turned to stone?"

The Judge had been listening to their whole conversation.

He nodded. "If you stand around and talk long enough, anyone can find you."

The Judge stood. "I'll make this quick, now. I simply wanted to see the look on your faces."

So death was here at last. Jacobsen wondered if it would

be easier if he closed his eyes. He decided to leave them open.

He got to see the Grey Judge scream. The Judge writhed in agony before he began to shake so rapidly Jacobsen could no longer follow the movement. It only lasted a moment until the magician disintegrated into dust.

"You may thank me if you wish," a new voice remarked.

Qert now sat beneath the single torch. He smiled.

"The best way to get rid of a melodramatic Judge is with some melodrama of one's own."

"And where did you come from?" Summitch demanded. The Gnarlyman actually sounded a little annoyed.

"Well," Qert replied, "when I saw Jacobsen pop down to that trapdoor, I thought, why not? It seemed a new way of approaching the battle."

"First Jacobsen, now Qert?" Summitch muttered. "The entire Green army will be down here soon."

"Well, they need to be somewhere. I think the battle is finally turning against us. Even Gontor won't be able to stand against the combined might of both Purple and Grey." Qert looked quizzically at the others. "You're thinking about not going back, aren't you?"

Summitch shuffled his feet. "Well, it had crossed our minds."

"Excellent!" Qert cheered. "Mind if I tag along?"

Summitch looked like he'd had all the wind knocked out of him. "But your position—"

"At the bottom of the pecking order of a castle full of stuffy Judges?" Qert finished for him. "What a life to look forward to!"

"But you're a Judge. That's the sort of thing—"

Qert shook his head. "Too much power corrupts the

soul. Who wouldn't give it all up for a life of adventure? A life like yours.''

Summitch shook his head more firmly. "Look, kid. I don't have much of a life at all. Ask Jacobsen. He has even less of a life than I do.''

"Yes," Jacobsen asked. "Now that I think about it, where *are* we going?''

"Well, there are certain places that don't look twice at a talking Gnarlyman. And I have—certain plans.''

Qert smiled in admiration. "I don't think I've ever heard a more indirect answer in my life.'' He jumped down from the ledge. "Let's look at the facts, here. One's options are rather limited in a world at war. I believe the Green will have to retreat and regroup. We could even leave with official approval. We could be, say, a scouting party!''

Summitch grimaced. "This wouldn't be safe at all. We are headed behind enemy lines.''

"That's one of the greatest things about this war. Almost every place around here is behind enemy lines.''

The Gnarlyman looked to the ceiling. "Why does everyone want to come with me? I've spent my whole life trying to be as unpleasant as possible.''

"Well, you've failed. I say let's get out of here before the Grey decide to look down here for stragglers.''

Jacobsen looked from Qert to the Gnarlyman. He wondered if Summitch could coexist with someone who could be so cheerful.

"I'll pop off a message to Dantis. The Grey will be sending other Judges down here to follow the first. Once one gets this sort of idea, they all want a piece of it. Perhaps we can lead a few more astray.''

Summitch sighed. "Come on, then.'' He strode across the chamber past Qert.

The young Judge smiled at Jacobsen as the two hurried

to follow the Gnarlyman. "It appears we'll have some time together. You'll have to tell me about your homeland. When we're not being chased by Judges, that is."

Summitch started to mutter again.

XERIA ALLOWED COUNSEL to do much of the interviewing for those who would join them against the world above. She wanted to make sure that certain other projects were maintained in her absence. Who was more qualified to lead the raid than Xeria herself?

It was only now, with a day free from the Great Judge, that Xeria was beginning to gain some perspective. When one's society was brand new, every action was a learning experience. And an adventure. Every Judge in the chamber wished to join them on the quest. It was their first chance to test their strength and to win back whatever honor they might have lost when the Great Judge was surprised by those from above. But large groups could not move easily through the narrow tunnels, and concocting a spell to move any more than a couple dozen would give off enough energy to have the chamber's ceiling collapse on their heads.

Finally, Xeria took Counsel and the first half-dozen he had chosen and sat them down to talk about their collective goals. They were up against four Judges and less than a dozen guards and soldiers. Oh yes, and a high-born lady. Such a pampered creature was almost beneath notice, were she not of use. They would grab her quickly, ignoring her screams and pleas for mercy, and put her someplace safe for their experiments.

But the others held potential danger. While far less powerful than any party Xeria might send, the four enemy Judges had vast superiority in practical experience. As to the others? Even a soldier could get lucky against a Judge.

And they had already discovered that these tunnels held hidden dangers.

In the end, they decided their raiding party would number twenty.

She told Counsel to choose the others quickly, then consulted the young Judge who had first identified their targets.

"Does the lady remain at that same place?" Xeria asked.

"I believe so. Their energy has remained more or less the same since I first discovered them."

Xeria frowned. "More or less? What does that mean?"

The young Judge answered slowly. "For a short time, their energy—wavered. Perhaps they attempted to place a protection spell of some sort to hide themselves from us." He smiled at that. "It is a shame they concocted such a spell far too late to do them any good."

Counsel joined them, immediately adding, "So they do not move for now. It will take us some hours to reach them. What is to keep them from some further subterfuge before we arrive?"

Xeria noted that Counsel had included himself in the raiding party. She decided not to make it an issue—yet.

"I have solved that problem," she replied instead, "by consulting with some of our fellows. We will approach the enemy with a low-level spell, essentially a series of jumps that will transport our entire party. Our spell will target the High One, so we will not become displaced. Wherever they might travel, our spell will find them."

"And what of their defenses?" Counsel challenged.

"Even if they detect our sorcery, they will have no time to prepare. We will arrive a moment after the spell is complete."

She thought it an excellent solution. They would surprise

those who attacked them without warning. The children of
the Great Judge would see justice served.

There was no further comment. Xeria thanked the young
Judge and turned to pursue her other projects.

Counsel pursued her. "I have been thinking. While we
are taking a powerful force to capture this High One, there
are still dangers in this raid. For the good of the leadership
of our group, one of us should stay behind."

"What do you mean?" Xeria asked.

"You are our chosen leader. If something should happen
to you in the raid, who would the other Judges turn to?"

"It is because of my position that I should lead the raid.
We must reclaim the honor of the Great Judge. But you
raise an important point. There is much to be done while I
am gone. You will stay behind. I am trusting you with
completing our greater work."

Counsel opened his mouth to object, but said nothing.
He bowed.

He did not seem pleased. But Xeria's job was not to
please her followers.

Xeria's job was to give them glory.

KEDRIK FELT A coldness deep within.

Basoff had arrived in his chamber as he was preparing
for bed. The Judge spoke of an urgent message from the
front.

It had not been time for his sons' report, but apparently
they could not hold the news. They had surprised the
Green, and would soon overwhelm them. In their enthusiasm, they would ruin everything.

Basoff completed relaying the report, and blinked, once
more regaining his own voice. "Sire?"

Kedrik was reluctant to speak.

He had found the effects of bathing in blood a bit . . .
unfortunate. In the past, the process had done nothing more
than rejuvenate him. But this time? He had flown into
rages, insulted his staff, sent a Judge to the dungeons.
While a lord's will was never questioned, he saw his earlier
outbursts as a sign of weakness; the sort of sign noticed,
perhaps, by others at court. Basoff would be able to smooth
over any small problems with the Judges. But what of his
counselors and retainers, his high military advisors, and
those who wished to curry favor with his children? Basoff
would have to take some decisive action to make those
around him forget this little incident.

He realized, as the effects began to wear away, that he
had acted rather like his hotheaded son, Zibor. Or, Kedrik
admitted, as he had been in his early days as a mercenary,
before he learned how to handle himself at Court.

"This is great news," Basoff insisted, commenting on
the narration he had just reported. Kedrik pulled himself
back to the business at hand. "The Grey army will conquer
the Green. Your last great foe. The remaining houses will
crumble one by one."

It was what they had wanted, but he felt no joy. Kedrik
decided he needed to speak quietly of his own fears. "They
will also drive Gontor back into hiding. Why must they
succeed so quickly?"

Everything these days seemed to point to weakness. His
body was failing him at last. He was hiding with his pets
or lashing out at his underlings.

"There are other ways of dealing with Gontor," Basoff
replied.

But what would Basoff know? How could he imagine
that Gontor was the one thing Kedrik had to face personally?

Basoff was partially responsible for Kedrik's current

condition—the ever more arcane antiaging spells and those playthings the Judge introduced to fill his lord's time. Kedrik was well aware how the Judge had sought to make himself indispensable, and how, someday, the High Lord of the Grey should kill his first Judge for that attempt.

But he needed Basoff now.

And all because of Gontor. Instead of lashing out he should have been making plans. Now, he would curse his sons for their success.

He could not place blame or make excuses. The responsibility rested upon the High Lord of all the Grey.

"My lord?" Basoff prompted.

Kedrik shook his head. He had stopped talking, once again lost in thought.

No more. He would focus on what must be done. He would have to take command directly.

"Enough of the report," he snapped. "How can we reach the front most quickly?"

"Quickly?"

He found his anger beginning to rise again against this Judge. When he said quickly, he wanted it done! Why did Basoff pry him with questions?

Perhaps, Kedrik thought, a bit of the bloodbath remains in my veins.

"Within the hour," he replied.

"Your plans would have to change." Basoff shook his head. "With that speed, we cannot take a full complement of your guard."

"How many, then?"

"Safely and quickly?" Basoff asked. "Perhaps I can take four, you and I included."

"Four it will be. Gontor shall not escape me."

"Very well. I think this is a good decision, my lord. The Judges of the Grey will find a way to capture this metal man. And we will be present for the Grey's greatest victory.''

　　Yes, Kedrik realized. This was what they had been striving for all this time. Why did it now feel so hollow?

· 23 ·

"**S**O LET ME GET THIS
straight. When this guy starts pulling our strings,
there's nothing we can do?"

The voice jarred Savignon. Where was he? He blinked,
forcing his eyes to focus and interact with his brain. He
was walking down these same underground corridors, following the rest of the lady Karmille's growing party. Lepp
was at his side. And the spirit within Lepp spoke to him.

"The Judge Sasseen sometimes controls us more
directly," he explained. "When this is so, yes, we must
do his bidding. I imagine he believes he controls us all
the time."

Sav heard a chuckle deep within his head.

"Hey, I don't think the guy's got a clue that I'm even
here. How high and mighty can he be, anyway?"

Sav had to admit that the being called Ernie had a point.
Sav was still doing the Judge's bidding, but he could think

again. The longer the spell wore on, the more it appeared to unravel, first through Savignon's great anger, and now from this strange spirit from another world.

"Okay, so this Sasseen doesn't have a clue what's goin' on in this end of the world. We just got to wait for one of those times he's not payin' attention. And then somethin' comes up, and we make a break for it!"

"Break?" Sav didn't quite understand.

"We leave! Take off runnin'! Kapish?"

"I understand." They now walked at the rear of Sasseen's procession. Should there be a distraction, they would fall back out of sight and try to hide themselves in the tunnels. The Judge Sasseen needed their services too much to destroy them outright.

If he was busy elsewhere, the two of them just might get away. Whatever happened, they would never again surrender to the Judge's control.

Savignon smiled within. Ernie was a fitting entity to inhabit his dead friend's form. Whoever this being was, he seemed to hold some of Lepp's spirit.

Even if he was from another world, he appeared very resourceful. Savignon should follow his example.

They would be free, free to return to the Green and fight again. And no Judge or highborn lady of the Grey would stop them.

WHILE BRIAN DIDN'T mind talking to pass the time, he was beginning to wish this Rouss would just shut up. This former servant of the renegade Judges didn't simply say his life was boring—he proved it in detail. He talked about every single minute of his daily routine.

"Not that we are allowed to see much of the outside world. It is always 'kitchen boy do this' and 'kitchen boy do that!' Well, y'know, it wasn't really outside, either, just a big chamber—''

"Yeah," Joe cut in. "We were there. We remember."

Apparently others in the party were growing as tired of Rouss as Brian was.

Brian wished he could hear from the others in the party of refugees that marched behind them. Why had they all become so quiet? Not that they had gabbed away at any time, but earlier, when they were prompted as a group, they had spoken a fair amount.

Aubric held up his hand. "There is an enchantment in the chamber we are about to enter."

"Is that a good thing?" Joe asked.

"It is neither good nor bad. It was left by Karmille's party, I think to confuse those who follow her. If the enchantment is looked upon a certain way, it appears that Karmille's party is still in the chamber."

"A certain way?" Brian asked.

"The Judges' way," Aubric replied. "All their magic follows a certain pattern, and that pattern can be fooled."

"Is there any danger in going in there?"

"The spell is benign. It is also the quickest way for us to reach our goal."

Aubric's goal, Brian thought. It was very important for the beings inside the warrior's form to confront Judges and test their power. It all sounded a little dangerous to Brian, but Aubric was the one who knew the way down here. They had to follow him if they were ever going to find Summitch. And Aubric had seemed more than capable of handling everything so far.

"Karmille is not far, and we have walked a great distance." He glanced at Rouss. "Including those who follow. Perhaps we might rest for a bit in the chamber. I sense water nearby. Unfortunately, at the moment, I lack the means to find us other sustenance."

"Hey," Joe assured the warrior. "Water's better than nothing."

Aubric's eyes glowed. A door opened where Brian had seen nothing but wall before. Aubric led the way into the room, a good-sized chamber the size of a high school gym. Brian and Joe found a quiet corner and sat down upon the packed dirt. Runt stayed close by Aubric's side. Brian was less than pleased when Rouss wandered their way. Wouldn't the kitchen lad have friends among the other servants?

The crowd of servants filed in slowly, but crowded over close to the door.

Aubric looked up, eyes ablaze. The creatures in his head buzzed like a hive of angry bees. He grabbed Runt's elbow and drew her back closer to Joe and Brian.

"Stand back! We have visitors!"

A swirling blackness filled the middle of the chamber. Brian noticed Joe had drawn his gun.

The servants on the far end of the room fell to their knees.

Rouss collapsed to his knees as well. "I knew you would be back. I was the one who told you where to come! I live to serve."

Twenty men and women dressed in black—Judges!—appeared from the swirling mist.

"Where is the High One?" a woman who stood before the others called. "The lady Karmille?"

"She isn't here?" Rouss looked about in confusion. "I was the one who called you, y'know! Now you can get your servants back! I want my chance to join the other Judges!"

Aubric stepped forward. "You do not belong here. These people are under our protection."

Rouss ran forward to collapse again before the woman Judge. "Please! Take them all! Then accept me as a Judge!"

The woman frowned down at him. "You are not a Judge."

"But I can make magic!" Rouss held up his hands. "Only one of my parents is a Judge. But my blood is pure enough. I'll prove it!"

The Judge looked away.

Rouss's voice was growing ragged. "I was the one who called you here! You owe me that!"

"No one called us here. We came seeking the lady Karmille. But we will take our servants back."

Aubric strode forward. "No, you will not. I have always wanted to face the Judges."

The woman barely even looked at him. She waved to her fellows. "Seize all of them."

The others around her rose from the ground, floating toward every corner of the chamber. Many among the servants screamed.

Joe stood up and aimed his gun. "Let's see how they handle this." His gun boomed.

The nearest Judge exploded.

"Who-hoo!" Joe cheered. "I guess this thing doesn't just work on beasts!" He pointed the gun at the next nearest man in black. He, too, blew into a million bits.

He swung the piece around, aiming at a third.

His gun made an empty, clicking sound.

Joe looked down at the weapon. "Well, I guess that answers one question."

The gun was empty?

"Hand it to me," Brian said. "Maybe I can do it again."

Joe eagerly gave him the gun. "What have we got to lose? In the meantime, it looks like the Judges are staying away from here."

Brian looked down at the metal in his hands. How had he made it work last time? He wished he could remember. He looked out into the room.

Most of the other Judges were swooping around the servants, herding them into an ever-smaller space.

The woman who had spoken and two other Judges faced Aubric.

"You will leave this place now," the many voices of Aubric said, "or I will have to destroy you."

The woman was not impressed. "No one destroys those who follow the Great Judge." She nodded to her fellows. "Take him captive. Perhaps we can learn something of his power."

One of the two stepped forward. The buzzing sound within Aubric grew, sounding more now like a chain saw than the soft insect noise of before.

Two gouts of fire spewed from his eyes to bathe the Judge in silver light. The Judge shrieked, his whole form looking as if it were lit from within.

The fire leapt back within Aubric, the twin fire streams bringing the glowing Judge with them. In an instant the silver form disappeared, absorbed within Aubric's form.

"You bring me nourishment!" the things within Aubric roared. "Give me more!"

The woman Judge looked frightened then. She looked about for something, anything, to defend herself from the beings of light. She grabbed the simpering Rouss and threw him at the warrior.

Aubric simply stepped aside, allowing Rouss to fall

heavily to the floor. "Not enough," the buzzing voices called. "I need the power of Judges!"

"This is our true enemy!" the other Judge at her side called. "Judges! We must join together and defeat him!"

The other Judges turned then, leaving the servants behind to rush across the room to face Aubric.

Aubric's tongues of fire hit one Judge, then a second. But the Judges only struggled and screamed for an instant. The fire died, drawing none of the Judges in. The black robes swarmed around the warrior.

They would overwhelm Aubric. They would kill all of them.

The gun was heavy in Brian's hand.

"Joe!" He handed the gun back. "Try it now!"

Joe picked off a single Judge at the edge of the throng. He exploded as spectacularly as all those before.

But Aubric had fallen to his knees in the midst of all the Judges. The creatures of light could not handle so many at once.

"They'll kill him!" Brian called. "Do something!"

Joe swung his gun back and forth, but didn't fire a shot. The Judges were packed too tightly around the warrior.

"I'm afraid I'll hit Aubric with this thing!"

Brian looked around the room for something, anything, he could do.

He saw a glowing circle maybe twenty feet away.

He pointed. "Look at that!"

"What?" Joe asked.

"Don't you see that glow?"

Joe shook his head. "I see something or other drawn in the dirt. Is that what you're talking about?"

Brian guessed that it was. And the fact that he saw it glowing meant that it was important.

What if he did something to it? Would it change things in here?

He rushed over to the glowing symbol. The Judges were piling atop Aubric like vultures after raw meat. Things couldn't get much worse.

Brian rubbed out the sign with his shoe.

"What?" the woman who led the Judges cried.

And the Judges were gone, the black robes turned back to fog, which evaporated in another instant.

Aubric pushed himself to his feet. "Thank you, Brian. You have removed the enchantment from the room, and it has taken the Judges with it."

Runt had already rushed to Aubric's side. "Are you hurt?"

"I will be fine." He brushed the dirt from the sleeves of his shirt. "Feeding upon a Judge has given me a great deal of power. There were too many Judges, coming at me too quickly. Those within me must learn how to use that power they gain."

So, in other words, Brian thought, the things inside Aubric *ate* the Judge? He wasn't sure if that was cool or creepy.

"Wait a moment," Joe said. "I still don't understand this." He looked down at his gun. "Like I understand anything around here."

"The Judges came here in error. They were looking for Lady Karmille. Her party had left behind an enchantment that prevented the Judges from discovering her true location. When the enchantment was removed, the Judges were pulled to their true destination."

"So the lady must deal with them now," Runt said with the slightest of smiles.

Rouss groaned.

A pair of the servants stepped forward.

"He is half a Judge."

"We will take care of him."

Rouss struggled to his knees. "They will kill me."

"That is perhaps what you deserve," Aubric replied.

For an instant, Brian wished there was something else they could do. Rouss was an outsider, like Brian, only looking to belong.

Rouss jumped to his feet and ran for Brian. Was he going to plead for his life? What should Brian do?

Rouss grabbed Brian roughly.

"Try to kill me and I'll kill your lord!"

"Lord?" Brian asked. "Like in the High Ones? I'm nobody's lord!"

"You tried to hide it from me, y'know. But I've got Judges' blood in me. I can tell who's important!"

Runt stepped next to him. "Don't you think you're being a bit hasty? Maybe we can talk about this."

Rouss laughed. "A minute ago they were going to kill me. Now you want to talk?"

Runt took a step behind him. "I simply don't think violence is the only answer."

"Where are you going?" Rouss demanded. "I—"

He made a gurgling sound deep in his throat. Brian felt Rouss's grip fall away.

He turned around as Rouss fell to the ground, a deep cut running across the width of his neck.

Runt wiped the blade off on the hem of her dress. She smiled sadly at the fallen kitchen boy.

"It is a small thing I have kept for my own protection."

Joe walked to his side. "How about you, Brian? How you doing?"

"Fine," Brian said, still not quite believing all that had happened. "He only grabbed me."

"We would still like the body," one of the two servants said.

"Very well," Aubric replied. "Dispose of it when you are done." He turned and called to the others.

"Come. I have power now. I will give you all something to eat."

Brian took a deep breath.

He bet this Summitch guy could have explained a lot of this.

"So are we done with Judges for now?" Joe asked.

"I think we will eat and wait a bit before we visit Karmille," Aubric replied. "But we do need to visit her. After all, that is where we'll find your cousin Ernie."

· 24 ·

Xeria blinked. They were elsewhere.

One minute, they had surrounded the Judge eater. The next, they were spirited away.

Why?

They had found the lady Karmille.

They were disorganized. They were weary from their struggle. In that place they had come from, they had lost five of their number in an instant.

She would rally the others to her cause. "Judges! To my side! Our goal is before us!"

She could see the whole group of them, a short distance ahead of them in the tunnel. The lady Karmille, with four Judges and nine others. They looked neither upset nor surprised.

"We have been expecting you," one of the Judges said. "Actually, you are a little late."

She would not be goaded further. "Well, we will kill and capture you quickly, then."

The tunnel was only wide enough for four of them to stand side by side. She called for one group of four to kneel before her, then gathered three more around her.

"Kill the soldiers first!" she called.

The Judges did as she bade. The power sprayed down the tunnel toward its intended targets—until it hit an invisible wall, the bolts of power dissipating harmlessly.

"What is this?" Xeria cried aloud. "They have erected some sort of barrier."

One of the kneeling Judges pitched forward, a knife in his chest.

They were ready for them.

"It is a simple spell!" Xeria called to those around her. "Our greater power will overcome it!"

A man to her side grunted, a knife in his belly. A second knife caught him in the throat.

Two of their number were killed by common knives. The barrier only protected against sorcery. No doubt they could throw knives the other way, if they only knew how.

Perhaps if she tried another tactic.

"Why do you resist us so?" Xeria called. "You are Judges! We belong together!"

"Nice way you have of introducing yourselves!" the Judge who had spoken before called back. "We are charged with the protection of the lady Karmille."

Xeria sighed. "Well, there we have a problem. I'm afraid we need the lady Karmille for our own purposes."

Two more of Xeria's Judges came forward to replace the dead. A third whispered in her ear: "I recognize the protection spell. I can defeat it."

"Do so!" she commanded.

The Judge chanted a quick string of words at her side.

The invisible wall glowed a bright red.

"So you do know your way around a spell!" Karmille's Judge called.

"Give up the lady!" Xeria called back.

"I'm afraid you will have to find us first!" was his reply.

The glowing red faded to nothing.

A bolt of power struck a wall above the lady's head.

Their spells could reach Karmille's party. The wall was gone.

But so was the enemy.

Where Judges and soldiers and Karmille had stood, there was nothing but bare ground.

They were all gone.

"We can follow them!" one of the others called.

Xeria frowned. Why hadn't the spell already sent them after their prey? No doubt the enemy Judges had left some other obstructive spell behind. And she had lost two more of her party.

"Xeria!" another called. "Look!"

No, she had been wrong. She saw movement in the shadows where torchlight should be.

One man stepped forward. One Judge was left.

He held out his hands. "I've decided to join you."

"SASSEEN!"

"He calls to us?"

"He asks us to move."

"He is distracted."

"He's under attack."

"Yes. His call is weak."

"This is our ticket out of here!"

Sav understood the intent, if not the precise language.

"Come with me then," he called to Ernie. "I saw a side tunnel in the passageway behind. We shall lose ourselves in the twists and turns of the maze."

"Sounds like a plan to me!"

The attack had come from the front, where Karmille and three of the Judges strode in the lead. Kayor and Sasseen had expected something of the sort, and had set up appropriate barriers that would fall into place at the first sign of trouble.

Once the trouble began, Sasseen's servants were forgotten. The Judges were too busy.

"Move away from the others," Savignon called. "Back into the tunnels."

Karmille, her Judges, and her soldiers were all watching the various spells the enemy threw at them as they stopped harmlessly at the barrier Kayor and Sasseen had put in place.

They congratulated each other heartily at the success of the protection spell, and every time one of Flik's knives found a target among the enemy. They were all too engrossed in the spectacle before them to watch anything happen to Sasseen's puppets.

Only Flik, the assassin, paused in his throwing long enough to turn at their soft, shuffling retreat.

"He sees us!" Ernie called.

Perhaps he did. But there was nothing else they could do but quietly retreat. Any commotion would uncover their plan.

Flik only grinned and waved.

"The guy's one of us!" Ernie enthused.

Was he? Sav thought it more likely that the situation appealed to the assassin's sense of humor.

They were soon around a turn in the tunnel, and were able to walk more quickly to the cross corridor.

"I can hardly hear Sasseen at all," Sav remarked. "Maybe with a little distance, he won't be able to find us."

"Fuckin' a!" Ernie agreed.

Whatever that meant.

"So where do we go from here?" Sav asked.

"To find Joe. Don't ask me how." Ernie chuckled. "These things have a way of working out."

XERIA DID NOT want to trust this Judge. She was tired from battle and deeply upset by her losses. How could their first raid have gone so wrong?

Yet the truth of the Great Judge was so great, how could she deny another of their kind from joining?

"You wish to join our group?"

The newcomer nodded solemnly. "Yes. I am a Judge, like you. We know we are the true power within the Castle. We were meant to rule."

"If you feel this way, why do you serve?"

The new Judge shook his head. "I have never had a choice in my life—until now. It was either serve the High Ones, or perish. With your group, at last, Judges have a chance to be free."

He said all the right words. And yet . . .

"Why should we believe you?" Xeria demanded.

The Judge grinned at that. "Because I'm telling you to get out of here. You have lost many of your number. If you pursue this course without proper planning, you will lose more." He shook his head again. "You need my experience, or you will be made fools of every time."

This, unfortunately, made the most sense of all.

"Very well. You can come with us. I am called Xeria."

"And I am called Kayor," the new Judge said with a

smile. "With your potential power—our potential power, now—we can rule the world. You just need a little help to show you the way."

"And what of those you leave behind?" another of the Judges asked.

Kayor's smile grew even broader. "They should know you can never trust a Judge."

"THEY DO NOT follow us, m'lady," Sasseen said after consulting with the other two Judges.

"And what of Kayor?" Karmille asked.

"He has left us, m'lady," Eaas replied, "of his own volition. And we believe he has taken Sasseen's servants as well."

"The two soldiers of the Green?" Karmille frowned. "Why would he do that?"

Why indeed? Sasseen wondered. First Basoff destroyed his Imp, and now Kayor makes off with his playthings. He had come upon this journey to gain independence. Instead, he would apparently see all his spells stripped away from him.

"We do not know, m'lady," Eaas replied. "Kayor has always gone his own way."

"Judge Basoff is usually a very sensible leader," Nallf added. "Frankly, though, his choice of Kayor as a part of this party has always been beyond us."

"Whatever has happened to Kayor," Sasseen said. "And I do not think we can rule out foul play on the part of those other Judges. They are many and their experience is varied. Whatever has happened to Kayor, I feel it only makes it more important to get our lady from these tunnels to a place of safety."

"Yes!" Eaas agreed. "We must bring her back to the Grey Keep at once!"

"I said a place of safety," Sasseen replied pointedly.

"We can discuss all of this later," Karmille interjected, "while we are walking to a place of safety—wherever that may be."

"I bow to the lady's wisdom," Sasseen said.

Enough for now. But he would not see her placed again under the power of her father. After all, her future was his future.

But much had transpired. One of the new Judges had mysteriously vanished, and the others seemed to have accepted it without question.

Many things might happen in these tunnels that would defy explanation. One Judge was gone.

Who could say what might happen to the other two?

THE COUNSEL DID not look pleased.

"You have returned! What has happened? Where is the lady?"

Xeria briefly related what had transpired. First, how the Judges had left behind an enchantment that had misdirected them to confront the being who contained the Ancient Race, who now had claimed protection of all their former servants. She spoke of the battle, and their losses, including the strange weapon that had made some of them explode. And she mentioned the very annoying young man, who claimed he had sent for the Judges.

"Yes," Counsel replied, "that is how we discovered the servants. The child of the Judge has a gift. He should be brought into our community."

Xeria stared at the man. "That would be difficult, because I believe he is dead. Why didn't you tell me of this boy before?"

Counsel shook his head. "There is so much happening in our community. I did not wish to burden you with petty details."

"Like giving me information to help me succeed? Instead of having seven of our party killed in battle?"

"Seven?" Counsel frowned. "Oh, dear. That never should have happened."

She went on to describe how the spell had finally sent them to their true destination. "We found Karmille's party but they were prepared for us, repelling our attack, killing two of our number with knives. And then they escaped again. That is, all escaped save one."

The newcomer stepped forward. "I am Kayor, and I've come to join you."

"Think of it!" Xeria said. "A new convert to the Great Judge. No doubt the first of many."

Counsel looked even less pleased than before. "But he has just come from the enemy."

"All Judges save your group serve the High Ones above," Kayor pointed out. "But won't you accept us if we learn the truth and leave our former life behind?"

"I do not know," Counsel replied. He turned to Xeria. "I believe he should be tested, perhaps confined for a period. And if there is the slightest question, he must be eliminated."

Kayor studied the other Judge coolly. "I believe this one deserves to die right now."

Counsel's mouth fell open.

"He spreads distrust and misinformation," Kayor continued. "He seeks to usurp your authority."

"Why do you listen to this newcomer?" Counsel demanded.

Xeria looked to Kayor. "Isn't death a little severe? He could just be stripped of his rank and rejoin the others working together."

Kayor shook his head. "You have made him your second in command. Once he has tasted this power, he will not give it up easily."

Xeria realized that she had felt this way before, although she had not been able to put it into words. Kayor's experience was already a benefit.

"This is absurd!" Counsel appeared red in the face. He paused to gasp for breath.

"He is pompous and inefficient," Kayor continued. "He spreads incorrect information. Why do you think your raid failed? Because it was not planned well. That was this man's responsibility."

"I will not have—" Counsel clawed at his chest. "What?" His eyes grew large as the blood drained from his face. His fists clenched as he fell to his knees, then flat on his face.

He was no longer breathing.

"You did something to him, didn't you?" Xeria asked calmly.

"In a manner of speaking," Kayor agreed. "It is a simple spell that speeds up your opponent's heart. Especially effective on arrogant, argumentative types. In the end, they kill themselves."

Xeria studied the newcomer for a moment before speaking again.

"You certainly are direct in your dealings."

Kayor shrugged. "In order to gain with the Judges above, you must think like them."

"And you can do that for us?"

"I live to serve the Great Judge."

"Perhaps you do," Xeria agreed. "Perhaps you do. I

will find someone to make you comfortable in your new home.''

The other Judges spoke to Kayor upon Xeria's command, but most kept a very respectful distance. She would watch him, too. He seemed a most dangerous man. But that could make him a most valuable asset.

That night, in Xeria's dream, the Great Judge returned and spoke to her.

. 25 .

IT HAD TAKEN HOURS TO TIE
up the first loose ends on the murder—and it was a murder.
After it was all over with the Chief—the police cars, the
coroner, the staties, the reports—Jackie Porter came back
to the same diner where she had met the Chief the night
before. She didn't know why. Maybe she expected a walk
through the restaurant would jar her memory, give her a
clearer picture of those men who had followed the Chief,
let her recall some clue buried in the Chief's words. Maybe
she was looking for a peace denied her by that corpse out
in the marshland. The Chief had wanted to tell her something. Why had he been so afraid of speaking out?

The Chief was a contradiction. He was a competent ad-
ministrator who'd run the department for a dozen years. A
man who fought to get innovative procedures like Jackie's
accident specialization into his department. She was sure
that, in his heart, he wanted to be a good man. And yet he

had gotten himself under the thumb of a slime bucket like Smith. What could cause a man to make that kind of mistake?

The diner was a wash. She hadn't found any answers in the old red leather booths and overhead fluorescents. So far, all she had found here was a bagel and some coffee.

A shadow crossed her table.

"Ah. I was told I would find you here."

She looked up. The stocky, middle-aged man above her had a slightly Oriental cast to his face. He was very well dressed, with a dark, pinstriped suit and deep red tie, a cashmere overcoat, and a couple of expensive rings on his fingers. He also looked vaguely familiar.

"Yes, you probably have seen me," he said with a smile before she could make any reply. "I'm the Reverend Billy Chow."

Really? He was one of those late-night evangelists. Jackie had seen his photo in ads in *TV Guide*. REVEREND CHOW'S MIDWESTERN CRUSADE, midnight, channel 36. "Give it all for the Lord!"

She'd never particularly had time in her life for bible thumpers. Some of them only seemed out for a fast buck, but she'd heard some of the biggest names were totally legit. She shouldn't prejudge. After all, she had been taught to look at all the evidence.

"What can I do for you?" she asked as pleasantly as she could muster.

"I just want to tell you how sorry I am about what happened to your Chief." He smiled too easily. He slid into the seat opposite her without invitation.

Jackie shook her head. "I'm sorry. How did you know about all this?"

Chow placed his hands together on the Formica tabletop as if he were about to pray. "Let's just say I have friends

on the force. In my line of work, you meet people everywhere.''

She supposed that made a certain sense.

"It seemed there was a lot on the Chief's mind recently,'' Chow continued.

And where was this going, she wondered. But she
wouldn't give this stranger anything until she'd learned
something about him first.

"Really? I hadn't noticed.''

"So he hadn't talked to you about any of his problems?'' Chow prodded.

What was this character trying to prove? "Had he talked
to *you* about his problems?''

"Many people come to the Reverend Billy Chow with
their problems. I'm a noted spiritual advisor.''

"You didn't answer my question.''

The reverend smiled. "Nor have you answered mine.''

Jackie shook her head. "I only met you two minutes
ago. Give me a reason why I should answer anything.''

"I'm sorry. Perhaps we've gotten off on the wrong foot
here. I have to admit a certain—personal interest in this.
The Chief and I had mutual friends, friends that were not
simply concerned with his welfare, but his mental state.''

"I'm sorry. I still don't see what you're driving at.''

The Reverend Chow frowned ever so slightly. "It
seemed the Chief was delusional. Or so I'd heard. Whatever
he was involved in—''

"You mean outside the force? Do you know anything
about that?''

"Only the vaguest of rumors. I really shouldn't listen to
rumors, and I certainly won't repeat them. Anyway, I know
you met with the Chief shortly before his death, and—''

The faint alarm bells that had been ringing in the back
of Jackie's head since Chow had arrived became much

louder. She leaned forward across the table. "How? How could you know something like that? When the Chief and I were in here, this place was almost empty!"

The Reverend pushed himself back against the red leather seat cushions. "Oh, dear. Perhaps I've come to you too soon about this. You're obviously distraught." He moved out of the booth. "I just wanted to—"

"What? Quiz me to see if the Chief dropped anything damaging? Who are you working for, Reverend?"

"What?" Chow looked most upset. "I'm not working for anyone, Officer. I just had some friends who were concerned about—"

"I think I would like to meet your friends, Reverend. I'm glad you stopped by. I'm not going to answer any more questions now, but I'll be asking more of you in the near future. I think you'll be seeing a lot more of me."

The smile fell from Chow's face. "Officer Porter. That would be unwise. I'm sorry if I disturbed you."

He turned and walked from the diner.

Now what had all that been about? Jackie wondered if she had overreacted to the reverend. But there was just something so evasive, so smarmy, so demanding—heck, she had to face it. She didn't like the Reverend Billy Chow.

And she did believe she'd be doing a little checking into the Reverend, too. Because Chow had made one thing clear. This was all about the Chief.

Maybe, even from the grave, the Chief could finally tell her what was bothering him.

JOHNNY T COULDN'T believe it. They hadn't done a thing to him.

Oh, they grabbed all his guns, knocked the air out of him, carried him into this bare room where they'd tied him to a chair and then locked the door. But compared to what they could have done? Hell, he and Vinnie had probably taken out twenty of their guys in the last few minutes.

Then they let him sit here for a while. A little intimidation. Roman used to do that sort of thing to guys at Funland all the time. Used to work better than outright torture; the stuff those guys would think was gonna happen was far worse than anything Johnny T would come up with.

So there he was, tied up and alone. Right then, Johnny T had no idea what Smith and his guys were going to do to him. So he wasn't going to sweat it.

Instead, he closed his eyes and got some sleep.

He woke up, though, as soon as the lights came on. Took him only a second, too, to remember where he was. So he was on top of it when the pale guy walked into the room.

Johnny recognized him, too, from the time he had barged into Delvechio's. It was Mr. Smith himself.

"You won't do anything foolish, will you, Mr. Tutwillow?"

Johnny T took a shallow breath. Nobody used his last name. Nobody. But how would Smith know something like that?

"Call me Johnny. What could I do?"

"A wise response. You have already seen a small sample of my strength."

Smith coughed politely. "We have a friend of yours here. Why don't you come in, Ernie?"

Oh, yeah. Johnny T was sure he was going to see Ernie again. Big creep factor here. The totally expressionless guy who looked just like Ernie walked stiffly into the room.

"Why don't you untie him, Ernie?" Smith said.

Well, this was a surprise. Johnny T guessed Smith took him at his word. Then again, in Johnny T's line of work, your word is all you've got.

Ernie walked behind Johnny T. He could feel the big guy's fingers moving roughly but methodically over the ropes around his wrists. It wasn't fast.

"So, can you answer a question?"

"Anything, Johnny," Smith replied.

"What have you done to Ernie?"

Smith smiled at that. Johnny T didn't like his smile in the least.

Before tonight, Johnny T had thought he could take just about anything. That's why he had taken it easy, waiting for the door to open. But he knew one thing now. He didn't want to end up like Ernie.

"Let me tell you a few things, Johnny. Nothing happens around here without my say-so."

Oh, yeah? he wanted to say. What about taking out a couple dozen of your goons? As weird as they were, it had been a kick to mow them down.

But right this minute, considering his situation, he didn't feel quite as good about it.

"You don't think your friend—Vinnie, yes?—could have escaped unless we wanted him to?"

What? So Smith had let Vinnie escape? That didn't make sense.

"Yeah, but," Johnny objected, "all those guys you put up against me—"

"A small demonstration of what I can do when I need to."

Johnny T had to get this straight. "You demonstrated that you can get guys killed?"

Smith laughed. That was even worse than the smile.

"I wished to be rid of many of them. They had passed their usefulness."

So he just hypnotized people and let them become targets in a shooting gallery?

"Do not worry about your friend," Smith continued as if he could read Johnny T's thoughts. "Ernie will not be harmed. He is too valuable—to all of us."

"And what about me?" Johnny T asked.

"You, Johnny?" Smith replied. "Well, I'll probably let you go."

Johnny T couldn't believe this for a minute. "Really?"

"I'll even let you return to Mr. Petranova."

Okay. Here it came. "What's the catch?"

There went that smile again. "It's a very small catch, Johnny. You can make it all worthwhile by agreeing to a small proposal of mine."

This didn't sound so bad.

After all, what choice did he have?

. 26 .

H E HAD HOPED IT WAS A
ghost.

"Father!"

Limon realized he was staring, openmouthed. He closed his mouth and snapped to attention.

His father strode into the command tent, trailed by his personal Judge and two of his guard. This was no ghost. It was simply unthinkable.

Kedrik threw his heavy coat upon the rough-hewn table at the tent's center. "I have arrived to take command."

"But we have the Green on the run."

"And you may continue to pursue the Green," his father replied without expression. "I am here for one reason. To capture the metal man, Gontor."

"Gontor? That is his name, then?" How, Limon thought, did his father know the metal man's name? But he had been trained not to ask. "I'm afraid we haven't seen him in hours. Not since the Green quit their camp.''

"Oh, I'm sure he's still somewhere nearby. After all this time, he's no doubt waiting for me.''

GONTOR AND TSANG looked out over the last of the retreating Green. Their tents were gone, their fires out. And the front line of the Grey was only minutes away.

But Gontor would have something to say about that.

"Are you sure you want no more support?'' Etton called from where he stood with the last of the soldiers. "Some of us could stay behind and drop covering fire from the hills.''

Gontor shook his metal head. "I have unfinished business in this valley. Do not fear for me. I can move quite quickly when I need to.''

"Very well,'' Etton replied. "You have done more for the Green than I can ever possibly repay. If I can ever do anything for you in return, do not hesitate to ask.''

"No doubt we will see each other again, Lord Etton,'' Gontor replied. "This war is far from over.''

With that, Etton gave the two a final wave, then led his men quickly away from the field of battle.

Gontor looked to the warrior of Orange.

"What say, Tsang? I think it is time to slow the advance of the Grey one final time.''

Tsang nodded and drew his great curved blade.

"Excuse me for a moment.''

With that, Gontor stepped behind a convenient boulder. It was a foolish trait, no doubt, but he never liked to change in front of others. He again used the secret he had learned in captivity, to shimmer, to shift, to grow.

He stepped back out to Tsang's side, now a being fifty feet tall.

"What say we go to battle?"

He stepped quickly to the forward edge of the hillside. A great cry greeted him from below—the forward line of Grey troops acknowledging his presence. It was, Gontor decided, good to be appreciated.

He moved forward quickly, grabbing a pair of soldiers and tossing them aside. Most of his little drama here, though, was to intimidate the other soldiers, to get them to fall back and let Etton and his fellows gain a little distance from their pursuit. Well, that and to call some final attention to himself.

He heard the clash of swords behind him. Tsang was still back on the hilltop, ready to kill any of those who might slip past Gontor's large hands.

The Grey troops before him fell back slightly, but the line held perhaps fifty paces down the hill. More troops, both Grey and Purple, climbed up from the valley below. Soon they would be around him in such a concentration that they might overwhelm even a fifty-foot giant. He hoped he didn't have to wait that long.

He was only looking for one particular member of the Grey.

And it looked like he wasn't going to be disappointed. Gontor would have smiled if he could. Far down the hillside, he could see a Judge and a lord, floating above the mass of soldiers, slowly rising past the troops in his direction.

Kedrik had taken the bait. Now, if Gontor could find a way to make the High Lord of all the Grey just a bit more careless—well, that would come with time. This meeting was simply to set events in motion.

"Greetings, Kedrik!" Gontor pitched his voice to boom out across the entire valley.

Kedrik and his Judge settled down to the ground just

before their front line of soldiers. Kedrik did not seem happy to see Gontor. The High One's expression filled Gontor's heart with joy—well, it would have, if Gontor had a heart.

"I was hoping you were dead!" were the first words from Kedrik's mouth.

"After all this time, this is how you greet me?" Gontor shot back. "My dear Kedrik, is that any way for brothers to talk?"

Kedrik, if anything, looked even paler than before. Sibling rivalry had always been an issue with him.

"It is a thousand years," Gontor continued, "but you are alive, and so am I. I wonder if either one of us can die without the other."

Gontor had to admit he was enjoying this. "You could not kill me, so you chose to imprison me forever. I left that prison behind some time ago. Now I thought it time for a family reunion. A lot can happen in a thousand years. I learned a great deal from that place."

"I have no interest in what you have learned!" Kedrik shot back. His brother had lost none of his bitterness. "We struggled for power when we were young. You lost. We will struggle for power again."

Gontor shook his head. "I made a mistake when I was very young. I'm planning to make the world—all the worlds—right again."

"I'm not going to let you plan anything!" Kedrik shot back. "Now that I've found you again, I'm going to kill you!"

Gontor heard a shout from further up the hill. It was Tsang. Gontor spun around to see a row of Judges behind him.

"You are not so invulnerable as you appear!" Kedrik called up the hill. "We both know things about the other, brother. We know each other's weaknesses.''

That, Gontor thought, was too true. Perhaps it was time to go elsewhere and reevaluate the situation.

"Tsang!" he called. "To my side!"

The Judges made way for the warrior to join him. Perhaps they were planning to kill both of them together. The line of men in black had already begun to chant something complex and rhythmic, no doubt quite deadly if he had planned to stay around.

But Gontor and Tsang were already fading. "I will see you again, brother."

Kedrik shook his fist. He always was so melodramatic.

"You won't escape me that easily!" he called. "I can follow you anywhere!"

Actually, with his resources, Kedrik probably could. Well, almost everywhere.

Perhaps, Gontor thought, this little talk had been a bit of a mistake.

"CAN'T YOU FEEL it?" Ernie called.

Actually, Savignon could indeed sense something nearby. The spell was wearing away. Sometimes Ernie's thoughts within his mind would be so faint that he could barely understand them. Soon they would have to talk with their voices rather than their minds.

But he still knew exactly what the being named Ernie spoke of. There was something very powerful nearby, something whose energy seemed to cause the air of the tunnels to vibrate with its coming. Sav hoped it was a good thing, because they were going to meet it one way or another.

The fading of the spell caused problems as well. Savignon had eaten very little in the last few days. Now he realized that Sasseen's magic had sustained him. He felt more tired with every passing step, his arms and legs like lead weights. But for all his problems, he was still alive. Lepp, on the other hand, was animated entirely by sorcery—or at least he had been until the spirit of Ernie had arrived. Now, as the magic faded, Lepp would occasionally stumble at his side, Ernie's faint voice cursing softly. Soon, Sav imagined, Lepp might not be able to move at all, his limbs stiffening with that final death so long denied him.

Both of these problems meant they could do little in the way of movement. Sav felt he needed to rest before he could go on, but if Lepp stopped walking, he might never be able to move again.

So they struggled onward, waiting for the power to come.

"They are just ahead." A rough voice, like a hundred angry bees, echoed down the tunnel toward them.

"Here it comes!" Ernie cheered faintly. "About fuckin' time!"

Lepp leaned heavily against a wall.

Savignon walked a short distance farther down the corridor, looking for the source of the voice.

He saw two points of light and heard the sound of many feet. The man with glowing eyes led a multitude.

As they grew closer, he saw that the light came from a man's eyes. As they came closer still, he realized he knew the man.

"Aubric?" he called.

"Who?" the bees responded. "Savignon? Is that you?"

"Yes, it's your old friend." Sav could feel his face twisting into a grin. "I never thought I'd see you again."

"I have changed," Aubric replied.

"We have all been through much," Sav acknowledged. "But I am alive, and will recover."

"I am more than alive," Aubric said in turn. "I have many plans, but I do not know my fate. And what of Lepp?"

Sav shook his head. "I fear that his body still moves, but his spirit is gone. His shell is inhabited by another, a being named Ernie."

Another man in strange foreign garb stepped up next to Aubric. "Ernie? No shit?"

Sav recognized that pattern of speech. "Ah. You must be Ernie's cousin Joe."

"Joe?"

The voice was weak behind him. Sav turned around. Lepp crawled toward them on all fours.

"Hey," Ernie's voice said through Lepp's mouth. "I knew we'd find you."

He collapsed on the ground. Aubric strode quickly to his side. "He has been sustained by sorcery. His energy is almost gone."

"Can you do something?" Sav asked. "We knew you were coming. We could feel your power."

Aubric paused for a moment before he replied. "Did you feel my power, or Brian's? He is the greatest sorceror among us."

A young man stepped forward from among the others. "I am? But I don't understand—"

"You were sent here to learn," Aubric reassured him. "I'm sure understanding will come."

"In the meantime," Joe said, "you do great work on guns. But what's going on with Ernie? Is he going to be all right?"

Aubric's eyes glowed. "I can restore the life force to this form for a time. Is that what you wish?"

"I can't have found Ernie to lose him now," Joe replied. "Hell, yes."

Aubric nodded. "Everyone should stand away. There will be a substantial exchange of energy."

Sav took a few steps back, wondering, only now, what had happened to his old friend. A part of him was still Aubric. But only a part.

Those who stood behind Aubric also walked some distance down the corridor. There were so many of them. Sav realized he had a lot of questions to ask. And only now, free of the Judge's spell, would he be able to ask them.

Aubric leaned down over the still body of Lepp. He turned the body over, laying both his hands over the heart.

Sav saw a blinding flash, like the tunnel was filled with lightning.

The light returned to normal. Lepp groaned with Ernie's voice.

"What was that?" Ernie said. The words were stronger now.

Aubric smiled. "Simply something to keep you with us, Ernie Petranova."

"Hey!" Joe called. "Brian? Where's Brian? Did your magic send him someplace?"

Aubric paused, the lights in his eyes flaring.

"He is gone. But no, Joe Beast. It was not my magic that took him."

"What do you mean?"

"I think he has finally gone where he has always belonged."

"Hey," Ernie complained. "Help me up on my feet, would you?"

Joe shook his head and walked over to his cousin. "Sure. You get somebody back, you lose somebody else. Sometimes, I think this place is the pits."

Sav would have to agree with that.

. 27 .

S̲ᴜᴍᴍɪᴛᴄʜ ᴄᴏᴜʟᴅ ʜᴀᴠᴇ ɪᴛ all.

He was finally free of all that fighting, not to mention the questing with Gontor for all those keys. And what were they going to do once they found all the keys? Probably start looking for a bunch of locks.

But Summitch, and Jacobsen, and Qert had walked away from all of that. Now he could go back and live in that style he had always wanted, with a little previously enchanted gold. Jacobsen already knew about it, but what of the others? Gontor might be able to find some way around the curse. It was a shame that Tsang, no doubt, would demand all of it.

And Qert? He just seemed to be tagging along for the adventure.

He had had enough of oversized personalities. So he

would have to limit himself to working with the malleable sort, like Eric Jacobsen.

Fabulous wealth awaited, if he could only avoid Mrs. Mendeck and survive this nasty little war. It was these little comforts that made life worth living.

Of course, Qert would be a bit of a problem. Still, he seemed agreeable to many things. And they all had to find a way to live, didn't they?

Summitch had a most pleasant thought. Maybe Qert could find a way to remove the curse of the Orange. Then they could spend the gold right here.

If he hopped worlds, Mrs. Mendeck would find him for sure. But should they be able to spend their wealth in a certain disreputable port city—ah, life could be good!

What?

Summitch blinked. He was no longer in the tunnels. Instead, he stood on a grassy hillside in the midday sun.

"Very impressive," Qert was saying. "You brought all three of us here, just like that."

"Only a little something I learned in my captivity," the voice of Gontor boomed.

Summitch should have known it was all too good to be true.

"It was good of you to get away like that," Gontor continued. "It gave everybody else a little push. Unfortunately, the Green had lost that particular battle. But a battle is not the war."

Summitch turned to see Gontor, once again a reasonable size, and Tsang. "Is that why you called us here?"

"Do I sense a little bitterness in your voice, friend Summitch? Remember, our destinies are intertwined." He laughed heartily. "Besides, friend Jacobsen has something I gave him for safekeeping."

Jacobsen reached inside his shirt. "Oh, yeah. The keys!"

He had forgotten all about the keys. Gontor would follow those things anywhere.

"I thought it best to track these down and hide them for safekeeping."

Hide them? After all they'd been through?

Gontor accepted the pouch from Jacobsen, opened it, and extracted two small pieces of metal. The keys' true aspect, Summitch guessed. Before, they were always being disguised as spiders or something.

"This will take but a moment," the metal man announced. He took a key in either hand and lifted both arms high overhead. Two birds appeared in either palm, one a snowy white, the other deepest black. Gontor shook his hands. The birds flew away.

"Those were the keys?" Jacobsen asked.

"They were indeed, hidden now in the open air, until I call for their return."

"But why couldn't we just hold onto them?"

"Gontor has made a slight miscalculation," the metal man admitted. "Even a god might have an occasional failing. I have someone chasing me whom I would rather avoid for the time being. So we must go somewhere that I will not be followed."

"But why not take the keys?" Jacobsen insisted.

"Because we will hop between worlds. It is not advisable to take too many things of value on such journeys, especially since we go there to retrieve another key and bring it home."

"Hop between worlds? Does that mean—"

"Yes, Eric Jacobsen. We must go to your world now, or face the wrath of the Grey."

Oh great, Summitch thought. That meant that Kedrik was still on their trail.

"What about me?" Qert asked.

Gontor regarded the young Judge. "A worthy addition. Have I called us the noble four? Perhaps we will become the noble five. Not everyone will get a key, of course. But perhaps Gontor will be better with his hands free."

The noble five? Summitch was beginning to think Gontor was making this all up as he went along.

"But come," Gontor added. "We need to make final preparations. I am afraid, friend Tsang, we will need to borrow a little of your gold."

Gontor knew about Summitch's gold, too?

The Gnarlyman sighed. What could he do? He was forced back into adventure.

Some days, you could never win.

THE REVEREND BILLY Chow did his best to smile at Mr. Smith.

"What did you find?" the pale man asked in his cold voice.

"She was not cooperative at all," Chow replied. "I think the Chief told her something."

"Then she must be eliminated."

"What, and kill a second police officer this soon? There might be a certain heat that even you can't handle."

"This one will not be rushed. This one will truly look like an accident."

"How do you know that?" the reverend asked.

"Because you will be the one to plan it. And do it quickly."

Chow thought he understood. "You want me to get her before she gets to the Petranovas?"

"No. I have taken care of that. The Petranovas are no longer a problem." Mr. Smith smiled. "Get rid of Jackie Porter. You will be richly rewarded. And I will achieve everything that I desire."

JACKIE PORTER HAD to admit it. She was glad for the call.

She had spent the day at the station, talking with the other cops about the Chief and seeing what she could dig up on the Reverend Billy Chow. Her conclusions so far? The Chief was a very private man. And nobody wanted to talk about Chow. The smiling evangelist seemed to scare people.

After a day of dead ends, it was great to hear from Mrs. Mendeck.

"Oh, Officer Porter. I'm so glad to find you in. We could really use your help right now. We're expecting visitors."

"Visitors?" Jackie had asked. "From out of town?"

Mrs. Mendeck had laughed. "Yes, these folks are from very far out of town. They'll need your help to get acclimated. We should all be working together now, anyway. You do know that your life is in danger?"

Jackie tried to get Mrs. Mendeck to explain that last remark, but the old woman said she'd only have time to explain it later.

So Jackie got back in her car to drive across town. Visitors? She wondered if any of the newcomers would know anything about Smith or Chow.

She bet they would.

This could be most interesting.

Epilogue

Brian WAS IN THE DARK.

One minute, he'd been watching Aubric zap the dead man. The next, he was nowhere.

"Hello?" he called. "Is anybody here?"

Sorry to bring you here this way, but I felt it was past time.

Brian was confused. "Bring me where? Past time for what?"

I can step inside another spell and use it for my own purposes. It is one of my gifts. When Aubric sent his energy into the other, I saw my opportunity.

"Are you Summitch?" Brian asked.

Summitch works for me. Or at least, he should. I'm afraid our Summitch has been a little delinquent in his duties of late. No matter. He would have brought you to me.

You are here now. Now, your true training can begin.
 Brian still wasn't sure he liked this.
 "And who are you?"
 Me? Oh, you can call me Growler.